Emma fell against the door, thrown off balance by the speed of the turn. "Slow down," she snapped, fumbling for her seat belt.

"I can't." Sawyer ground the words out. He adjusted his white-knuckle grip on the steering wheel and pressed the limp brake pedal into the floorboard. "My brakes are out."

"What?" Her eyes widened.

Before them, a line of cars plugged away behind a slow-moving school bus on the road. He jammed his thumb against his emergency flashers and started a battering assault on his horn. His truck was out of control, and if the cars didn't move, he was going to take them all out with him.

One by one, the cars veered sharply to the shoulder. Tiny horrified faces came into view, staring back at him through the dusty emergency exit of the bus.

Sawyer couldn't stop. Couldn't slow. Couldn't hit a busload of children at his current speed or they would all be dead, thrown over the mountain or fatally injured on impact.

With no other choice, Sawyer gritted his teeth and resolved to leave the road at any cost.

[excerpt is from *Missing in the Mountains*]

HIGH-STAKES MOUNTAIN REFUGE

USA TODAY Bestselling Author

CASSIE MILES

&

JULIE ANNE LINDSEY

2 Thrilling Stories

Murder on the Mountain
and *Missing in the Mountains*

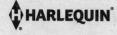

ISBN-13: 978-1-335-74495-1

High-Stakes Mountain Refuge

Copyright © 2022 by Harlequin Enterprises ULC

Murder on the Mountain
First published in 2006. This edition published in 2022.
Copyright © 2006 by Kay Bergstrom

Missing in the Mountains
First published in 2020. This edition published in 2022.
Copyright © 2020 by Julie Anne Lindsey

Recycling programs
for this product may
not exist in your area.

For questions and comments about the quality of this book,
please contact us at CustomerService@Harlequin.com.

Harlequin Enterprises ULC
22 Adelaide St. West, 41st Floor
Toronto, Ontario M5H 4E3, Canada
www.Harlequin.com

Printed in U.S.A.

CONTENTS

Cassie Miles, a *USA TODAY* bestselling author, lives in Colorado. After raising two daughters and cooking tons of macaroni and cheese for her family, Cassie is trying to be more adventurous in her culinary efforts. She's discovered that almost anything tastes better with wine. When she's not plotting Harlequin Intrigue books, Cassie likes to hang out at the Denver Botanic Gardens near her high-rise home.

Books by Cassie Miles

Harlequin Intrigue

Mountain Retreat
Colorado Wildfire
Mountain Bodyguard
Mountain Shelter
Mountain Blizzard
Frozen Memories

The Girl Who Wouldn't Stay Dead
The Girl Who Couldn't Forget
The Final Secret
Witness on the Run
Cold Case Colorado

Visit the Author Profile page
at Harlequin.com for more titles.

MURDER ON THE MOUNTAIN

Cassie Miles

To Kayla and Landon.

And, as always, to Rick.

Chapter 1

Deputy Paul Hemmings stood at the edge of the cliff looking down. Far below, a midsized sedan was wedged upside down against a tall pine. Morning sunlight reflected dully on the muddy undercarriage and tires. A bad accident. Not uncommon on these mountain roads. Especially at this time of year, early December.

Yet there were no skid marks. The pavement was dry. Ice wasn't a hazard. Why, Paul wondered, had this vehicle gone off the road?

The woman who had flagged him down asked, "Can I leave now?"

"I've put through a call for assistance, ma'am. The rescue team should be here soon."

"But I'm supposed to meet my husband at Vail Village in fifteen minutes."

"Sorry. You have to stay so you can give a report to the investigating officers."

"There's really nothing to tell," she said. "I pulled onto the shoulder to take a picture of that frozen waterfall. I'm an amateur photographer, and it's a beautiful morning and—"

"Stop." Paul held up a hand. "I can't take your statement. I'm off duty."

He glanced at his Ford Explorer SUV. The faces of his two young daughters, Jennifer and Lily, pressed up against the windows. They'd been on their way to the ice-skating rink for their lesson when this witness signaled him to stop. His girls were going to be plenty ticked off about arriving late to Saturday practice.

And so was this witness who stabbed at the buttons on her cell phone. "I can't even call my husband. I've got no signal."

"Accidents are inconvenient," he said. "Especially for the person driving."

Had that person survived?

Highly unlikely. However, if the driver had survived, it was Paul's duty to offer assistance until the rescue team arrived. He stepped over the ridge of dirty snow that marked the shoulder of the two-lane mountain road.

The descent was rocky and steep, but this was the sunny side of the valley and much of the snow had melted. So far, this had been a mild winter. Too mild. The workers at the ski resorts were praying for a blizzard.

He sidestepped down the slope. Though he was a big man—over six feet four and weighing more than was good for his cholesterol—Paul moved with surefooted balance. He'd been born and raised in these mountains; climbing was in his DNA.

As he approached the overturned car, he noted that the earth was torn up from the car's plummet, but there were no footprints. None leading away from the wreck. None leading toward it.

At the driver's side, he hunkered down. Though the car rested on the roof, the interior hadn't been crushed too badly. The driver's-side window was broken out. There was a man inside. And blood. A lot of blood.

"Sir?" Paul reached inside the car to touch the shoulder of this man. Half of his forehead was a bloody pulp. His complexion had the waxen sheen of a death mask. His lips were blue. He couldn't still be alive. If his injuries from the accident hadn't killed him, exposure to the night cold would have finished him off.

Yet, he moved. His eyelids twitched. He whispered one word. "Murder."

I'm going to murder this guy. FBI Special Agent Julia Last glared daggers into the broad shoulders of the distinguished, silver-haired man who had started making demands the minute he walked through the door.

After eleven years with the FBI, she didn't appreciate being treated like a housemaid. Julia was the agent in charge here. The operation of this two-story, nine-bedroom FBI safehouse in Eagle County, Colorado was her responsibility, and she'd managed it well enough to receive several commendations. Dozens of protected witnesses had come under her care. She'd also provided a haven for agents and officers who had been injured in the line of duty and needed recuperation time. Never once, during her two-year tenure at the safehouse, had security been breached.

Her latest guest—the silver-haired jerk—regarded his second-floor bedroom with blatant disdain, then turned to face her. "I'll take my first cup of coffee at six in the morning. Low-fat milk and one teaspoon of sugar. Not a sugar substitute. Delivered to my room along with *The Wall Street Journal*."

"We don't provide room service," Julia said through gritted teeth. "All meals are family-style in the dining room."

"My coffee at six," he repeated. "And the *Journal.*"

"You might have noticed that this is a rather remote location." The safehouse was four miles down a graded gravel road through a heavily forested wilderness area. "Newspaper deliveries are much later than six."

He glanced around the clean but relatively plain bedroom. "Where's the television?"

"We have a TV downstairs."

"Unacceptable. How am I supposed to keep up on the news if I can't watch CNN?" He tapped his chest. "I need to stay abreast of developments. Do you know who I am?"

"Yes, sir." Senator Marcus Ashbrook from Wyoming had been mentioned as a possible candidate for president. Needless to say, if Julia had resided in that state, he wouldn't get her vote.

"I'll need a television in my room." He flashed his photogenic smile and held out a five-dollar bill. "That will be all."

He was offering her a tip? This was too much. Julia snatched the bill from his hand and slammed it down on the knotty pine dresser. "I'm not a concierge, sir. And this is not a hotel."

"You're supposed to make me comfortable."

"It's my job to keep you safe," she corrected him. "This FBI safehouse might look like a rustic mountain lodge, but we're equipped with state-of-the-art security. While you're here, I will expect you to abide by our rules and to accept our restrictions."

"Will you now?" He looked surprised; the senator wasn't accustomed to having underlings tell him what to do.

"If it's necessary for you to leave the premises, I must be notified. No guests permitted. Three meals a day are served in the dining room. And, of course, tell no one that this is a safehouse."

"Why not?"

Could he really be that stupid? She didn't think so. Senator Marcus Ashbrook hadn't risen through the ranks of national politics by being a moron. "The whole purpose of a safehouse is to provide a covert location to keep the 'guests' safe. Security depends on keeping our mission secret from the bad guys."

"Good answer." Again, the photogenic smile.

She eyed him suspiciously. "Were you testing me, Senator?"

"I was indeed. I've heard that you're good at your job, Agent Last."

She dredged up an insincere smile of her own. "Thank you, sir. I prefer to be called Julia."

"Of course you do."

She turned on her heel and left his bedroom. This was going to be a long, strenuous, annoying week. The only "guests" at the safehouse were five high-ranking individuals who were involved with a Homeland Security project. In addition to the senator, there was a four-star Marine general, a former Navy SEAL who was now CIA and two senior FBI agents.

Though Julia didn't know the precise agenda for this group, she was certain that she and her live-in staff of two agents were going to have their hands full. Managing all these egos wouldn't be easy.

"Excuse me, Julia."

Now what? She turned and saw Gil Bradley, the CIA agent, standing in the center of the hallway. She could have sworn that the door to his room was closed, and she hadn't heard it open. Nor did she register the sound of his footsteps on the creaky hardwood floor. He'd just appeared. Like the spook that he was.

Gil Bradley was obviously the muscle in this group. His massive shoulders and well-developed arms suggested that he was capable of bench-pressing a giant redwood. But he was still able to move silently. Spooky, indeed. "What can I do for you, Gil?"

"I'm allergic to shellfish." His rasping voice made it sound like he was imparting a state secret.

"Thanks for telling me. I don't think we have shrimp on the menu for this week." Apparently, he was *not* allergic to dirt. His jeans were streaked with mud. "Have you been out hiking?"

"I run five miles every day. Rain, shine or snow."

"Admirable."

His gaze rested on her full hips. "You should come with me. Lean and mean, Julia. Lean and mean."

He zipped back into his room. The door closed with an audible click before she had a chance to tell him that she might not look like the Barbie version of GI Jane but would gladly match her physical conditioning and stamina against anyone. Even him.

At the foot of the staircase, she stalked through the great room, past the long oak dining table and into the kitchen. Roger Flannery, a young agent who had been at the safehouse for three months and discovered a talent for cooking, stood at the counter, chopping with the speed and aplomb of a sushi chef.

She should have been pleased with Roger's dedication to providing a semigourmet dinner every night, but Julia was still cranky after her encounters with Senator Ashbrook and Gil Bradley. When she was in this kind of mood, it was better not to stop and chitchat. She made a beeline through the kitchen toward the back door.

"Hey, Julia," Roger said.

She growled a response and kept walking. If Roger had any self-preservation instinct at all, he wouldn't say another word.

"Wait a sec," he said. "I could use some help with dinner."

She muttered a negative, but that wasn't sufficient for peppy Roger-Dodger. "What's eating you?" he asked. "You look like a grizzly that swallowed a wasp nest."

Slowly, she turned. "A grizzly?"

Roger chuckled. "Yeah."

"Is that a reference to my hair?" Her long brown hair was notoriously curly and wild even when pulled back in a ponytail.

"N-n-no."

"Or maybe you were thinking of my size when you said I look like a grizzly." Nearly six feet tall in her hik-

ing boots, she had a broad-shouldered, muscular frame
that made comparisons to a bear somewhat plausible.
"Gil thinks I should step up my exercise program."

"You look g-great," Roger said, frantically back-
pedaling as his gaze darted, taking in the details of
her jeans, white turtleneck and plaid wool shirt. "Nice
outfit."

"Can't say the same for you." He'd stripped down to
a black T-shirt revealing his shoulder holster. Hadn't
she just lectured the senator about keeping the true purpose of the safehouse a secret? "Put a shirt on. Cover
that weapon."

"But it's hot in here."

"Do it." She shoved open the door that led onto a
spacious cedar deck at the rear of the safehouse.

The December air cooled her face as she walked
across the deck to the railing. The sight of clear blue
skies above a wide valley bordered by forest gave her
a momentary surge of pleasure. She loved the rugged
majesty of the Colorado mountains, especially at this
time of year when swathes of drifted snow gleamed
pearly white in the afternoon sunlight. Though the ski
areas were open and had a solid snow base, much of
the snowfall near the safehouse had already melted
into the thirsty earth.

In the midst of all this grandeur, did she still feel
annoyance at the way she'd been treated by the senator? Or at the thinly veiled criticism from Gil? Was
she still mad? Yes, most definitely. And she needed
to lose this attitude before confronting the Homeland
Security hotshots over dinner.

Unfortunately, there wasn't time to run down to the

barn, saddle up one of the horses and ride. The next best thing for blowing off steam was chopping wood.

She tromped heavily down the stairs and along a path to a storage shed where several cords of logs were neatly stacked and waiting along with work gloves and a well-honed ax. After pulling on her stiff leather gloves, she carried a couple of fat logs to the outdoor chopping block where she would split them into an appropriate size for the fireplace in the great room.

With the log positioned on the block, she drew back and swung with all her strength. The ax head made contact and the wood split. A satisfying jolt went through her body. Again and again, she attacked the logs. This was a better workout than a heavy punching bag. She imagined the senator's face before the ax descended in a fierce and graceful arc. *Take that, you jerk.*

Julia caught a glimpse of movement in her peripheral vision and turned. There was a man watching her with his arms folded across his chest. He wore the brown uniform jacket for the Eagle County Sheriff's Department.

"I didn't want to interrupt." He came closer and held out his hand. "I'm Deputy Paul Hemmings."

"Julia Last."

Their gloved hands met. His grip was strong, and she appreciated that he didn't hold back because she was a woman. Though she'd seen the deputy in town when she shopped for supplies, Julia hadn't appreciated those broad shoulders and barrel chest until this moment. Paul Hemmings was a very tall, very impressive man.

Despite his extra-large dimensions, he wasn't hulking or threatening. He had an easygoing smile. His strong white teeth contrasted his tanned complexion. Sunlight glistened in his thick black hair. She wished he'd take off his sunglasses so she could see the color of his eyes. "What brings you here, Deputy?"

"I've been wanting to pay a visit," he said. "A friend of mine, Mac Granger, stayed here a couple of months ago. He liked the place."

"I remember Mac." He'd been involved in a sting operation that turned ugly. "Got himself into a bit of trouble."

"That's putting it mildly." He bent and picked up the chunks of wood she'd split. "I'll help you carry this load inside."

Which was a subtly clever way of getting an inside peek at the safehouse. She didn't for one minute believe that Deputy Paul Hemmings had popped in for a casual howdy.

Julia rested her hand on the ax handle. "Why don't you tell me the real reason you stopped by?"

"You like to get right to the point."

"I do," she said. "So?"

"There was a car accident last night. The driver went off the road, flipped his rental car. He was DOA at the hospital."

"Sorry to hear that."

"He had a note in his wallet with the phone number for your lodge written on it."

Her protective instincts were immediately aroused. Though the safehouse had a regular phone listing, the message was always the same: Sorry, we're booked. There were never outside guests. Feigning disinterest, she said, "Maybe he was looking for a place to stay."

"Or he might have wanted to contact one of your guests. The man who died was from Washington, D.C."

As were all the people involved in the Homeland Security project. Julia didn't like where this conversation was headed. "I hate to have you bothering my guests."

"I promise to be quick, Julia. Is it okay if I call you Julia?"

"If I can call you Paul."

"You bet." He glanced down at the logs in his arms. "Where do you want these?"

"We have enough wood inside. Just bring them into the storage shed."

Inside the dimly lit shed, she watched as Paul methodically placed the logs in a neat stack. Though he seemed like someone who could be trusted with a secret, she didn't want *anybody* to know the true purpose of the safehouse. Not even the local law enforcement. If one person knew, then another would and another. Then word would leak. Security would be compromised.

As Paul finished with the woodpile, he took off his sunglasses and turned to her. His eyes were a beautiful chocolate-brown. When she gazed into their depths, Julia felt something inside her begin to melt. For one fleeting second, she imagined what it would be like to be held by those big, strong arms. The broad expanse of his chest would provide ample room for her to snuggle. His flesh would be warm. His lips would be gentle.

She blinked, erasing these inappropriate thoughts. Where did that little burst of wild-eyed lust come from? It had been a long time since she'd been with a man, mostly because her responsibilities at the safehouse made dating difficult. But that was her choice. Her career. And the lack of a meaningful relationship didn't bother her.

But maybe it did. Maybe that was the real reason why her emotions were all over the place. Maybe she needed more than chopping wood to control her anger. Maybe she needed to get laid.

"What's wrong?" Paul asked.

"Nothing," she said quickly.

"I should talk to your guests now."

When he gave her a broad smile, his cheeks dimpled. He was just too sexy for words. Her repressed imagination again caught fire. She wanted to kiss those dimples, to taste his mouth.

He took a step toward her.

Julia's breath quickened.

She heard, very clearly, a gunshot.

Chapter 2

Paul charged through the door of the shed with his gun drawn. "Julia, stay back."

"No way."

Another gunshot. Paul looked up.

Standing on the cedar deck behind the lodge was an older man, bald with a neatly trimmed fringe of graying hair around his ears. His posture was ramrod straight. He stood with legs apart and one hand behind his back. With the other hand, he aimed a chrome automatic handgun into a nearby stand of trees. What the hell did he think he was doing?

"Freeze." Paul sighted down the barrel of his gun. "Police."

The bald man looked down his nose. "Nothing to worry about, young man."

Paul thought otherwise. Without lowering his gun,

he climbed the staircase to the deck. "Drop your weapon."

"You're overreacting." He squatted and carefully placed his gun on the deck floor. "I was just taking target practice, shooting at a rabbit."

"Hunting season is over." Paul scooped up the weapon. A Colt Double Eagle. A nice piece. And well cared for.

Julia stepped onto the deck behind him. "Deputy Paul Hemmings, I'd like to introduce General Harrison Naylor."

The general's squint and his square jaw seemed familiar. His formal bearing gave Paul the feeling that he was supposed to snap to attention and salute. But he had guns in both hands, so he merely nodded. "Army?"

"Marines," the general said.

Which still didn't give him the right to take potshots off the deck. "I'm sure you don't need a lecture on gun safety, General. In future, if you want to take target practice, choose a less populated location."

"Away from the barn," Julia added. "We have several horses, and they're not accustomed to gunfire."

Reluctantly, Paul returned the Colt Double Eagle. The general took a white handkerchief from his pocket and wiped the moisture from the gleaming silver gun. Though dressed in a casual cardigan, the man was impeccable. His trousers held a razor crease, and his shirt was buttoned all the way up to the collar.

Paul cleared his throat. "I'm here because of a car accident. The driver was from Washington, D.C., and I have reason to believe he was looking for someone staying here."

"I'm stationed in D.C.," the general said.

"The driver's name was John Maser."

The general paused for a moment. His lips moved as he silently repeated the name several times. "That's Maser as in Maserati?"

"Yes, sir."

"It's hard to remember all of the men I've had under my command. You said there was a car accident. What happened to Maserati?"

"He was killed."

"A shame." The general shook his head. "Can't say that I know the gentleman."

Paul was dead certain that he'd seen the general before. "Do you come to this area often? Maybe for skiing?"

"This is my first time. I usually ski in Utah."

"General Naylor, have we met?"

"I don't believe so."

"You might have seen the general on television," Julia said. "He does a lot of expert commentary."

"You can't believe everything you see on TV," the general said. "Nothing they've said about me is the truth. Not one damned thing."

He executed a sharp turn and marched through the door into the lodge.

Paul exchanged glances with Julia, who seemed as puzzled by the general's statement as he was. "Interesting guest."

"Very," she said.

"How many other people are staying here?"

"Four. And I have two full-time guys who help me run the place."

Since it was obvious that she didn't want to invite

him inside, Paul took the initiative. He held open the storm door. "After you."

As she sauntered past him, her curly ponytail came so close that he could smell the fresh scent of her shampoo. There was no other perfume on Julia. She didn't seem like the type to fuss with girlie things. And yet, she was all woman.

When he'd seen her chopping wood behind the resort, Paul's heart had pounded harder than thunder across the valley. He'd been stunned, unable to do anything more than stand and stare as this Amazon raised the ax over her head and swung down with force. She'd been breathing hard from her exertions. Inside her white turtleneck, her full breasts heaved. Damn, but she had a fine figure. An hourglass shape.

She reminded him of the early settlers in these mountains—women who were strong, resourceful and brave. And beautiful. Her complexion flushed with abundant health. Her eyes were blue—the color of a winter sky after a snowfall had washed the heavens clean.

Unfortunately, it seemed that she didn't particularly want him around. Not that she was rude. Just standoffish. He wondered if one of the men who helped her run the lodge was her boyfriend.

In the kitchen, she introduced him to a young man who was doing the cooking for dinner. Though Paul was pleased to see that their relationship fell into the category of boss and employee, there was something disturbing about this guy. Young Roger Flannery had the bulge of a shoulder holster under his flannel shirt. Not illegal. But worrying.

A small, sleek woman entered the kitchen, and

Julia introduced her. "Another of our guests. This is RJ Katz."

She looked like a cat with a button nose, a tiny mouth and wide, suspicious eyes. As Paul shook her thin hand, he asked, "Where are you from?"

"I travel a lot."

That was an evasive answer if he'd ever heard one. "Business or pleasure?"

"Both."

Just like a cat. Snooty, cool and independent. When RJ Katz sidled toward the fridge, he half expected to see her take out a bowl of cream and lap it up with her tongue.

If the car crash of John Maser turned out to be something more than an accident, Paul would put RJ at the head of his suspect list. "I need to see your driver's license, Ms. Katz."

"It's in my purse. In my room." She popped the tab on a cola and took a sip. "What's this about?"

Paul explained about the car accident and the victim from Washington, D.C. He watched for her reaction when he mentioned the name John Maser.

She was unruffled. "Don't know him."

"I'd still like to see your license."

"I suppose you're wondering if I live near D.C. Well, I do. My address is Alexandria, Virginia. But I assure you, Deputy, I don't know your victim."

There was a lot more he wanted to ask, but Paul had promised Julia that he wouldn't harass her guests. "Enjoy your stay."

Before they left the kitchen, Julia directed a question toward RJ Katz. "Do you know if David is in his room?"

"He's in the basement," she said, "playing with his precious computer."

"I'd appreciate if you asked him to come up here and speak with the deputy. So we don't have to go downstairs."

An unspoken communication passed between the two women, but Paul couldn't guess why. He was beginning to think that something strange was going on at this rustic little resort. There was the cook with a shoulder holster. And the feline Ms. Katz who seemed determined to hide her identity. And, of course, a general who gunned down jackrabbits from the porch.

When Paul first arrived, he had noticed three satellite dishes that might be for extra-fine television reception or for some other kind of communication. Clearly, he needed more information about Julia and the lodge.

She led him through the dining room to the front area where a cheery fire burned in the moss rock fireplace. Comfortable was the first word that popped into his head. The sturdy leather sofas and chairs looked big enough to sink into and relax. "Nice," he said. "I could see myself sitting in that big chair on a Sunday afternoon watching the football game."

"How about those Broncos?"

"Are you a fan?"

"Actually, I prefer hockey."

"Me, too."

Damn, he liked this woman. He really hoped there was nothing sinister going on here.

She stepped in front of him and looked him directly in the eye. "I want to level with you, Paul."

"Go ahead."

"All five of my guests are from the Washington, D.C., area. They're here for a retreat and meetings."

The presence of the high-profile general who appeared on talk shows suggested a topic for those meetings. "Something political."

"I really shouldn't say."

"What you're telling me is that any one of your guests might be acquainted with the man who was killed."

"Yes," she said.

Paul was sure that if they knew anything about the death of John Maser, these people wouldn't be forthcoming with information. More in-depth questioning and investigation was necessary. He needed to verify their alibis and arrival times.

On the other hand, he might be bothering these people for no reason at all. John Maser might have died as a result of careless driving. Nothing more.

After the autopsy, Paul would have a better indication of foul play. Right now, his only evidence was the whispered word of the dying man who might have been out of his head. *Murder.*

"I have a thought," Julia said. "It's almost time for dinner, and everybody will be gathered in one place. You can talk to all of them at the same time."

Not a great idea from the aspect of police procedure. One-on-one questioning was a more effective tool. But this wasn't really an investigation. Not yet anyway. "Fine with me."

This time Julia held the front door open for him. "After you."

He stepped onto the covered porch that stretched all the way across the front of the lodge. From this vantage

point, there was a clear view of the gravel drive leading up to the lodge and the vehicles that were parked in
the front, including a Hummer that probably belonged
to the general.

He sat in one of the rocking chairs, and Julia climbed
onto the porch swing. She didn't speak right away, but
the silence wasn't uncomfortable. He liked her self-as-
surance—a maturity that didn't require the constant
chatter that filled his house when his girls got revved.
"How do you feel about kids, Julia?"

"Love them." Her face lit up. "My one regret about
living here is that I don't get to spend more time with
my niece and nephew back in Wisconsin. They're practically teenagers now."

"I have two daughters. Seven and nine."

"They must keep your wife busy."

"Not so you'd notice. My ex-wife left a long time
ago. I guess we didn't have much in common." *Not like
you and me,* he wanted to add.

"Raising two little girls on your own must be hard."

The way she looked at him, giving him her full attention, made Paul feel like spilling his guts. He wanted
to tell her about how frustrated he got when the girls
burst into tears for no reason he could understand. Or
how confused he was when they changed clothes five
times before walking out the door. He wanted to tell
Julia about the feeling of sheer happiness when one of
the girls hopped onto his lap and told him he was the
best daddy in the world.

Julia's smile encouraged him, and he wanted to tell
her everything, wanted to hear her laugh. Or maybe
he just wanted to sit here on the porch and watch as
the last rays of sunset tangled in her thick, curly hair.

His gaze stuck on her lips, and his thoughts turned toward kisses. Caresses. Making love in the afternoon.

"What are their names?" she asked.

"Who?"

"Your kids."

"Jennifer and Lily." His thoughts had moved far beyond the kids. "Maybe sometime when you're not busy, you'd go out to dinner with me."

Those beautiful lips pinched, and he was pretty sure she was going to tell him to take a hike. Instead, she said, "Next week?"

"It's a date."

He leaned back in the rocking chair and grinned. A date with Julia. Damn, this was going to be good.

A glint of sunlight caught his eye. When he looked toward the roof of the covered porch, he spotted the camouflaged lens of a surveillance camera. Again, he wondered what was really going on here.

She shouldn't have agreed to go out with him. Alone in the kitchen, Julia loaded the last of the dinner dishes into the washer. And she thought about her date with Paul Hemmings. The pros and the cons. Her mind seesawed.

A chirpy little voice whispered in one ear, "Go on the date. Paul's a good-looking man. Have some fun for a change."

In the other ear was a stern professional tone. "Paul is too smart. He'll figure out that this is a safehouse. Your career will be ruined."

She couldn't take that chance. Julia had worked too hard to get to this level. Her FBI career was her whole life.

"That's pathetic," said the chirpy voice that sounded a little bit like her mother. "You're thirty-two years old. Don't you want to have a family? Children of your own?"

Paul already had a family. Two girls.

Julia shook her head. She was getting way ahead of herself. He hadn't asked her to marry him, after all. It was only a date.

David Dillard, the FBI computer specialist, sauntered into the kitchen. "Any coffee left? I'm going to be up late."

"I was just about to make a fresh pot." Julia and the other two agents at the safehouse would be staying up all night in shifts to monitor the surveillance cameras that were posted in the hallways and outside. To stay alert, caffeine was a necessary evil.

David pushed his glasses up on the bridge of his nose and took a seat at the kitchen table. Of all the Homeland Security specialists who were staying here, she liked David best. He was an average looking guy— pleasant and unassuming. "This is a excellent facility," he said.

"You've hardly been outside."

"I was talking about the lower level."

"The basement? But it's all white and sterile."

"For a computer geek like me, that's heaven."

To each his own. Julia spent as little time as possible in the basement where the charming, rustic lodge transformed into a high-tech operation with computers, communication devices and surveillance monitors. Most of the meetings for the Homeland Security group would take place in a bland windowless room on the lower level.

"I thought you brought your own computer with you," Julia said. "And that collapsible screen thing."

"Tools of the trade." He gave her a weary grin. "I'm setting up a series of simulations over the next several days."

"Simulating what?"

"Our project is to establish a protocol for first response teams handling crisis situations. We want to set up five-person teams of experts who can step in and run things in the chaos following a disaster. They would be the ultimate authority."

Thus far, no one else had bothered to explain the purpose of this meeting. Though Julia had been curious, she was accustomed to FBI people who played it close to the vest. Apparently, David didn't have reservations about talking.

"Isn't there already a chain of command?" she asked as she ground the fresh beans for coffee.

"Too many commanders," he said. "That's the problem. The people who are here represent various authorities. The senator to handle political issues. The general for military. RJ is a financial specialist. I'm a communications person. And, of course, there's Gil representing the CIA."

"What's Gil's specialty?"

David shrugged. "He looks like an assassin to me."

A charming thought. But she suspected David was correct. The sneaky but muscle-bound Gil Bradley looked like the kind of guy who could be dropped behind enemy lines to take out the opposition.

"What kind of crisis would you deal with?" she asked.

"There's the obvious big stuff, like a terrorist bomb-

ing. I have that simulation set up for the last day, and
it's got really amazing effects. But there are smaller issues. Attacks on a high-profile target, like the Golden
Gate bridge. A siege at a survivalist compound. Hos-
tage-taking."

Julia shuddered as she watched the coffee slowly
drip through the filter into the pot. "That's the worst,"
she said. "Hostages."

When it came to her own personal safety, she was
fearless. But a threat to someone she loved? To her
mother and father? She remembered the horror and
pain she'd felt when she learned of her older brother's
death three years ago. He'd been a Marine. In harm's
way.

"Setting up an official response team is an exciting
project," David said. "On paper, it looks like a snap.
The problems come in dealing with all these authoritative personalities. Like the general, for example. His
plan is always the same—Send in the Marines."

"Like my brother," she said. "He was a Marine."

"No kidding," David said. "Mine, too."

"So you know that the Marines are well trained
for crisis."

"If it's a military crisis, yes. But there's so much
more to consider. RJ with her financial expertise brings
a whole different perspective."

The aroma of brewing coffee filled the kitchen.
"What do finances have to do with homeland security?"

"If you close down the money spigot, the terrorists
are left high and dry."

The coffee was done, and she poured a mug for

David. "Thanks for the explanation. It's nice to have some idea about what's going on."

"Simulations are only half of what we're doing. There's also going to be team-building stuff."

"So you'll all learn to like one another?"

"That's too much to hope for," he said with a wry grin. "We'll be doing well if we don't all kill one another by the end of the week."

He grabbed his coffee and disappeared into the lower level. Julia probably should have followed him. There were daily reports she needed to file, but they weren't due until morning and that computer work would give her something to do while watching the monitors.

In spite of the coffee, it was nine o'clock when she fell into bed exhausted. Her alarm was set for three, when she was scheduled to take her shift at the monitors.

When she closed her eyes, her thoughts immediately flashed on Paul Hemmings. In her mind, she saw his chocolate eyes and the deep dimples in his cheeks. And his body. His large muscular body.

Her arms wrapped tightly around her pillow, and she imagined what it would be like to embrace him. It would take at least three pillows for that simulation.

It wasn't safe to feel this way. If only he hadn't asked her out, she could dream about Paul without regret. But he wanted to see her again, and that might be her undoing.

The next morning, everyone was up early except for the general, which seemed odd for a military man who ought to be accustomed to morning exercises. Julia was a bit worried when she stood outside the locked door of the general's bedroom and knocked. "Sir? Are you awake?"

She pressed her ear against the door and listened. There was no sound from inside.

Though she hated to disturb his privacy, Julia unlocked the door to the general's bedroom.

He was flat on his bed, dressed in his uniform with medals and ribbons arrayed across his chest. In his right hand was his Colt Double Eagle handgun. General Harrison Naylor had shot himself in the head.

Chapter 3

Early Sunday morning, Paul had the girls loaded in the Explorer and on their way to another practice session at the ice-skating rink near Vail. The kids had a performance tonight, and their coach wanted to use every possible minute on the ice for practice.

When they passed the spot on the highway where they had been flagged down yesterday, both girls stared in silence through the car windows. Though Paul had gotten them away from the scene of the accident before the emergency rescue team went into action, they knew what had happened. Word spread fast in their community. Though they were close to Vail, they were separate. Redding was the kind of town where everybody knew everything.

"Daddy?" Jennifer, his nine-year-old, sounded subdued. "That man in the crashed-up car died, didn't he?"

Like every parent, he wished to shield his kids from death and tragedy. There was no easy way to talk about these things. "Yes, Jennifer. The man died."

"But you tried to rescue him."

"I tried, but I was too late. It was a very bad accident."

From the back seat, seven-year-old Lily piped up, "It's okay, Daddy. I love you."

"Me, too." Jennifer reached over and patted his arm.

"I love you back." Apparently, they'd decided that he needed comforting, and he appreciated their effort. His daughters weren't always so sweet and sensitive. These two adorable, black-haired girls with porcelain complexions could be hell on wheels. "Have I ever mentioned that you kids are pretty amazing?"

"Yes," Lily said firmly. "I'm very pretty."

Jennifer groaned. "That's not what he meant, dork-face."

"Is too."

"Is not."

So much for sweet and sensitive.

"Daddy," Jennifer whined, "you've got to make Lily change clothes before we get to the rink. Nobody wears their performance outfits to practice."

"I do," said Lily. "I look like a figure-skater princess."

"You're a cow!" Jennifer leaned around the seat to snarl. "I don't even want to be your sister."

"Daddy, make her stop."

Jennifer went louder. "She's sooo embarrassing."

Paul pulled onto the shoulder of the road and slammed the car into Park. He took a sip of black coffee from a thermal mug that never managed to keep the liquid hotter than tepid. From the CD player came the music that Jennifer was using for her latest figure-skating routine. "I Enjoy Being a Girl."

"We can't stop here," Jennifer said desperately. "We're going to be late. Again."

"We got to hurry," Lily echoed. "I have to practice my double axel."

"You wish! You can't do a double."

"Can too."

"Not. Not. Not."

Not for the first time, Paul wished his daughters had been interested in a sport he could get excited about. Skiing or rock climbing or mountain biking. If they had to strap on ice skates, why the hell couldn't they play hockey?

He waited until the car was quiet except for the perky music from the CD, then aimed a stern look at Jennifer, whose rosebud mouth pulled down in a frown. "Don't ever say that you don't want to be Lily's sister."

"But she's—"

"Never say it. We're family. You. Me. And Lily."

"And Mommy," Jennifer added.

"Right." Wherever Mommy was. His ex-wife had taken off before Lily was out of diapers and didn't stay in touch. "We're family. Understand?"

"I guess." She flung herself against the seat and stared straight ahead through the windshield.

He peered into the rear where Lily, the selfproclaimed princess, plucked at the silver spangles on the leotard she wore under her parka. "Why are you wearing your fancy outfit to practice?"

"Coach Megan wanted to see it before tonight."

"Show it to her, then change into your other clothes.

I don't want those sparkles to get ruined." That scrap of fabric had cost a pretty penny. "Promise you'll do that."

"Yes, Daddy."

He nodded. "Both of you. No more fighting."

"Daddy?" Jennifer was still scowling. "Is Mommy coming to our performance tonight?"

"She lives in Texas, honey. That's a long way from here. Besides, I'll be there." His presence felt insufficient.

"Who's going to help me put on my makeup?"

"You're wearing makeup?"

The girls exchanged a glance and rolled their eyes. "Everybody wears makeup for performance," Jennifer informed him.

"I'll take care of it," Paul said as he merged back onto the road and drove the last couple of miles to the new indoor ice-skating rink. He waited until the girls had scampered inside. After skating practice, they were scheduled for an all-day play date with a friend, another little ice-skating princess.

Paul had to work today. And, apparently, he also had to figure out a way to get lipstick and mascara on his girls. He shuddered at the thought.

Wheeling around in the parking lot, he headed back toward home. There was just enough time to grab a shower, change into his uniform and report for duty. After he checked in, his first order of business would be filling out reports on the five people he'd interviewed at Julia's place—a waste of time. All five came from the Washington, D.C., area, but none of them recognized John Maser's name.

Though Paul had suspicions about these people, he'd have to wait for more evidence before pursuing this investigation further. John Maser's accident could have been just that—an unfortunate vehicular accident.

Still, that single dying word kept repeating in Paul's brain. *Murder.*

As he pulled up in front of his house, his cell phone rang, and he picked up. Immediately, he recognized Julia's rich, alto voice. She sounded agitated.

"Paul, I need for you to come here. Right away."

"What's wrong?"

"I can't explain. Just come. Please."

If she'd been anybody else, he would have insisted on more details. But he liked that she'd called him. He wanted to be the knight in shining armor who could solve all her problems. "I'll be there in twenty-five minutes."

Julia had never been in such a complicated situation. The general was dead. He was in his locked bedroom, all alone with the gun in his hand. He'd left a suicide note.

Yet, she knew in her heart that his death was murder.

Her duty as a federal agent was to encourage an investigation. But if the local law enforcement got involved, her safehouse would be exposed. She'd have no choice but to recommend closing down the entire operation, and she didn't want that to happen. She was proud of her work here and loved the mountains. The safehouse felt more like home than anywhere she'd ever lived, and she'd do anything to protect it. Even if it meant misleading Paul.

When she opened the front door for him, she forced herself to look him in the eye. Inside her rib cage her heart was jumping like a jackrabbit, but she kept her voice steady, "Thank you for coming."

"No problem." As he stepped across the threshold, his gaze flicked around the room, taking in every detail. "What's up?"

"Come with me."

She led the way up the staircase to the second-floor bedrooms. Their boot heels echoed on the hardwood floor. She and Paul were almost alone in the house. Her so-called guests—the Homeland Security experts— were horseback riding as a team-building exercise. Julia had suggested that everybody lay low while the police were here.

Using her key, she opened the door to General Harrison Naylor's bedroom. The death scene was carefully arranged. Wearing his Marine dress blues, the general lay stretched out on the bed. In his right hand, he gripped his silver Colt Double Eagle pistol with sound suppressor attached. The fatal bullet had gone through the back of his skull, leaving his face unmarked. His eyes were closed. His lifeblood stained the pillows and the linens.

On a small desk, his laptop was open but not turned on. A note rested beside it.

As Paul stepped gingerly into the scene, Julia told her first lie. "I found him like this."

When she first discovered the body, she had closed and relocked the bedroom door behind her. Standing over the body of the general, her FBI training kicked into high gear. Her brain cleared. Her priorities sorted. Much to her shame, her first thoughts centered on the security of the safehouse.

She forced herself to focus. A man was dead. A

heroic military man. A man who led other brave Marines, like her brother, into battle. There were procedures to be followed.

Her trained gaze had gone to the rows of medals on this fallen soldier's chest. At that moment, she realized that the general had not committed suicide. The medals were not in proper order.

A Marine would never be so careless. When her brother was laid out in his coffin, she had studied the Marine Corps Manual to make sure his ribbons and medals were in correct alignment. The general would never make such a mistake. Therefore, she could assume that someone else had pinned those medals to his chest. This wasn't a suicide.

However, if the general was murdered, it meant a prolonged investigation by local authorities. A simple suicide would be an open-and-shut case. She could carefully escort the local lawmen through their duties without revealing the real business of the safehouse.

And so, she had decided to change the medals, putting them in proper order. As if this tampering with the crime scene wasn't bad enough, she'd done more.

Under the sink in the general's bathroom, she found a pair of latex gloves, slipped them on and returned to the body.

The general's shoes had been scuffed. A true Marine would never consider himself to be fully in uniform with dirty shoes. She'd removed the shoes from the general's feet, polished them and put them back on.

Guilt coursed through her veins like poison. How could she have done such a thing? Her life was dedicated to fighting crime, and she was no better than any other criminal, hiding evidence. How could she allow the general's family to believe that he'd killed himself?

She watched as Paul prowled around the bedroom, being careful not to touch anything. He leaned over the general's body for a closer look. "This is strange."

"What?" She halfway hoped that he'd see through her tampering and confront her. "What's strange?"

"He's wearing his hearing aid," Paul said. "If I was going to shoot myself in the head, that would be the first thing to go."

Her lips pinched together, holding back an urge to confess to him. Not only was she guilty of rearranging a crime scene but she was also betraying Paul, deliberately misleading him.

He asked, "Was his bedroom door locked?"

"Yes." That much was true. "And we have a security camera in the hallway. I've already checked the tape. There was no one who came into or out of his room."

"A security camera?" He turned toward her. "Why?"

"Security," she said as if it were the most obvious thing in the world. Julia knew that most people in nearby Redding didn't even bother locking their doors. "There was already a lot of security equipment when I moved here."

"And you still keep it running?" he said. "Have you been bothered by theft? Vandalism?"

There wasn't much likelihood of anyone sneaking up on the safehouse. If they came within a hundred feet of the property, they'd be met by armed agents.

"I've never had any problems," she said, trying to shrug off his questioning gaze. "The camera came in handy this time, right?"

Paul circled the bed, went to the window and

glanced out at the eaves. Julia knew it was possible for the murderer to have come across the roof and entered the general's room through this window. Such an action would require the expert skill of a rock climber who was accustomed to clinging to tiny ledges. She'd immediately thought of Gil Bradley, the former Navy SEAL who had the look and the manner of an assassin.

If Gil had murdered the general, she didn't want to shield him from justice. But she had to keep her secret; she couldn't let people know this was an FBI safehouse.

Paul inspected the double-paned window. The lower half was designed to be pulled up over the upper half in summer to let in the fresh air. "This window doesn't have a lock."

"There's no way to open it from the outside without prying it loose."

"After the sheriff gets here, I'll need to check it out."

"Surely, you don't think someone crept in here during the night and murdered the general."

She held her breath, waiting for his response.

"I doubt it," he said. "There are no signs of a struggle. It appears that the general was shot where he lies because there aren't blood spatters in the rest of the room."

"So it's suicide," she said.

"Apparent suicide," Paul corrected her. "We still need to go through the drill. Taking fingerprints. Checking the room for fibers, hairs and tiny spots of blood. I'll need to interview your guests to see if any of them heard or saw anything unusual."

"I'd really appreciate if this could be handled with as little fuss as possible. It's bad for business and—" She paused midsentence. Her gaze turned to the dead man. How could she be scheming in his presence? "God, I sound cold. I shouldn't be thinking about business."

"I understand," Paul said.

"My other guests knew the general. I don't want to upset them any more than necessary."

"They'll probably call off their meeting," Paul said.

That was what she had expected. But the senator had been adamant about moving forward with their mission; he had no other free time in his schedule. "They've decided to carry on."

Clearly taken aback, Paul said, "Doesn't sound like your other guests are concerned about the general's suicide."

"They're task-oriented people from Washington. It's not up to me to approve or disapprove of their decision."

Her job was to keep them safe. And she'd failed miserably. As she glanced at the lifeless body stretched out on the bed, her heart ached with the weight of her guilty secrets. *I'm sorry, General. So horribly sorry.* He deserved to have his death investigated. Suicide was looked upon as the coward's way out. A Marine deserved better.

She felt Paul's arm encircle her shoulders. Gently, he guided her toward the bedroom door. "Don't worry, Julia. I'll take care of everything. We'll be as discreet as possible."

Standing in the hallway outside the bedroom, she allowed herself to accept his comforting embrace, leaning her head into the crook of his neck. Her arms wrapped around his huge torso. He was so big and solid.

Though his touch was in no way inappropriate and he patted her shoulders in an almost impersonal manner, she felt a surge of erotic tension. Her breasts rubbed against his chest. She inhaled his masculine scent. Gazing up, she noticed that his chin was marked with morning stubble. Though he was in his deputy uniform, he had to have come here immediately without even stopping to shave.

He was anxious to help, and she repaid him with lies, using him for her own purposes. Julia stepped away from his embrace. There was a depth of meaning in her voice when she whispered, "I'm sorry."

"No need for you to be sorry. This isn't your fault."

If only he knew what she'd done. In his warm brown eyes, she saw the glow of kindness. She didn't merit his friendship. "What happens next?"

"I'll call the sheriff. He's not going to be happy. Two fatalities in two days."

"Is that unusual?"

"Not for a city," Paul said. "But we're a fairly quiet little county."

"I hate to bring this up," she said, "but there will be media attention. General Naylor was well known. He did commentary on a lot of news programs."

"Which means the sheriff is going to be talking to the press," Paul said. "He can handle it."

She envisioned television trucks with satellite dishes and reporters with microphones. A nightmare! "I really don't want my lodge to be the backdrop for those interviews."

"No problem. We'll evacuate the body to the hospital before autopsy. The sheriff can make his statement to the press from that location."

For that, she was endlessly grateful. The last thing she needed was a mob of curious interviewers crawling all over the safehouse.

"Yesterday," Paul said, "the general reacted strangely when you mentioned his television commentaries. What did he say? Something about not believing everything you hear. It was like he thought he was being unfairly criticized."

"Paranoid," she said. "That fits with suicide, doesn't it?"

"Did you notice anything else unusual about his state of mind?"

"Other than shooting at rabbits off the deck behind the lodge?"

"Strange behavior," he said.

"But not typical. The general kept to himself. He got here a day ahead of the others and spent most of that time in his room."

Paul glanced down at his boots, then looked up at her again. "How much do you know about makeup? You know, lipstick and stuff."

That question came out of the blue. "On occasion, I've been known to use cosmetics."

"You don't need that stuff," he said quickly. "I like the way you look. Healthy. And your eyes…well, your blue eyes are beautiful."

His gruff compliment took her off guard. Had he really said that she was beautiful? Her eyes were beautiful? Self-consciously, she glanced away. "Thank you."

"This is about my two daughters. They have an ice-skating performance tonight at the rink near Vail, and they need to put on makeup. That happens to be a topic I don't know much about."

She peeked up at him. Though he was trying to scowl, the dimples in his cheeks deepened. Adorable. "I'd like to help you, Paul."

He waved his hand back and forth as if to erase his words. "Forget it. You have enough to worry about."

"Tell you what. I'll put together a little makeup kit for you to take with you."

"Thanks a lot, Julia."

His gratitude was utterly sincere. The sheepish expression on his face almost brought her to tears. For the first time in her life, Julia had purposely done wrong. She was lying to this terrific guy, and it was tearing her apart.

Unable to look in Paul's trusting eyes for one more second, she pivoted and headed down the staircase.

In the kitchen, they found Craig Lennox, the other FBI agent who worked with her at the safehouse. Craig, a computer expert, was nearly as concerned as Julia about the true purpose of the safehouse being discovered. The office on the basement floor—filled with high-tech surveillance and computer equipment—was his domain, and he didn't want anybody touching anything.

His dark eyes darted nervously in his thin face. He nodded to Paul, who he'd met yesterday. "Is there anything I should be doing?"

"Sit tight," Julia said. "The police will be here soon."

He held up a videocassette. "I made copies of the surveillance tapes that show the hallway outside the general's room."

"For all night?" Paul asked.

"From eleven o'clock when the general went to bed until this morning when Julia opened his door."

"Nobody entered the room?"

"Nobody," Craig said. "These tapes are time coded on the bottom. There's not one second missing."

Paul took a cell phone from his utility belt and punched in a number on his cell phone. "Jurisdiction can be complicated up here, but your resort is well outside Vail's city limits so the Eagle County sheriff will be handling this incident. There's no need to call in the state investigators for a suicide."

A suicide. Paul seemed convinced. She could only hope that the other county officials would also be satisfied by that explanation.

Chapter 4

That evening at half past five o'clock when Paul herded everybody out of the house, the girls were wearing their sparkly costumes under their parkas. Their black hair was done up in curly ponytails, and their makeup was perfect thanks to makeup kits assembled by Julia and expert help from Abby Nelson. Abby was an FBI agent recently assigned to the Denver office so she could be near Mac Granger, a homicide detective, who was one of Paul's oldest and best friends.

Earlier today, Paul had called Mac and asked if he and Abby would drive up to Redding for the performance that night. "It would mean a lot to Jennifer and Lily."

"Count on us," Mac said.

Though it wasn't the same as having their mother

attend, Paul knew the girls would be pleased to have a decent-sized cheering section in the audience.

Another good friend, Jess Isler, was also coming along. Jess had been staying with Paul while recuperating from a serious injury. Being with Jess—a ladies' man—usually meant there were several adoring females in the vicinity. Jess was on the Vail ski patrol and was so ridiculously handsome that he regularly dated the supermodels and movie stars who showed up on the slopes. Right now, however, Jess seemed to be spending a lot of one-on-one time with a nurse from the hospital who had promised to meet them at the rink.

Paul looked over the entourage. "We should take two cars."

Jennifer batted her eyelashes. "Me and Lily want to ride with Abby."

Teasing, Jess clutched his heart. "You don't want to ride with me? I'm hurt."

"We see you every day." Jennifer had already linked her hand with Abby's. "Mac and Abby drove all the way up here from Denver to watch us skate."

"But we love you, Jessy-Messy," Lily said happily. Her lipstick was already smeared. "You go with Daddy."

"If I don't see you before the show," Jess said, "break a leg."

Lily gasped. "Huh?"

"That means good luck," Jess said. "It's an expression. Break a leg means—"

"Everybody knows that," Jennifer said. "Come on, Lily."

When Paul got behind the wheel of the Explorer, he surreptitiously watched as Jess climbed into the passenger seat. Six weeks ago, Jess had been shot in the chest. For a while, Paul was as scared as hell, afraid his friend wasn't going to make it. Though he wasn't a particularly religious man, he'd prayed hard and long. Jess and Mac had grown up together; they were closer to him than brothers.

So far, Jess's recovery seemed to be going well, but he wasn't back to full strength, and he had a bad habit of overexerting himself. That habit was the main reason Paul had insisted that Jess stay with him in Redding even though he owned a condo in Vail. Though it was driving Jess crazy to know there was fresh snow and mountains to be skied, Paul kept him safely on the sidelines.

Jess slammed the car door and turned to Paul. He was pale but grinning. "Where did you get the lipstick?"

"I have my ways." Paul quickly changed the subject. "You had therapy today. How are you doing?"

"The doc said I could try skiing next week, but I have to wear this girdle contraption to protect my busted ribs." He cocked an eyebrow. "The lipstick?"

"A lady friend."

"I knew it," he crowed. "Who is she?"

"Forget it." Paul pulled out of the drive and led the way so Mac could follow. "I'm not going to introduce you. Because she'd be all gaga over your skinny butt."

"Don't go there, Paul. I'm doing my best to convince Marcia that I'm not a hound dog."

"Getting serious about her? Maybe thinking about marriage?"

"Whoa, buddy. Marcia and I haven't even been, you know, intimate."

Paul offered wry condolence. "Poor you. I guess it's complicated to make love with broken ribs."

"It's been almost six weeks. That's the longest time I've gone without since we were in high school."

"A little abstinence is good for you," Paul said. "If you decide to marry Marcia, it's going to be a day of mourning for the other women of Eagle County."

"You're full of crap."

"Not really."

Paul was a realist. He'd never been popular with women. In spite of his size—or maybe because of it—he tended to be shy. Then, when he finally spoke, he'd blurt out something stupid. Around women, he was clumsy, always tripping over his own big feet.

All the way from grade school to high school graduation when he, Jess and Mac had been best pals, the girls had flocked around handsome Jess with his streaked blond hair and blue eyes. Mac's relationships tended to be more monogamous and intense. And Paul was relegated to the role of the perpetual fifth wheel.

It was ironic that he'd been the first one to settle down into a marriage and have kids. And unfortunate that the marriage had fallen apart in spite of his best efforts to hold things together.

"Come on," Jess said, "tell me who gave you the lipstick."

"Her name is Julia Last, and she runs that resort where Mac stayed when he was in town."

"Did you ask her out?"

"Dinner. Next week." Paul figured he might as well take advantage of Jess's vast dating expertise. "Where should I take her?"

"That depends. Tell me about her."

"She's strong." That was the first word that came to mind when he thought of Julia. "The first time I saw her, she was chopping wood, handling an ax like a lumberjack. But that's not to say she's masculine. She's got long curly brown hair that smells great. And the prettiest blue eyes I've ever seen. She's tall. With an hourglass figure. Full, round hips and full, round..."

His voice trailed off as a picture of Julia took shape in his mind. Throughout this morning's investigation with the sheriff, the coroner and the ambulance team that removed General Harrison Naylor's body, he hadn't been able to take his eyes off her. Though she'd obviously been tense, he admired her composure as she served up coffee and muffins all around.

Julia only relaxed after the forensics were done and the sheriff agreed with Paul's conclusion that the general's death was a suicide. The note he'd left behind stated his regrets for wrong decisions he'd made in the heat of battle.

"What does she like doing?" Jess asked.

"There are horses at the lodge." He took a moment to imagine Julia on horseback with her hair flying loose around her shoulders. A very sexy image. "She likes football, but prefers hockey."

"Just like you."

"When I'm around her," Paul said, "I want to tell her everything about me and the girls. Every little detail. At the same time, it's nice to just be near her. She's a woman who knows how to be quiet."

"You've got it bad," Jess said. "Here's what you do on the first date. Order a catered picnic basket and pick up some decent wine. Then you charter a plane. I know I guy who flies for cheap. And then—"

"What? Charter a plane?"

"Think big. You want to impress the woman."

"I don't want her to think I'm abducting her," Paul said.

"Women like a man who takes control and sweeps them off their feet."

Paul's instincts told him that Julia wouldn't appreciate a lot of fuss. "I think a simple dinner is going to be enough."

He pulled into the parking lot outside the ice-skating rink, met up with the others and escorted the girls into the backstage area. The new skating rink had been a huge success with lots of kids interested. Backstage, a couple of dozen skaters, ranging in age from five years old to high school, were doing stretch exercises and giggling wildly. There were few other men in this preparation area and Paul made a hasty retreat after wishing Jennifer and Lily good luck.

He returned to the bleachers surrounding the rink. From the way Mac and Abby were smirking, he guessed that Jess had blabbed to them about Julia. Swell.

Guilt had driven Julia from the safehouse. After sitting at the dinner table with the others who had known General Harrison Naylor and had offered respectful toasts to his memory, she had to leave. How could she have tampered with the crime scene? How could she, in good conscience, allow the world to believe this brave old Marine had committed suicide?

She needed to confess, and that need lead her to the ice-skating rink near Vail where she knew she would find Deputy Paul Hemmings. She hoped that he would understand, that he wouldn't hate her for what she'd done. Inside the arena, she took a seat by herself on the bleachers and watched as these seemingly delicate skaters performed their athletic spins and leaps.

Checking out the audience, she immediately spotted Paul. Unfortunately, he was with Mac Granger and Abby Nelson—two people who knew about the safehouse. No way could Julia face them. It had been a mistake to come here.

As she rose from her seat, intending to slip away before she was noticed, Paul spotted her. He bolted from his seat and came toward her. She couldn't run away, had to face him.

He took a seat on the bleachers beside her. His huge thigh brushed against hers. "I'm glad to see you, Julia."

"Did you get the girl's makeup put on straight?"

"Abby did it." He pointed back toward the others who were all staring in their direction. "Abby Nelson. I think you know her. And Mac."

"Yes." Julia gave them a small wave. "They stayed with me. How are they doing?"

"Good. They've got a good relationship. I've never seen Mac so open."

They sat quietly for a moment and watched the tiniest skaters go through a simple routine with only a couple of slip-ups. Julia's anxiety ratcheted higher with each passing second. In spite of the cold from the ice, she was sweating. Her mouth was dry as cotton. Her feet were itching to run.

"Something wrong?" Paul asked.

She had to face up to what she'd done. "Could I talk to you in private for a minute?"

They climbed down from the bleachers and went toward the area where hot dogs and pretzels were being sold to benefit the Eagle County Skaters. From what Julia had heard, this newly built facility was a tremendous success—booked solid with figure-skating lessons, hockey teams and recreational time. She wished she could enjoy the evening, but the cheers from the audience only heightened her tension. She knew that once she spoke out, her words could never be reclaimed. The secrecy of the safehouse would be in Paul's hands. "Can I trust you?"

"A hundred percent."

"Even if I might tell you something that could cause conflict with your job?"

He gave her a friendly little pat on the shoulder. "I guess that depends. If you tell me you've got twenty dead bodies buried in your backyard, I'll probably have to dig them up."

She'd expected that response. Paul was a deputy, sworn to defend the law. And so was she. "It's about the resort."

"I'm listening."

"My resort offers something more than lodging and meals." She bit her lip. *Now or never. Just tell him.* "I'm running an FBI safehouse."

"You're an FBI agent?"

"Yes."

He didn't seem surprised in the least. Instead, his expression was visibly more relaxed. "That's a relief."

"You suspected something?"

"You've got surveillance cameras all over the damn place, and your employees wear shoulder holsters. Mac was real secretive about the resort when he was staying there." He grinned, showing his dimples. "I was worried that you might be protecting a bad secret."

"Twenty bodies buried in the backyard?"

"Something like that."

"Nobody else can know about this."

"Understood. A safehouse isn't much good if everybody knows it's there." He took both her hands in his and gave a squeeze. "Don't worry, Julia. Your secret is safe with me."

Suddenly, his head jerked up. "That's Jennifer's music. Come on, we have to see her routine."

As they hustled back to the rink, her emotions were in turmoil. She'd taken the first step toward the truth. Would Paul be equally sanguine with her confession about tampering with crime-scene evidence?

The music was "I Enjoy Being a Girl." Four slender young skaters, dressed in pink-sequined leotards with short skirts, took the ice. Holding hands they skated in a figure eight.

"The one in front," Paul said, "that's my Jennifer."

"I can tell." Jennifer had her father's black hair and dark eyes. And his dimples. "She looks like you."

"God, I hope not."

She glanced up at his profile. Every bit of his attention focused on the ice as he watched the skaters glide to the center. Each did a spin. Then a spread-eagle leap. After his Jennifer successfully completed her double axel, Paul gave a cheer and pumped his fist. "She did it. Damn, I'm glad. There'd be no living with the girl if she slipped up."

He applauded enthusiastically as the routine completed and the skaters left the ice, then he turned to

Julia. "That's all for my kids until the grand finale. Can I buy you a hot dog?"

She nodded, wishing that she could relax and share the joy of this proud father. Though Paul was a deputy who carried a gun and dealt with crime, everything about him seemed wonderfully sane and normal—the very opposite of her daily routine.

At the safehouse, there was constant surveillance, the ever-present threat of danger. She was always looking over her shoulder. Especially now, with her suspicion that the general had been murdered.

She slathered mustard on a fat bratwurst and took a healthy bite, which she immediately regretted. Her throat was too tight to swallow. And her stomach twisted in a knot.

Forcing herself to gulp down the brat, Julia realized that she had to be really, truly upset if she was having trouble eating. Usually, she had a cast-iron stomach. "Paul, there's something else."

"Okay." He led her to a round table, and gallantly held her chair while she sat.

Though there was no one nearby, she lowered her voice. "It's about the general. I have reason to believe he was murdered."

"Tell me why."

She hesitated. Supposedly, confession was good for the soul. But she hated admitting what she'd done. Throughout her career with the FBI, she'd been an exemplary agent. No mistakes. No black marks on her record.

Quietly, Paul said, "All the evidence points to suicide. The door to the general's bedroom was locked. Your surveillance tapes show that no one entered or exited. We checked the window, and it showed no sign of tampering. There were other fingerprints in the room, but none on the gun. No sign of a struggle. No blood spatters to indicate he was shot somewhere else, then laid out on the bed."

"I know," she said miserably.

"Only one of your guests, Senator Ashbrook, who had the room right next to the general, reported hearing anything unusual. A thud that could have been the gunshot with the silencer. That was around midnight."

She nodded.

"Those are the facts, Julia. Nobody else was in that room with the general. Nobody else pulled that trigger."

For a moment, she doubted her own suspicions. Everything Paul said was correct. It seemed physically impossible for the general to have been murdered. She set the bratwurst on the paper plate. "Maybe I'm wrong."

"If I had to guess," Paul said, "I'd say you were feeling guilty that he died on your watch."

That thought hadn't occurred to Julia. Her feelings of failure about having the general commit suicide at the safehouse might have caused her to make too much of her observations. A couple of misplaced medals and scuffed shoes didn't override all the other evidence. "What about the note?"

"It seemed like a straightforward apology," Paul said. "He felt bad about mistakes he'd made in battle."

"It was a printed out page from his laptop."

"But he signed it." Paul pointed to her bratwurst. "Not hungry?"

"I guess not."

"Do you mind if I finish that off for you?"

"Go right ahead." She liked watching him eat. A big man with big appetites. No problem was too large for him to handle. When she was with him, her burden of responsibility seemed lighter. "Thanks, Paul. You've put my mind at ease."

He finished off her bratwurst and grinned. "Would you like to go back to the ice and join the others? I'm sure Mac and Abby would like to say hello."

She shook her head. "I've already been gone too long. I don't want any more trouble tonight."

"Are you expecting problems?"

"Not really. The others knew the general well. Over dinner, they were subdued. Not sad enough to cancel their meetings, though." She rose from the table. "Good night, Paul."

"I'll walk you out to your car."

Though it wasn't necessary for him to escort her, she appreciated the gesture. At the exit from the rink, he held the door for her, and she realized how long it had been since anyone had treated her like a lady.

To the other agents at the safehouse, she was the boss. Her gender didn't matter. And her "guests" treated her like a function—somebody who was there to facilitate their needs.

In contrast, Paul was gentlemanly and courteous, taking her arm to guide her through the parking lot. She wanted desperately to believe he was right about the general's death. It was suicide. No one else was in the room. It had to be suicide.

When they reached her car, she turned toward him. Her head tilted back. She had to look up to gaze into his face, dimly lit by the lights in the skating rink parking lot.

"You should get back inside," she said. "It's cold out here."

"That's strange. I feel nice and warm."

So did she. The comforting warmth that radiated inside her held the December cold at bay.

"I'm glad you came to me, Julia."

"Me, too." His calm statement of the facts had gone a long way toward reassuring her. Impulsively, she reached up and rested her hand on his cheek.

He responded in kind. His hand glided along her jawline and rested at her nape under her ponytail. He leaned closer, and she knew he intended to kiss her. She wanted him to.

Their noses rubbed. His mouth brushed lightly against hers. His lips tasted of mustard, and she was hungry—hungry for him. His gentle kiss left her longing for more. But he stepped away, hesitant and shy.

His voice was husky. "I might have to stop by your place tomorrow. You know, to follow up."

"I'll be there."

"Not that I think the general's death was murder," he said.

"Probably not," she agreed.

"If it was," he said with a frown, "that would mean the murderer was one of the people staying at the house."

A shudder went through her. "All my guests would be in danger."

"And you," he said.

With all her heart, she hoped he was wrong.

Chapter 5

The next day when Julia sat down to lunch with the four remaining participants in the Homeland Security project, she remembered Paul's words. One of these people might be a murderer. They certainly looked angry enough. The hostility around the long table in the dining room was palpable. They sat where she had laid the plates—two on each side with Julia at the head of the table.

Senator Marcus Ashbrook poked his fork into his salad. "Is this lettuce organic?"

"It doesn't matter," said RJ Katz. Her sleek helmet of calico-colored hair fell forward, hiding her delicate features. "Lettuce approved by the FDA isn't going to kill you."

"I'm with Ashbrook," said Gil Bradley. His body was his temple. "I want fresh, organic produce."

He glared accusingly at Julia who said, "As a matter of fact, all our produce is certified free from artificial additives or pesticides. We purchase from the same source as one of the exclusive Vail hotels."

Ashbrook was appeased for the moment. He took a bite, chewed thoroughly and swallowed. "What about the chicken?"

"Free range." Because the safehouse budget for food was subsidized by the FBI, she was able to buy the highest quality. Unlike other struggling little resorts, she was under no pressure to turn a profit. Julia's pressures were different and more deadly.

Gil glanced across the table at David Dillard, the computer expert. "What's our agenda for this afternoon?"

"I need to reprogram the simulation exercise," David said. "It was originally set up for input from five people."

"We agreed," Gil said, "that I would take the general's position. My background as a Navy SEAL qualifies me to speak to the military view."

"My simulation doesn't work that way," David said. "I present you all with a Homeland Security situation, and you need to concentrate on your own responses. Political from the senator. FBI and financial from RJ. And the CIA response from you, Gil."

"What happens to the military response?" Ashbrook asked. "We need to know what the generals would require."

"I'll program in the most likely response." David pushed his glasses up on the bridge of his nose. "It's not a perfect solution, but the alternative is to cancel the entire exercise."

"That's not an option," Ashbrook said. "General Naylor would have wanted us to continue."

"You don't know that." RJ's wide catlike eyes narrowed. "None of us can guess what was going through the general's mind."

"We were close," said the senator. "The general and I served on two other committees together."

"Then maybe you can tell us," RJ said. "Why did he kill himself?"

"My dear young lady, you have no idea of the pressures that come from great responsibilities."

"None of us can guess what he was thinking," Gil said. Though he seemed an unlikely peacemaker, his tone was placating. "We can only mourn his passing."

There was a moment of silence as they attacked their food. They almost seemed sad, and Julia was glad for this small show of humanity from this group.

"The general's absence," David said, "doesn't ruin the project. Our purpose here is to create a prototype for communication."

"Waste of time," Ashbrook muttered. "I can already tell you what you're going to learn from these computer simulations."

"What might that be?" David asked.

"It's obvious. The first response to a Homeland Security situation is the need for leadership. One man." Ashbrook held up his index finger. "One acknowledged leader."

"That might well be our conclusion," David said. "Unfortunately, when there's a threat to national security, several branches of government are involved."

Ashbrook returned his attention to his food. "I fully

intend to lead this first response team when it is organized."

"Do you?" RJ's voice was cool. "Why should you be the leader?"

"That's what I do." Ashbrook jabbed a fork across the table in her direction. "I lead."

"I always thought the job of a senator was to represent the interests of his state."

"It's within the interests of Wyoming to deal with Homeland Security."

"Right," RJ muttered. "As if Wyoming is a major target for international terrorism."

As Julia watched their sniping, she wondered if this power struggle might be a motive for murder. The general—another man who was accustomed to being the leader—would have been a formidable adversary for Ashbrook.

"In any case," David said, "I'd appreciate if we could take a break after lunch so I can work out the bugs in my program. Maybe start up again around two-thirty."

There were murmurs of agreement around the table. RJ added, "There's no need for more team building. Right?"

"Certainly not," Ashbrook said.

From the atmosphere of tension evident around the dining table, Julia guessed that the exercises designed to build trust and cooperation among these people had been a dismal failure. They were all too high-powered, too focused on their own agendas, their own secrets.

She offered, "If any of you would like to use the time off for recreation, I can arrange horseback riding."

When they all refused, she was relieved. The less time she spent with these people, the better.

* * *

As it turned out, Paul had a legitimate, police-oriented reason for visiting Julia's resort. He needed to talk with the senator in conjunction with his investigation into the vehicular death of John Maser.

A background check on the deceased man had revealed some interesting information. He had started out as one of the good guys and received an honorable discharge from the Marines. Then his life went to hell. His rap sheet showed three arrests and one conviction on fraud. His primary activities involved gunrunning and dealing in illegal weaponry. Currently, he was in touch with a survivalist group based in Wyoming. That fact formed a tenuous connection to the Wyoming senator who was staying at Julia's place.

When he parked in front, Paul saw the pretty little resort through a new focus. This was an FBI safehouse where protected witnesses were secreted away and surveillance was high.

The agent who opened the door at the safehouse, Roger Flannery, informed Paul that the guests were resting and Julia was with the horses. *No problem!* Paul would much rather talk to her, anyway. He left the front porch and followed a well-worn path around the house to the barn.

Though the sun was shining and the temperature was in the low forties, misty gray clouds smeared across the skies. The forecasters were calling for major snowfall tonight. Not that anybody took those predictions too seriously. Colorado weather was notoriously fickle. His buddy, Jess, described the sudden changes in temperature and precipitation as Rocky Mountain

PMS—ranging from heat wave to ice storm in a matter of minutes.

In the heated barn, Paul found Julia saddling up a dappled mare. She wore a short leather jacket, giving him an enticing view of her voluptuous bottom in snug-fitting Levi's.

He glanced over his shoulder toward the safehouse, wondering if they were being observed on surveillance cameras right now. If he reached out and patted her butt, would the other agents at the house have a front row view?

Hands in pockets, he looked back toward Julia. "Going for a ride?"

"A short ride," she said.

He leaned close to her and whispered, "Are we being watched right now?"

"We have a camera in the barn, but it's not turned on right now. During the day, we rely on sensors in the fence surrounding the property to let us know if anybody is approaching."

"So nobody would know if I did this." He glided his hand down her arm, caught her hand and squeezed lightly.

"Nobody's watching," she said.

"Or this?" He gave a little tug, pulling her closer to him. "Nobody would know."

"No one but me." She slipped into his arms for an embrace. Though her lovely face tilted up toward him and her smile was welcoming, she moved away before he could kiss her. "Do you ride, Paul?"

"Hell, yes." Though his arms were empty, the fresh scent of her hair tantalized his senses.

"Come with me."

"You bet."

In minutes, he'd saddled a big black stallion with a blaze of white on his chest. Together, he and Julia led their horses from the heated barn and mounted.

"What's my horse's name?" he asked.

"Diablo."

"The devil. Bad temper?"

"Not at all. Most of these horses are gentle, accustomed to being ridden by strangers. I do have a pregnant mare who's really cranky. Poor thing."

On horseback, Julia was as striking as he'd imagined. She sat tall in the saddle with shoulders back. The cool December wind brought roses to her cheeks, making her blue eyes look even more beautiful.

Last night, Jess had teased him about having a bad case of the hots for her, and he was dead right. Paul couldn't find a single flaw in this woman.

He rode beside her. "Mac and Abby say hi."

"They seem to have a good relationship," she said. "I'm glad."

"They have a lot in common with both of them being involved in law enforcement." *Like us,* he wanted to add.

"There's a lot of stress that goes along with their work," she said. "Especially for Abby. She was undercover a lot. That's hard."

"Have you ever done undercover work?"

"I'm not the right personality type." She tossed her head, sending a ripple through her long, brown ponytail. "I've never been good at lying."

"But you've kept the safehouse a secret for a couple of years."

"Keeping a secret is different than out-and-out lying.

Until yesterday, nobody paid much attention to this little resort. And then, when I was under pressure…" Her blue eyes focused on him. "I had to tell you."

"I'm glad you did. I wouldn't like having a lie between us."

When they reached the open meadow, both horses were frisky, tossing their heads and tugging at the reins. They seemed to know that this was their time to run hard.

Julia pointed to a distant outcropping of jagged boulders shaped like the head of a rabbit with two ears sticking straight up. "I'll meet you there."

Leaning forward in the saddle, she made a clicking noise. With her heels, she gave her mare a nudge. The horse took off in a shot, leaving Paul and the stallion behind.

He flicked his reins. "Let's go, boy."

Diablo charged forward. His powerful sinews flexed and extended as they flew across the open land, closing the gap between himself and Julia.

The exhilarating sensation of speed shot through him like a jolt of electricity. Paul loved going fast whether it was downhill skiing, racing a car or riding a stallion. The wind swirled in their wake. The arid landscape, dotted with snow, flashed in his peripheral vision.

Though Julia had a head start, Paul reached the outcropping at the same time she did. Pulling back on the reins, he announced, "It's a tie."

"This wasn't a race," she scoffed. "If we'd been racing, there's no way you would have caught me."

"I'd have won," he said. "My horse is bigger than yours."

"It's not about size."

"Too bad. I'm usually the biggest guy around."

"I'll bet you are."

They rode side by side at the edge of the forest. Though the ground was dry, there were still patches of unmelted snow. The white-trunked aspen had lost their golden autumn leaves, and the shrubs were bare. "I like winter," he said. "Everything gets quiet and still."

"And dead."

"Just resting. Building up strength for the spring-time." He relaxed in the saddle, enjoying the rhythm of the stallion's gait. It had been a while since he'd gone horseback riding. "Now that you've had some time to think about it, how are you feeling about the general's death?"

"If it was murder, I couldn't have handpicked a more suspicious bunch than my so-called guests. They're at one another's throats, especially the senator. He wants to be leader of this group. That could be a motive for murder."

"How so?"

"The general would have threatened his claim to leadership. Senator Ashbrook is hoping these meetings will result in an important position, something he could use to further his plan to be president." She shuddered. "I hate to think of that man running our country."

"He's the reason for my visit today," he said. "The guy who was killed in the car accident is suspected of supplying illegal weapons to a survivalist group in the senator's home state."

"You think Ashbrook has something to do with that?"

"Maybe." He shrugged. "Or he might be able to give me some info on the survivalists."

"Good luck finding out anything from him. He's as slippery as a…" She paused, trying to find the right word. "Slippery as a politician."

It worried him that Julia hadn't completely given up on her suspicions of murder. Did she know something she hadn't told him? "Let's suppose the senator does have a motive. How could he commit the crime?"

"I've thought about that," she said. "What if the killer knocked the general unconscious, then laid him out on the bed and pulled the trigger. The bullet wound would destroy evidence of being hit on the head."

"That still doesn't explain how the killer got into and out of the room."

"I know," she said.

"And the medical examiner would find evidence of a prior contusion."

The general was scheduled for autopsy today so his body could be released to his family for burial. Very likely, John Maser's autopsy would also be done today, though nobody was clamoring for his remains.

These two deceased men were unlikely partners in death. The general was a hero. John Maser was, from all that Paul had learned, a thug.

Both bodies had been transported to the medical examiner in Denver where they had the facilities for a sophisticated analysis. The Eagle County coroner had been glad to see them go.

Julia looked across the meadow toward the safehouse. "We should head back if you want to catch the senator before this afternoon's meetings start."

"What kind of meetings are these?" Paul asked.

"I'm not really sure. And I couldn't tell you if I was. The whole point of meeting here is secrecy."

"Understood."

"Paul, I'd appreciate if you didn't let on that I told you about the safehouse. Not even to Roger and Craig."

"Got it." He nodded. "Should we race back?"

Her blue-eyed gaze appraised him and the big, black stallion. "You're on. Go."

They took off together, their horses neck in neck. When Paul glanced over at her, he was distracted by her profile and the way she leaned forward in the saddle. But he kept up the pressure.

The gentlemanly thing would be to let her win. But he was pushing as hard as he could. Second place was never good enough.

They arrived at the fence at the same moment.

"I win," Julia said.

"In your dreams. I got here first."

She laughed as she guided her mare to the barn. "There's no shame in losing to a woman."

"No shame at all. Because I didn't lose."

"I guess we'll have to race again to see who's the clear winner."

"Guess so."

Next time meant he'd be seeing her again, and he was glad to settle for that solution.

Smiling to herself, Julia took the reins and led the horses into the barn while Paul went inside to catch the senator before the meeting started.

After she removed the saddles, she shooed the horses they had ridden into the attached corral along with two other dappled geldings. Julia decided to keep

Stormy, the pregnant mare, in her stall. Stormy had been skittish lately, and the vet said they should keep her quiet.

"How are you doing, Stormy?" Julia leaned into the stall. "Feeling okay?"

The mare's nostrils flared. She pawed the hay-covered floor of her stall. Her eyes were angry, impatient. This horse did not like being pregnant.

When Julia reached out toward her, the chestnut-colored horse nipped at her hand. Julia backed off. There were plenty of other jobs in the barn—hauling the saddles to the tack room, mucking out the other stalls, breaking open a fresh bale of hay.

As she worked, Julia's mind was busy. Her thoughts of the general's murder segued to a vision of Paul on Diablo. Most people were dwarfed by the size of that big, black horse. Not Paul. The breadth of his shoulders and the span of his thighs were perfect for Diablo. Paul's thick, black hair was the same color as the stallion's coat.

She heard a noise and stood up straight. "Who's there?"

Was that a mewing sound? One of the barn cats?

Julia went to investigate. She stepped into the open doorway and looked around. Such a lovely day. The sun had appeared from behind the clouds, bathing the yard and the house in a glowing, golden light. "Anybody here?"

No answer. Nothing seemed to be moving.

As she turned, she heard the creak of hinges. The heavy barn door was crashing toward her. It was too late to move. She felt the impact on the back of her skull. A ferocious pain. The brilliant sunlight faded to black.

Chapter 6

Waiting for Senator Ashbrook, Paul paced the length of the porch and back again. He couldn't stop thinking about Julia's persistent suspicion that General Naylor had been murdered. Her theory about how the general might have been knocked unconscious before he was shot was a possibility. But why was he dressed in his uniform? And how did the killer get into the room without being seen on the surveillance tapes? And the window? It hadn't been forced. Maybe Paul should go upstairs and take another look at that window frame.

Senator Ashbrook emerged from the front doorway and closed it behind him. As he approached, his manner was cordial but reserved. "How can I help you, Deputy?"

Mentally, Paul changed gears, leaving his questions

about the general's suicide for another time. "I'm still looking into the vehicular death of John Maser."

A frown appeared on the senator's forehead beneath his gleaming white hair. "The gentleman who hailed from Washington? What about him?"

"He had ties to your home state of Wyoming." Paul took his time in phrasing the next question so it wouldn't sound like an accusation. "John Maser was involved with a survivalist group that calls themselves the Lone Wolves. I hoped you might have information on them."

"As a matter of fact, I do." Ashbrook's frown deepened. "Their leader's name is Henry Wolf, hence their moniker. And they made a significant monetary contribution to my last campaign."

He couldn't believe the senator had admitted to this association. "Are you aware that the Lone Wolves have been in negotiations to purchase high-powered weaponry?"

"No."

His response was unusually emphatic and direct for a slippery politician. Paul followed up. "How much do you know about their activities?"

"Very little."

The senator either didn't mind being linked with survivalist whack balls who were apparently building an arsenal, or he had a clever ulterior motive. Paul suspected the latter. "Why did you tell me about this?"

"Their contribution is a matter of record—something you would discover fairly quickly. I must hasten to add that as soon as my campaign manager discovered that the Lone Wolves were a fringe group with an antigovernment bias, we returned every penny of their money. Here's the truth, Deputy." He made a pointing gesture as though he were addressing a throng. "I'm a card-carrying member of the NRA, and I believe these groups have a right to exist. But I don't support their rhetoric."

"Do you believe the Lone Wolves are dangerous?"

He shrugged. "Probably not. They seem more like a bunch of guys who get together on the weekends to spout conspiracy theory and play soldier."

"I assume you're no longer in contact with them."

"What's their connection with your dead man? Was he a supplier of weaponry?"

It didn't escape Paul's notice that although Ashbrook was careful to deny knowledge of weapons, he hadn't repudiated all connection to the Lone Wolves. But of course, he wouldn't. Even the members of a fringe survivalist group were Wyoming voters.

"Senator, now that you've had a few days to think about it, are you sure you don't know John Maser?"

He shook his head slowly. The sunlight glinted in his silver hair. "I meet a lot of people in my work, Deputy. The name John Maser doesn't sound familiar."

"I appreciate your time, sir."

Paul went down the stairs from the porch to his Explorer. Julia had been right about one thing. The senator acted like a man who was up to something.

Julia's eyelids opened slowly. She saw nothing but murky gray. Where was she? What had happened to her?

A fierce pain radiated from the back of her head, and she winced. The muscles in her arms and shoulders tensed. She realized that she was curled in a ball. Facedown in a pile of hay.

The barn! She was in the barn. The heavy door had swung shut, crashing against her skull, knocking her off her feet.

A shrill whinny pierced the air. She lifted her head, looked up and saw Stormy. How had Julia gotten in here? Why was she in Stormy's stall? The pregnant mare pawed the floor, tossed her head.

When Julia moved her arm, Stormy reacted. She reared back on her hind legs. Her hooves came down hard. The floor shook. Julia trembled. If she wasn't careful, she'd be trampled by this nervous mare.

Slowly, she rotated her shoulder and placed her palm on the floor of the stall. She pulled her legs up under her until she was on her knees. Even though her movements were slow and careful, Stormy was spooked, shaking her head and snorting as she rocked back and forth. Her swollen belly swayed. She danced on sharp hooves capable of crushing bone.

The horse reared again.

This time, Julia sprang into action. She bolted to her feet. The sudden movement made her dizzy. Her head throbbed. Her peripheral vision was darkness. The sheer, overwhelming black threatened to overwhelm her.

As Stormy plunged toward her, she dodged clumsily, backed into the corner of the stall.

Julia tried to speak, to whisper reassurance to the horse. Her throat was too tight to squeeze out a single word. Her strength was fading. Her legs were rubber. She braced herself against the stall. "Stormy, hush."

The horse jolted back and forth. Her eyes were wild. She was panicked.

Julia shook her head to clear the cobwebs and was rewarded with a searing pain. Damn it! This shouldn't be happening. Not to her. She was a trained agent.

Her anger brought a surge of adrenaline and gave her the strength she needed. She edged her way around the stall. Reaching through the slats, she unfastened the latch, pushed open the gate and stumbled through. When she'd relatched it, she turned and scanned the barn.

No one else was here.

Gasping, she rested her hand on her breast and felt the heavy thud of her own heartbeat. She could have been killed. If she hadn't gotten out of that stall, Stormy might have trampled her to death.

But this wasn't the horse's fault. Someone had knocked Julia unconscious and dragged her into that stall. Someone wanted her dead.

After she got Stormy calmed, Julia went into the house and directly to her third-floor bedroom where she locked the door behind her. Would locking up do any good? It hadn't saved the general.

Her suspicions coalesced into dire certainty. General Naylor had been murdered. And the person who killed him was after her.

The assault in the barn had been clever. Julia hadn't seen her attacker. Not even a small glimpse. If she hadn't wakened when she did, her death by trampling would have looked like an accident. Investigators would assume she'd been careless.

Not Paul. He'd know. He'd be smart enough to realize that she knew how to handle horses and would never put herself in a dangerous position. She wished he was here right now, holding her in his big, strong arms and telling her that everything would be okay. *Oh, Paul, I need you.* It seemed like she'd been alone all her life, fighting her own battles. The ache in her head intensified. Her eyelids squeezed shut and a tear slid down her cheek.

Angrily, she rubbed the moisture away. Crying wouldn't do any good. *Pull yourself together. You've got to be strong.* A highly trained FBI agent didn't whine and weep. It was her duty to act—to figure out who killed the general and attacked her, to bring the guilty to justice.

At the same time, she had to protect the sanctity of the safehouse.

She peeled off her clothes, filthy from rolling around in the stall, and slipped into her terry-cloth robe. Taking her gun with her, she went down the hall to the bathroom.

The third floor where she and her staff stayed was a bare bones arrangement. Four small bedrooms and one shared bathroom for herself, Roger Flannery and Craig Lennox.

Should she tell the other two agents what had happened to her? Though Julia was the senior agent and they were supposed to take orders from her, Roger and Craig had ambitions of their own. If she outlined the situation to them, they would very likely report to their superiors. And Julia would have to admit she'd tampered with the crime scene. Her career would be over. The safehouse would be closed down or turned over to someone more competent.

Gingerly, she unfastened her ponytail. When she touched the knot on the back of her head, the result was a shooting pain. But the skin hadn't been broken. No doubt, her thick ponytail saved her from more serious injury.

Inside the medicine cabinet, she found a bottle of aspirin and gulped down three tablets. She'd been unconscious, which meant a slight concussion. Head wounds were tricky; she ought to have it looked at. But what if the doctor wanted to keep her overnight? What if she had to explain how she'd been injured?

No doctors. She sure as hell didn't intend to end her FBI career in a hospital bed like a sad little victim. She was tougher than that.

Gritting her teeth, she turned on the water for a shower. It was usually a little warmer on the third floor than in the rest of the house, but she was burning up. She glanced at the locked bathroom door. It was very little security. Julia was no expert, and she could pick that lock. Did she dare step into the shower? Separated from her gun?

Instead, she switched the water flow to a bath. In the tub, she could keep her weapon nearby and could see the door. She lowered herself into the hot water and scrubbed until her skin was pink. Her energy was returning. And her determination.

She wasn't beaten. Not yet. Julia would find the murderer. And she would maintain the safehouse. But she couldn't do it alone. She needed help. She needed Paul.

Though he was glad to get another phone call from Julia, Paul was also worried. There was an intensity in her voice that bothered him, and she was acting mysterious—insisting that she couldn't talk on the phone, had to see him in person.

Of course he'd meet her. At a few minutes after four o'clock in the afternoon, he parked outside the Sundown Tavern in Redding—a local hangout with a bar in the front area. Pool tables were in the back room where nonalcoholic beverages were served. This musty old log building at the edge of the trees had been here as long as Paul could remember, and some of the patrons sitting at the bar under the neon beer signs seemed as deeply rooted as an old growth forest. There was a man with a grizzled, gray beard who always sat by himself, scribbling in a spiral notebook. A couple of construction workers in steel-toed boots. A guy in a battered cowboy hat looked up at the television screen where the Bronco game was winding down to the last quarter.

He spotted Julia, sitting alone at a corner table. In the dim light of the tavern, her healthy complexion seemed as out of place as a blooming red rose in a storage attic. She lifted a coffee mug to her lips and sipped.

He sat opposite her and signaled to the bartender that he also wanted coffee. Technically, Paul was still on duty for another hour.

She started talking. "Paul, I need your help. I know it's unfair for me to ask, but I have nowhere else to turn. I'm putting my career in your hands. Everything I've worked for. My reputation. My years of service. My dreams. Everything."

He didn't feel worthy of such trust. Still, he said, "I'll try not to disappoint you."

"You couldn't," she said. "It's the other way around. I'm the one who messed up. Big time."

His coffee was served by the burly bartender who knew Paul well enough to add two containers of cream and three packets of real sugar. "What's the score?" Paul asked.

"A blowout. Twenty-six to seven. Broncos."

"Good deal." Life was always better when the home team won. As Paul doctored his thick dark coffee, he said to Julia, "Start at the beginning."

She glanced around nervously, then leaned toward him. Her voice was low, barely more than a whisper, though he was fairly sure nobody could hear them over the television. "When I discovered the general's body, I saw two things that made me think he'd been murdered. As you recall, he wore his Marine Corps dress blues."

Paul would never forget the sight of General Harrison Naylor decked out in his full uniform, lying on his bed with a bullet through his head. "Go on."

"Right away, I knew something was wrong. His shoes were scuffed, and his medals were in the wrong order."

"How would you know about the medals?"

"My brother was a Marine, killed in action three years ago. I was responsible for laying him out in the coffin, and I studied the manual to make sure his medals were correct. Marines are very careful about their uniforms. It's a point of pride. The general never would have dressed himself incorrectly. Somebody else pinned those medals on his chest."

"I remember the general's shoes," he said. "They were freshly polished."

Julia drew a ragged breath. A flush turned her cheeks a bright crimson. "After I found the body, I removed the general's shoes and polished them. And I changed the medals so they would be in the correct order. I tampered with a crime scene."

He was stunned. This confession wasn't what he'd expected. Not from FBI Special Agent Julia Last. "Why?"

"Protecting the safehouse. A murder investigation is intrusive, to say the least. It would have meant the end of Last's Resort."

"To say the least." Anger washed over him as he realized that she'd played him for a fool. He remembered how he'd readily believed the general's death was suicide. Paul had urged the sheriff toward a speedy acceptance of the suicide theory so Julia wouldn't be bothered or upset. "Was there anything else you tampered with?"

"Nothing. I swear."

"So the room was locked. There was no further cleaning up of evidence. The surveillance tapes were correct. You didn't rewrite the suicide note."

"I only touched the medals and the shoes."

"Wearing gloves," he said.

She nodded. "I know better than to leave fingerprints."

His blood began to boil. Harshly, he said, "Very thorough. Nobody will pick up on that clue. You should be proud of yourself."

"Pride is the furthest thing from my mind."

"I've heard it said that former lawmen—and women—make good criminals because they know how to manipulate a crime scene."

"I made a mistake."

"Manipulate," he repeated. "As in jerking me around."

"You're angry," she said.

"Hell, yes." He stared across the table at her. If she hadn't looked so damned miserable, he would have slapped the cuffs on her and marched her out the door. "Why are you telling me this now? You could have gotten away with it. Could have saved your precious safehouse."

"Please listen to me."

So she could tell him more lies? He'd been completely gullible, putty in her hands. His instincts told him to bolt. *Get away from her. Run as fast as you can.*

He could no longer gaze into her beautiful blue eyes and imagine a future with her. Julia was a liar, someone who had committed a criminal act, someone he could never fully trust. He needed to treat her like any other suspect.

"I rationalized at first," she said. "Like you said, it was an impossible crime. I tried to tell myself that I was mistaken, and the general's state of mind was such that he was careless with his uniform."

"Not your call," he said. "The sheriff should have been given full evidence."

"Do you think it's likely the sheriff still would have concluded that the general committed suicide?"

His rising temper made it hard to think straight. "I don't know."

"What about you? Would you have called it suicide?"

"Maybe."

"The facts," Julia said, "didn't change. No one entered or left the general's room. There were no signs of a struggle."

He shot her a stern glare. "That doesn't excuse your actions. You shouldn't have tampered with the scene."

"I know. I can't turn back time and do things differently no matter how much I wish I could." Her lips thinned to a straight line. "The thing I feel worst about is you. I lied to you."

It was more than just a lie. She'd purposely summoned him to the crime scene first. She knew he was sympathetic to her, knew he'd be easy to manipulate. "You used me."

There was a halfhearted cheer from the other patrons in the tavern as the Broncos made another touchdown. A blowout.

She looked down into her coffee mug. Ashamed to look him in the eye? Damn it, he hoped so. He hoped she was hurting half as much as he was.

"I'm sorry, Paul." When she looked up, he saw the shimmer of unshed tears in her eyes. "I have no right to ask you for help."

Her pain and regret reached through his anger and touched him. He didn't want to feel empathy for her. She'd treated him like a chump, and he ought to hate her for that. But he didn't. God help him, he cared about her.

"When I first sat down," he said, "you said you needed something."

"It's wrong to ask you."

"I'm here. And I'm still listening."

She cleared her throat. "I want you to help me catch the general's murderer."

"If there is a murderer," he said. "The facts still point to suicide."

"I know he was killed," she said.

"Why are you so sure?"

"This afternoon, the killer came after me."

Chapter 7

Back at the safehouse, Julia didn't join the Homeland Security team for dinner. She didn't trust herself to sit across the table from someone who had tried to kill her without betraying her anger and frustration.

In her third-floor bedroom, she stood at the window, looking out. The snow was starting to fall. Flakes as large as popcorn swirled in the lights outside the house. By tomorrow, a pristine white blanket would cover the meadows, mountains and trees. She loved waking up to a fresh snowfall that made the world look clean and beautiful.

Exhaling a sigh, she rubbed at her nape. The throbbing in her head had subsided, replaced by a brand-new kind of pain. Heartache.

She'd disappointed Paul. As she sat across from him in the tavern, she'd watched his dimples disappear.

The approving light from his dark brown eyes faded to a cold, angry glare. He would never trust her again.

And yet, he didn't abandon her. When she told him about the attack in the barn, his concern for her physical safety took precedence over his hostility. He had pointed out that she couldn't stay at the safehouse with a murderer on the loose.

Though Julia liked to think she could protect herself, especially when forewarned, she had to agree. This killer had managed to slip into and out of the general's bedroom without being seen. She wasn't safe behind a locked door. If she intended to get any sleep at all tonight, she had to be somewhere else. Paul insisted that she stay with him.

Their plan was for him to pick her up at eight o'clock tonight. She would return to the safehouse at five in the morning.

She looked out at the snowfall. Right now, the storm seemed benign enough, but a blizzard was predicted. The people at the ski lodges would be happy.

At a quarter to eight, she figured the Homeland Security people would be safely tucked away in their meeting room in the basement. She took a small, canvas bag containing her overnight necessities and went downstairs to the kitchen where Roger was still cleaning up the dishes.

"How's the headache?" he asked.

"Much better," she said. "So much better that I'm going out tonight."

He turned away from the sink so quickly that he dripped soapy water on the floor. "On a date?"

"That's right," she said with bravado. "And I probably won't be back until morning."

She expected him to object. They were operating on a round-the-clock schedule, which meant one of the agents needed to be awake and on surveillance duty all night. Instead of grumbling, Roger dried his hands on a dish towel and patted her on the shoulder. "Good for you, Julia."

"You and Craig will have to take my shift tonight."

"Is it that deputy? Paul Hemmings?"

"Yes."

"Excellent. You need to get out."

"Need to?" Her lack of social life was evident to anybody who worked here, but she hadn't thought it was a problem. "What are you suggesting?"

"It's just that I've been here for three months, and I haven't seen you take any time off. Nobody can be an ace FBI agent 24/7. You've got to take some time for, you know, recreation. It'll improve your mood."

It didn't take much reading between the lines to understand what Roger was implying. He thought she needed to get laid. Then she might not be superbitch.

Unfortunately, Julia didn't think sex would be included in her night with Paul. He could barely stand to look at her. "Thanks for understanding, Roger. I'll be back in the morning."

After donning her heavy parka and scarf, she went out on the front porch to wait for Paul. The cold air stung her cheeks. Reaching into her pockets, she pulled out her ski gloves. Though the snowfall was continuous, it wasn't yet heavy. The graded road leading to the safehouse was relatively clear.

"Hey, Julia." David Dillard sauntered from the house. "Pretty night, huh?"

She forced a smile. "David, what are you doing here? I thought you were in session."

"The others are busy with my simulation, and I thought I'd take a break." He removed his black-frame glasses to peer into the dark and snow. "I get restless after being indoors all day."

"Everyone else got a break after lunch." During the time when she was attacked in the barn. "You were busy with your computers in the basement."

"The time was worth it. This simulation is excellent. Even RJ is having trouble figuring out the details on this terrorist attack scenario. The takeover of a nuclear power plant."

"Should you be telling me about this?"

"There's nothing top secret about the big picture. It's got lots of bad guys running around. Several possible escapes and solutions."

"You make it sound like a computer game."

"That's what it is. Only with more accurate detail. Before I joined the FBI, I used to write software gaming programs."

As he shivered inside his heavy-knit sweater, she noticed how skinny he was—the typical computer guy who couldn't be bothered with stopping to eat or to exercise. There were dark circles under his eyes. "Are you taking care of yourself, David? You look tired."

"A little tired," he admitted. "I have trouble getting my brain to shut down so I can go to sleep."

"Insomnia?"

"Yep, and I'm not the only one. I tried one of RJ's sleeping pills last night, but I don't think I'll do that again."

"Why not?"

"They gave me weird dreams. Paranoid stuff."

When she saw Paul's headlights coming up the drive, Julia's heart gave a joyful little leap. This evening might have been a real date. She might have been looking forward to an evening of warmth, friendship and maybe…something more intimate.

"Going out?" David asked.

"Just for the evening."

When she reached for her overnight bag, he had already clasped the handle. "I can carry this for you."

"That won't be necessary." She tugged it away from him. "Good night, David."

"Okay, then. Have fun."

She tromped down the steps. As soon as Paul parked, she went around to the passenger side and yanked open the door. When she looked back at the safehouse, David was waving. Roger had also come out on the porch to watch her departure. Good grief! Their attention made her feel like a teenager on her first date.

She fastened her seat belt before glancing toward Paul. He had no smile for her tonight as he nodded toward the porch. "What's with those guys?"

"I told them this was a date."

"So they're seeing you off," he grumbled. "As if you're not a grown woman."

"I don't go out much." How pathetic! She sounded like an old maid. In a more up-beat tone, she added, "It's the general opinion of the male agents at the house that I should get out more. They think if I had a boyfriend, I'd be easier to live with."

He made no comment as he backed the Explorer around and drove away from the safehouse.

Unlike the other times they'd been together, the silence that spread between them was decidedly uncomfortable. She felt a desperate need to fill the air with words. "It's not true that I *need* a boyfriend. A woman doesn't *need* a man to be happy and fulfilled. I do just fine on my own. By myself."

"I don't believe you."

His comment surprised her. "What?"

"Don't get me wrong. This has nothing to do with whether you're a woman or a man. Everybody's happier when they're in a good relationship. That's a fact."

"A fact, huh? It doesn't sound scientific to me."

"Call it a theory," he said. "Everybody needs somebody. Whether it's their kids, their friends or a special person. It's what we're all looking for."

"Love?"

"Love, approval, sharing, caring. Whatever you want to call it."

"Do you have any proof for this theory?"

He almost grinned. "Late at night, when I look in my daughters' bedroom and see them sleeping like angels, that's my proof. The way I feel about Jennifer and Lily makes my life worth living."

Oh, how she liked this great, big man! The picture he painted was wonderfully simple and complete. But the deep love he had for his children was far different than a relationship between a man and a woman. "Is that how you felt about your ex-wife?"

"Not all the time. That's for damn sure. Remember, I said a *good* relationship. You know what I mean."

Actually, she did know. At age thirty-two, Julia had done her share of thinking about whether her future included marriage and family. Her career was great, but she wanted children. And a home. And a partner—

a man who would become an inseparable part of her life. "A good relationship is hard work."

"Seems to me it's just a matter of finding the right person."

"How? There are millions of people on the planet. How do you find the right one? It's like panning for gold. You sit by the creek, sifting through a million grains of sand and never find the one tiny particle that sparkles. And if you do? Half the time, it turns out to be pyrite. Fool's gold."

"You're cynical," he said.

"I call it practical."

"Whatever." He shrugged. "We need to make a stop at the skating rink. Lily forgot her bag last night, and I need to pick it up."

Surreptitiously, she watched him as he concentrated on the road where the conditions were worsening by the moment. Not only was he good-hearted and kind, but Paul was a fine-looking man—big, strong and masculine. Especially big. He was so tall that the crown of his head almost touched the roof of the SUV. His gloved hands on the steering wheel were huge.

When she was growing up, she had reached her full height by the time she was twelve. Her brother had joked that it would take a big man to handle her. Like Paul? Was he everything she'd been looking for? Had she stumbled across a solid gold future?

When he parked at the door outside the skating rink, she noticed there were no other cars in the lot. "It doesn't look open."

"It's not. But I have a key. Sometimes, when the coach can't make it, I'll open up early for practice."

"Do you coach, too?"

"Not figure skating," he said. "I help out with hockey on occasion."

She followed him inside. When he turned on the lights, the big empty building echoed like the inside of a cavern. She was drawn toward the huge mirror of ice. "It's been a while since I've gone skating. I used to be pretty good."

"Figure skating?" he called out as he went toward the counter where ice skates were rented.

"I've been known to do a couple of spins," she said. "But I really like to go fast."

"Me, too." He waved a pink gym bag. "Found it."

She stood at the edge of the rink, gazing wistfully at the smooth surface. Back home in Wisconsin, she and her brother had skated on the frozen pond at the edge of town. The first skate of the winter was always the most dangerous because the ice might crack and you'd be dumped in the freezing water. She remembered a time when it snapped under their feet. They both came to a halt, afraid to move a muscle. Cautiously, they dropped to their knees and crawled across the frozen surface—scared to death and laughing at the same time. She missed her brother's laughter most of all.

Paul came up beside her. He held out a pair of well-worn white ice skates. "I brought you a size ten. Is that right?"

"Good guess."

"Put them on and show me your stuff, Julia."

Though he wasn't smiling, this was a friendly gesture. A step toward reconciliation. "You're skating, too. Right?"

"You bet."

* * *

As Paul jammed his foot into his own skate, he told himself that he was making a big mistake. It wasn't smart to forgive Julia. She'd lied to him, manipulated him and used him.

When she first told him about tampering with the crime scene, he should have turned her over to the sheriff and walked away fast. Breaking the rules wasn't his thing, especially not in the case of a suspicious death that might be murder.

But he couldn't desert her. Whether or not it made good sense, he cared about this woman. And when she told him she'd been attacked, he had to protect her.

But he was done playing the fool. After they left the rink and went to his house, after the kids were in bed, he intended to sit her down and make her understand what they had to do. This investigation should be turned over to the proper authorities even though she might be in a lot of trouble and it meant the end of her safehouse operation.

"I'm ready," she said as she peeled off her parka. Standing firmly on her skates, her smile was bright and warm enough to melt the ice. Wisps of curly brown hair had escaped her ponytail and framed her face. Her blue eyes shimmered.

If the safehouse closed down, she'd leave the area and go on to her next FBI assignment. He was damn sure he'd never see her again. *That hurt. He didn't want to lose her.*

With sure strokes, she glided across the smooth white surface. Her blue sweater outlined her hourglass figure. She was great to look at. Not like those skinny little girls that twirled like twigs in a storm. Julia's breasts thrust forward. Her movements were strong and steady, more like a speed skater than a figure skating twinkletoes. Her hips rotated from side to side. When she reached the far end of the rink, she crossed one leg in front of the other to make the turn. Nice move.

He plowed across the ice with little grace and a lot of muscle, slowing to round the curves and picking up speed on the straightaway. The exercise felt good, stretching his muscles after sitting too long in the car. He circled the rink. He was flying. His heart beat faster.

When he looked over, Julia was right beside him. She was doing a good job of keeping up with him, matching him stride for stride.

At the curve, she slipped and let out a yelp, almost falling. He reached over and placed an arm around her waist. It seemed natural when she snuggled against him.

He knew he was making a mistake when he pulled her close, but he couldn't resist. Without even trying, they skated in tandem. A perfect fit.

Though there wasn't any music, they moved to a synchronized beat, knowing each other's rhythm. It was almost like dancing, especially when she turned in his arms so they were face-to-face with Julia skating backward.

"Show off," he teased.

"You try it."

They switched positions, and he glided toward the center of the ice where they spun in a slippery circle and came to a stop.

Julia was breathing hard. She held both his hands in

her own. "Let's stay here all night. Let's forget about everything else and just skate."

As he gazed down into her face, he wished that life could be that simple. But it wasn't. They both had responsibilities. Not to mention a possible murder to solve. "We need to get going."

"Once more around the rink. Please."

Before he could reply, the lights went out. They were standing in the middle of the rink in pitch darkness.

"Hey," Paul yelled. "Who's there?"

Julia released her grasp on his hands. "I don't like this," she said.

"It's somebody playing a joke."

"If not," she said quietly, "I'm drawing my weapon."

"You have a gun?"

"I'm always armed."

Any illusion he might have had about Julia being sweet and defenseless was gone. He unholstered his own gun and shouted again, "Turn on the lights."

He felt her tug on his sleeve. "We should get off the ice," she said. "We make an easy target here."

"You're right." He tried to orient himself using the faint glow from the few windows in the rink. But he wasn't sure which way they were heading. Toward the exit? Toward the dressing rooms?

He could barely see Julia beside him. She slipped. He heard her fall with a thud and a soft curse.

When he tried to help her up, his feet went out from under him. He sprawled. The cold ice surface bit into his hands. Side by side, they crawled toward the waist-high guardrail. They moved fast. No time for nonsense.

"I'm at the edge," Julia said quietly. "I'm climbing over."

"Right behind you." He grabbed the rail and pulled himself to his feet.

The lights came on. The sudden burst of illumination blinded him. After an instant of disorientation, Paul went into a crouch and aimed his weapon toward the front door where the light switches were. Behind the guardrail, Julia did the same.

He saw a figure in a black ski mask. He had a gun of his own. This wasn't a joke.

"Police," Paul shouted.

The figure took a few steps toward the ice.

"Throw down your weapon," Paul shouted. "Do it. Now."

Instead, the dark figure pivoted and ran toward the exit. He was getting away, and there wasn't a damn thing Paul could do to give chase. Not on ice skates.

From across the arena, he heard the door of the skating rink slam. Their would-be assassin was gone.

"I guess we scared him off," Julia said as she stood behind the wall.

"He had a gun."

"So do we."

And they were a formidable twosome. Though Paul should have been thinking about filing reports and alerting the sheriff to this incident, the rush of adrenaline was exciting. He was proud of Julia and of himself.

They'd been threatened. And they had won.

Next time, it might not be so easy.

Chapter 8

Julia tore off her ice skates and followed Paul across the arena to the entrance. Still holding her gun at the ready, she positioned herself as tactical backup as he whipped the door open.

The wet, cold air blasted into the arena, momentarily blinding her. Bracing her gun in both hands, she stepped up beside Paul. The heavy snowfall and blowing wind had already begun to erase the footprints of their would-be assassin. Though it had been only minutes since he left the arena, he was out of reach. His taillights vanished in the storm. The tire prints were nearly obliterated.

"Too much snow," Paul said as he pulled the door closed. "There's nothing out there we can use as a clue."

Compared to the storm raging outside, the arena was utterly silent. Julia allowed her gun hand to drop to her side. She scanned the area where they were standing. The man in the black ski mask had worn gloves, which meant there would be no fingerprints. And he didn't fire his weapon. So there would be no shells or bullets that could be used in ballistic analysis.

If she hadn't experienced that instant of panic when the lights went out, she might not have believed they'd been threatened. "Any idea of his identity?"

He shook his head. "In Eagle County, the usual suspects don't include armed assassins in ski masks. Our local troublemakers are drunks, druggies and guys with bad tempers. Not professional criminals."

"You're assuming the man in the ski mask was a hired gun?"

"A hit man."

She had to agree. The Homeland Security people at the safehouse were in a meeting, and none of them would have taken this kind of risk. Instead, they'd hired someone else to do their dirty work. "Not a very effective hit man. As soon as he saw we were armed, he retreated."

"A wise move," he said. "When he turned the lights back on, he probably expected to find us floundering around on the ice. Easy targets."

"But we were ready." She and Paul had been side by side with weapons aimed. It had been a very satisfying moment. "Armed and dangerous."

"He must have followed us from the house." Paul glided his hands up and down her arms as if reassuring himself that she was unharmed. "Are you okay?"

"Fine." Her heartbeat was accelerated, and she had the hyperawareness that came from being threatened.

"You know he was here to kill you, Julia."

That realization bothered her far less than the fact that Paul had been with her. She'd dragged him into this web of danger. The hit man would never have allowed Paul to escape unharmed. He was a witness. He could have been shot, and it would have been her fault.

"If you want to call in the sheriff," she said, "I'll understand."

"What's the point? We've got no evidence. There's not a damn thing the forensic people can investigate."

"I was thinking about protection."

"For me?"

"He would have killed you, too." An even worse possibility presented itself in her mind. "What if we hadn't stopped at the skating rink? What if we'd gone directly to your house?"

They might have unwittingly pointed a professional killer toward his home. His children. Oh God, his children! Danger to herself was nothing. It was part of being a federal agent, part of the job. But her actions were responsible for putting innocent children in harm's way.

When she remembered that beautiful little black-haired child spinning on the ice, pure dread coiled tightly around her heart. No horror was more intense than a child in jeopardy. Julia hated herself for what she had brought upon this family. "You've got to take me back to the safehouse."

"Now that I know you're being stalked, there's no way I'm going to leave you."

"That hit man could have come to your house. He could have—"

"It didn't happen," he said.

"I was wrong to ask for your help. I wasn't thinking

about anything but my own needs." Her decision to approach him might have resulted in unthinkable tragedy. How could she have been so blind to the possible consequences? To endanger his children? "I'm so sorry."

"I know."

At the ragged edge of emotional restraint, her breath came in gasps. Her gaze met his, and she searched the depths of his eyes for a sign. He had every reason to hate her. "Can you ever forgive me?"

Gently, he pulled her into his arms. "I can try."

That was the best she could hope for. She trembled against him, needing his solace and comfort.

His voice was quiet. "The important thing now is to figure out what we do next."

In spite of the threat, Paul's mind was clear. His two girls might be in danger. He needed to make the right decisions.

The first thing was to make sure they were protected and safe. If guarding his children meant sitting on his front porch with a shotgun across his lap, that was what he'd do. Gladly. But he couldn't desert Julia. She was in the direct line of fire.

"I can contact the sheriff and demand protective custody." He thought about the guys he worked with. They were a small staff. The sheriff couldn't spare even one deputy to stay at his house night and day.

Julia shivered in his arms. "I never should have touched the general's body."

"You made a mistake." He wasn't about to let her off the hook for that. "I don't know if the evidence you tampered with would have made a difference. It's still an impossible crime. The general's death still looks like suicide."

"Then why is a hit man coming after me?"

He thought for a moment. "Because you're a trained agent on the inside. Frankly, you're the only person who could hope to figure this out."

"Me?" He felt her shaking her head. "I'm not that good. Not a forensic investigator."

"But you know these people." The picture was becoming clear to him. "If there had been a full-scale murder investigation, your four guests would have thrown up all kinds of barriers. Think of the senator. He wouldn't sit still for an interrogation. And the other three are high-ranking people in the FBI and CIA. Their agencies would have closed ranks to protect them."

"What are you saying?"

"We don't have evidence, facts and clues. The only way this killer will be caught is by someone on the inside, someone who can talk to these people, get them to open up."

"Like me?"

"Exactly like you."

Paul knew what had to be done. He gave Julia a squeeze and pulled away from her. "First, I make sure there's no danger to my kids."

Her face was pale, stricken. "How?"

"Mac and Abby are still in town."

He took the cell phone from his pocket. His good buddy Mac was a Denver cop and an expert marksman. Abby was a trained federal agent with several years of undercover work under her belt. They were the perfect twosome for keeping his girls safe. "Mac owes me a big favor. And this is the payoff. He's going to be watching my kids until we have this sorted out."

"And what are you going to do?"

"I'm going back to the safehouse with you."

"Why?"

"Because we're going to solve this murder. You and me, Julia. Together."

It was just after nine o'clock when Julia followed Paul up the snow-covered sidewalk outside his house. Apparently, the kids were still awake; lights shone from nearly every window in the two-story clapboard house.

On the porch, he turned to her. "We're not going to talk about any of this in front of the kids."

She nodded. After her emotional turbulence at the rink, she felt drained, exhausted.

"With Mac and Abby keeping watch, the girls will be safe. And there's no reason to start them worrying about me. They've already lost one parent."

"Your ex-wife doesn't stay in touch?"

"Not often enough." He frowned. "Anyway, not a word."

"Understood."

As soon as Paul opened the door, the two little girls raced toward him for hugs. The older girl, Jennifer, wore a long flannel nightie with bunny slippers. The seven-year-old, Lily, had on purple pajamas with a fairy princess on the front.

Paul lifted them off the floor, holding one girl in each arm. "I thought you two would be in bed. Tomorrow's a school day."

"Uncle Jess said we could stay up."

Julia glanced toward the man who sat on the plaid sofa in front of the television. She knew that Jess Isler was a good friend of both Paul and Mac. But she'd never actually met him. He came toward her with his hand outstretched. "You must be Julia."

"And you're Jess." With his streaked blond hair and twinkly blue eyes, he was too pretty for her taste. "How's your recovery going?"

"Very well, thanks." After he released her hand, he went to the front window, pushed the curtain aside and peered out at the snowfall. "Next week, I get to start skiing again."

The older of Paul's daughters wriggled out of his arms. Mimicking Jess's move, she held out her small hand toward Julia. "I'm very pleased to meet you."

"Same here," Julia said. The child was adorable. "I saw you skate last night. You were good."

"And me?" Lily hopped out of her father's arms and braced her fists on her hips. "What about me? I didn't fall down once."

"I'm sure you're fantastic."

"However," Paul said gruffly, "you forgot your gym bag at the rink."

He held it up the pink bag, and Lily snatched it away from him. "Thank you, Daddy." She whipped it open, reached inside and pulled out a half-eaten candy bar.

Before she could take a bite, Paul said, "Freeze."

Lily went completely still. So did Jennifer.

Paul lifted the candy bar from Lily's fingers. "Not right before bed."

Lily groaned.

"No moving," he said. "You know the rules. When I say 'freeze,' you don't move until I say...okay, un-freeze."

"Please," Lily whined. "I'm starving to death."

"We had dinner," Jennifer said. Her dark brown

eyes—the same color as her father's—studied Julia. "Do you like to cook, Julia?"

"Very much. And I especially like to bake. Breads and cookies."

"Would you show me how?"

"I'd love to. Nothing smells as good as baking bread."

As Julia took off her parka and boots, Jess came over beside Paul. "The sheriff called. He wanted you to call him back at home as soon as you got in."

"Wonder why he didn't use my cell phone." Paul shrugged and turned to the girls. "I need to take care of this business, and you two kids need to be in bed."

"We can stay up," Jennifer said. "There's not going to be school tomorrow. It's a blizzard."

"You wish," he said. "I want those teeth brushed and faces washed."

Jennifer latched on to Julia's hand. "Come with me."

Lily took her other hand. "And me."

As they marched up the staircase to the second floor, the girls chatted about how school would for sure be canceled tomorrow.

Inside the bathroom, Lily tugged on Julia's hand and motioned for her to come close. When she leaned down, Lily asked, "Are you Daddy's girlfriend?"

"We're friends."

"I think he likes you," Lily said. "You're big like him."

"Jeez, Lily." Jennifer rolled her eyes. "She didn't mean that you look like a man."

"I didn't say that. I think she's pretty."

Julia cut in. "Aren't you two supposed to be brushing your teeth?"

The girls took turns at the sink. More than once, Lily caught Julia's eye in the mirror and smiled sweetly. It was becoming obvious that these two young ladies wanted another female in the house; they missed having a mother.

Lily led the way down the hall to their bedroom. "It's the master bedroom," she said. "Because there's two of us and only one of Daddy."

Their room was an explosion of pink with white four-posters on opposite sides of the large room and lots of shelves for a play area in the middle. Herds of stuffed animals lurked in the corners.

Lily hopped up on her bed. "Tell me a story."

"Do you have a book you'd like to read?"

"Make up a story. About a princess."

Jennifer said, "You don't have to if you don't want to."

"Not a problem," Julia said. "Let's all sit over here on Lily's bed, and I'll tell you a story about skaters. Have you ever heard of Hans Brinker?"

"Never," Jennifer said. "Is he a famous ice skater like Timothy Goebel? He does quads. I love him."

With one girl on either side, Julia started to tell the story she only vaguely recalled. "Hans Brinker was from Holland and his family was very poor…"

She invented most of the details about a contest to win a pair of beautiful silver ice skates and how much Hans wanted those skates. Then came the part about sticking his finger in the dike and staying there all night long.

"Wait a minute," Lily said. "Did he miss the contest?"

Julia wasn't sure, but she decided this story would

have a happy ending. Hans was a hero. He saved his little town. "Even though he was really tired from staying at the dike all night long, he won the contest the next day. And he had his silver skates."

"Is this a true story?" Jennifer asked.

"It's a legend. Maybe true. Maybe not. The important thing is that Hans did the right thing even though it was really hard."

She looked up and saw Paul standing in the doorway. He smiled with infinite gentleness. His dimples appeared and softened his rugged features. The glow from his dark eyes showed pure affection. He adored these children. As he'd told her earlier this evening, the girls were what made his life worth living, and she was honored to be a part of this family if only for a moment.

When Paul joined her to tuck the girls under their comforters, she savored the special warmth that surrounded them—the warmth that came from unconditional love.

Before Paul left the bedroom, he switched off the overhead light. "Sleep tight, girls. I need to go out tonight for work, and I might not be back in the morning. But Mac and Abby are coming over to stay with you."

"Okay," Lily said. "Daddy?"

"What is it, honey?"

"Is Julia your girlfriend?"

"She's a friend and a girl." He tossed a grin over his shoulder toward Julia, then looked back at his children. "I guess that makes her a girl friend."

"I like her," Jennifer said.

"Me, too," Lily piped up.

"Good night." Paul eased the door closed. "I love you both."

"Love you back."

Though the children weren't asleep and there was no particular need to be quiet, Julia tiptoed down the hallway. She didn't want to risk disturbing this unexpected aura of family and belonging. His children liked her. They accepted her and thought she was a good match for their father. Because she was, as Lily pointed out, a big woman. Julia grinned to herself. Never before had the breadth of her shoulders counted as a virtue.

In the living room, Paul went to a worn armchair—similar in style to some of the heavy furniture at the safehouse. He sat and leaned back. His eyes closed. He rubbed at his forehead.

She sat on the sofa. Jess was nowhere in sight.

When Paul looked over at her, she couldn't tell what he was thinking. He had so many faces. With the girls, he was a good father. On the job, he was a hard-working deputy. At the ice-skating rink, he had been her protector. Could he ever be her lover? Was that expression in his repertoire?

She wanted to be Paul's girlfriend—a real girlfriend with commitment and relationship. But so much negativity had passed between them. She'd betrayed him. She'd brought danger to his family.

Telling him that she was sorry wasn't enough to regain his trust. She knew that.

"That phone call from the sheriff," he said. "It was about the preliminary autopsy results."

Though solving the possible murder of the general should have been her number-one priority, she didn't want to think about crime. She'd rather stay here in this cozy house with the comfortable clutter of children's toys. Still, Julia asked, "What did they find?"

"The general had no external injuries that might suggest he was knocked unconscious. The cause of his death was gunshot wound to the head." He exhaled a heavy sigh. "No evidence points to murder. The medical examiner believes this was suicide."

"But you and I know that's wrong. If the general wasn't murdered, no one would be coming after me."

"There were two autopsies done. One on the general. The other on John Maser."

"The victim from the car accident."

"It wasn't careless driving that made him go off the road," Paul said. "The tox screen showed a high level of morphine in his system but no indication that he was a user. On his left arm, there was a hypodermic puncture wound. He was shot full of drugs and turned loose on a dangerous mountain road."

"Murdered," she said.

"The sheriff wants me to do further interrogation on the people staying at your safehouse. That gives me a reason to stay there."

She wished the reason was because he wanted to be with her. *Every*body *needs somebody.*

Chapter 9

The snowstorm continued unabated. Road conditions were miserable, but Paul had driven in worse. He eased his four-wheel drive SUV along the road at a slow, steady speed to avoid going into a skid. His windshield wipers whipped back and forth. Visibility through the swirling snow was almost nil. "Jennifer might have been right. This could be a blizzard."

"It's good for the skiers," Julia said.

"For them, it's perfect."

And for Paul? Extreme weather was never good news for the sheriff's department. There were always emergencies. Lost cross-country skiers. Car accidents. Power outages.

This time, however, these problems weren't his responsibility. The sheriff had ordered him to investigate the possible connection between the morphine-related death of John Maser and the four remaining guests at Julia's lodge. Not an easy task.

He carefully negotiated the turn onto the road leading to the safehouse. Within an hour, these back roads would be impassable. It was lucky that Mac and Abby had gotten to his house when they did. Paul had no qualms about leaving his daughters in their care.

"You're going to be snowed in at the safehouse," Julia said.

"I expect so."

"It's no problem. We have available bedrooms on the second and third floor. You'd probably prefer the second floor. You only have to share a bathroom with one other person and—"

"I'm staying in your room, Julia."

"Oh."

Though the car heater blasted on high, there was a chill in the car. He'd avoided thinking about what might happen if they shared a bedroom. Making love to Julia was a strong temptation. He couldn't deny that he'd been imagining what it would be like to hold her strong, sexy body in his arms and to kiss her sweet pink lips. But he couldn't forget that she'd used him, played on his gullibility and dragged him into a threatening situation. If he made love to her, he'd be an even bigger fool than he was before.

"We can't stay in the same room," she said. "I'm the senior agent at the safehouse. It sets a bad example if I have a guest of the opposite sex in my bedroom."

If he'd dared to take his eyes off the road, he would have glared at her. They had a murderer on the loose. And a hit man who came after them at the rink. This was no time to worry about her reputation. "I'm staying in your room," he repeated. "I can't protect you if I'm sleeping down the hall."

"I can protect myself."

"Not this time. We have a killer who walks through locked doors."

"Of course, he doesn't, but—"

"The main reason I'm coming back here with you is to keep you safe. Which means I'm staying in your room."

She exhaled a prolonged sigh. "I guess you're right."

"You're supposed to be my girlfriend," he reminded her. "If our cover story is going to work, you'll need to pretend that you're glad to have me in your bed."

"I can do that."

He was surprised to hear a smile in her voice. "I'm not expecting an Academy Award performance."

"That's good because I'm not talented enough to do convincing undercover work. But I can act like your girlfriend. I'll give you little hugs and kisses on the cheek." Her gloved hand rested on his shoulder. "This might be the best assignment I've ever had."

"Being my girlfriend?"

"Having you in my bedroom."

Snow drifts completely covered the road ahead of them. There weren't any other tire tracks to follow. Paul squinted through the windshield, through the curtain of falling snow. "Did you just say that you want to go to bed with me?"

"You heard me."

His fingers tightened on the steering wheel. This was one hell of a way to find out that she was as interested in sex as he was. Paul wasn't sure how to deal with this information. So much had changed since he'd first seen Julia chopping wood and had thought she was the perfect woman.

Gruffly, he said, "Tell me about the surveillance system at the safehouse."

"You already know about the exterior cameras protecting the perimeter and the cameras in the hallways." Her hand withdrew from his shoulder. Her tone became crisp and businesslike. "We also have interior cameras focused on the front door and kitchen door. The lower level where we have our office isn't monitored."

"That's the area you kept secret when the sheriff and paramedics were picking up the general's body."

"Right."

"What else?" he asked.

"On occasion, with some of our more infamous protected witnesses, we've used listening devices in their bedrooms. All the phones are, of course, bugged."

"So I can assume that somebody might be listening or watching all the time."

"I'll make sure my bedroom is clear," she said. "The rest of the time, we need to be careful about what we say."

"What about your other two agents? Roger and Craig."

"What about them?"

"As far as I'm concerned, they're suspects in the general's murder. They know their way around the safehouse better than your guests. One of them could have tampered with the surveillance camera outside the general's room."

"Not possible," she said firmly.

"How much do we tell them?"

Again, she sighed. "We'll have to admit that you

know about the safehouse. And you're investigating John Maser's murder. We won't mention the general."

"Sounds good to me."

The lights of the safehouse flickered before them. In the midst of the raging storm, the lodge looked like a warm, peaceful sanctuary. It was hard to believe a killer lurked inside.

As Paul slowed, his tires went into a skid, which he managed skillfully as he parked. "Nobody else will be leaving here tonight."

They fought their way through the storm to the front door. When they stepped inside, Roger Flannery greeted them. "What are you two doing back here?"

"You were waiting up for me," Julia accused. "Honestly, Roger. I'm not a teenager on a first date."

"That's a negative on waiting up," he said. "We saw your headlights approaching."

Of course. Roger and Craig would have been watching the monitors, doing their job. She was the one disobeying the rules and acting irresponsibly. Her blatant disregard for her duties bothered her a great deal. Until now, she'd been an exemplary agent.

Before removing her parka, she asked, "Have you tended to the horses?" she asked.

Roger gave a nod. "They're all bedded down for the night. I tried to clear a path to the barn, but the snow kept drifting. It's bad out there."

"A blizzard," Julia said. "We're going to be snowed in. That's why I came back. If I didn't return tonight, I knew I'd be gone for a while."

Paul stepped forward. "There's no way I can drive back to my house. Looks like you're stuck with me."

Roger's mouth twitched nervously. His eyes darted toward Julia as he said, "Welcome, Paul."

When she saw the look of doubt painted on Roger's face, Julia got a sinking feeling in the pit of her stomach. The first lesson she drilled into the agents who worked at the safehouse was keeping their mission secret. Now she was about to break her own rule. She confronted Roger directly. "Deputy Hemmings knows we're an FBI safehouse."

"He does?"

"In addition to being my friend," Julia said, reminding herself to give Paul a flirtatious little pat on the arm, "the deputy has official business. He's investigating the death of that car-accident victim."

"Who?"

"John Maser," Paul said. "He's from Washington, D.C.—like all your guests."

"It's a big city," Roger said defensively. "None of them had a connection with him, did they?"

"Nothing they'd admit. The sheriff was willing to let it drop. But we have new information. I'm going to need more detailed alibis from your guests."

"Good luck," Roger muttered.

Julia asked, "Are they done with their meeting?"

"Not yet. They took a break about a half hour ago, came upstairs and scarfed down half the cookies I made for tomorrow's dessert." He looked pained at this blatant disregard for his well-planned menu. "Then they went back into session."

She checked her wristwatch. It was half past ten o'clock. "Did they say how long they'd be working?"

"Not to me."

She gave him a nod. "The deputy and I will be going

upstairs. Would you please tell Craig that I'll take the three a.m. surveillance shift?"

"Okay." Tight-lipped, he shot a glance at Julia, then at Paul. It was obvious that Roger wasn't sure how to react to the news that his by-the-rules boss intended to spend the night with an outsider.

There was no justification for her behavior. No excuse that wouldn't sound lame. Julia could see her career slipping away, inch by inch. Maybe Roger would be the next senior agent to run this safehouse. Linking her arm with Paul's, she gave him a little wave. "G'night."

With a shrug, he turned back toward the kitchen.

After Julia and Paul hung their wet parkas on pegs near the door, she led him up the staircase past the second floor to the third, then down the hall and into her bedroom, where she shut the door behind them.

The small space was hardly bigger than a monk's cell. She glanced at Paul. The top of his head was less than a foot away from the ceiling. His shoulders seemed cramped. He couldn't take a full stride because most of the floor space was taken up by her full-size bed.

The bed! Oh yes, that was another problem. The bed was barely big enough for her. If Paul stretched out full length on that mattress, his feet would dangle over the end. There was absolutely no way the two of them could lie on that bed without touching.

As she watched him edge around the foot of her bed, she could tell that he was thinking the same thing. One small bed. Two tall people. Not a good fit.

"Perhaps," she said, "we should move downstairs to the empty bedroom. It's bigger."

"Bigger bed?"

"Not really."

"On the second floor," he said, "we're one step closer to the murderer."

Feeling trapped and uncomfortable, she dropped her overnight case on the floor beside her tiny desk and peered out the window. A fierce blast of wind hurled snow against the pane. This should have been a good night to curl up in bed, pull the covers over her head and sleep until the storm passed.

"We're not all that much safer in this room," she said. "It's just up one flight of stairs."

"Fine. Let's check out that bigger room."

They descended the staircase to the second-floor landing where there were six bedrooms. Julia used her set of master keys to open the door to the unoccupied room. "This room shares a bathroom with Gil Bradley. There are locks on either side."

Though the bed was no larger, the floor space was almost double her room. In one corner, a cornflower blue armchair and ottoman were arranged beside a brass standing lamp for reading.

Paul strode across the floor to the bathroom, unfastened the lock and went inside.

When she followed, she saw him standing in front of the open medicine cabinet. The shelves were lined with plastic bottles. Paul picked one up and read the label. "Enchinacea and goldenseal." He picked up another. "Garlic pills. And here's vitamin C, E and B12."

"Gil's a health nut."

"I wonder how he feels about drugs."

"Like morphine?" She wouldn't be a bit surprised if Gil had access to all kinds of substances—legal and illegal. He was the kind of agent who worked on the shadowy fringes, which meant he was also smart enough to be careful. "I hardly think he'd leave his hypodermic kit lying around."

Paul went to the door that opened to Gil's bedroom.

"What are you doing?" she asked.

"I want to search these rooms, and I'm pretty sure our suspects aren't going to give permission." The door handle turned easily in his hand, and he grinned. "Let's see what Gil might be hiding."

"What are we looking for?"

"Anything suspicious."

They didn't have to look far. In Gil's bottom dresser drawer was an automatic handgun and ammunition. Under the bed, they found a leather case with a repeating rifle and a night scope, useful for a sniper.

Gil Bradley was a dangerous man, and these sophisticated weapons reminded her just how scary he was. Apprehension tickled the hairs on the back of her neck. "Maybe he brought the rifle for hunting."

"Not a .50-caliber rifle. Not unless he's going after rhino."

In the back of his closet was a small, locked suitcase. "He could have anything in there," Paul said.

"Don't even try to open it," she advised. "He's CIA. It'll probably explode if tampered with."

"It's one of those combination locks. You think he'd use 007?"

The longer they stayed in Gil's room, the more her tension increased. "Let's get out of here."

Paul replaced the suitcase in the closet and followed her toward the bathroom. "This is a nice room. And that's a queen-size bed."

"I can't ask Gil to move." Standing inside the bathroom, she motioned for him to hurry. "Come on, Paul."

The door to the bedroom crashed open. Gil Bradley charged inside. Moving at top speed, he was a dangerous blur in Julia's vision. His arms rotated like a windmill as he thrust at Paul's throat with an open hand.

The shock of this unexpected attack left her paralyzed. All the terrifying stories she'd heard about CIA assassins coalesced into one second. Trained killers. With one swift blow, they could kill, blind or permanently disable their opponents.

Paul defended himself with surprising skill. After he dodged the first assault, he caught hold of Gil's arm near the elbow and used his forward momentum to throw him off balance. The muscular CIA agent recovered and immediately went into an attack stance.

"Hold it," Paul said as he backed away. "I'm on your side."

"What the hell are you doing in here?" Gil's voice was low and seething.

"I can explain." Julia broke through her shock to rush forward. "We're snowed in. Deputy Hemmings and I were looking at the unoccupied bedroom next door."

"You're in my damn room."

He looked angry enough to kill them both, tear them limb from limb and sauté their remains for dinner.

"It's all about the size of the bed," she said desperately. "We were checking out your bed."

The senator appeared in the doorway. "Is there a problem?"

Gil aimed a ferocious glare in his direction. "Nothing I can't handle."

"Julia," Senator Ashbrook snapped in his most officious tone, "why is the deputy here?"

"Glad you asked," Paul said as he wisely moved away from Gil's striking range. "I'm here because I'm investigating the murder of John Maser."

"Murder?" Ashbrook's eyebrows pulled into a scowl. "I thought that was a car accident."

"Get out of my room," Gil said. "All of you."

They moved onto the landing where RJ Katz and David Dillard were standing. Gil whipped the door to his room closed with a sharp click.

"Good," Paul said. "I'm glad you're all together so I only have to say this once. We have new evidence on the death of John Maser that indicates foul play. I need to ask you further questions."

"I don't believe this." RJ Katz widened her eyes. "Are you saying we're suspects?"

"A suspect?" Ashbrook echoed. "Outrageous! I refuse to answer any questions without my lawyer present."

"Same here," RJ said. "Frankly, Julia, you should know better. I'm appalled that you've put us in this position."

Even the mild-mannered David Dillard complained. "It's been a long day. Can't this wait until morning?"

"I can wait," Paul said. "We're snowed in tonight. Nobody's going anywhere."

Julia backed him up. "A very good plan. I suggest we all go to bed and start fresh tomorrow. Sorry for the disturbance. Good night."

RJ turned on her heel. Her slim hips twitched back and forth as she went into her room and slammed the door. The senator matched her huffiness. More calmly, David said good-night.

Julia and Paul stood on the landing with Gil Bradley. His square jaw clenched with barely suppressed rage. Unlike RJ and the senator, Gil would never call on lawyers to protect him.

He looked Paul in the eye. "Let's talk."

Chapter 10

The smallest room on the first floor of the safehouse was a library with several shelves of well-worn books and a couple of comfortable looking armchairs. In the center of the room was a square table and four sturdy wooden chairs that looked like they'd been stolen from a high school. A huge dictionary lay open on a lectern beneath the window. It wasn't the most comfortable room in the house but one of the most private—a good place for Paul and Julia to have a talk with Gil Bradley.

When Paul lowered himself into one of the hard wooden chairs and stretched his long legs out in front of him, he realized how tired he was. It had been a hell of a long, stressful day. His limbs felt heavy, weighted down with exhaustion. And his forearm ached where he'd blocked the jab that Gil had aimed at his Adam's apple. If that blow had connected, Paul's windpipe might have been crushed. He looked across the table at the former Navy SEAL.

In spite of the fact that Gil was the one who said he wanted to talk, words weren't pouring through his tight lips. He leaned forward in his chair, elbows resting on the tabletop in front of him, tense from head to toe. Cold intelligence gleamed through his squinted eyes.

Paul spoke first. "John Maser. You knew him."

"A jerk," Gil said. "A wannabe mercenary who didn't have the guts to pull it off."

"He was convicted of fraud," Paul pointed out. "So he must have done something."

"Lying. He was good at that."

"What about weapon smuggling? We have information indicating he was involved with the Lone Wolf survivalists."

Gil gave a snort. "Smuggling weapons to Wyoming? That's like smuggling milk to Wisconsin."

"Hey," Julia interrupted. "I'm from Wisconsin. Let's not pick on my home state."

Her attempt to lighten the mood fell flat. Paul was too tired to respond, and Gil had no sense of humor.

"My point," Gil said, "is that guns—even high-powered weapons—are relatively easy to come by in Wyoming. It's a hunting state."

Paul cut to the chase. "Was Maser coming here to see you?"

"No way. I met with Maser about three years ago, decided he was a poseur and didn't want anything more to do with him. He was, however, on the CIA watch list. Probably on the FBI list, too."

Which meant that RJ Katz and David Dillard might also be acquainted with him. It was entirely possible that every person staying at the safehouse knew Maser—a circumstance that irritated Paul. Each of these people had looked him in the eye and denied knowledge of John Maser.

He glanced toward Julia. Did she know? Was this another lie she'd told him?

Leaning forward in his chair, Paul matched Gil's aggressive posture. "Were you aware that Maser was in this area?"

"No."

"Did you kill him?"

"Hell, no."

"Why should I believe that? You already lied to me about knowing him."

"If I'd taken him out, it wouldn't be a sloppy kill. There'd be no details for you to investigate."

That was a scary assertion, especially since the second murder—that of General Harrison Naylor—had been completely free from damning evidence. "Are you an assassin?"

"Can't answer that question."

Another terse response. Trying to pull information from Gil wasn't easy. Paul leaned back in his chair. "Why the hell did you want to talk to me?"

"I meet problems head-on. You have suspicions about me. That's why you were in my bedroom." His gaze hardened. "You're wrong."

"Assuming I believe you," Paul said, unsure of whether or not he could trust a CIA assassin, "maybe you can help me."

"Sure. Why not?"

"Maybe if I tell you a little bit about this crime, you can give me a profile of the killer."

"Shoot."

"Maser's car went off the road at a fairly deserted spot. In regular circumstances, it might not have been found for days. But it happened that a tourist pulled off to take photographs and noticed the wreck. She flagged me down. I called it in."

"How do you know the accident didn't take place days ago?" Gil asked.

"Maser rented the car in Denver earlier in the day." Paul stared into Gil's fathomless eyes. "Maser wasn't there long. He was still alive when I climbed down the hill to offer aid."

"Did he say anything?"

"One word." *Murder.*

Paul allowed the pause to stretch between them. If Gil Bradley was nervous that Maser might have implicated him, he didn't show it. His posture was rock solid. It didn't even seem like he was breathing.

"He was covered in blood," Paul said. "His car flipped on the way down the hill, and he wasn't wearing a seat belt. He was banged up pretty bad."

Julia shifted in her chair, clearly uncomfortable with this description.

Gil said, "Sounds to me like nothing more than a car accident."

"That's the way it appeared," Paul said. "Even though there was no snow or ice on the night Maser went over the edge, these mountain roads are treacherous. The sheriff wasn't inclined to push the investigation until we found more evidence."

"Which was?" Gil asked.

It went against interrogation procedure to give information to a suspect. But Gil wasn't a regular suspect. Paul needed something to draw him in. "Usually, with this kind of car accident, we wouldn't bother with an autopsy. The Eagle County coroner would mark down cause of death due to external injuries and loss of blood. But it so happened that we were transporting the general for autopsy in Denver and Maser went along. Autopsy results showed Maser was drugged."

"Usually," Gil said, "you wouldn't have noticed."

"Whoever killed Maser was unlucky twice. For one thing, we found the wreck more quickly than we should have. For another, Maser's body had a detailed and expert analysis." He didn't take his eyes off Gil. "What can you tell me about the profile for this assassin?"

"It wasn't a professional job. A trained killer leaves nothing to chance." Gil's posture seemed to relax as he considered the murder. He steepled his fingers. "There's a cowardly aspect to this murder. The killer filled his victim full of drugs and sent him off a cliff."

"Why is that cowardly?"

"At the moment of dying, the killer didn't have to look his victim in the face. He didn't see the fear. The pain. The eyes bugged out in surprise. The gaping mouth."

Though Gil's voice was a low monotone, the picture he evoked was vivid. He'd been there. Paul knew, without doubt, that Gil had killed before.

And now? Was he an assassin for the CIA? Had he looked into the eyes of the general before he pulled the trigger?

"You know what it's like," Gil said. "You're a lawman, Paul. I'm sure you've seen your share of violent death."

Too often, he'd dealt with the victims of accidents or

natural disasters. The crushed body of a cross-country skier caught in avalanche. The charred corpses of the firejumpers on Storm King Mountain. Hell, yes. He'd seen the aftermath of violence. But Paul had never killed another human being. He hoped with all his heart that it would never be necessary for him to do so.

Abruptly, Gil pushed back his chair and stood. "Good luck on your investigation, Deputy."

"I appreciate your cooperation."

In a few quick strides, Gil was at the library door. Over his shoulder, he said, "Even Johnny Maserati deserves justice."

"What did you say?"

"Johnny Maserati," Gil repeated. "That's what Maser used to call himself. Maserati. Like the fast car."

Paul had heard that name before. When he first mentioned John Maser, the general had referred to Maserati. General Naylor had known Maser well enough to use his nickname. These two murders were connected.

In the relative safety of her bedroom, Julia locked the door and turned toward Paul. "Johnny Maserati. That's what the general called him. Right?"

"Right." He detached the holster from his belt and placed his handgun on the nightstand. Then, he sat on the edge of her bed to pull off his boots. "Did you know him, Julia?"

She couldn't believe he'd even ask that question. "Of course not."

"Maser was on the FBI watch list. I assume you have access to that information."

"I'm not a field agent. The watch list is nothing to me."

Without looking at her, he asked again. "You're sure you didn't know Maser?"

His doubts reminded her of her own deception and lies. After what she'd done, she probably deserved to be treated with suspicion. But she didn't like it.

She came around the bed to stand in front of him, planted her fists on her hips and waited until he looked up. It was important to her that he understand what she was saying. "I'm telling the truth about Maser. There are no more lies between us, and there never will be again."

"What about your FBI buddies? RJ and David? They probably knew Maser."

"I can't answer for them."

With his boots off, he sat on her bed, leaning back against the pillows and the headboard. His extra-large body and long legs took up a lot of space. "I'm pretty damn sure that everybody else in this safehouse is lying to me. FBI. CIA. A senator. All your so-called guests have their own special little agendas to protect."

"What about Gil?" she asked. "He seemed to be straightforward in his responses."

"He didn't admit to much. And I didn't question him about the general's death—a murder in a locked room. That kind of complicated assassination seems like it's more in line with an expert kill. The kind of work Gil might be real proud of."

She had to agree. "You're seeing a link between the two murders. The general. And Johnny Maserati."

"Yeah. Maybe." He nodded slowly. His eyelids were beginning to droop. "I'm too tired to think any more tonight."

So was she. But there were issues that needed to

be handled before she got into bed beside him. "We're still in danger. One of us should stay up and keep watch while the other sleeps."

Paul rose from the bed and went toward the locked door. With a shove, he pushed her dresser so the edge blocked the entrance. "Anybody trying to get in here will make enough noise to wake us. And nobody is coming through the window. Not in this blizzard."

If that was his idea of protection, she wasn't impressed. Obviously, she could have managed this precaution all by herself. She reminded him, "I'm supposed to take the three a.m. surveillance shift."

"I'll go with you." Paul stretched out flat on the bed. He was lying on top of the comforter. "Turn off the light and wake me when it's time."

The other important issue was sex. Julia wanted to clarify their relationship before she climbed into the bed beside him. Her gaze traveled the length of his body—from his thick black hair to his feet, which were almost off the end of the bed. Her attraction to him was undeniable, but she didn't intend to make love to a man who thought she was a liar.

Julia had never been the sort of woman who indulged in casual affairs. If she and Paul made love, it had to mean something. "We need to talk."

"Not now."

His eyelids closed. In contrast to her own lustful thoughts, he wasn't showing the least bit of sexual interest in her. No subtle winks. No dimpled smiles. Paul looked like he was ready for sleep. And nothing more. *Damn it.*

Didn't he like her? When they first met, he'd asked her out on a date. He'd kissed her in the parking lot outside the skating rink. Was that sexual magnetism gone? Dead?

Irritated, she turned off the overhead light. There was enough illumination from the window to find her way around her small room. Should she change into her nightie? Peering through the dark, she saw that Paul's eyes were closed. His breathing was slow and steady. In about two minutes, he'd be fast asleep. *Damn it!*

Opening the top drawer of her dresser, which was now halfway in front of the door, she took out her long, totally unsexy flannel nightgown. She pulled her sweater over her head and peeled off her jeans, which were still slightly damp from being outside in the snow. In her bra and panties, she glanced over her shoulder at the bed. Paul didn't move a muscle. This total disregard was not what she had anticipated. With an angry tug, she pulled her gown over her head.

It was probably for the best that he wasn't interested in sex tonight. They'd been through a lot today, and it was too soon to be intimate. *Damn it!*

To be sure, she was physically drawn to him—his broad shoulders, barrel-sized chest and long legs. More than that, she approved of his profession, his lifestyle, his family. He embodied many qualities she looked for in a mate.

If they'd had a chance to date and gradually develop their intimacy, having him in her bed would have been cause for champagne and celebration. Tonight, it was obvious that nothing was going to happen.

After setting her alarm for three—less than five hours from now—she slipped under the comforter. With this very big man in the bed, there was only a sliver of mattress left for her. She nudged against him, trying to make room.

And then, he surprised her.

He turned to his side. His arm draped across her waist, and he pulled her against him. They fit together like two large spoons. His breath tickled her ear as he whispered, "You're beautiful, Julia."

"You watched me undress."

"I'm tired," he said. "Not dead."

In the darkness, she felt a smile spread across her face. *He thought she was beautiful.* The attraction wasn't gone. She snuggled more firmly against him. Through the comforter that separated them, she felt his belt buckle pressing into her back. If she rolled over and faced him, she knew they would kiss.

"Your hair…" He exhaled a sigh. His voice sounded utterly exhausted. "It's like silk. Smells so clean."

"It's too curly," she said.

"It's perfect." He lifted his hand to stroke the back of her head. "You've got a bump back here."

"It's where I was hit by the barn door."

"Does it hurt?"

"A little."

"Should I kiss it and make it better?"

"I wish it was that easy."

If she gave him the slightest encouragement, she knew he'd respond with all the passion that had been building between them since the first moment they laid eyes on each other. His arm wrapped around her again. His hand lightly massaged her torso below her breasts. She placed her hand atop his and anchored him firmly.

Moments ago, when she'd thought he wasn't interested in her, she was confused and frustrated, even angry. Now, he'd put her doubts to rest. He wanted her, too.

Her womanly instincts urged her to become his lover. What was she waiting for? They were two consenting adults, spooning in a too-small bed. Why not make love?

Because the timing was wrong. He wasn't with her because of their relationship. His concern was to protect her from physical danger. And he still had residual anger about the way she'd deceived him. Before they made love, they needed to talk. And they were both too tired.

"We should sleep," she said.

"If that's what you want."

"I do."

I do not. She wanted ever so much more. All his kisses. All his caring. She longed to hear him tell her a thousand times that she was beautiful.

And yet, she decided to wait. Her relationship with Paul had the potential of becoming something precious, and she would treat their moments together with the utmost consideration.

"Thank you," she whispered, "for being here."

"Good night, Julia."

Though she wouldn't have believed it possible for them to fall asleep in each other's arms without having sex, his embrace was warm and comfortable. The sound of his steady breathing was a lullaby. She felt herself drifting gently into slumber.

Her dreams flowed in pastel images. Flowers opened to the sun. Pink and yellow butterflies fluttered on the breeze. She stood at the edge of a waterfall. The cascading torrents played a soothing rhythm. The shimmering droplets moistened her cheeks. When she reached into the water, it was warm and soft.

A claw thrust out from the waterfall and grabbed her outstretched arm. In an instant, the skies turned dark and threatening. She was being pulled into the waterfall. She couldn't breathe.

She was struggling to escape when her alarm clock sounded and she woke up.

The comforter no longer separated her from Paul. She was snuggled against him. Her head rested in the crook of his neck. Their long legs entwined. His large hand cupped her breast.

Her alarm clock continued to beep.

Struggling away from his embrace, she hit the alarm and sat up. A weary groan pushed through her lips. The back of her skull ached. She needed to go to the bathroom. She wanted more sleep. Hours and hours more sleep.

Behind her back, she heard Paul moving. "Come back here," he growled.

"I can't." She turned on the bedside lamp, hoping that the light would erase the memory of her dream. "I promised to take the three o'clock shift."

"Let the other guys do it. You're the boss."

Which was exactly why she had to fulfill her responsibilities. Though she doubted that Roger or Craig were anywhere near as tired as she was, Julia needed to start behaving like the senior agent in this safehouse. To step up. To take charge. "Gotta do it."

Grumbling, he roused himself. His movements were slow and lumbering. He reminded her of a big, old bear coming out of hibernation as he stumbled toward the dresser and pushed it back where it belonged.

When he reached for the doorknob, she said, "Wait. We need to be careful."

"I'm just going to pee."

She reached for her handgun. "I'll cover you."

"For a trip to the bathroom?"

"Can you think of a better time for an ambush?" She didn't need to remind him that there was a murderer locked inside the safehouse with them. A murderer who had probably taken two lives.

He stretched his shoulders and rolled his head from side to side before he turned toward her. The hint of a smile touched his lips. "Julia?"

"Yes, Paul."

"We need a bigger bed."

Chapter 11

In the kitchen, Paul leaned against the counter and watched as Julia made a fresh pot of coffee. In spite of the fact that it was three o'clock in the morning, she looked good—neatly dressed in jeans and a V-neck red sweater. Her thick brown hair was pulled back in a neat ponytail.

Last night, his fingers had tangled in those wild curls. He'd held her close and felt her heart beating against him. Her body was full, strong and supple. Her skin was smooth as satin. Warm satin.

As she filled a mug for herself and for him, she was humming.

"You're a morning person," he said accusingly. "One of those people who do the rise-and-shine routine."

"It's my wholesome Midwestern heritage. I like getting an early start on the day, baking bread, keeping a clean house."

But she also carried a gun. "How did a wholesome girl like you decide to join the FBI?"

"My psychological profile says I'm a self-motivator with a highly developed sense of right and wrong."

"You like chasing down the bad guys?"

"Not so much," she admitted. "I was a field agent for a while, and it wasn't real satisfying. I like helping people, but there's no big thrill in slapping the cuffs on a bad guy."

"Why did you stay in?"

"I really like being in authority." She grinned. "That means bossy. So, come with me. Now."

He followed her down the narrow staircase to the basement of the safehouse. At first glance, this looked like any other semifinished basement with furnace, storage and several well-stocked pantry shelves. There was a laundry area with washer, dryer and folding table. Nothing special.

Julia unlocked a plain wooden door and pushed it open.

He'd never been in this room before, and his first impression was of white. White walls. White desktops. White tile floor. This office space had several computers and a bank of monitors showing surveillance from the many hidden cameras.

Agent Craig Lennox looked up when they entered. Nervously, he glanced toward a computer screen across the room from where he was standing. Then, he threw up his hands. "You caught me."

Julia went directly to the screen. The picture showed David, RJ, Gil and the senator sitting around a table.

"What's this?" Julia demanded.

Craig dragged his hand through his sandy hair. His skinny shoulders hunched. If he hadn't been wearing a holster clipped to the belt of his khaki trousers, he might have passed for a high school computer nerd. "I was curious about the Homeland Security meetings, and I planted a camera in the room and recorded them."

"You were spying," Julia said.

"Yes, ma'am."

"You know that's a breach of security."

He stalked toward the computer monitor. "I'll erase this disk and remove the camera."

"Not so fast."

She glanced toward Paul, and he gave a quick nod. It might be handy to know what went on in these meetings.

"I'm curious, too," she said to Craig. "Did you record this earlier today?"

"This afternoon. It's mostly arguing. But from what I could see of the computer simulation, it's brilliant." Craig visibly brightened. "David Dillard is some kind of genius. He's set up an interactive program, posing a terrorist situation. Each of the other participants has their own laptop, providing them with additional information not seen by the others."

He crossed the room and pointed to the image on the computer screen. "See. At this point, they were all punching information into their computers. Then they'll discuss the problem and come up with solutions, deciding how to set up a task force to deal with the terrorist simulation."

"Sounds like a computer game," Paul said.

"A really amazing computer game," Craig said.

"David has time limits imposed. When the participants respond, the situation changes. For better or worse. Or another event might disrupt their discussion. I'd really like to discuss the programming with David."

"But you won't," Julia said. "At least, you won't tell him that you've been secretly recording the sessions."

"Should I disconnect the meeting room camera?"

"Not yet," she said. "I can justify this covert observation on the basis of security. But let's not share that information with the others. Understood?"

A loopy grin stretched the corners of his wide mouth. "Thanks, Julia."

"Get some sleep," she ordered. "It's still snowing, and we're going to be busy tomorrow with the snowblower and the plow."

When Craig left the room, Paul went to the bank of six monitors. "I know you've got more cameras than this."

"Dozens of cameras," she said. "And dozens of sequences we can run them in. We pretty much keep the interior cameras going all the time. Plus one in the front of the house and one in the rear."

"What if somebody approaches from across the meadow?"

"We have a motion-sensitive system for outdoors. If anybody touches the fence, the surveillance camera comes on and we get a warning light on this grid." She pointed to another computer with an electronic diagram of the property. "Most of the time, those cameras record charming wildlife videos of deer or squirrels crawling over the fence, but we still need to respond and check it out, then record the security breach in our log report."

"Sounds like a lot of work."

"It is," she agreed. "We usually keep the exterior system turned off."

Paul nodded. There was such a thing as too much surveillance. These computers and electronic equipment must have cost the FBI a small fortune.

She took a seat in front of the monitor bank and tapped in a code on the keyboard. "I wish this camera had been on when I was attacked."

The screen showed the interior of the barn where the horses appeared to be comfortably bedded down for the night. As Julia watched the monitor, she smiled.

"You love those horses," he said.

"If I get reassigned and have to leave the safehouse, I'm really going to miss them." There was a softness in her blue eyes. "I love just about everything about the mountains."

"Even the weather?" He pointed to an outdoor camera at the front of the house that showed a steady snowfall. "It's really coming down. We've probably already got ten inches. The roads are going to be hell tomorrow."

"On the plus side," she said, "I don't think we need to worry about that guy who came after us at the skating rink showing up here."

The downside was that they were snowed in with a very clever murderer.

On the indoor surveillance monitors, he watched Craig's progress as he left the kitchen, went through the lower level, then up the staircase to the second floor and then to the third. Throughout the rest of the house, there was zero activity.

Paul took a sip of his coffee and glanced toward

Julia. "What's your procedure? Is there anything special you do when on surveillance duty?"

"We'll walk through the house a couple of times at unscheduled intervals. And keep an eye on the monitors."

He glanced at the screens. Nothing had changed. Three hours of this was about as exciting as watching paint dry.

Crossing the room, he focused on the prerecorded session of the Homeland Security meeting. Nothing happening there, either. David, RJ and Gil were punching information into their individual computer keyboards. The senator leaned back in his chair, looking bored.

"Here's a thought," Julia said as she moved to one of the desks. "We can check out the FBI information on John Maser, also known as Johnny Maserati."

He stood at her shoulder and watched as her fingers dashed across the keyboard. The FBI logo flashed across the screen. "Is it legal for me to watch you do this?"

"Probably not recommended, but I'm not accessing any top-secret information. I imagine this is pretty much the same data you have in police files and the National Crime Information Center."

A mug shot of John Maser popped up on the screen. He was an average-looking guy, age forty-two. Quickly, Paul scanned his record. "Check his military history. Maser was a Marine. Let's see if he ever served under General Naylor."

Like all Marines, Maser was a marksman. He'd attained the rank of lance corporal before he was honorably discharged.

While Julia cross-referenced his postings with those of General Naylor, Paul wandered back over to the wall of monitors. Nothing had changed. Nothing had moved. The surveillance system provided a comprehensive look at the interior of the safehouse. How had a murderer gotten past this surveillance to enter the general's bedroom? "Is there any way of doctoring these tapes? Overriding the system?"

"Sure," Julia said. "But it didn't happen on the night the general was killed. Trust me, Paul. Nobody went through the door into his room."

"And he didn't share a bathroom?"

"Both the general and the senator have private bathrooms."

The murder was physically impossible. If that was true, why had Julia been attacked? Why had an assassin come after them at the skating rink? There had to be something they weren't seeing.

"Here." Julia pointed to the computer screen. "John Maser and the general served at the same time in the same place. They could have known each other."

"A lowly lance corporal and a general?"

"This was almost twenty years ago. Naylor wasn't a general then. Only a lieutenant."

"Let's assume they were buddies." It was a starting point. "Maser could have been coming here to meet with the general. Why?"

"To warn him." Julia clicked off the FBI Web site and swiveled around in the desk chair to face him. "In Maser's gun deals, he might have come across information that indicated the general was in danger."

"Why would he care? According to our records,

Johnny Maserati was little more than a fraud and a petty criminal."

"He was a Marine," she said as though that explained everything. "During that one period in his life, he behaved honorably and served his country. If the general was in danger, it was Maser's duty to warn him."

He remembered that her brother had been a Marine, and she had a lot of respect for the Corps. "Why wouldn't Maser warn the general with a phone call?"

She shrugged. "His message might have been too important to convey on the phone."

Paul understood that reasoning. Messages delivered in person were more effective. He took another sip of his coffee and rubbed his eyes. This was too much thinking. His brain hurt. He missed his usual seven hours of sleep. "Where does this logic lead us?"

Brightly, Julia replied, "Maser came to Colorado to warn the general that he was in danger. The killer intercepted him, drugged and watched as he drove off the side of a mountain. Then the killer carried out his original plan to murder the general."

Paul drained the rest of his coffee. "Now all we need is to ID the murderer."

Julia turned toward the screen where Craig's secret camera caught the four members of the Homeland Security team in action. "One of them. We'll know more after you interview them tomorrow."

"If they choose to cooperate."

He didn't expect these interviews to be easy.

After they completed their surveillance shift, Paul and Julia went back upstairs and got ready to face the day. After his shower, Paul was still wearing yesterday's clothes. But he'd borrowed a razor from Craig and felt fairly clean when he left Julia's bedroom.

As he descended the staircase, he smelled breakfast—bacon, coffee and freshly baked muffins.

The others were already eating. RJ and David sat on one side of the long table. The senator and Gil were on the opposite side. Julia presided at the head. When Paul entered, she indicated an open seat beside David Dillard. "Please join us, Deputy. We were discussing the weather."

"Still snowing," David said. "The whole area is socked in. Airports are closed. The chain law is in effect over the passes."

"It happens," Paul said as he took a seat and immediately helped himself to pancakes and crisp bacon. Until this moment, he hadn't realized how hungry he was.

"I hate being confined," said RJ Katz. Her small hands busily sliced her food into tiny pieces. "This session has been a disaster. First, the general commits suicide. Then, we're snowed in."

In a sadistically cheerful voice, Paul said, "Don't forget the murder of John Maser, also known as Johnny Maserati."

The only one who showed any reaction to the alias was David Dillard. "Hey, I know something about Johnny Maserati. Isn't he involved with illegal weaponry?"

Ashbrook scowled at Paul. "I told you last night that I refuse to answer any questions without a lawyer present."

"I heard you, Senator." Immediately, Paul looked away from the politician and gave his complete attention to David Dillard. "I appreciate your willingness to cooperate. You and me need to have a little talk after breakfast. Pass the syrup."

While Paul chatted about the food and potential for skiing after a blizzard and other mundane topics, he watched the senator out of the corner of his eye. Ashbrook dropped his fork loudly against the plate, sipped at his coffee and cleared his throat. His body language showed that he didn't like being ignored.

"David," Ashbrook snapped, "we should be getting started."

"Not for another half hour."

Pointedly, Paul said, "And David needs to talk with me. Shouldn't take long."

Again, he turned away from the senator. Without the proper warrants and probable cause, Paul couldn't compel Ashbrook to talk to him, especially since the senator demanded a lawyer be present. Ashbrook would have to decide for himself that he'd rather cooperate than be left out of the loop.

With breakfast done, Paul escorted David down the hall to the library where he'd talked with Gil last night. Taking a seat at the wooden library table, David appeared calm. He removed his black frame eyeglasses, took out a hanky and cleaned the lenses before placing them back on his pug nose.

Though Paul was only a few years older than David, he had a paternal attitude toward the wide-eyed computer specialist. Unlike Gil, David seemed inexperienced and eager to please.

Paul folded his hands across his comfortably full belly and said, "Tell me about Johnny Maserati."

"I never actually met the guy, but I ran across his

name when I was doing research to create one of these simulations. It's the one we're doing today, and it involves a survivalist group."

Paul remembered the Wyoming survivalists associated with Ashbrook. "The Lone Wolves."

"I'm surprised you've heard of them," David said. "From what I can tell, they aren't dangerous. Their primary objective is to avoid paying taxes."

"Maser was supplying them with weapons."

"Possibly." David leaned across the table. "I don't like to point fingers, but Ashbrook has been involved with the Lone Wolves."

"How so?"

"Campaign financing."

David's information neatly validated facts that Paul already knew. "Is there anything else you recall about Johnny Maserati?"

"Not really. The only reason I recalled the name was because of the car. Maserati."

"Anything about his record when he was in the Marines?"

"Sorry," David said.

"Were you in the military?"

"My brother was a Marine. But not me. I went to college, got a degree in computer science and worked in Silicon Valley before I got recruited into the FBI."

"Recruited?"

"The gaming software I was developing had applications the FBI thought might be useful. When they contacted me, I jumped at the chance to get my hands on all the high end government technology."

They were getting off the subject. If Paul wasn't careful, he'd end up getting a lecture on megabytes and RAM. He brought the focus back to his inquiry. "How well did you know the general?"

Behind his glasses, David's eyes darted. "We met only a few times before this weekend. I still can't believe he committed suicide."

"Why is that?"

"General Naylor had a giant ego. It was more than self-confidence. He didn't think it was possible for him to make a mistake—surely not a big enough mistake to justify killing himself."

Though Paul hadn't known the general well enough to form his own opinions, he wasn't surprised by David's analysis. General Naylor had the reputation of being a leader of men. "Strong ego is probably a good trait for a general."

"Yeah? Tell that to Custer's troops."

"Sounds like you know something about the general's record. Can you give me some examples of his giant ego?"

"It's all in his book."

"I wasn't aware that he'd published a book."

"Every lamebrain pundit on television has a book deal," David said bitterly. "The general's book isn't in print. Not yet, anyway. He said that he planned to work on his manuscript while we were here."

Paul mentally reviewed the items he'd removed from the general's bedroom: clothing, the usual toiletries, a vitamin supplement, sleeping pills, three hardbacks including one on war strategy, a case for the general's hearing aid, a photo of his grandchildren. He hadn't found manuscript pages—nothing resembling the rough draft of a memoir. There had been, however, a laptop that was used to print out the general's suicide note. The manuscript must have been stored in the computer, which was now in the custody of the sheriff's department.

"I won't keep you much longer," he said to David. "Tell me when you arrived in the area and came to the safehouse."

"I came here the night before the exercises were supposed to start."

The night John Maser was killed. "What time?"

"It was after nine. I spent the day in Vail where I tried snowboarding."

"Did you like it?"

"Not much," he admitted. "I'm a whole lot better at computer sports than the real thing."

"After the snowboarding?"

"I had dinner and came here."

"Were you with anyone?"

He pushed his glasses up on his nose. "Sorry, Deputy. I haven't got an alibi until I arrived at the safehouse around nine or ten."

"Were any of the others here?"

"I don't know," David said. "I went directly to bed."

"Tired from the snowboarding?"

"Wiped out."

Paul recalled something Julia had mentioned. David suffered from insomnia. "So you didn't need a sleeping pill."

His eyebrows arched above his glasses. "How did you know about that?"

"It's my job to know. Did you take a pill?"

"I don't exactly remember."

David leaned back in his chair, withdrawing from

the conversation. There was a wariness in his expression. Until now, he'd been cool and steady, even though he had no alibi. What was it about those sleeping pills?

Chapter 12

After her "guests" were back in session, Julia pulled on her boots, gloves and parka. Though Roger had already been out to the barn, she wanted to check on the horses. Stormy, the pregnant mare with the bad temper, wasn't expected to deliver for a week or so, but Julia was still concerned.

This marked the first time she'd been back to the barn since the attack, and she was glad that Paul had decided to come with her. Not that she was afraid to return to the barn. A well-trained federal agent didn't give in to fear. But she was definitely uneasy. Apprehensive.

Being confined in the safehouse with these four angry people—one of whom was likely a murderer—amplified her tension. Every word they spoke seemed to have a double meaning. Every gesture appeared threatening. Julia desperately wanted this impossible crime to be solved.

And when it was? She'd try to scrape together the shreds of her career and convince her superiors that she was still capable of running the safehouse.

"Ready?" Paul asked.

"Let's do it."

She shoved open the front door, and they stepped onto the covered porch. The storm raged before them. High drifts reached up to the porch railing. Though Craig had been out here with the snowblower clearing a path to the barn, the mounting snow had almost wiped away his efforts. It was white and cold.

"It's beautiful," she said.

"If you're a polar bear."

"I love when it snows like this. Unstoppable and fierce."

In comparison to the storm of tension inside the safehouse, the snow was wonderful and natural and clean.

She went down the steps from the porch and spread her arms wide, allowing herself to feel the full force of the storm. The heavy wet flakes pelted her cheeks and clung to her. If she stood like this for five minutes, she'd be covered in snow, turned into Frosty the Snowwoman.

Out here, there were no subtle motives. No secret ploys. The cold was real and exhilarating. When she laughed, puffs of vapor escaped her lips.

Paul tromped down the stairs. His shoulders hunched against the storm. "You're not going to flop down on the ground and make a snow angel, are you?"

"I might." But she had a better idea. Bending, she picked up a handful of snow and packed it into a ball.

"Don't throw that," Paul warned.

"Or else?" She shaped the ball with her gloves. "What are you going to do?"

"Lady, I will have to take you down. I happen to be the king of snow fights. Born and bred in the mountains, and I—"

She lobbed her snowball into his chest. "You're a nice, big target."

"Shouldn't have done that." In his huge hands, the making of a snowball took two seconds. He fired, hitting her on the shoulder. Before she could react, he pitched another one.

"You missed." Stumbling, she plowed through the drifts toward the end of the house. The wind pushed her forward. Scooping up another handful of snow, she packed it, turned and fired.

Paul retaliated with a direct hit on her shoulder. But she'd gotten a head start on him and easily escaped his next missile.

Behind the house, she ran as best she could through the knee-deep snow, stopping at the chopping block, which was almost buried. When she paused to make another snowball, Paul was right on top of her. Stumbling through the heavy snow, he caught up and wrapped his arms around her.

"What are you doing?" she demanded.

"You can't throw snowballs if you can't use your arms."

She struggled halfheartedly. In this moment, her mind was blissfully free from worry. She looked up into his handsome ruddy face. "Think you're so tough?"

"I know I am."

"Tough guys don't have dimples when they smile."

"Are you making fun of me?" His dimples deepened. "Now, you're in real trouble."

When he caught her under the knees and lifted her off her feet, she couldn't have been more surprised. Julia was a big woman. Carrying her through a blizzard wasn't easy. She dropped her snowball and wrapped her arms around his neck. "Don't drop me."

Staggering, he headed toward a huge drift.

"I mean it, Paul. Don't you dare—"

When he tried to plop her down in the snow, she hung on tight and pulled him down with her. They were both wallowing in the snow. The hood of her parka fell back. Her hair was wet.

She should have been freezing cold. But when his lips claimed hers, an amazing heat flowed through her. This kiss had been building inside her for a long time—since last night when they lay together and throughout yesterday when she admitted she'd lied and saw anger in his dark, brown eyes.

Despite the raging blizzard, she was hot. A furnace flamed inside her. Apparently, all she needed to protect her from the elements was his kiss.

When he separated from her, she saw the reflected warmth in his chocolate-brown eyes. He wanted her as much as she wanted him.

He pulled her to her feet and glanced over his shoulder to the house. "Do you suppose we gave them a show?"

"Do you care?"

"Not really."

When they entered the relative warmth of the barn, she stamped her feet and brushed off snow. It was quiet in here. And peaceful.

And she was incredibly wet. Melted snow trickled down the back of her neck. When she unzipped her parka and pulled it off, a shower of snow fell to the barn floor. Rolling around in a blizzard hadn't been the smartest thing she'd ever done, but it was worth it. She'd gotten the kiss she'd been waiting for.

She saw Paul glance toward the corner where he knew a camera was placed. "Do you suppose the surveillance is operational?"

"It is." After her attack, she'd given instructions to run the barn camera 24/7. "But there aren't any microphones. We can talk freely out here."

"That's what I was hoping for."

Actually, she'd been *hoping* for more kisses. She was disappointed when he took out his cell phone. "Who are you calling?"

"First, the kids. Then, the sheriff."

"Did you get new information when you talked to David?"

"A book," he said. "According to David, the general planned to work on his memoirs while he was here this week. Since we didn't find any manuscript pages in his bedroom, he must have had it stored on his laptop."

"A memoir," she said. "The story of his life."

"Let's hope this book can tell us the story of his death. Who he loved. Who he hated. Who might have a good reason to want him dead."

Leaving Paul to make his phone calls, Julia went to Stormy's stall. Her gaze went to the far corner where she'd been left to be trampled in the hay. The mare paced nervously, pawing at the floor.

"Hush, Stormy. It's okay."

The horse whinnied. She reared up and came down hard. If those heavy hooves had connected with Julia while she was unconscious, she could have been killed.

Nonetheless, this was an inefficient murder method. She couldn't imagine Gil Bradley doing anything so haphazard. When he set out to perform an assassination, nothing was left to chance. Or was it? Maybe he'd claimed to be a cold-blooded killing machine to throw them off. Maybe Gil Bradley had lost his nerve. He'd been anxious to talk to them, and he made a point about looking into the eyes of your adversary at the moment of death.

In Gil's view, hitting her on the back of the head and dragging her body into a dangerous situation was cowardly. Similar to the way John Maser was killed. A supposed accident. There was little doubt that the same person was responsible for both assaults. The same murderer. And then, they'd hired a hit man.

Stormy calmed. She sidled up to the edge of the stall. Her big brown eyes seemed almost apologetic as she waited for Julia to stroke her nose.

"It's okay," Julia murmured. She took a piece of apple from the pocket of her parka and held it out. "I know you didn't mean to hurt me."

Stormy nuzzled her hand as she ate the apple.

"Being pregnant can't be much fun. Not that I'd know."

While Paul talked on the phone, she puttered in the barn, straightening the tack, checking the heating system, talking to the horses. There weren't any real chores to handle. Roger and Craig had done a good job out here.

Paul sat on a bench near the door, and she came across the barn to stand before him. "How are the kids?"

"They don't miss me at all. They're having a great time with Mac and Abby."

She was immensely glad his family hadn't been touched by the danger that surrounded the safehouse. "How much have you told Mac about the murders?"

"As little as possible."

"And how does he feel about babysitting?"

"He's trying to be cynical, telling me that I owe him big time for getting snowed in with the girls. But he's having fun. I can hear it in his voice."

"He and Abby make a good pair."

"Yeah, I'm expecting wedding bells real soon."

From the bench, he gazed up at her, and she saw the tension behind his easygoing expression. Their problems weren't over. Not by a long shot. "What did the sheriff say?"

"Because of the blizzard, he hasn't yet returned the general's personal effects, including the computer, to his family."

That sounded like good news, but Paul's smile faded. His dimples disappeared.

"What's wrong?" she asked.

"The sheriff isn't inclined toward more investigation on the general's murder. I asked him to send me the memoir on e-mail, and he refused. We won't have that memoir to use for clues."

She hated to give up that potential lead. "It's possible the general brought the manuscript with him."

"Did you see him with the pages?"

"No, but he was the first to arrive. Came a day early, in fact. And he spent a lot of time in his room."

"There was no manuscript in his room," Paul said.

"But there might have been one," she said. "If the killer managed to slip into the general's room without being seen, it would be easy to steal away with the manuscript."

"In which case, we'll never find it," he pointed out.

"Not necessarily. Keep in mind that nobody but me has left the safehouse since the general's death."

"What are you saying?"

"We need to make a search of the bedrooms to see if we can find that manuscript." She pushed up the sleeve of her sweater to check her wristwatch. "They'll be in session for another hour before they break for lunch."

Paul was on his feet, ready to go. Though she'd wished they could spend a bit more private time together in the barn, the room search took top priority.

There were no snowball fights or kisses on their way back to the house. Now they had a mission. Search the rooms.

Inside the front door, Julia discarded her wet clothing quickly. In stocking feet, she padded toward the kitchen. Roger leaned over the stove, putting the last spicy flourishes on a huge pot of chili.

"Hey," she said, "good job with the horses."

"Is Stormy okay?"

"She'll be fine." She inhaled the spicy aroma. "That smells fantastic."

"The key is in the peppers," he said. "I made two versions. One with no meat."

Paul entered the kitchen and went directly to the stove. "Can I taste?"

Roger held out a spoon. Paul tasted, licked his lips and made a low, prolonged groan—a sound that Julia suspected was more appropriate for the bedroom than the kitchen. Wryly, she said, "You like chili."

"I like food." Paul proudly stroked his barrel chest. "Especially chili. This is excellent."

"I like it hotter," Roger said, "but I figured these people from back east wouldn't appreciate three-alarm chili."

Paul nodded. "Serve it with hot sauce on the side. What brand have you got?"

Roger flipped open a spice cabinet to show off a row of Tabasco and hot sauce. As Paul started picking up each small bottle and studying the contents, it was clear to Julia that he was enthralled with Roger's collection.

She cleared her throat. Time was running out before the morning session ended, and they needed to get their room search underway. "I'm going upstairs to change linens on the beds. Paul, would you like to help?"

"You bet." He dipped the spoon for another taste of chili. "Be with you in a sec."

She headed upstairs to get started. Changing bed sheets and towels was a good excuse to be in the rooms of her guests, but it wasn't her favorite chore, especially since the dirty linens would then need to be laundered. She started with RJ's bedroom.

After the bed was stripped, Julia carefully went through the dresser drawers and closet. RJ's clothing was simple and well cut. No frills. Her underwear drawer showed a different side to her personality. Thong-style panties. Skimpy bras in exotic colors.

Under RJ's tightly wrapped exterior beat the heart of a sexy vamp.

Beside the desk, Julia found RJ's briefcase. It was large enough to hold a manuscript, but when she lifted the locked case, it wasn't heavy enough to hold a ream of paper. Julia ignored the many other computerized devices stored in the drawers of the desk. Her goal was to find a manuscript.

Her search proceeded quickly. Not under the bed. Not between the box spring and mattress. Not behind the dresser or desk.

When Paul entered, she was already tucking the new sheets onto RJ's bed. "Nothing in here."

"How about the bathroom?"

"She and David share the bathroom. There aren't many hiding places. It's a plain, functional room."

He went through the bathroom door.

As soon as she smoothed the down comforter on top of the bed, Julia joined him. "Anything interesting?"

He was going through the contents of the mirrored medicine cabinet above the sink. "It's hard to tell who belongs to what. Everything is jumbled together."

"Let's assume the cosmetics are RJ's."

He shot her a grin. "It might be more fun if they weren't."

"Paul, we need to hurry."

"Apparently, both RJ and David suffer from insomnia. There are two different brands of sleeping pills."

"David mentioned that," she said. "RJ gave him one of her pills, and he didn't like the effect. It gave him bad dreams."

"The general took sleeping pills, too."

She suspected their high stress jobs were the cause

of insomnia. Or ulcers. Or any number of nervous disorders. "I don't think it's all that unusual for these people to have trouble sleeping."

"There's an added significance," he said. "The autopsy tox screen on the general indicated that he'd taken two sleeping pills. They weren't his regular brand."

This really didn't seem like a big deal. These three people shared a common condition. Likely, they'd talked about their insomnia and swapped medications.

"It was this one." Paul held up an amber prescription bottle. "The general had taken two of these. The label says they belong to RJ."

"What's the dosage?" she asked.

"One or two per night. As needed."

An extra sleeping pill, especially in a different prescription, might have caused the general to sleep more soundly than usual. Still, it was hard for Julia to imagine him staying asleep while the murderer dressed him in his uniform and shoes. "Did the autopsy indicate an adverse reaction to the medication? Like a stroke? Or a coma?"

"No."

As she gathered up the used towels in the bathroom and replaced them with fresh ones, she repeated, "We need to hurry."

David's room was messier than RJ's. Yesterday's clothing draped carelessly over the back of the desk chair. The contents of his pockets, including breath mints and a couple of hankies, lay on top of the dresser. Like RJ, he had several electronic devices, including one that stored and played music. In his underwear drawer, she found a couple of condoms. She held one up for Paul to see. "Is it possible that David and RJ are having a fling?"

"I don't get that impression."

She carefully replaced the condoms in the exact place she'd found them. "Maybe David is indulging in a little wishful thinking."

They finished up in his room and went to Senator Marcus Ashbook's larger bedroom with the private bathroom. Despite the lack of a television, this was considered the luxury corner suite.

While Julia picked up the used towels and stripped the bed, Paul searched in the nooks and crannies. He paused at the window that overlooked the driveway leading up to the house. "Still snowing."

"Thanks for the weather report. Keep looking. We've only got a couple of minutes."

"Ashbrook has good taste," he said from inside the closet. "Nice clothes and shoes."

She carefully remade the queen-size bed. The senator would surely complain if his covers weren't neatly tucked in.

Paul rummaged through the desk drawers. "Got it."

He held up several printed pages. The manuscript.

Julia rushed over to join him. Ashbrook had to have taken these pages from the general's room. This was more than a juicy piece of evidence. This was an indictment. Ashbrook had killed the general. She didn't know how or why. But she was certain that the honorable senator from Wyoming had somehow engineered General Naylor's suicide. Relief flooded through her.

She took a deep breath. Then she gasped as she read the title page. *"My Life in Politics* by Marcus Ashbrook."

"These are his own memoirs."

"Are you sure? Flip through the pages."

Paul scanned quickly. "Growing up on the ranch. His first vote on the floor. His work with Homeland Security."

Her short-lived satisfaction imploded and crumbled. "This isn't a clue. It's an ego trip."

Too bad. She really disliked Ashbrook. It would have pleased her immensely to place this murder at his doorstep.

Chapter 13

After lunch and the afternoon chores were done, Julia and Paul went into the basement office where Craig was watching the Homeland Security session on his hidden camera.

Julia pulled up a desk chair to sit beside him. "You know we shouldn't be doing this. Spying on the spies."

"Should I turn it off?"

"No way," she said. "What's going on?"

"Today's computerized simulation deals with a bunch of survivalists. They're holed up in a compound in Wyoming and are refusing to come out."

"Similar to what happened in Waco." Julia shuddered, remembering the terrible consequences of that siege. "I'm kind of surprised. This isn't something I consider a terrorist issue."

"True," Paul said as he took a seat behind her. "I'm

never quite sure what kind of situations fall under the jurisdiction of Homeland Security."

Craig pointed to the screen. "That's exactly the point they're debating. Jurisdiction."

"Turn up the volume," Julia said.

The three of them leaned forward to watch the real-time transmission from the room down the hall. In normal circumstances, Julia would never condone this covert observation. Not only was their unsanctioned camera a breach of the rules, but there was something creepy about spying. At the same time, it was fascinating. The picture on the computer monitor was like a made-for-television movie. They ought to be watching with a bowl of popcorn.

The petite RJ Katz came across very well on the screen. Her edgy hostility seemed almost attractive. Like a crusader, she was vehement in her insistence that a siege with an extremist group within the borders of the United States should be handled by the FBI.

Gil argued back that strategic groups within the CIA were better trained and equipped to infiltrate the perimeters of the survivalist compound and take control of the situation.

The senator sat quietly, biding his time. Like a poisonous spider, Julia thought, waiting to strike.

On the large screen behind the Homeland Security people, a well-defined graphic showed the outer walls of the computer-generated compound where the survivalists were under siege—several plain, clapboard buildings encircled by a high chain-link fence.

"We need more information," Gil said. He typed a command into the laptop in front of him. "I'm calling for aerial surveillance with heat-sensing capability to see how many people are inside and where they are."

Immediately, the computer graphic of the compound was replaced by an aerial photo.

"Wow," Paul said. "How was that done?"

"I told you," Craig said. "David is brilliant. Every probability is accounted for. They mention a strategy, and it's there."

Using his computer, Gil zoomed in on one sector. He squinted at the image on the screen. "That looks like a bomb. David, am I right?"

David Dillard stepped away from the wall. "You're right, Gil. There is a bomb within the compound."

RJ typed on her keyboard. "I'm getting the data. Inventory of weapons. Warheads. Missiles."

"How can you do that?" Gil asked.

She gave him a smug look. "Follow the money."

"I don't get it."

"How many times do I have to tell you? This is my area of expertise. I can access inventory, bank accounts and transfers. All of it." She glanced up at David. "You've made it easier for me. Usually, this type of research would take hours."

They all watched as she typed, occasionally muttering to herself.

Her fingers leaped off the keys as though they had suddenly become red hot. "Oh my God!"

"What is it?" Gil demanded.

RJ's eyes were wide. She appeared to be genuinely alarmed, drawn into the computer simulation. "This bomb could be a nuke. We can't risk a violent takeover. They might detonate the device."

"We need immediate action," Gil said. "We send in

my CIA team using extreme caution. The team will include a specialist to disarm the bomb."

As Julia watched, she was getting caught up in the drama of their simulated situation. Real lives were not at stake, but she felt the rising tension.

"Are you with me?" Gil asked.

"I don't think we should provoke them." RJ looked toward David, who was leaning against the wall, apart from the others. "As a technology expert, what would you suggest?"

"If the firing mechanism on the device is computerized, I might be able to jam it. But that's risky. I could just as well set it off."

"No good," RJ said. "What else?"

"Brainwashing techniques," he said. "We soften them up by bombarding the compound with audio messages, suggesting their surrender."

"What if they can't hear us?"

"That's a problem," David conceded. "We might find a way to introduce narcotics into their drinking water."

Gil scoffed. "How long would this brainwashing take?"

"It could be awhile," David said. "And I have to admit that these techniques aren't efficient with a large, diverse group."

"We go on the offensive," Gil said in a low, urgent tone. "There's no other way."

The senator rose to his feet. With a practiced gesture, he brushed the silver hair back from his forehead. "We need to talk with the people in that compound."

"Forget it," Gil said. "The United States government does not negotiate with terrorists."

"It's not a negotiation," Ashbrook said. "They've made no demands other than to be left alone on their own land."

"Which they refuse to pay taxes on," RJ said. "Not that tax evasion is important compared to the fact that they might be in possession of a nuclear weapon. They must be disarmed."

The senator signaled David with an imperious wave of his hand. "Show us the photograph of their leader."

David tapped a few computer keys, and the screen transformed to a picture of a rugged-looking character with stringy blond hair.

"He doesn't look very terrifying," Ashbrook said. "He's not a devil. Not a genius. He's just a man."

"Get to the point," RJ snapped. "What's your plan?"

Ashbrook stood beside the projected photograph of the leader. "My solution is political. Man to man. I walk up to the door of the compound and talk them into disarming."

"Without negotiating," Gil said firmly.

"I'll be reasonable but firm. These men aren't really terrorists. They're Americans. Just like a lot of other people I represent. I can talk sense into them."

RJ gave a decisive nod. She turned to David. "Let's follow Ashbrook's scenario. What's the outcome?"

"It depends." He circled the room and held the senator's chair. "Have a seat. You'll need to type in your dialogue with the leader."

While Ashbrook returned to his position behind the laptop, Craig explained what was happening to Julia and Paul. "These interface sessions are cool. The dialogue appears on the screen. I don't know how David comes up with the responses."

"Sure, you do." Julia stood and stretched. "When you were in training, you took classes in profiling and hostage negotiation."

Craig's thin face pulled into a scowl. "All that psychology stuff."

"I'm sure that's the data David will use. He can program typical responses in a high stakes conversation."

Both Craig and Paul seemed mesmerized by the screen, but she'd seen enough of this simulation to understand the most important factor. This wasn't about a simulated group of survivalists in Wyoming. The reality was the dynamic of the small group of people in the room down the hall. Their mission was to set up a first response advisory team. And Senator Marcus Ashbrook had taken control. He'd assumed the leadership position. He'd gotten what he wanted.

If the siege had been real and Ashbrook solved the problem—as he'd said, man to man—he'd be a hero. Wouldn't that be a fine launching pad for a presidential campaign?

She hated to think of Ashbrook in a position of power within Homeland Security. His motivations seemed to be entirely selfish. He wanted to be front and center, standing before dozens of television cameras and proposing his solutions.

Julia wished that Gil or RJ had put up more resistance to him. If the general were still alive, he wouldn't have relinquished his authority so easily. When he was killed, the balance in the group was thrown off, tilted in favor of Ashbrook.

Was that enough motive for Ashbrook to arrange the general's murder?

She glanced back toward Paul and Craig, who were both glued to the computer monitor.

"Ashbrook is good," Paul said. "He's making progress in convincing the leader."

"But he hasn't mentioned the bomb," Craig said. "That's the real concern."

Julia returned to stand behind them. "You know this is only a computer exercise, don't you?"

"It could happen," Paul said. "There are a lot of extremist groups and conspiracy theory people. Even here in Eagle County. We've got our share of wackos."

"If this was happening in Eagle County, would you want Ashbrook handling the negotiations?"

He pulled his gaze away from the screen and turned toward her. "I don't trust him."

"Nor do I," she said. "Let's leave Craig to keep an eye on the monitors."

Barely interested in their departure, Craig waved goodbye.

In the cozy living room, Julia flung herself into one of the matching rocking chairs in front of the fireplace. "Ashbrook is using this group to gain a position of power within Homeland Security. He's manipulating the others."

"You've got to admit," Paul said, "his solution of confronting the leader was a hell of a lot better than Gil's assault team or that mumbo-jumbo David was spouting."

"Mind control isn't so strange," she said. "True, it's hard to pull off with a group. But one-on-one, it can be very effective."

With a sigh, he sat in the rocking chair beside hers.

It seemed almost too small to hold his large frame. "How do you know about this stuff?"

"FBI training," she said. "Forensic psychology is really interesting. The profiling. Interrogation techniques. If you punch the right emotional buttons, you can make a person do just about anything."

"Like hypnosis," he said.

"Kind of."

An excess of nervous energy coursed through her veins, and she rocked vigorously. Though it was too soon for her to be experiencing the effects of cabin fever, she felt trapped in this house. And frustrated by their lack of progress in solving the general's murder. If only they'd found the manuscript for his memoirs.

Pushing out of the chair, she paced to the front window and looked out. Though snow was still falling, the storm's fury had abated. "It's letting up."

"We're running out of time." Paul left his chair and joined her. "How much longer are these people going to be here?"

"Two more full days." Through the window, she saw Roger with the snowblower, clearing a path. "When we're not snowed in, you won't have a good reason to stay here."

"Protecting you." He eased up close behind her. Gently, his arms encircled her waist. "That's all the reason I need."

Leaning against his broad chest, she drew warmth and comfort from his nearness. Though he might want to stay with her, she knew it was impossible. Paul would be required to get back to his job. His children needed him. "There's no way I can justify keeping you here as a bodyguard. Not without explaining my sus-

picions. If I make that explanation, I'll have to confess
that I tampered with the crime scene."

"Not necessarily." He nuzzled behind her thick curly
ponytail to whisper in her ear. "We were threatened at
the skating rink. If I tell the sheriff about that guy in
the ski mask, he'll want me to stay with you."

And she wanted him to stay, wanted to keep him
close. Tilting her head, she encouraged him to nibble
at her ear. His breath was hot and moist against her
throat. A shiver coursed through her—a shiver that
had nothing to do with the cold. She longed for release. Sexual release.

Outside the window, Roger made another pass with
the snowblower. "Nobody's watching," she said. "Craig
is engrossed in his spying. He's not keeping an eye on
the house monitors. Roger is outside."

"Then no one will see if I do this."

He spun her around in his arms and pulled her
against him. Her arms stretched to wrap around his
huge torso. She loved the way she fit against him, the
way he held her close felt so good. So right.

"We shouldn't be doing this," she murmured. "I'm
in charge of the safehouse. I should be setting an example."

His lips silenced her. With his kiss, he exploded the
apprehension that had been building inside her. Her
defensive wall of propriety crumbled to dust. With a
soft moan, she gave herself completely to this fierce,
demanding passion.

Her mouth opened hungrily. His probing tongue
thrust inside. She couldn't breathe. Didn't want to. She
was overwhelmed. Blissfully overwhelmed.

When he separated from her, she gasped. Her heart

beat throbbed like a big bass drum. It took a big man to sweep her off her feet. Paul was that man.

"Nobody's watching," he said.

His hand slid inside her sweater and cupped her breast. His thumb flicked across her taut nipple causing an electric thrill to chase through her.

"We should use this time to search."

As soon as the words left her lips, Julia couldn't believe she'd said them.

"What?" His eyebrows pulled into a frown.

"The manuscript."

"The general's memoir?"

"We can search the lower floor of the house. Nobody will question what we're doing."

His large hand gently squeezed her breast. "That was the last thing on my mind. But you're right."

She didn't want to be right. She wanted him to kiss her again, to throw her down on the leather sofa, tear off her clothes and make love to her. "Damn it."

Paul kissed her forehead and stepped away from her. "Tonight," he promised.

"Yes. Tonight."

When she turned away from him, her legs wobbled as if she were intoxicated, drunk with passion. She blinked, forcing her eyes to focus. "Let's start in here."

They looked under chairs and behind shelves for the manuscript. While Paul checked the upper shelves in the hall closet, Julia stared into the fireplace where bright flames danced across her hand-split logs. "If I were the killer, I would have burned the manuscript."

"What would be the point? I'm sure there are other copies. Probably on the general's laptop."

"That could take months to surface." And they needed proof now. "Let's try the library."

It seemed like a very logical place to find a manuscript. Julia was familiar with the shelves and the books, which were half fiction and half reference books. Since the usual residents at the safehouse were protected witnesses involved in legal proceedings, there was a row of law books. At first glance, the library looked the same as always.

On shelf after shelf, she reached behind the rows of books and felt around, hoping her fingers would touch the loose pages of a manuscript. But there was nothing. Not on the shelves. Not inside the closed lower cabinet.

Paul stood beside the table where he'd sat to question David and Gil. The wood grain on the top was scratched and worn. In the middle was a drawer. He pulled it open. "Julia, come here."

Inside the drawer was a red pen and a stack of white paper. The page on top read: *Memoir of Harrison Naylor*.

"This doesn't seem like a hiding place," she said.

"Too obvious," Paul agreed

"He must have left it here."

Her mind formed a picture. She imagined the general sitting in the library with his red pen, editing his memoirs. She lifted the pages and flipped quickly through them. The first fifty were heavily marked in red. There was nothing after that.

"He stopped here," she said. "Chapter Six."

"It's like he was planning to come back to it," Paul remarked. "That doesn't sound like the action of a man who intended to commit suicide."

Carefully, she placed the pages on the table. Finally,

they had a tangible piece of evidence. She could only hope that the general's written words about his life would be enough to spark a full investigation into his death.

Chapter 14

In the kitchen, Paul helped Julia prepare dinner. Stuffed pork chops for the carnivores. Plain stuffing for the vegetarians. The side dishes included peas with pearl onions, buttered squash and a salad of romaine lettuce and artichoke hearts. Dessert was a chocolate cake. It was a simple but hearty meal. Comfort food to soothe the belly on a cold winter night.

Likewise, the next step in their investigation was uncomplicated. While everyone was gathered around the table for dinner, Paul would mention that they had located a copy of the general's life story. From the response, they might be able to figure out who knew about the memoir and who might be threatened by the general's remembrances.

It wasn't definitive evidence. No smoking gun. But they didn't have much else to go on. Forensic evidence was nil, and the murder didn't even look like a murder. Their best hope was that one of their suspects would open up.

He telephoned his kids to see how they were doing and got a blow-by-blow report on the day's activity. The high point was when they caught Mac and Abby kissing. Then, Jennifer asked to talk with Julia.

Paul handed over the cell phone. He watched as Julia smiled and chatted, completely at ease while talking to a nine-year-old. Most people didn't know how to deal with kids. They either came across as stuffy advice-giving adults or they tried too hard to relate and acted like overgrown teenagers. Julia was perfectly natural—easygoing and pleasant with a great sense of humor.

Over the phone, she described their dinner preparations in detail. When she got off, she was smiling. "Don't be surprised when your daughter adds artichoke hearts to your next pizza."

"Why?"

"She thought it sounded gourmet. That's her word. Not mine."

"Swell," he muttered. "Were they complaining about my cooking?"

"Not at all. In fact, they said Abby is worse than you are. Apparently, she burned the microwave popcorn."

"The kids want to learn how to cook. And how to bake. And sew. And put on makeup." This refrain was familiar. And painful. "I can't teach them any of that stuff. I'm not, you know, a woman."

"Excuse me?" She bristled. "Are you saying housework is woman's work?"

"Hell, no." He'd stuck his foot in it this time. "I

never got trained. My mom was traditional and never bothered showing us kids how she worked her magic."

Though Julia shot him a warning glare, she let the subject drop. "Where are your parents now?"

"They moved to Flagstaff about ten years ago. It was just after I got married, and I bought their house."

"The house where you're living now?"

"That very one."

It had been a sweet deal, requiring zero down payment. But Paul often wondered what his life might have been like if he hadn't been tied down so young with a house, a wife and kids. He loved the mountains. And he was well suited for his job as a deputy. But sometimes, he wondered what might have been. "I haven't led a very adventurous life."

"Some people say that raising kids is the best adventure of all."

"You know what I mean. I haven't seen the world, haven't tried a lot of things."

"Like what?" she asked. "Do you have an urge to go parachuting? Bungee jumping?"

"I've done those two," he said. "Didn't much care for the bungee jump."

"Come over here and sit." She directed him to the kitchen table and placed two cooled layers of chocolate cake in front of him. "Would you please frost these and stick them together."

"I can do that."

Wryly, she added, "It doesn't exactly require the skills of a pastry chef."

Using a flat knife, he smeared a glop of frosting on the top of one layer. "My friend Jess is always telling me about exciting stuff. He spent one summer in Baja, lying in the sun and swimming with the whales."

"Is that something you'd like to do?"

"Maybe." But he wasn't much of a beach person. And he knew that any travel plans would have to include the kids. If they weren't with him, he'd miss them too much to enjoy himself. "What about you, Julia?"

"On my vacation last year, I worked in a rural community that had been destroyed by a tornado. Rebuilding the houses, repairing the water system and electric."

"Doesn't sound like much of a vacation." He carefully placed one layer of cake on top of the other.

"Sure it was." She stood over his shoulder. "Hauling cinder blocks is a better workout than I'd ever get in a spa. I met some fantastic people. And I had the great satisfaction of seeing a completed project. A couple of brand-new houses for people who needed them. Fresh water pouring out of a faucet. It was a good adventure."

He tilted his head and looked up at her. "Hauling cinder blocks? Repairing plumbing?"

"That's right." She raised an eyebrow. "That's what I call women's work."

She was one hell of a fine woman. Too good to be true. When she talked about disaster relief work, it sounded like something he wanted to do. "Where have you been all my life?"

"Down the road twelve miles from Redding."

She reached around him, dipped a finger into the frosting and popped it into her mouth. Though he was sure she didn't intend for that gesture to be sexy, his eyes were drawn to her rose-colored lips. Slowly, his gaze traveled south. Over her shoulders. Down to the swell of her full breasts under her sweater.

Tonight, he reminded himself, they would be alone in her bedroom. Tonight, he would unfasten her wild, curly hair. He'd yank that ridiculous flannel nightgown off. Tonight, they would make love.

When she dipped again into the frosting, he objected, "Hey, save some for the cake."

She gave him a wink and started carrying dishes into the dining room.

It didn't take long for the troops to gather. Even Roger and Craig joined them at the long table. The mood tonight seemed more positive than be-fore, partly due to the fact that the snow had finally stopped. According to the forecasters, they could expect sunshine tomorrow.

The attitude among the Homeland Security people was different. Almost friendly. Gil and RJ teased David about how they had outsmarted his simulation and averted disaster. The senator basked in his leadership role, and Paul had to admit that Ashbrook wore that status with dignity. He was gracious, steady and concerned. It seemed that a pecking order had finally been established in this group. Ashbrook was on top.

Paul waited until the cake was served to drop his bombshell. "Julia and I happened to find an interesting document today."

"Tell us about it," Ashbrook said.

"A memoir." He watched for their reaction. "General Harrison Naylor's memoir."

"I knew he was working on it," David Dillard said.

Gil and the senator commented on how the general's life story was especially important in light of his recent passing. They lifted their glasses in a toast.

RJ remained silent.

* * *

"I wish RJ had spoken up." Julia flopped crosswise on the bed in her room. "There was something on her mind. That's for sure."

Paul closed and locked her bedroom door behind himself. Tonight, he wanted to be sure there would be no interruptions. He placed the general's memoir on top of her dresser. "RJ had her opportunity to come forward. I asked her again if she'd sit down for a talk, and she turned me down."

"What's she hiding?"

"The answer might be in here." He tapped the top sheet of the manuscript. "RJ was the only one who seemed worried that we'd found the memoir."

"The only one who *showed* concern," Julia corrected him. "I guess we should start reading."

"In a minute."

"Did you have something else in mind?"

She turned to her side, bent her elbow and propped up her head. Her sweater outlined the womanly curve of her waist and the fullness of her hips.

Though Paul was plenty tired after being trapped inside the house all day, her hourglass figure enticed him. The promise of tonight was the only thing that had kept him going through another long day. He stretched out on his belly beside her. The bedsprings creaked under their combined weight.

Paul shifted himself around, trying to find a comfortable position. No matter which way he turned, his feet dangled off the edge of the mattress. He rolled onto his back. "At my house, there's a king-size bed."

She snuggled up close. "There are certain advantages to a small bed."

"Like cold feet that stick out from under the covers?"

"Like this," she whispered.

Her long legs straddled his hips as she climbed on top of him. The weight of her breasts pressed against his chest. Her action surprised him, but he was glad she made this move. Very glad.

"Wait," he said. "Unfasten your ponytail."

She tore off the barrette and her thick hair cascaded around her shoulders. He glided his fingers through the silky length. Reflected glow from the overhead light shimmered in the vibrant curls.

Her lovely face loomed above him. If she wore any makeup, he couldn't tell. Her complexion was fresh, clean, beautiful. Her blue eyes darkened with a sensual promise meant only for him.

When they kissed, he was immediately aroused. He'd been waiting all day for this. Maybe longer. Maybe he'd been waiting all his life for Julia.

There was a knock at the bedroom door.

"Not now," he grumbled.

Another knock. He heard RJ's voice. "Excuse me? Deputy Hemmings?"

He wrapped his arms more tightly around Julia. "Maybe if we ignore her, she'll go away."

"You know we can't do that." She dropped a kiss on his cheek and climbed off him.

Oh, man! Paul squeezed his eyes shut, willing his frustration to go away. Every cell in his body wanted to make love to Julia. Why was this so impossible? He liked her. She liked him. If there was any justice in the world, they should be lying together naked.

Instead, there was RJ. She'd picked the worst moment to intrude.

Julia opened the door and confronted her. "What is it, RJ?"

"I'm ready." Her mouth drew into a prissy little bow. "I've decided to answer questions from Deputy Hemmings."

He couldn't say no. But he sure as hell wasn't going to invite her into the only privacy he had with Julia. Paul grabbed the memoirs from Julia's dresser and tucked them under his arm. No way would he leave this evidence unprotected. "Let's all go down to the library."

By the time they entered that familiar room, Paul's patience was at an end. He sat across from RJ and fired off questions to determine her whereabouts during the time frame when John Maser crashed his vehicle. RJ had no alibi. None of these people did. That would be too easy.

Paul charged into his next line of inquiry with all the subtlety of a bull elephant. "You were upset when I said we'd found the general's memoir. Why?"

One of her small hands rubbed across her mouth, and her gesture reinforced his first impression that she was like a cat. She might be preparing to lick her fingers and groom herself.

Her small hands folded neatly on top of the table. "I wasn't on friendly terms with General Naylor."

"Something in the past?"

She nodded and lowered her head, staring down at her own hands. It was obvious that she was having trouble getting the words out, but Paul wasn't in the mood for gently leading her toward a confession. "You wanted to talk to me, RJ. What do you want to say?"

"It's a long story."

Julia sat beside her and placed her hand atop RJ's. "It might be easier if you started at the beginning. How did you first meet the general?"

"At Arlington Cemetery."

"At a funeral?" Julia prompted.

"Four funerals. There were four Marines killed in the line of duty because Naylor had made a stupid mistake in judgment. A failure in leadership."

"Did you know these men?"

"No." She raised her head. Her hazel eyes widened as she looked at Julia. "I was there with my former fiancé. A Marine sergeant. The men being buried were his friends. He'd been injured in the same incident. He lost his left arm below the elbow."

"I'm sorry." Julia felt RJ's small hands trembling. Her skin was icy cold. "What was your fiancé's name?"

"Garret. He shouldn't have been out of the hospital, but he insisted. He needed to be with his men."

Julia understood her former fiancé's motives. Her brother had been the same way. "The Marines put duty first."

"And Garret loved being a Marine. It was his whole life. With his injury, he knew that he'd never be cleared for active duty. He was devastated."

Julia nodded. Though RJ wasn't her favorite person, she sympathized with her tragedy. Someone she loved had suffered a terrible loss. "Was General Naylor any help?"

"Not one damned bit." Her tone was as furious as the harsh winds that rattled the windowpanes. "When

I met him at Arlington, he gave me the standard 'sorry for your loss' speech. And he told Garret to pull himself together. As if he could. As if he could grow another arm."

She pulled her hands away from Julia's grasp and folded her arms below her breasts. A tremor rocked her shoulders as she continued, "Naylor was an insensitive bastard, and I told him so. Right there in Arlington in front of those long rows of white crosses, in front of everybody. I never thought our paths would cross again."

"But they did?"

"Several times. The general never returned to the field. For the past couple of years, he has been focused on Homeland Security, which is also my area. Whenever I could, I made it my business to put General Naylor in difficult situations."

"Like this weekend?"

Her eyes glittered with suppressed hostility. "I was looking forward to these simulations. I wanted to show Naylor what an incompetent fool he was." She turned toward Paul and repeated those words with careful enunciation. "Incompetent. Fool."

"Got it," Paul said.

"But not likely to commit suicide," RJ said. "That's why you're really here, isn't it? You think Naylor was murdered."

"Is that why you were concerned about the memoir?" Paul asked.

"He might have mentioned me. Something derogatory. To tell the truth, I'm not sorry Naylor's dead. But I didn't kill him."

Julia waited for this angry outburst to settle. It bothered her that she hadn't picked up on this feud between

RJ and the general. When she'd seen them together, they hadn't acted like sworn enemies. Paul asked, "Did you know John Maser, also known as Johnny Maserati?"

"No."

He fired off another question. "RJ, do you have insomnia?"

A puzzled look crossed her face. "I do."

"You're not the only one."

"David's worse than I am," she said. "He's always so wired that he can't sleep."

Julia asked, "Do you and David share information about insomnia?"

"Sure. We even swap pills."

"What about the general," Paul asked. "Did you give him some of your sleeping pills?"

"No," she said coldly.

"Why not? He also had trouble getting to sleep."

"Too bad for him. There's no way I'd help him. If he was drowning, I wouldn't throw him a rope." Her eyes narrowed and she glared at both of them. "But I wouldn't shove him overboard. I'm not a murderer."

She most certainly had motive. Julia couldn't remember the last time she'd seen such venomous hatred. "You never finished telling us what happened between you and Garret."

"After he lost his arm, he was a changed man. The psychologists said he suffered from survivor's guilt and posttraumatic stress. Depression. I pleaded with him to get help. To learn to use his prosthesis. But he wouldn't do anything." Her spine stiffened. "Garret never really recovered. He quit the Marines. And he quit our relationship, too. He kept pushing me away until I finally gave up."

"You don't stay in touch?"

"The last I heard, he was living on disability. Hardly ever leaving his apartment." She shrugged. "If you want more information, you'll have to ask David."

"How does David fit into this picture?"

"Garret is David Dillard's brother."

Chapter 15

Instead of one motivated killer, they had two. Both RJ and David might blame General Naylor for what had happened to Garret.

After RJ left the library, Julia closed the door behind her. She should have known about this connection, should have asked more questions. David had mentioned his brother in the Marines. He and RJ were friendly enough that they volunteered to be in the rooms that shared a bath. "If I had talked to them, I could have gotten this information a lot sooner."

"Don't blame yourself." Paul glanced toward an upper shelf in the library where they both knew a surveillance camera was situated. "Is there audio surveillance in this room?"

"A bug?"

He nodded.

"Not usually." But she was well aware of Craig's secret audio and video in the meeting room. And the safehouse was occupied by other agents—Gil, David and RJ—who were capable of planting their own listening devices. "If you'd like, I could do a sweep and find out if anyone is listening."

"I'd appreciate that," he said. "Seems to me that we should stay down here and start reading these memoirs."

A twinge of disappointment went through her. "Instead of in my bedroom?"

"I think we both know what will happen if we go to your bedroom."

She knew. They'd make love. The inevitability of their passion was an awesome force, constantly surging through her. She wanted him. But she also wanted to solve this crime, and there wasn't much time left. These suspects would check out of the safehouse in two days. As soon as the blizzard stopped, Paul would be gone.

Glancing over her shoulder at the almost-invisible lens of the surveillance camera, she reined in her natural urges. Paul was right. The general's memoir was a clue they couldn't ignore. They should stay here. "You're right. We need to look at the memoir."

"I'd feel a lot better if I didn't have to worry about being recorded."

"I'll be right back."

She went down the hall and through the dining room to the basement staircase. In the office, she found Roger in front of the monitors. "Nice dinner," he said. "The cake was really good."

"Thanks. It's my mother's recipe."

He swiveled in the desk chair. "Julia, what's going

on? I know Paul's here to investigate that car crash, but what does that have to do with the general's suicide?"

"I hope there's no connection." She opened a cabinet where electronic equipment was stored.

"Do you think the general killed himself because of that guy from the car accident? John Maser?"

"I don't know what to think."

"Me, neither. But I'll tell you this. I'm going to be real glad when these Homeland Security people are gone. They're too intense for me."

"Ditto." She found a handheld bug sweeper and closed the cabinet. "I'll take the three a.m. shift again."

"Fine with me. I'll leave a note for Craig."

As she hurried back to the library, it occurred to her that Roger and Craig should also be considered among their suspects. She didn't really know much about either of these young agents. They might have reason to hate the general. Buried secrets.

In the library, she found Paul hunched over the table, reading the manuscript pages. "Anything interesting?"

"This is about the early years. His sainted mother and stern father who was a lawyer."

Quickly and efficiently, she swept the room and found no evidence of a listening device. "We're clear. What did you want to talk about?"

"The sleeping pills." He leaned back in his chair with his long legs stretched out in front of him. "RJ swears she didn't give the general her pills. But the autopsy showed he had taken a couple of pills with that formula."

"RJ could be lying."

"Why? It's not like the sleeping pills were poison or anything."

Julia remembered a conversation about insomnia. "David said he had a bad reaction when he tried RJ's pills. Bad dream. Paranoia."

"Unreasonable fear," Paul said. "That pretty much describes the way the general was acting the first time I met him."

"When he was shooting rabbits off the deck." That incident seemed like a hundred years ago. "He said something about the media."

"He thought they were after him," Paul said. "Paranoia."

"Maybe that's a side effect of the sleeping pills, but it still doesn't explain why RJ might have given them to the general. If she intended to kill him, wouldn't she want him to be unsuspecting?"

"Good point." He straightened the pages of the manuscript. "Maybe another side effect is really deep sleep. So the general wouldn't wake up when somebody came into his room and shot him in the head."

"That doesn't explain why he was dressed in his uniform." Even though she knew the library was free from audio surveillance, she lowered her voice. "With his medals incorrectly displayed and his shoes unpolished."

"What happens to a Marine who isn't up to snuff?"

"A reprimand," she said. "Especially for a general. It would be humiliating."

"Whoever killed him might have done the medals wrong on purpose. To show that General Naylor didn't deserve to be a Marine."

"Whoever killed him." All of their investigation came back to the same thing. The murder was impossible. There was no evidence to indicate that anyone had entered the general's bedroom.

Paul divided the manuscript in two and held out a stack of pages toward her. "Dig in. We need to get lucky and find a clue."

She went to one of the comfortable chairs in the library, turned on the lamp beside it and sat. Her belt holster jabbed her in the back. She unclipped it and placed her handgun on the small side table beside the lamp. Settling into the recliner chair, she popped up the footrest, got comfortable and started to read. The chapter heading was: "My Silent Battle."

In these pages, the general described a battlefield explosion resulting in a head trauma that caused him to lose sixty percent of his hearing. His writing style was straightforward and almost completely devoid of emotion. He wrote about the hospital where he stayed but never mentioned his pain. Or his family. "Paul, was the general married?"

"At least once." He looked up from the pages. "He mentions getting married in his twenties and calls her the first wife."

"What about his next of kin? Who claimed the body?"

"A sister," he said. "That makes me think there isn't a current wife. And probably no children."

"His whole life was the military," she said.

Though the general had achieved a great deal and traveled the globe and had innumerable adventures, his life story didn't seem to be a happy one. She flipped through the pages, wondering if he'd written them himself or if this was an "as told to" memoir.

Julia's eyelids were drooping before she got to the

end of the chapter. She leaned back in the comfortable recliner. It had been another long day. She needed a second wind. A burst of energy. Maybe if she rested her eyelids…

It seemed like only a few minutes later when she heard Paul gently calling her name, and Julia opened her eyes and saw him hovering over her. His huge hand rested on her shoulder. His dark brown eyes looked directly into hers. "Are you awake?"

"Just resting my eyes."

"It's almost three. Time for your surveillance shift."

That couldn't be. Her brain struggled toward consciousness. "I've been sleeping? How long? Four hours?"

"Just about." He leaned down and kissed the tip of her nose. "Has anybody ever told you that you're pretty when you first wake up."

"Pretty embarrassed," she said.

He stood, went to the library table and picked up the manuscript pages. "Let's go downstairs. I found some good stuff in the general's memoir, and I want to tell you about it."

"Good stuff?"

"Important pieces of evidence." He held up two fingers. "Two of them."

She hauled herself out of the recliner, stretched and yawned. "I feel guilty for not helping."

"No problem. I even caught a couple of hours sleep myself."

"How did you wake up without an alarm?"

"I'm a light sleeper."

Paul had always been able to fall asleep when he

wanted and wake up on time. That skill came in handy when the kids were sick.

He hustled Julia through the kitchen where they grabbed hot coffee. Then they went to the basement level. He waited while she settled herself at one of the swivel chairs and did a routine check on the monitors, including a peek into the barn where the horses rested peacefully.

The information he had uncovered in the general's memoir wasn't enough to solve the murder, but it might be enough to push for further investigation. *Really good stuff.*

"Ready?" he asked.

"You're excited," she said. "Did the general outline the murder method and point a finger at the killer?"

"Not quite. But this might be enough to get you off the hook for tampering with evidence."

Her beautiful blue eyes flashed. "Tell me."

"Here's what the general says." Paul held up a manuscript page and started reading. "'I never claimed to be infallible. I have made mistakes in my life and in my career. My deepest, most heartfelt regret came when—'"

"Wait," Julia said. "This sounds familiar."

"He goes on to talk about an error in strategy that caused the death of four Marines. That must have been the incident RJ was talking about."

Julia nodded so vigorously that her ponytail bounced. "I've heard this before."

"Not exactly." He handed her the page. "You've read it before. This was the general's suicide note."

As soon as Paul had seen those words, he recognized the context. They were printed on a plain sheet of paper, signed by General Harrison Naylor and left on the desk in the bedroom where he died.

One of the most important pieces of evidence in the investigation of a suicide was the note. When the general's note talked about regret and failure, it went a long way toward convincing the sheriff that his death was self-inflicted.

Shaking her head in disbelief, Julia studied the page. "It was a page from his memoir."

"Anyone could have printed it."

"But he signed it," she said.

"I'm sure he's left a lot of signatures for someone to copy. When I turn this over to the sheriff, it'll be enough to reopen the investigation."

"Are you sure?"

"One hundred percent sure," he said confidently. "Here's how these things work in Eagle County. We aren't equipped to handle a complicated homicide. We don't have all the fancy equipment or handwriting analysts on the payroll. The sheriff will turn this over to the state investigators. Or to the FBI. Your own people can look into the general's death."

"Which means the true nature of the safehouse can still be kept a secret."

"This probably fake suicide note will be their reason to suspect homicide." He gave her a smile. "Nobody ever needs to know that you tampered with evidence."

She should have been cheering and dancing up and down. Instead, Julia looked worried. "It doesn't seem right. I ought to report my actions."

He came around the desk and took her hand. "Let it go, Julia. There's such a thing as being too responsible. If you make a full report, you'll likely lose your job here."

"Very likely."

"That would be a damn shame. I'd hate to have you shipped out of town when I'm just getting to know you."

She squeezed his fingers. "I'd hate to leave."

"Besides, you told Jennifer that you'd teach her how to bake. You don't want to break that promise."

When she stood and wrapped her arms around his neck, Paul couldn't help thinking of the other unspoken promise between them. Their need to make love, fulfillment of the attraction they felt for each other.

She broke away from him. "What else did you find in the memoir? You said there were two things."

"The other one isn't so dramatic. The general is talking about the 'threat at home,' which he says is as important as the threat abroad. He mentions the Lone Wolves survivalist group and how Senator Ashbrook has been shielding them. It's a tirade against Ashbrook and all other politicians."

"Enough to give Ashbrook motive to kill the general?"

Her voice was hopeful. Clearly, if Julia had the chance to pick, she'd choose Ashbrook as the murderer.

"We could ask him," Paul said. "It's only a couple of hours until breakfast."

In a matter of hours, this could be over and done with. Paul would present his evidence to the sheriff, and the feds would take over. He and Julia could step back quietly. If they could make it through the next few hours, the threat to them would be gone.

Chapter 16

After breakfast, Paul stepped onto the front porch to join Senator Ashbrook. Once before, they had met on the porch and talked about the Lone Wolves. Today, they were both drinking coffee. Both maintained an uneasy edge of hostility.

The view that spread before them was spectacular. It was the kind of morning that should have gladdened Paul's heart. The snow had stopped, and in its place was a magnificent blue sky. The sunlight glistened on mounds of crisp white snow. Perfect for skiing.

"Beautiful scenery," the senator said.

"It is."

"The weather report said we had twenty-six inches of new snow."

"I believe it." Paul should have felt better than he did. He and Julia had done their part in setting up a further investigation. They'd survived being snowed in with a killer. It was almost over. Still, he had a sense of foreboding. Even on this sunny day, a dark shadow seemed to hang over him like a shroud.

"What's on your mind, Deputy?"

"Last night, Julia and I had a chance to read General Naylor's memoir. He didn't much like you, Senator Ashbrook."

"Lucky for me, he's not a voter in my state."

"The general made some harsh accusations about the way you handled the Lone Wolf situation. Said you were sympathetic to terrorists."

"Sympathetic?" he scoffed. "It's unfortunate that you didn't have a chance to see me in action during yesterday's simulation exercise. Believe me, Deputy, I know how to handle so-called terrorists."

"Tell me about it."

"Sorry. It's classified."

Not really. With Craig's hidden camera, Paul had seen plenty. "If those memoirs get published, it could damage your reputation. Did General Naylor tell you that he was going to mention you in his book?"

Ashbrook tried to look down his nose, but he couldn't really manage the superior look because Paul was so much taller than he was. He settled for a sneering curl to his upper lip. "Let me explain something to you, Deputy. I'm a senator, a campaigner and, most of all, a politician. People take potshots at me all the time."

"That must tick you off."

"I've learned to deal with it."

"Do you ever want to take revenge?" Paul asked.

"I can't allow myself that luxury. I need to be circumspect and careful."

"I guess so." Like Julia, Paul didn't like the senator personally. He was condescending and manipulative. "I guess if politicians started murdering every person who said bad things about them, they'd all be serial killers. Enjoy your day, Senator."

Leaving his coffee mug on the porch, Paul went down the steps to the path leading toward the barn. Though he doubted that he could solve this impossible murder by himself, there was something in him that hated giving up.

In about an hour, around ten o'clock, he'd put in a call to the sheriff and tell him that the general had likely been murdered. And that murder was likely connected to the death of John Maser. He'd also have to explain about the FBI safehouse. That was going to make their conversation messy, but it was necessary for the sheriff to know what was going on.

At the same time, Julia would talk to her superiors. The feds would take over. Then he and Julia could sit back and watch the show.

Though it was all for the best to let the experts make the case, it didn't feel right to simply hand over their hard-won bits of evidence and conjecture to other investigators. Not until he knew the truth. It would have given him great satisfaction to take the murderer into custody.

Outside the barn, he met Julia coming out the door. She was dressed in snow gear from head to boot, but the hood of her parka was tossed back and wisps of curly hair bounced around her face. She tromped through the deep snow and directly into his arms. Though he held her tightly, an embrace through all these layers of clothing was like hugging a pillow.

"It's almost over," she said.

"You'll be safe. And I'll be heading for home." He wanted to believe that, wanted to be certain that everything would turn out fine. "Will you miss me?"

"I hope we'll be seeing each other again."

"Count on it."

"It's kind of a shame," she said. "We've spent all this time together and haven't had much chance for fun. Are you up for an adventure before we make our phone calls?"

"That depends." He recognized the mischievous gleam in her blue eyes. "What have you got in mind?"

She led the way to the large garage beside the house. Though the snowdrifts piled high as the windows on the north side, she pushed open a double wide doorway. Inside, she lifted the covers off two gleaming snowmobiles. One was black. The other, metallic blue. "I've only had these out once this season."

"Let's make it twice."

He loved snowmobiling, especially on a day like today. It took only a minute to haul the machines outside, climb on board and point the runners toward the open field.

"Follow me." Julia started her engine.

Until they were a good distance away from the house, he followed her at a slow speed. In the snow-covered field, Paul revved his engine and let loose. He swooped across the open snow, spraying a wake of champagne powder.

At the edge of the forest, Julia followed a wide path into the snow-laden trees, climbing the hillside. The route was tricky; these weren't manicured ski slopes. But these snowmobiles were made for navigating through rugged terrain.

He wished the kids were with them. Lily was still too small to operate a snowmobile, but Jennifer could do this. She was a decent skier, though she preferred figure skating.

At the top of the hill, Julia waited for him. They were surrounded by conifer forest, snow-covered peaks and a pure blue sky. He glanced back over his shoulder. From this distance, the safehouse was tiny. A plume of smoke rose from the chimney.

He was glad to be far away from the tension that had been building while they were snowed in. But he couldn't quite shake the feeling that the danger wasn't over. Not yet.

"Do you see that cabin?" She pointed through the trees and across the hillside.

Throughout these mountains were a system of warming huts used by backpackers in the summer and cross-country skiers in winter. "I'm surprised to see a hut so close to civilization."

"The only habitation around here for ten miles is the safehouse. If you follow the regular trails, it's a long hike to this cabin." She grinned. Her cheeks were red with cold, and her eyes were as blue as the sky. "Race you to it."

"What do I get if I win?"

"Me."

She cranked up her engine and took off.

No way was he going to lose this race. Paul dodged around rocks and trees, taking the steep hill at a precarious angle. He nearly overbalanced but adjusted his weight and kept going.

He beat her to the cabin with five yards to spare. He parked the snowmobile, got off and raised both hands over his head. "The winner and new champ is Deputy Paul."

"Real gracious," she said wryly.

"And now, the winner claims his prize."

"A trip to Disneyland?"

"A trip to Julia." He plowed through the deep snow and pulled her off the snowmobile into his arms. In spite of the wet cold that penetrated his jeans, he kissed her hard.

"You're freezing," she said as she struggled out of his grasp. "I'm wearing my snow gear. But you've just got jeans."

"Take me inside," he murmured. "Warm me up."

"With pleasure."

It was a small, one-room cabin with two bunk beds, a table and a fireplace with the logs already arranged to start a fire.

Paul found matches in a moisture-proof container on the mantel. "Whoever stayed here last did a nice job of preparing for the next visitor. The fire is ready to go. It's nice and clean."

"It was me," she said. "I like to come here to get away."

It was obvious that she knew her way around the cabin. She quickly pulled the mattresses from the lower bunks and dragged them close to the fireplace.

While he nursed the flame, she arranged several blankets and comforters on top of the mattresses. "Take off your pants," she said.

"That's pretty direct."

"I'm not talking about sex, Paul. Your jeans are wet and cold. Take them off."

"You first."

"No problem."

She peeled off layer after layer of clothing. Boots. Parka. Snow pants. Sweater. Regular slacks. Wool socks. It was like watching a butterfly emerge from a cocoon.

Her straightforward gaze challenged him, and Paul started taking off his own clothes. It felt good to get the cold, wet denim away from his legs.

Stripped down to her thermal underwear, Julia dove under the blankets on the mattress near the fireplace. In two seconds, he was beside her.

They held each other for warmth, sharing the combined heat of their bodies and waiting for the warmth from the fireplace.

"We're finally alone," she said. "No one knows we're here."

"Not exactly." He snuggled her lush body against him. "The snowmobiles made a lot of noise when we left the safehouse. And we've got smoke coming out of the chimney at this cabin."

"We're safe," she said firmly.

In Julia's mind, the danger was over. Nobody was coming after them. She intended to claim the next hour with Paul for herself. This would be their time.

She kissed the deep dimples on each side of his mouth, then she kissed his lips. It was a long, slow kiss to warm them up, and it worked well. When she separated from him, heat flowed through her.

Together, they removed their last layer of clothing.

His huge arms enveloped her naked body. His tree-trunk thighs wrapped around her. She had never been with a man as big as Paul. He was overwhelming.

Her breasts rubbed against the crisp black hair on his chest. The friction of their bodies was amazing and arousing. Her nipples peaked. A groan of pleasure escaped her lips.

She wanted to be on top. Exerting all her strength, she rolled him to his back and eased herself across his chest. All the while, she rained kisses upon him.

He cupped her breasts, and a shudder went through him.

"Beautiful," he growled.

His hands roved her body. His touch was strong and demanding. He squeezed her bottom and fitted her against his hips so she could feel his hard erection. He was big all over.

When he flipped her onto her back, she let out a shout of surprise. "Hey, what are you doing?"

He teased her with a smile. "I'm claiming my prize."

"Do you think you can toss me around like a rag doll?"

"Yeah."

"Think again."

She shoved back. They rolled off the mattresses onto the hardwood floor. She should have been cold. The crackling fire hadn't yet warmed the small cabin. But her blood boiled; she had never been hotter in her life.

Paul lifted her from the floor. They were standing. His body pressed hard against hers. He kissed her with mind-numbing passion. Just as hard, she kissed him back.

Wild and abandoned, they staggered against each

other, intoxicated with the enormous desire that had been building for days. Her need was voracious and fierce. He retreated, and she pursued. His back slammed against the log wall of the cabin.

She heard a thudding noise. "What was that?"

Paul turned away from her to peer through the window. "We knocked the snow off the eaves."

When she looked out, he captured her again. She faced the window. Her fingertips touched the icy glass. From behind, he pressed against her. He held her breasts.

She spun in his arms, gave herself completely to their embrace. His touch consumed her body, her world, her consciousness. She whispered, "Take me."

"I didn't hear you."

Louder, she said, "I want you."

"What was that?" he teased.

"Make love to me." She was shouting. "Now. Paul. Now."

Her feet left the floor as he scooped her up and carried her back toward the fireplace. Together, they sprawled on the mattresses. He tried to cover her with blankets, but she threw them off. Too hot. Too damn hot.

She yanked him down on top of her. The weight of his body aroused her. She clawed at his back.

He groped for his jeans.

"What are you doing?" she demanded.

"Condom."

"Don't need it." Though she hadn't made love in years, had never made love like this, she was on birth control pills to regulate her cycles. "I'm protected."

There was a moment of stillness as they gazed into

each other's eyes. She was gasping for breath. Her heart crashed against her rib cage. She was smiling, happy. Amazingly, utterly happy. Julia knew she had found the man she was supposed to be with. She whispered, "I'm yours."

When he spread her thighs, she was moist and ready for him. He entered her with a slow, tantalizing penetration. Her back arched. She called out his name. Softly at first, then louder.

He thrust against her. And she rocked back, echoing his fierce rhythm. Goosebumps covered her naked flesh. She tingled all over. The combined heat of their passion ignited in an earth-shattering eruption. Fireworks exploded behind her eyelids. More skyrockets than the Fourth of July. It was beautiful. She exhaled a ragged sigh.

He collapsed on the mattress beside her, pulled up the blankets and lightly kissed her forehead.

There was no need for talking. She lay quietly beside him, allowing the shivering aftermath of their lovemaking to pleasure her.

Moments passed before she opened her eyes. He was gazing down at her.

"You're loud," he said. "I like that."

"So are you."

"I hope all our racket didn't start an avalanche."

She grinned into his big, handsome face. "An avalanche of lust."

"The best kind."

She couldn't imagine being apart from him ever again. But he'd be leaving the safehouse today, after the other investigators moved in. "I wish we could have solved these murders."

"So do I." He lay on his back and stared up at the low ceiling in the cabin. "Do you feel like talking?"

"Maybe."

"We should try to get our facts straight before I call the sheriff and you contact your boss."

"I'll listen. You start."

"We've got good motive for all our suspects. RJ and David blamed the general for what happened to David's brother, Garret. Ashbrook wanted the general out of the way for political reasons."

"And Gil?"

"A man like Gil doesn't need a reason to kill," he said. "He just needs an order."

Usually, after lovemaking, Julia was lethargic. But she felt strangely invigorated—not enough that she was ready to jump up and run a mile, but her mind was alert and sharp. "Somebody like Gil would know other assassins. Like the guy who came after us at the skating rink."

"Right," Paul said.

"How is the general's death connected to John Maser?"

"Maser or Maserati knew all these people. And they knew him. My guess is that he got wind of a scheme to kill the general and was coming here to warn him. After living most of his life as a criminal, Maser was doing the right thing, trying to rescue his commanding officer."

"Once a Marine, always a Marine." But this explanation was still too vague. "How did Maser know?"

"Supposedly, he was in contact with the Lone Wolves, and they have information."

"About what?"

"That's what a more in-depth investigating team would uncover. Let's just assume the Lone Wolves knew the general was in danger and they told Maser."

"That seems to point to Ashbrook." Much as she'd like to pin the murder on the senator, Julia added, "Gil knew them, too. And David used them as a prototype for his simulation exercise."

Paul pushed himself to a sitting posture. "Our main problem is that we still don't know how the murder was committed. Nobody went into that room."

"The general must have pulled the trigger himself," Julia said. "It's the only way."

"But why? It's not like he was brainwashed or anything."

"Maybe he was drugged." She sat up beside him, proudly naked. "We know the general took RJ's sleeping pills because they turned up in the autopsy. Sleeping pills that David said made him paranoid."

"It's a long step from paranoid to suicide." Paul leaned over and kissed her cheek. "We should get back to the safehouse and turn this over to the big-shot investigators who can put all the pieces together."

"Do we have to? I'd rather stay in this cabin forever."

His dark eyes turned serious. "We have a future, Julia. You and me. This won't be the last time we're together."

"Is that a promise?"

"You bet."

Though it seemed a shame to put out the fire they'd started only moments ago, they took care of cleaning up the cabin, leaving it ready for the next wayfarers.

Outside in the pearly snow, Julia looked back at the cabin. Their wild lovemaking had dislodged the snow on one side of the sloping roof—a fact that gave her an unexplainable burst of pride. She and Paul were good together. Really good.

She threw her leg over her snowmobile and reached for the starter.

"Wait," Paul said. "Do you hear that?"

A mechanical whine sliced through the crisp, clean air. Another snowmobile was approaching.

She saw him coming through the trees. A man in a black ski mask. He stopped at the edge of the trees. He was a good fifty yards away from them.

As she watched, he reached over his shoulder, bringing forward the rifle that was slung across his back. He raised the barrel and aimed.

Chapter 17

In an instant, Paul reacted. He drew his handgun. Before the man in the ski mask could position himself, Paul fired three shots. At this distance, his accuracy was unreliable. Still, his bullets were enough to make the man in the ski mask duck.

Paul climbed aboard his snowmobile. "Go, Julia. Back to the house. Fast as you can."

"I'm not leaving you." She'd already drawn her weapon.

"He's got a rifle," Paul said. "Better accuracy. Better range."

"Then we need to get closer."

She started her snowmobile and drove directly toward the assassin. What the hell did she think she was doing? He had no choice but to follow. Gun in hand, he leaned down behind the windshield and raced after

Julia, praying she wouldn't get shot. *Please don't let her be hurt.* If anything happened to her, he didn't think he could go on living.

Their would-be assassin retreated. Down the hillside, he dodged through tree trunks until he swooped into the wide open expanse of the valley. His black snowmobile swerved away from the safehouse and disappeared into the trees.

At the edge of the forest, Paul and Julia halted. He leaped off his snowmobile and charged through the snow toward her. "Don't ever do anything like that again. You could have been killed."

She stepped off her snowmobile to confront him. "I figured he wouldn't have time to aim."

"You took a risk."

"What was the alternative? To run? To present my back as a target?"

Her cheeks flushed bright red. Her jaw thrust out in a stubborn line. He loved her strength and her fire. But there was danger that came along with her headstrong attitude. "You scared me half to death."

"I didn't mean to."

He guided her over to the shelter of a thick tree trunk. They needed to make plans. "This attack was a repeat of what happened at the rink. We made a show of force, and he ran. But this time, he's got superior firepower. He can hide and wait to pick us off when we cross the meadow."

"We could stay in the trees," she suggested. "Use the forest for cover."

Paul wished he knew the caliber and make of the assassin's rifle. He might be capable of pinpoint accuracy. He might be taking aim right now. "You head back to the house on a back route. I'll keep him busy, won't let him follow."

"You'd stay here? Exchanging fire with a hit man who has a superior weapon and probably unlimited ammo?"

"Right."

"I won't let you take that risk." She held out her hand. "Give me your cell phone. I'll call Roger and Craig for backup."

"No good," he said. "If they come racing out here, they'll be in as much danger as we are."

A gunshot echoed through the thin, cold air. The bark of the tree trunk beside him splintered.

He pulled her down behind an outcropping of snow-covered granite. They were trapped. There was no way to escape without taking a risk.

"I saw him," Julia said. "He's hiding behind the rocks shaped like rabbit ears."

From there, Paul knew the sniper had a clear view of the entire meadow. "You mentioned staying in the trees. Is there a path?"

"The long way around," she said. "But I'm not sure that's the best option."

"It was your idea," he said.

"That was before he almost shot our heads off from nearly a hundred yards away. That rifle has a telescopic scope. A good one."

"Like the rifle we found in Gil's bedroom."

"That's not Gil," she said.

Paul agreed. "He'd never turn tail and run."

"The problem," she said, "is that our sniper doesn't have to be close to be deadly accurate."

He understood exactly what she was saying. As soon

as they started their snowmobiles, the assassin would know they were on the move. And he would follow. When he got within range, he could pick his shot.

Julia had another idea. "We could abandon the snowmobiles and try to sneak through the trees on foot."

"Not in this deep snow. We can't move fast enough."

"What are we going to do?"

"We have an advantage," Paul said. "There are two of us. And only one of him."

A plan began to form in his mind, but he didn't want to use Julia as part of his strategy. He wanted her safe and protected, shielded from harm. Though she was a federal agent, trained to react in dangerous situations, she was also his woman.

"We need to move fast," she said. "We don't want to give him time to set up and take aim."

"We'll start out like we're trying an escape through the forest," he said. "He'll follow us."

She nodded. "And then?"

"After we find a vantage point—like the top of a hill—you peel off. I'll keep going. Our sniper is going to stop so he can take aim at me. That's when you shoot him."

"I ambush him?"

"Right."

"I hate this plan." Her blue eyes were troubled. "You'll be a target."

"Not if you don't miss."

"It makes more sense for me to be the one who keeps going. I know the trails up here."

"No way. I promised you a future."

"Without you?" Her gloved hands grasped his shoulders, and she stared deep into his eyes. "I don't want to think about the future if you're not part of it."

"That's crazy talk."

She shook him. "I mean it, Paul. Until you showed up, I didn't even know I was looking for a man. But here you are. Pure gold. You're the man I've been waiting for all my life."

"And you—" inside his chest, his heart expanded; it was their destiny to be together "—you're everything I want."

"I can't lose you," she said. "I can't."

He gave her a quick kiss. "Don't miss."

Hunched over her snowmobile, Julia set a course through the trees behind the cabin where they had made love for the first time. With any luck, it wouldn't be the last.

There were two big flaws in Paul's plan. The first and most obvious was the danger to him. The second lay with her. She'd never shot anyone before. Of course, she knew how to use her weapon. On three other occasions, when she was acting as backup, she had aimed her gun at the bad guys. But it had never been necessary to pull the trigger. She didn't even enjoy hunting.

She told herself to be fearless, to be strong. This was a matter of life or death. Paul's life. She had to be accurate. If she got a chance for a first shot, there probably wouldn't be time for another.

Too soon, they approached the area where she would make her stand. Julia knew these backwoods trails well; this was her backyard. Near the top of a hill— the best vantage point for the sniper—the trail widened into a one-lane road. This route was used by forest rangers and BLM trucks, but there would be no traffic today. Mounds of snow covered the rocks and clung to the overhanging branches of trees.

At the edge of the forest, she guided her snowmobile behind a huge boulder. Glancing over her shoulder, she saw the tracks from her snowmobile. If the sniper came this far, he'd know she pulled off the trail. There might as well be a big red arrow pointing to her location.

Paul raced ahead, then doubled back. He was laying down two tracks through the snow so it would look like she'd kept going straight.

As she scrambled up the hill behind the boulder, his words echoed in her brain. *Don't miss.*

She had only seconds to position herself. Frantically, she pulled out her handgun and removed her heavy gloves. The weapon was as cold as death in her bare fingers.

She heard the drone of Paul's snowmobile pulling away. At the same time, the other snowmobile approached.

At the top of the trail, the man in the ski mask appeared. He killed the motor and pulled off the goggles that covered his ski mask. The place he'd chosen to stop was almost exactly where she had expected.

Weapon in hand, she braced her arms on a waist-high boulder. *Take your time. Don't panic.*

Then the unexpected happened. The sniper spoke out loud. "I have a visual on one of the subjects. Should I take the shot?"

What was he doing? He reached up, touched his ear and said, "It's the deputy. The woman must be farther ahead."

The sniper was in communication with someone.

Wearing an earpiece. She gasped as a sudden realization hit her. She knew how the general had been
killed. The most damning clue had been right there
in front of them.

"You got it," the sniper said as he whipped his rifle
into position and braced the barrel with his left hand.

No more time to think. Julia fired her handgun.

The sniper yelped. His left arm flung wildly. She
had to have hit his hand. He threw himself off the
snowmobile.

She took another shot. And missed.

When he rose from behind his snowmobile, he had
an automatic pistol in his gloved fist. He was steady,
professional. If he was in pain, he didn't show it.

Julia shot first. A direct hit in the center of his chest.
He fell back.

Her pulse beat in triple time. Had she killed him?
As she stood for a better look, she heard the approaching whine of Paul's snowmobile.

The sniper was back on his feet. Not dead. Though
his left arm hung at an odd angle, he wasn't disabled.
He had to be wearing a Kevlar vest under his parka.

He turned and aimed downhill. Though she couldn't
see Paul's approach, she knew he was racing back to
help her. He could be killed.

"No," she said through gritted teeth. "Hell, no."

Her hand was steady. She took three more shots.

The sniper got off a couple of shots, then he darted
into the forest on the opposite side of the trail.

The sound of Paul's snowmobile died. For one terrible moment, there was silence. Had he been hit? A
gust of sheer terror blew through her, and she was
chilled to the bone.

Then she heard a loud bellow. "Julia! Where the hell are you?"

"Here! I'm back here!"

"Cover me."

He stepped into her field of vision. Her focus was on the trees where the sniper had disappeared. She watched for any sign of movement, any indication that he might attack again. The branches of a conifer trembled, dropping a load of heavy snow. Though Julia couldn't see the sniper, she fired a warning shot into the forest.

Paul approached the sniper's snowmobile. He stayed low, keeping an eye on the forest, holding his handgun at the ready. His surefooted progress through the heavy snow showed a lifetime of experience in the mountains. Not too fast. Not too slow.

Leaning down, he grabbed the sniper's rifle. Using the snowmobile for cover, he aimed into the trees, peering through the telescopic sight.

"Come out and throw down your weapon," he shouted.

His voice echoed into the pure blue sky above the frosted mountains. There was no reply.

"I know you're injured," Paul yelled.

She heard the crunching of snow and saw a tree limb far down the hillside waver. The sniper was retreating on foot.

Paul called to him again, "We'll get you medical assistance."

That wasn't going to happen. This guy was on the run.

She stumbled out from behind the boulders. Fighting her way through the drifted snow, she made her way to Paul's side. "He's gone."

He slung an arm around her shoulders. "You're okay, aren't you?"

"Fine. You?"

He pointed to the torn sleeve of his parka. "He came close."

"Too close."

Though Julia loved her work as a federal agent, she never wanted to go through anything like this again. If she lost her assignment at the safehouse, she intended to apply for a desk job.

Paul said, "I thought I told you not to miss."

"I didn't. First I got him in the arm. Then here." She pointed to the center of her chest. "A direct hit. He must be wearing Kevlar."

"Figures."

Though the sniper was probably a professional assassin, she was relieved that he wasn't dead. Even in the line of duty, she didn't want to be a killer. What was it Gil had said? To see the fear in their eyes. Their gaping mouths.

She shuddered. "What do we do next?"

"We could track him through the forest. He's probably leaving a trail of blood."

"He's still dangerous," she reminded him. "He might not have his fancy rifle, but he's got a handgun."

"You're right. We'll leave the tracking to a posse. I'll notify the sheriff." He stood. "Let's get back to the safehouse."

"One thing first." She pulled the key out of the snowmobile and slipped it into her pocket. "Now he won't be able to follow us."

"Smart," he said. "And we'll take a different route back to the safehouse so we stay clear of him."

He was already headed back to his snowmobile before she could tell him that she'd figured out how the general was murdered. The crime was solved. She had the answer.

Her revelation would have to wait.

Chapter 18

Paul had serious concerns about the escaped assassin. If he made it out of the back country on foot, he'd be desperate. He could try a carjacking. Innocent people could be hurt.

Outside the safehouse, Paul used his cell phone to alert the sheriff. His boss wasn't happy. In the aftermath of the blizzard, the sheriff's department was busy—stretched to the max with accident reports, helping people with stranded vehicles and dealing with dozens of other snow-related problems. The last thing they needed was an armed and dangerous fugitive on the loose.

By the time Paul disconnected the call, the sheriff had made it damned clear that he was in trouble up to his eyebrows. And Paul knew it would only get worse when he started talking about how the general's suicide was actually murder.

Standing beside Julia, he looked toward the safehouse. "I don't want to go back in there."

"I can't leave," she said. "It's my job."

No job was worth getting killed for. "Let's get the hell away from this place. We'll go to the sheriff, turn over our evidence and let somebody else take over."

"Not quite yet." She reached up and gently touched the side of his face, compelling him to look at her. "Do you remember when we were talking about how we wished that we had solved this case?"

Those moments weren't something he'd soon forget. Everything that had happened in that little log cabin was branded in his memory. Every touch. Every taste. The way she had called out his name. "We were naked. In front of the fireplace. We'd just finished making love."

She nodded. "You said you wanted the crime solved. It was important to you."

"I suppose I did."

"What if I told you I have the answer? That I know how the general was killed?"

"I'd say you were hallucinating."

She took his hand and gave a light tug. "I want to go inside, talk to these people, clear up a few details and make an arrest."

He balked. Investigating on their own had proved disastrous. They'd nearly been killed. "If you really have this figured out, we ought to turn the evidence over to the sheriff. For once, we should follow procedure."

"And let these people lawyer up? You said it yourself. As soon as they know they're officially under investigation, they'll find ways around it. I want this to be over." Her eyes shone with determination. "I want to wrap up this case in a neat little package with a bright red bow on top. Please, let's give this a try. Trust me."

In his experience, when anybody played the "trust me" card, it meant trouble. Still, he agreed to go along with her plan. Because—God help him—he did trust her. She was strong, brave and smart. Especially smart.

As soon as she entered the safehouse, Julia informed Roger and Craig that they were on high alert. The situation was dangerous. No one was to enter the safehouse. Then she led the way down the staircase into the basement and down the corridor.

Without knocking, she shoved open the door to the meeting room. There were no windows. Floor-to-ceiling shelves lined the wall nearest the door. There were framed black-and-white photographs on the wall.

As Paul followed, he had the sense that he was being drawn in the wake of a curly haired speedboat, churning through perilous waters.

The senator sat at the head of the conference table. Gil stood beside the large screen at the far end where a computer image showed a Navy carrier. David and RJ sat side by side at the table.

"Please don't get up," Julia said. "There are a few things we need to discuss about the deputy's investigation."

"How dare you interrupt!" Ashbrook bolted to his feet. "We're in the middle of a session."

"Murder is inconvenient," Julia said.

"I intend to file a complaint with your superiors, Julia. You were supposed to provide a quiet place for us to meet. Instead, we've been—"

"Sit down, Senator."

"You can't order me around."

Paul stepped forward. He was cold and wet. In no mood for the senator's prissy objections. "Yes, she can. And you're going to sit there and listen."

The senator's eyes narrowed as he assessed Paul's attitude. Apparently, he decided that Paul was serious because he returned to his seat and stared pointedly at his wristwatch. "We can spare a few minutes."

"First," Julia said, "I'd like Paul to summarize your connections to John Maser, the man who was killed in the car accident."

Though he wasn't sure exactly what she was doing, Paul was more than willing to vent his frustration. While dealing with these people, he'd been thwarted at every turn. "The first time I talked to you people, every single one of you lied."

"What do you mean?" RJ asked.

She knew damned well what he meant. "You all told me that you'd never heard of John Maser, alias Johnny Maserati. Then I come to find out that he was on the watch lists for the FBI and CIA. You knew him. You all knew him. Gil was the first one to come forward with the truth."

He glanced toward the former Navy SEAL. His arms hung loosely at his sides. His weight was balanced on the balls of his feet, ready for quick action. Gil sure as hell had the contacts to hire a hit man. Was he behind these murders?

"According to Gil," Paul said, "Johnny Maserati was a mercenary trying his hand at gunrunning. And that's where you come into the picture, Senator Ashbrook."

Ashbrook waved his hand dismissively. "If you're

talking about my tenuous connection to the Lone Wolves, that's old news. Everybody knows about it."

"Especially David," Paul said. "He talked to the Lone Wolves when he was researching his simulation. And if David had information, he probably told RJ. These two are a lot closer than you might expect."

"What do you mean?" Gil asked.

"Not that it's any of your business," RJ snapped. "But I used to be engaged to David's brother."

Gil scoffed. "There was a man willing to marry you? Hard to believe."

Julia waded into the conversation. "If you don't mind, Deputy, I have a few things to add."

"Be my guest."

"RJ and David are not only close friends, but they share a common ailment. Insomnia. Isn't that right, David?"

"Yes." His eyes flicked behind his glasses. His arms folded defensively across his chest, and he tilted back in his chair.

"Sometimes," Julia said, "you even share medications. I believe RJ let David try some of her sleeping pills."

"There's no law against that," RJ said.

"Do those pills have any side effects?"

RJ shrugged. "None that affect me."

"I believe David mentioned bad dreams and a sense of paranoia."

"When you first start on these pills," RJ said, "that might be a side effect. But it goes away."

"There was another person who suffered from insomnia," Julia said. "General Naylor."

At the mention of his name, Paul noticed a sharpening of attention as if everyone in the room gasped at the same time.

Julia continued, "We know that General Naylor took RJ's sleeping pills. They showed up in his autopsy. It's likely to assume he might have suffered a side effect. He might have been paranoid."

The senator spoke up. "I fail to see any connection between the unfortunate suicide of the general and the investigation into Johnny Maserati's death."

Julia glanced toward him, and Paul took over again. "There's a link. They were together in the Marines. In spite of what Maser became in his later life, there was a time when he served his country with honor. I suspect he cherished that memory. That was why he came here. He'd heard rumors, perhaps while he was dealing with the Lone Wolves. Maser knew the general was in danger."

Ashbrook slammed the flat of his hand against the tabletop. "Not the Lone Wolves, again. They're harmless. You're making too much of them."

"In a further investigation, we'll be talking to them. Exploring the connection between John Maser and each one of you."

It was Julia's turn again. "John Maser knew the general was in danger. Someone was planning to kill him."

"This is absurd," Ashbrook said.

"And irrelevant," Gil added in his low, dangerous voice. "It doesn't matter who wanted the general dead. There was no possible way to murder him."

"That was part of the plan. Using my safehouse as an alibi for murder." Her angry gaze swept the room. "The plan was for the general to die in a locked room with a surveillance camera watching."

"Still doesn't explain the method," Gil said.

"You heard the answer in your simulation of the Waco siege," she said.

RJ surged to her feet. "How do you know what we heard?"

"We have a camera in your meeting room." Julia pointed toward the shelves by the door. "Right up there."

Every single one of them voiced an objection. Their work was supposed to be confidential. They were very important people. Spying on them was a terrible offense.

Paul listened to their complaints for a minute before he spoke. "Settle down. We're talking about the murder of General Harrison Naylor. That's a whole lot more important than your computer games."

Disgruntled, they quieted.

Paul finally had an idea of what Julia was talking about. He sure as hell hoped she had more than a theory.

"In that session," she said, "one of the solutions proposed was brainwashing. Mind control."

All eyes focused on David. He was the expert in that area. He gave a nervous laugh. "You can't be serious. Do you think somebody hypnotized the general?"

"Something like that," she said.

"It doesn't work like that. Mind-control techniques are complex and subtle. It takes a long time to work into a subject's subconscious."

"You know all about mind control, don't you? You've been working on the general for a long time. And when the fatal night came, you made sure that he'd taken the sleeping pills that made him even edgier than usual. What was the next part of your plan, David?"

"How did this get to be my plan?"

"I'm guessing what happened that night," Julia said. "First, you suggested that the general print out a page from his memoir to use as a suicide note. And to sign it."

"How would I know what was in his stupid memoir."

"You hacked into his computer."

Paul was impressed with her reasoning. It all made sense.

She continued, "You chose the page where the general expressed regret for a mistake in strategy. A mistake that cost your brother his arm and threw him into a depression."

David stood. His arms were straight at his sides. His fists clenched.

Julia approached him. She was tall enough to look him directly in the eye. "Then, you suggested to the general that he dress in his uniform."

"No."

"You even told him to put the medals in the wrong order. Because he didn't deserve to be a proper Marine."

"You're wrong."

"You told him to lie on the bed and put the gun to his head. You were always talking to him."

"She's wrong." He appealed to the others. "How could I do these things?"

"Even at night when he slept, you were filling his head with subliminal messages and suggestions." Julia put her hand to her ear. "Through his hearing aid. It was more than a hearing aid, wasn't it? That piece of plastic that the general always wore was a transmitter. You could talk to him through it."

Paul blinked. The first thing he had noticed when he looked at the general's lifeless body was that he was still wearing his hearing aid. David had been using that transmitter to literally get inside the general's head, sending him mind-control suggestions.

No wonder the general was paranoid. He'd been hearing voices. It had to have felt like he was losing his mind.

Julia pressed David harder. "When did you make the switch? Was it when you talked to the general about the simulations? Maybe you even gave him a sneak preview. Put headphones on him and had him take out his hearing aid."

"No."

"Then you substituted the transmitter. It won't be hard to prove. The general's personal effects are still in the custody of the sheriff."

David took a backward step. Though Julia hadn't touched him, he reacted as though he'd been slapped. He held up his hands, warding off her words. "I didn't shoot him. I didn't pull the trigger."

"You slowly, methodically poisoned his mind."

"He deserved it. He cost good men their lives. His mistakes were heinous. I'm right. Aren't I, RJ?"

Her eyes were wide. "Oh, David. What have you done?"

"The general ruined my brother's life. I couldn't let him get away with it. He had to pay." He backed himself into a corner. "The old man killed himself. If he hadn't already felt guilty, he wouldn't have been susceptible to mind control."

Paul took the handcuffs from his back pocket. "David Dillard, you're under arrest for—"

"Listen to me," David said desperately. "I didn't pull the trigger. He committed suicide."

"Maybe so," Paul said. "John Maser's death was more clear-cut. He was shot full of morphine."

"I didn't do that. You'll never prove that I did."

"We'll find something in the car," Paul said. "Now that we know where to look. We'll find fibers. A hair. Fingerprints. Something."

"Search all you want. It wasn't me."

There was the sound of gunfire from upstairs. The assassin! Paul tossed the cuffs to Gil. "Take care of this."

"With pleasure."

Paul dodged into the corridor and ran. Julia was ahead of him. She was almost to the staircase.

A man dressed in black crashed down the stairs into her. She lost her footing and fell back, sprawled on the basement floor. The assassin stood over her and aimed his weapon at the center of her chest.

Paul's heart stopped. He couldn't get off a shot fast enough to save Julia. Desperately, he shouted, "Wait!"

The assassin looked toward him. The left arm of his parka where Julia had shot him hung limp. The sleeve was empty but not bloodstained. A one-armed man. He could only be Garret Dillard.

Paul could see the resemblance to David in his brother's face, but Garret's eyes were sunken, filled with an abysmal depth of misery. In his short life, he had seen too much. He had experienced combat, loss and too much pain.

In a low voice, Paul said, "Put down the gun, Garret."

"Why?"

"So I don't have to shoot you."

"I'm ready to die."

He limped a few steps away from Julia but kept his handgun trained on her. Silently, Paul cursed her unthinking bravery. He loved this woman. He wanted to spend his life with her. His life. Not death.

"Naylor's dead," Garret said. "He got what was coming to him."

"And Johnny Maserati?"

"That little snitch," Garret scoffed. "Running to tell the general what he'd heard. I gave him a chance."

"You filled him full of morphine," Paul said, "and sent him down a mountain road."

"He could have made it. I've learned how to operate a vehicle while I'm taking morphine."

Easing closer, Paul tried to gage his shot. He didn't trust his marksmanship enough to aim at the gun. And Garret was wearing a Kevlar vest. It had to be a head shot. From the corner of his eye he saw Roger sneaking down the staircase.

"You don't want to shoot her," Paul said. "Her family has suffered enough. Her brother was a Marine, killed in action."

Garret focused on Julia. "Is that true?"

She nodded.

"Here's the deal," Garret said. "My baby brother didn't do anything wrong. It was me. All me."

Paul doubted that was true. David had the expertise to hack into the general's computer and to use mind-control techniques. That wasn't Garret. Not this pathetic shell of a former soldier.

"I understand," Paul said. "Put down the gun."

"You won't arrest my brother?"

"Not if he's innocent."

"Then we're cool."

As Garret raised the gun to his own head, Julia dove toward him. They crashed to the floor together. In an instant, Paul was on top of Garret, wrenching the gun from his hand. He flipped Garret to his belly and twisted his good arm behind his back.

Garret offered no resistance. He had surrendered.

Behind his back, Paul heard Julia talking to Roger, asking if he and Craig were all right. They were. Gunfire had been exchanged, but no one was injured.

Paul leaned close to Garret. "How'd you get here so fast?"

"Trained as a mechanic," he muttered. "Hot-wired the snowmobile."

"You're a smart guy," Paul said. "Both you and your brother."

It was a damned shame that they had allowed revenge to consume them. When General Naylor pulled the trigger, following David's instructions, he'd destroyed three lives. His own. David's. And Garret's.

Three days later, after the Homeland Security people were gone, Paul tromped along the pathway to the front door of the safehouse. Under his parka, he wore the black suit he usually kept for funerals and a striped necktie that his daughters said was classy. This evening, he was here for a date. A real date with Julia.

When she opened the door, he was momentarily taken by surprise. Of course, he knew she was beautiful. But he'd never seen her dressed up. Her hair was straightened, sleek and shining. She wore a soft blue sweater with a deep V-neckline. Her matching skirt fell just below her knees. On her feet were high boots that outlined her shapely calves.

He swallowed hard. "You clean up real good."

She gave a twirl, and her skirt flared enticingly. "I even put on makeup."

"Lean close. Let me see."

When she did, he gave her a light kiss.

She backed away. "Don't smudge my lipstick."

Julia had put in some serious grooming time for their date, and she didn't want to ruin the effect. Not until later. "Where are we going?" she asked.

"Jess suggested that I charter a plane and take you someplace spectacular."

"That sounds like Jess. How's he doing?"

"Yesterday, he skied for the first time this season. Today, we moved him back to his condo in Vail." Paul grinned, and his dimples appeared. "He's going to ask Marcia—the nurse he's been dating—to move in with him. After spending all this time with my kids, Jess is ready to settle down."

"Just like Mac and Abby?"

Paul shrugged. "That leaves me as the fifth wheel."

"I guess that makes me the sixth wheel." Julia had some great news to share. "I'm not going to be reassigned, after all. Even though Ashbrook is still screaming for my head, RJ and Gil backed me up. I'll be staying here at the safehouse."

"Just twelve miles down the road from where I live."

When she took her coat from the front closet, he helped her into it, and he held the door like a gentleman. She wasn't accustomed to being treated like a lady, but it was something Julia decided she could get used to. "You still haven't told me where we're going."

"You'll see."

His first surprise was waiting outside. Instead of his Ford Explorer, there was a one-horse sleigh with a driver. In the back, they snuggled under warm blankets. In the cold December night, moonlight glistened on the snow, and the sky was filled with stars.

"I know you like the snow," he said.

"Love the snow."

With a jingle of sleigh bells, they lurched forward. When they turned onto a narrow path into the forest, Julia guessed where they were headed. "The warming hut."

"I wanted to take you somewhere secluded," he said. "So you could be as loud as you want."

As they neared the small log cabin, she saw the twinkle of lights strung along the eaves. "There's no electricity up here. How did you do that?"

"Generator. Mountain men are resourceful."

And that wasn't the end of his efforts. The interior of the cabin was something special. Light from the fireplace flickered on the log walls. There was a table set for two. Champagne. And, most marvelous of all, a king-size bed.

"All this for me?"

"I'd do anything for you, Julia."

"Promise?"

"You have my word." He took her into his arms. "And my heart."

She loved this mountain man. He was the man she'd been waiting for all her life, and she would never let him go.

* * * * *

Julie Anne Lindsey is an obsessive reader who was once torn between the love of her two favorite genres: toe-curling romance and chew-your-nails suspense. Now she gets to write both for Harlequin Intrigue. When she's not creating new worlds, Julie can be found carpooling her three kids around northeastern Ohio and plotting with her shamelessly enabling friends. Winner of the Daphne du Maurier Award for Excellence in Mystery/Suspense, Julie is a member of International Thriller Writers, Romance Writers of America and Sisters in Crime. Learn more about Julie and her books at julieannelindsey.com.

Books by Julie Anne Lindsey

Harlequin Intrigue

Heartland Heroes

SVU Surveillance
Protecting His Witness
Kentucky Crime Ring
Stay Hidden

Fortress Defense

Deadly Cover-Up
Missing in the Mountains
Marine Protector
Dangerous Knowledge

Visit the Author Profile page
at Harlequin.com for more titles.

MISSING IN THE MOUNTAINS

Julie Anne Lindsey

Chapter 1

Emma Hart couldn't shake the unsettling notion that something was wrong. The sensation had pestered her all day, needling away at her calm. Though she hadn't said so, her sister and housemate, Sara, seemed to feel it too. Sara had hunched over her cell phone and a notebook most of the day, barely speaking or touching her dinner. It wasn't like Sara to be inside short of a blizzard, yet there she was. All day.

Emma had thrown herself into the tedium of housework and the exhaustion of new-mommy duties, hoping to keep her mind off the inexplicable feeling that trouble was afoot. Nothing had worked. The prickle over her skin that had raised the hair on her arms and itched in her mind since dawn refused to let up, even now as the gorgeous setting sun nestled low on the horizon between distant mountains. If there was a silver lining, it was that the peculiar day was finally nearing its end, and tomorrow was always better.

She crossed her ankles on the old back-porch swing and shifted her attention to the beautiful gold and apricot hues spilling over everything in sight, including her perfect baby boy, Henry. Emma hoisted him off her lap and wiggled him in the air until a wide toothless grin emerged. There was the thing she lived for. A smile spread over her lips as she brought him down to her chest. "Someday I'm going to teach you to rope and ride, the way your granddaddy taught Sara and me." It would have been nice if Henry's father was around to teach him those things the way her father had taught her, but it didn't do to dwell on what wasn't, not when the things that were tended to be so fleeting.

Henry's daddy was a soldier on leave when they'd met, but he'd been raised a cowboy. Brought up on a ranch like hers, not too far from there, but he'd been deployed before she'd known she was pregnant, and despite the voice message she'd left asking him to call her, he never had. Of course, that wasn't a surprise since the next time she'd tried to call him the number was no longer in service. The local news hadn't announced his death the way they often did when a local soldier was lost, so she could only assume he'd survived that "eight week" mission he'd gone on nearly a year ago and had simply chosen to avoid her after his return. Whenever she thought of how his selfishness would force Henry to grow up without a father, Emma was glad he hadn't died on that mission. This way, if she ever saw him again, she could kill him herself.

Emma forced down the bitter knot rising in her throat and worked a pleasant smile over her lips. "You will always be enough for me," she promised Henry, "and I will be enough for you. Whatever that means on any given day. Always." She nuzzled his sun-kissed cheek, then stretched onto her feet as the last orange fingers of the sunlight slid out of view, replaced with the tranquil blues of twilight. "What do you say about a warm bath and fuzzy jammies before your night-time bottle?" she asked. Now she needed a distraction from the icky feeling that had followed her all day *and* from the frustration of a man who'd probably forgotten her name.

Emma jumped as the back door flew open, her knuckles colliding sharply with the handle. "What on earth!"

Sara stood on the threshold, one palm on the door, skin pale as the rising moon. "You need to come inside. Now," she gasped. "Hurry."

Emma obeyed, and Sara locked the door behind them, then checked the window locks and pulled the curtains. Without speaking again, she moved to the next room and did the same.

"What's going on?" Emma followed on her sister's heels, fear riding high in her gut. "Why are you doing that?" They only battened down the hatches if the news predicted heavy winds or rain. "It's a beautiful night. There's no storm coming."

"You're wrong about that," Sara mumbled.

Emma hurried around her sister, forcing herself into Sara's path. "Hey. What's that supposed to mean?"

Sara shot her a remorseful look, letting her gaze slide briefly to Henry, then back to her work. "I need you to listen to me and do as I say. We have to be quiet." Her hands trembled as she reached for the nearest light switch and flipped it off. Her face whipped back in Emma's direction a moment later. "Is your truck in the garage? Or the driveway?"

"Garage."

"Good." She nodded, her eyes frantic.

"Hey." Emma set her hand on Sara's. "Stop." Her sister never behaved this way. She was naturally calm to the extreme, cool in a crisis and found the positive in everything. Whatever had her so worked up was enough to make Emma want to pack a bag and move. "You're scaring me. Tell me what's going on."

Fat tears welled in Sara's eyes. "I can't."

"Sara," Emma demanded, using her most pointed tone without upsetting Henry, "you can tell me anything. You know that. I don't understand what's happened. You were fine at dinner."

Sara snorted, a derisive, ugly sound. "Was I?"

"Weren't you?" Emma grabbed hold of her sister's wrist, a lifelong stubborn streak piercing her forced calm.

Before she could answer, a set of headlights flashed over the front window, and Sara froze. "Don't make any noise," she said, looking half-ill. "We're not home."

Suddenly Sara's erratic behavior began making sense. "Is this the reason you're locking us up like Fort Knox?" Emma asked. "You knew someone was coming?" Someone who obviously terrified her. "Who?"

Sara jerked her arm free and went to peek through the living room curtain. "Hide," she seethed. "You're in danger. Henry's in danger. We all are. Now, go! Keep him quiet. Find his pacifier." Her rasping whisper cut through Emma's heart, and she pressed her back to the nearest wall, away from the front window.

"Not until you tell me what's going on," Emma shot back in a harsh whisper.

Heavy footfalls rumbled across the porch, and someone rapped against the door in loud, demanding strikes until Emma was sure the door would fall down.

"I'm calling the police," Emma said. "If you won't tell me what's going on, then you can tell them."

Henry started in her arms. He released a small whimper as the pounding continued.

Sara turned to them. Her eyes were wide, her face the perfect mask of horror and resolve. "Hide first. Call the police after." She rubbed her palms against her jeans and stepped forward, toward the rattling door.

"Where are you going?"

Sara gave Emma a pleading look, then swallowed hard. "I'm going to answer the door before he breaks it down. If you hide, he'll assume I'm alone, and you'll be safe, but I won't give him what he wants."

Emma's stomach twisted and coiled with nausea. "What does he want?"

Sara took another step.

"I won't leave you."

Sara shot one determined glance over her shoulder. "Your job is to protect Henry. Mine is to protect you. Now, hide."

Terror gripped Emma, and she snagged the cordless phone handset from the wall, immediately dialing the local police department. She ducked around the edge of the living room wall, hiding just out of sight in the long hallway that led to the bedrooms. "Come on," she urged, impatient for the ringing call to connect.

The dead bolt snicked back in the next room. The door swung open on squeaky hinges.

"I've already called the police," Sara said coldly in lieu of a proper greeting.

A choking gasp cracked through the silence a moment later.

Emma sucked air. Horrific images of what could have caused such a sound raced through her head. There were no more words in the silent home. Just the low gurgling of someone desperate for air. Emma prayed the sound wasn't coming from Sara.

A tinny voice broke through the phone speaker at her ear. "Knox Ridge Police Department."

Emma inched toward the end of the hall, ignoring the woman on the line. Desperate to know her sister was okay, she counted silently to three, then peeked her head around the corner, chest tight with fear.

A man in head-to-toe black, a ski mask and leather gloves had one giant hand wrapped around Sara's throat while she clawed uselessly at his fingers. Her eyes were wild, bulging, her mouth gaping for air. The man raised a pistol in his free hand.

Hot tears rushed over Emma's eyes. She had the police on the phone, but couldn't speak. If the man heard her, he might use his gun on Sara. *Or on Henry.*

Hide. Sara's desperate voice echoed in Emma's addled mind. *Protect Henry.*

"Knox Ridge Police Department," the woman on the phone repeated. Her small voice suddenly sounded like a booming gong.

Henry bunched his face and opened his quivering lips, a scream poised to break.

Emma took one last too-risky look into the living room, needing assurance her sister hadn't been choked to death while she'd stood helplessly by and deliberated over what to do next.

The man tossed Sara onto the couch like a rag doll and climbed on top of her in a flash. He lowered his face to hers and growled through the mask. "Who did you tell?" He pinned her hands overhead and pressed them hard into the cushions until they vanished from sight.

"No one." Sara choked out the words, still coughing and gasping for air. "No one. I have no one to tell. I swear it."

Henry released a warning cry, and the man's face snapped in Emma's direction.

Emma rocked back on socked feet and took off like a bullet down the hallway. Henry bounced and jostled in her arms as she pressed him to her chest and gripped the phone between one ear and shoulder. She slid and scooted as adrenaline forced her legs faster than her feet could find purchase on the hard, slick floors.

"What was that?" the man asked, footsteps already falling through the living room, nearing the hall at a clip.

"Cat!" Sara yelped. "It was only the cat."

Emma snatched their mean old barn cat off the hallway windowsill on her way to the master bedroom, and she threw him into the space behind her. He'd surely bite her the next time he saw her, but she'd gladly choose to face off with him rather than whoever was attempting to murder Sara.

The cat screeched and hissed, claws skidding over the wide wooden planks as he slid in the direction of Sara and the masked lunatic.

The footfalls stopped.

Emma barreled into her closet and pulled the door shut behind her. Her heart hammered and her chest ached. She climbed through the clothes racks, over boxes and blankets and shoes, then curled herself around her son and shushed him out of a fast-approaching fit.

Several wild heartbeats later, the footfalls retreated back toward her sister, who she hoped had had the good sense to run.

"Who did you tell?" the man's voice came again, impossibly angrier.

Emma's heart fell. Sara hadn't run.

"Ma'am?" the voice asked through the phone. "Miss Hart? Caller ID shows this as the Hart residence?"

What was happening? *Why* was it happening?

"Miss Hart," the woman persisted.

"Yes," she whispered, finally finding her voice. She cringed with each terrorizing demand of the intruder in the next room. *Who did you tell?*

Sara screamed.

Her gut-wrenching wail ripped through the rafters, the drywall and Emma's soul. "Someone is hurting my sister," she whispered. "Please, hurry."

Emma's gaze darted through the dark space. If only she hadn't moved her daddy's rifles into a gun safe after Henry was born. If only Henry was sleeping in his crib, and she could trust him not to scream. If only she could help Sara.

A deafening crack stopped her ragged thoughts. The sound of skin on skin. A brain-jarring slap. Or jaw-breaking punch. Every sound was amplified in the impossibly still home. Emma heard the muted thud of a collapsing body.

Then no more screaming. No more demanding growls. Just silence.

Outside, the rumble of an engine drew hope to Emma's heart. The psychopath was leaving. Whatever condition Sara was in, at least she hadn't been shot, and the police were on the way. Sara would be okay, and she would tell them everything so the son of a gun who did this to her would pay.

Emma crept from her hiding spot and raced to her bedroom window, confirming the empty driveway before racing back down the hallway, heart in her throat and preparing to provide triage while they awaited the first responders.

On a deep intake of air, she shored her nerve at the end of the hallway, tucked Henry tight to her chest and dared a peek into her living room.

But all that remained of her sister was a thick smear of blood on the polished wooden floor.

Chapter 2

Sawyer Lance, former Army Ranger and cofounder of Fortress Security, reached reluctantly for the ringing phone. It was late and he was tired. Protecting civilians was harder than he'd predicted when opening the private sector security firm. Far more challenging than similar work overseas where he could at least shoot the bad guys. He tossed another pair of aspirin into his mouth before blindly raising the phone from his desk.

What would it be this time? Another punk ex-husband or boyfriend bullying the woman he claimed to love? An unhinged stranger stalking a woman who didn't know he existed beyond the fact he harassed her anonymously with creepy unwanted gifts and the occasional break-in? "Fortress," he answered, his voice little better than a bark. "This is Sawyer Lance."

The long pause that followed was nearly cause for

him to hang up. Instead, he rubbed his forehead, knowing sometimes frightened folks needed time to gather their thoughts.

"Fortress," he repeated, becoming alert at the sound of soft breaths through the line. His muscles tensed. "If this is an emergency, you need to call 911 and get yourself to safety. Call me after. Police first."

He waited.

The quiet breathing continued.

"I can contact your local authorities if you're unable." Sawyer pulled the phone away from his ear and checked the caller ID. "Can you tell me your..." Two little words graced the screen and nearly ripped a hole through his chest. *Emma. Hart.* Sawyer's heart seized, and his lungs seemed to stop midexhale. "Emma?"

Emma Hart had been the only woman Sawyer ever imagined a future with, and a set of monsters overseas had stolen that from him. He'd been forced to say goodbye to her for the sake of a simple eight-week mission. That mission should have brought him right up to his last day in the service. Instead, it had gotten him captured and tortured. His team had gotten worse.

"You're alive," she said, a snare of accusation in her voice.

"Yeah." If she wanted to call it that. He'd fought six long months to get away from his captors and back to the secluded US military base. Another two months before he was debriefed and returned stateside. More weeks before the long-overdue discharge.

"Yet, you never called," she said.

Emma's message had been the last one left on his cell phone before the service was disconnected. The cell contract had ended while he was overseas, trapped for months past the contract's renewal date. He'd planned to get a new phone after the mission, after he'd returned stateside and been discharged. He'd even told himself Emma's number would be the first one he'd call. It was one of many plans his captivity had ruined.

"No," he answered finally, sadly.

He hadn't returned her call for multiple reasons. Part of him knew he wasn't ready to do normal things again, like date, or pretend he didn't wake up in cold sweats most nights. The rest of him doubted Emma was in the market for a 180-pound sack of misplaced anger, jangled nerves and general distrust. He couldn't make her happy anymore. *She'd sounded so darn happy on that voice mail.* Unlike now, he realized.

Instinct stiffened Sawyer's spine. "What's wrong?" Something in her voice set him on edge. She might've been mad at him, but there was something else there too.

"Sara's gone," she said, her voice breaking on the second word.

"Gone?" he repeated. His mind scrambled to make sense of the word. "How? When?"

"Tonight," she said. "He just came in here and took her."

Sawyer was already on his feet, gathering his things, shoving a fresh magazine into his sidearm. "Who?"

"I don't know. She told me to hide."

He slowed, pressing a folding knife and wallet into his pocket. "So, Sara's alive? Just missing?"

"I don't know if she's alive," Emma snapped, "but she's not *just missing*. She was choked, overpowered, hit and dragged away. There's nothing *just* about it."

"Of course." Sawyer shook his head hard, moving faster toward the exit. "I meant no disrespect. I'm only gathering facts." He stooped to grab his go-bag and a duffel of supplies from the closet floor. "What did the police say?"

"They're looking into it."

Sawyer blew out a humorless half laugh. So, the police were chasing their tails and waiting for Sara to appear on their laps. "I'm glad you called. I can keep you safe." He swung his laptop bag over one shoulder on his way out the door.

"You always talked about your plans to open Fortress Security with Wyatt," Emma said. "I figured he'd answer the call. I hoped he'd remember me and be willing to help. I didn't know what else to do."

"You did the right thing," he assured her.

"I know the last thing you probably want to do is see me—" her voice was strangled and tight "—but I'm scared, and I need help."

"I'm already on the way," Sawyer said, tossing his bags into his pickup, then climbing behind the wheel. "Are you home?"

"Yeah."

He gunned the engine to life and jammed the shifter into Drive. "I'm heading your way from the office. I won't be an hour."

"Okay."

He listened keenly to a few more rattling breaths.

"Sawyer?"

The quaver in her voice was a punch through his gut. "Yeah."

"You should have called."

* * *

Emma's words haunted him as he made the trip to her family ranch at a record pace, nearly doubling the posted speed limits whenever possible. The desolate country roads were poorly lit but easily navigated. At times, long stretches between darkened fields made visibility clear for miles, and Sawyer took full advantage. The hillier, curvier portions got a good cussing.

He hit the gravel under the carved Hart Ranch sign with a deep crunch and grind. Stones pinged and bounced against the undercarriage of his pickup, flying out in a cloud of dust behind him.

A small silhouette paced the porch. Long hair drifting in the wind around her face, exactly like the ghost from his past that she was. She went still when he started his walk across the lawn.

Sawyer pulled the cowboy hat off his head and pressed it to his aching chest. "Emma." His lungs seemed to fill fully for the first time since answering her call.

She gave a small nod, running the pads of both thumbs beneath red puffy eyes and brushing shaky palms over flushed cheeks. "Hello, Sawyer."

He took a step closer, and she wrapped her arms around a new, curvier figure. Sawyer tried not to stare, but the change looked damn good on her. So did the spark of ferocity in her eyes. He didn't know what had sparked the fire, but whatever it was, the change suited her. And it would help her get through the tough days ahead. Unfortunately, civilian abductions weren't known for their happy endings.

She appraised him as he climbed the steps. Her smart blue eyes scrutinized the visible scars along his neck and forearms, pausing briefly at the angry, puckered skin above his left eye. Then swiftly moving on to the lines of black ink circling his biceps beneath one shirtsleeve. "Thank you for coming."

"Of course."

Behind her, the small sound of a crying baby drifted through the open door.

Emma's chin ticked up. She turned immediately. "Come in. I've been through all of Sara's things, and I have something I want you to look at."

Sawyer followed. His heart clenched as the baby's cries grew more fervent. "Sara had a baby?" He tried to imagine it and failed. The willowy blonde had more interest in horses than men when he'd briefly known her.

"No." Emma grabbed the flashing baby monitor and shut it off as she passed through the dimly lit family room. "You can have a seat. I'll only be a minute."

"Are you babysitting?" he asked, ignoring her order and following her down the hall toward the bedrooms, unwilling to let her out of his sight and drawn by a strange tether to the infant's cry. "Was the baby here when Sara was taken?"

Emma opened her bedroom door and strode inside. A crib stood against the wall across from her bed. "No," she said, "and yes."

Sawyer paused at the end of the crib, puzzling over her unnecessary coyness. "You aren't babysitting?" he asked dumbly, watching as she raised the kicking blue bundle into her arms and slid a pacifier into the baby's mouth with practiced skill.

"No," she whispered, rocking the infant gently into sedation. "This is Henry." She turned a pride-filled smile in Sawyer's direction. "I named him after my father."

Sawyer's gut rolled against his spine. His jaw locked, and his fingers curled into fists at his sides. This was what had changed her. The carefree woman he'd known had been made into her own kind of soldier in his absence. Emma was a mother. "He's yours," Sawyer said, repeating the fact, trying to make it real for him. The words were bittersweet on his tongue. Any joy he might've felt for her was tainted selfishly with feelings of loss for himself. With regret. And thoughts of things that might have been. "You have a son."

"I do," she answered as Henry worked the pacifier in his tiny mouth. "And so do you."

Emma held her tongue as she waited for a response. She could practically see the wheels turning in Sawyer's head, adding up time, weeks, months. She ground her teeth against the need for an explanation. She hadn't been with anyone else since Sawyer. He'd barely left the States before she knew she was pregnant. If Henry's perfect olive skin and pale blue eyes weren't enough proof, then maybe Sawyer should look in a mirror.

"Mine?" His gaze jumped continually between her face and Henry's.

"Yes." She moved past him toward the hallway. "I need to sit down. You probably should too."

She led Sawyer back into the living room, giving a wide berth to the freshly bleached floorboards where Sara's blood had been spilled. She took a seat on the chair farthest from the couch where the monster had pinned her sister. It took effort to force the still-raw images from her mind.

Sawyer squatted on the floor in front of her chair, jeans pulled tight against his strong thighs, big hands dangling between his knees as he balanced, a look of shock and confusion etched on his brow. "Why didn't you tell me?"

Emma pursed her lips, culling the desire to scream. "I tried." She made each word stand on its own, tempted to recite all the one-sided arguments she'd practiced to perfection in the shower all these months since his "eight week" mission ended.

"I got a message from you," he said. "Did you know you were pregnant when you left the voice mail?"

The accusation in his tone ignited a fire in her belly. "That was why I called. I'd just confirmed with my doctor, and I was happy," she snapped.

"Then why didn't you tell me? Why would you keep something like this from me? I'm a father, Emma. A *father* and I had no idea."

"You could have returned my call," she said.

"You could've told me in the voice mail."

"I didn't want to tell you something this important in a voice mail. I wanted to tell you in person, and you were supposed to be home in two more weeks, and I spent every one of those last fourteen days deciding how I'd deliver the surprise. Maybe with some cutesy sign or a little custom-made onesie." She shook her head. "I can see it was stupid of me now, but I was *thrilled* to be having your baby, and you had your phone number changed."

"I didn't have my number changed." Sawyer ground the words through clenched teeth.

"Disconnected then," she conceded, "without the courtesy of letting me know first. You made it clear you didn't want to hear from me again, and you didn't want to call me either, or you would have."

"That isn't what happened."

Emma squinted her eyes, wishing she could scream and yell and lose control, but she refused to frighten Henry or give Sawyer the satisfaction of seeing her so rattled. Instead, she said, "I called your number every month after my prenatal appointment, and I listened to the notification that your number had been disconnected. I forced myself to remember you were done with me, even if my heart wasn't done with you, and you have no idea what that was like for me."

His frustrated expression fell slowly into a grimace. "I wasn't home when you left that voice mail. I didn't even get it until last month."

"Then you should have called last month."

"How could I have known this?" he asked, extending a hand toward the baby in her arms. "It's been more than a year since we've spoken. I assumed you'd moved on."

Her eyebrows shot up. "I did. I'm fine. We're fine," she said, casting a gaze at her son. "I had to get my act together, with or without you, and I had to find peace for Henry's sake. So I stopped calling you, and I let us go."

He fixed a heated gaze on her, his face wrought with emotion. Hurt, frustration, regret. "What would've happened if Sara hadn't been taken today?" he asked. "I would've just gone on with my life having no idea I was a father?"

Emma glared back, wind sucked from her chest. She wanted to shove him hard and knock him onto his backside, but there wasn't time for that. "We can fight about this later. Right now I need to figure out what happened to Sara," she said. "I found a notebook full of numbers hidden in her room. Will you look at it for me and see if it makes any sense to you?"

"How old is he?" Sawyer asked, unmoved by her change of subject. His gaze was locked on Henry. "When was he born? What did he weigh?"

Emma steadied her nerves and wet her lips. Those were fair enough questions. "His name is Henry Sawyer Hart. He's four months old, born June 8 at 8:17 a.m. He weighed eight pounds, eleven ounces. He was twenty-one inches long."

"You gave him my name."

"Middle name. It seemed like the right thing to do."

Sawyer pressed the heels of his hands to his eyes and dug them in.

"Why didn't you call?" she asked again, needing to know once and for all what had happened between their last passionate night of love declarations and the dead silence that began afterward and never ended.

Sawyer dropped his hands from his eyes. He stretched onto his feet and braced broad hands over narrow hips. Warning flared in his eyes. There was a debate going on in that head of his, but his lips were sealed tight.

Maybe he didn't have a reason. Maybe he didn't want to admit their time together had been nothing more than a fling. Not real to him like it had been to her. It was easy to see he wasn't the same guy she'd fallen in love with. The man before her was hard and distant. Not the man who'd swept her into his arms and twirled her until she was breathless with laughter.

Maybe that guy had never been real.

Emma's throat tightened as the look on his face grew pained. "Never mind. You don't owe me an explanation." She lifted Sara's notebook from the end table beside her and extended it to Sawyer. "Here. Let's just move on. Maybe there's something in there that will help the police figure out who took her and why. She's been gone twenty-four hours already, and our odds of finding her diminish significantly after seventy-two."

Sawyer caught the narrow book in his fingertips and held her gaze. "My team and I were captured. They were killed."

Emma's mouth fell open. "What?"

"They died. I didn't. I've only been home a few weeks. My cell service plan wasn't renewed on time because I wasn't home, so it was canceled. I didn't change the number or disconnect the phone. I wasn't thinking about any of that. I was trying to survive, and I don't want to talk about what happened."

She worked her mouth shut. Her own harsh words crashed back to mind like a ton of bricks. She'd blamed him for not returning her calls without bothering to ask why he hadn't. She'd assumed the worst, that he'd avoided her intentionally, played her for a fool, never realizing that him avoiding her was hardly the worst thing that could have happened. Her gaze snapped back to the scars. Thick, raised marks across his skin that weren't there a year ago. On his neck and arms. What looked like the results of a serious burn above his left eye. "Sawyer."

He lifted a palm. "Don't."

Emma cradled Henry tighter, comforting the one piece of Sawyer that would allow it. She'd heard stories, saw movies and read books about men who'd been through similar things, losing their teams, being held against their wills. There was a common thread to every man's story. Their experiences had wrecked them.

"I know what your sister is going through," Sawyer said, "not the physical details, but emotionally. Mentally." His serious blue eyes rose to meet her gaze. "I'll help find her," he said. "And I will keep you and Henry safe while I do."

Emma nodded. "Thank you."

He carried the notebook to the couch where Sara had fought with her attacker, and collapsed onto the cushions. He spread the notebook open across his palms, but his gaze continually moved to Emma's before sliding back to Henry.

"What?" Emma finally asked, her heart warming and softening toward the man she'd thought had tossed her away.

His eyes flashed dark and protective, but he didn't look away from his son. "You should've left that message."

Chapter 3

Sawyer didn't sleep. Emma had taken the barely manageable wreckage of his life and flipped it on its head. She might as well have flipped *him* on his head. He was a father.

The words had circled endlessly in his mind as he pored over the contents of Sara's notebook and made multiple trips down the hallway to check on Emma and Henry. *His son.*

A son he hadn't even known existed until a few hours ago. He might've never known about Henry at all if something horrible hadn't happened to Sara, forcing Emma to reach out for help. And Henry could've grown up thinking his father was the kind of man who would run out on a woman and his son.

It made him madder every time he thought about it. He'd nearly missed the most important part of his life because pride had stopped him from returning Emma's call. And it sure wouldn't have killed her to add the life-changing detail to her message.

The glow of a pending sunrise hovered on the horizon when he finally put Sara's notebook on the kitchen table and went to make coffee. Down the hall, he heard the stirring sounds of Emma and his baby. Sawyer set the coffee to brew, then opened the refrigerator. By the time Emma and Henry emerged from their shared room, Sawyer had a simple breakfast prepared for two. "I hope you don't mind," he said. "Restless hands."

Emma stopped at the kitchen's edge, Henry on one hip. She'd dressed in nice-fitting blue jeans and a long-sleeved thermal shirt that hugged all her new curves in the nicest of ways. Her straight brown hair hung over her shoulders and feathered across her forehead.

Sawyer longed to run his fingers through the strands and pull her against him. He wanted to comfort her. To make promises for Sara's safety that he couldn't keep. He'd promised to find her, but if he didn't do that fast… His mind wandered to images of his fallen team.

"You didn't sleep," Emma said, fastening Henry into a high chair.

"Rarely do." He lifted a pan full of eggs from the stove and flicked the burner off, forcing his thoughts back to the present. "Hungry?"

"I don't know." She went to the counter to make a bottle for Henry. A moment later she took the seat beside the high chair and poised the bottle to Henry's lips. "I feel like none of this is real. Like I'm waiting to wake up from a nightmare."

Sawyer cleared his throat. "You should try to put a little something in your stomach."

Henry sucked greedily on the bottle, peering at Sawyer with big blue eyes. His denim overalls had little horses embroidered on the knees, and his tiny brown socks were printed to look like cowboy boots.

Sawyer's hands itched to hold him, but he divided the eggs onto two plates instead, then poured twin cups of coffee for Emma and himself. The idea of holding something as precious as Henry frightened him, and Sawyer was rarely afraid. He took a seat beside Emma at the table and wrapped calloused palms around the small white mug. His hands had done awful things in the name of freedom. His hands were meant for hard labor, for holding rifles and following orders.

Emma took a slice of plain toast from the pile he'd plated and set between them, and bit into the corner. "What did you think of Sara's notebook? It was hidden so it must be important, right?"

"Maybe." Sawyer dug a fork into his breakfast. "Sara works at a bank, right?"

"Credit union," Emma said. "She's an account specialist, and she had that notebook with her all day before she was taken. I found it hidden in a basket of dirty clothes. She must've put it there when she realized that man was coming for her."

Sawyer cleaned his plate and grabbed a second slice of toast. "I want to visit her office today. I wasted a ton of time overlooking the obvious. I was looking at the numbers like a soldier. Trying to solve them like a cipher. First, I assumed they were a code. When that didn't work, I imagined them as dates and times or map coordinates, addresses, you name it." He gave a humorless chuckle. "Eventually I remembered Sara works at the credit union. Those numbers are probably a list of accounts. She's just jammed them all together, probably to disguise them."

Emma finished her toast and took away the empty baby bottle. "What are you going to do at the credit union?"

"I want to find out if she was working on any special projects. If any accounts or customers might've been giving her trouble, and if she seemed like herself the last few times she was in. I'd also really like to get a look at her desk. See if she kept any more notebooks like that one." He tipped his head toward the book on the table.

Emma unbuckled Henry from the high chair. "The police will probably be asking the same things today. The staff will be leery and guarded after that. Everyone loves Sara, and they don't know you. I doubt anyone will be candid with a stranger given what's happened." She turned Henry against her chest and patted his back. "I'll go. They know me. I'll ask to see her desk and try to collect anything that might be of interest. Then we can go through it here in privacy. If we find anything that leads to more specific questions, we can go back after lunch and ask."

Sawyer frowned. "I think you'd better let me be the face of this for you. As it is, whoever took Sara doesn't seem interested in you, and I'd rather you not get involved. Her abductor didn't even search the house while he was here. His mission was pointed. Not at you, and I'd like to keep it that way."

Emma chewed her lip, cheeks flushed with distress. "I'm Sara's only sister and I live with her. How long do you really think it will take before he comes for me?

For Henry? If she doesn't give up whatever it is that he wants from her?"

Sawyer locked his jaw. The abductor would be smart to use Sara's family as leverage if she gave him any trouble. Sawyer's captors had tried the same thing. Eliminating his men one by one, using their allegiances to one another to find the weakest link. But there had been no weak link, and they had died. One by one. "All the more reason for you to stay out of sight."

"But if Sara was keeping a secret book of account numbers," Emma said, "then someone at the credit union might know something about her kidnapping, and I don't want to draw any attention that will keep me from getting a look at her desk. You—" she lifted a narrow finger at him "—draw attention."

Sawyer sucked his teeth. It wasn't the first time he'd heard it. His six-foot-two-inch frame had been thickened, hardened and cultivated during his time in the service. The added scars and tattoos only served to enhance his dangerous appearance. Slowly, he relaxed against the seat back. He didn't like it, but she had a point, and while he would have preferred to go in and throw some weight around, Emma's idea wasn't a bad one.

Emma climbed onto the curb across the street from the credit union, Henry on one hip, his empty diaper bag on her shoulder. "I won't be long," she told Sawyer, who made no pretense of agreeing with her decision to go in alone.

She shut the door and hurried along the crosswalk before the light changed. Traffic was tight on the normally quiet streets of downtown Knox Ridge. The sidewalks teemed with people enjoying a beautiful Saturday morning. The weekly farmers market was set up a few blocks away, and barricades closed the street to traffic at the next intersection, making parking a nightmare. They'd gotten lucky finding a space in view of the credit union, but it was just another thing Sawyer had complained about. He'd wanted to be closer. Preferably right in front of the door. As if Emma was somehow in danger on a busy sidewalk at ten in the morning.

An exiting customer saw Emma coming and held the door.

"Thank you," she said, slipping inside.

The credit union's interior was quiet. A line of people stood between rows of velvet ropes, awaiting their turn with a teller. The air smelled vaguely of aged paper and new carpet. And despite the fact it was barely October, instrumental holiday music drifted softly overhead.

Emma scanned the room for a familiar face that wasn't already with a customer.

Kate, the assistant manager, came swiftly into view. Her eyes widened when she caught sight of Emma, and she cut through the space in a flash. "Oh my goodness. How are you?" she asked. "The police were here this morning. They told me what happened. I can't believe it."

Emma swallowed a painful lump in her throat. She hadn't expected to get emotional at the mere mention of *what happened*. She'd had a hold on herself at home, but out in the world, knowing other people knew made Sara's abduction seem impossibly more real. "What did the police say?" Emma asked. "Do they have a suspect? Or a clue?" If so, no one had bothered to call Emma with the information.

"No. They were asking a lot of questions. None I could answer. I just saw Sara a few days ago and she was fine. She looked tired, maybe distracted, but not enough that I even thought to ask her about it. I mean, we're all tired, right?"

Emma certainly was. She took a breath and prepared her practiced line to get into Sara's desk. "Did the police go through her things? Would you mind if I did? I think she has the spare house key," Emma lied, "and now I'm paranoid someone will come walking in at night while I'm sleeping."

Kate paled. "Oh no. Of course. This way." She walked Emma to a row of cubicles along the far wall and waved an arm toward Sara's desk. "There it is. Take a look. I wouldn't know where to start."

Emma gave Kate her most pitiful face as she lowered onto her sister's chair. "Sara did seem tired. I'd assumed it was work-related stress. She probably had a lot on her plate or an extra difficult account."

Kate puzzled. "We're all overworked, but she never mentioned a difficult account. She had about a metric ton of questions a few weeks back on how our banking system works, but I had no clue. I directed her to Mr. Harrison." She pointed to an open office door across the room. A bearded, middle-aged guy was on the phone and already watching them from his desk, brow furrowed.

"Do you want to talk to him?" Kate asked. "He can tell you more about whatever Sara was doing." Her bottom lip poked out. "You must be trying to get your mind around her last few days."

"They weren't her last days," Emma snapped, surprising herself with the force of her words.

Kate started. "I didn't mean that," she said. "Not like that."

Emma stared, biting her lip and collecting her calm. "Sorry. I'm on edge. You understand." She flicked her gaze to Mr. Harrison, a normally kind man who looked suddenly agitated inside his office. "I don't think I'm ready to talk to anyone else." It might've been her restless night, her emotional state or sheer paranoia, but the branch manager seemed to have fixed his angry eyes on her, despite the line of patrons moving between them. If Mr. Harrison had anything to do with what had happened to Sara, then Emma wasn't in a hurry to run in there and ask about it. Better to let the police or Sawyer do that.

She lowered her eyes to the tidy piles on Sara's desk. "Did the police go through her things?"

"They looked," Kate said, "but they didn't take anything. They were more interested in how she'd been acting lately or if anyone had come to see her here that potentially upset her. Angry ex-boyfriends, things like that."

Right, Emma thought, *because the police didn't have the notebook.* She'd only located it last night while waiting for Sawyer to arrive. The police didn't have a reason to wonder if someone at her work was involved when they'd visited. Maybe Emma didn't either. Maybe the notebook was something else completely, and Emma was reaching for threads, for some way to feel more useful, when in truth there was nothing to do but wait.

She'd get the notebook to the detective in charge as soon as possible. Let him take it from here.

A door slammed and Emma gasped. She and Kate swung in the direction of the sound.

Mr. Harrison's door was closed.

"Kate?" A teller waved from across the room.

Kate frowned. "Sorry. I'll only be a minute," she told Emma.

"I'll be fine." A minute was all Emma needed. She swiveled on her sister's chair and stared at the desk. "Drawers first," she told Henry. Then she opened his empty diaper bag on the floor and began dropping everything with Sara's handwriting into the bag. She took memory sticks from the middle desk drawer and the appointment book from the desktop. Anything remotely personal could be a clue, and maybe she'd see something in Sara's notes that the police hadn't. Then she might be able to give them a lead, in addition to the notebook, that would help identify Sara's abductor. Emma shuddered at the memory of the man's awful growling voice. *Who did you tell?* Her gaze jumped to Mr. Harrison's closed office door. Could he know who took her sister?

She blinked through another threat of tears.

A framed photo of Sara, Emma and their parents sat on the corner of her sister's desk. Their mom had been gone just over five years. Their dad had been gone much longer, but the holes their parents had left behind were permanent. Emma tucked the frame into her purse, unwilling to stow her parents' image with the hodgepodge of who-knew-what from Sara's desk.

Across the room Kate started back in her direction.

Emma kicked the bottom drawers shut on either

side of her, then heaved the bulging diaper bag back onto her shoulder. She gave the middle drawer a shove with her free hand.

"Did you find your key?" Kate asked, coming to a stop at the cubicle's opening.

"No." Emma tipped her head and stroked Henry's fuzzy brown hair. "I guess it's lost."

"Have you checked her car?" Kate offered. "If she's anything like me, it's probably in a cup holder. I find everything from hair ties to business cards in there."

"Good idea." Emma pushed Sara's chair in when she rose, then made a show of fussing over Henry on her way out, hoping to keep Kate's eyes on her adorable baby boy instead of her suddenly crammed diaper bag.

She hurried back onto the sidewalk with a feeling of victory and rush of relief. The local marching band played their high school fight song a few blocks away, adding an excellent backdrop to her enthusiasm. They were probably entertaining at the farmer's market to raise money again, but it certainly felt personal. Emma smiled a little wider.

She arranged the too-heavy diaper bag in the crook of her arm, having nearly dislocated her shoulder with the number of note pads and notebooks she'd confiscated. "I'm going to call this a success," she told Henry, dropping a kiss onto his tiny forehead.

Heavy fingers clamped hard around her elbow. "Don't say a word, or your baby's going to take a mighty fall." A man's low voice growled in her ear. He moved into her periphery, pulling her against his side and keeping pace there.

Ice slid through Emma's veins. It was *the* voice. *Who did you tell?*

She scanned the street for Sawyer, but the man's head turned at the eruption of a bass drumline. His thick arms crossed over his chest as the marching band carried their tune to a crescendo.

A moment later, the man tugged her around the building's edge and into a small alley.

"Don't hurt him," she pleaded.

"Give the bag to me." The man moved into her view; his face was covered in a black scarf from his chin to his nose. The dark hood of his jacket hung low over his forehead.

"No." Emma needed the things in that bag. The fact he wanted the bag was a sure sign that she finally had what she needed to find Sara. "Where's my sister?"

His hand moved from her elbow to the back of her neck, compressing and squeezing until shooting pain raced up the back of her head and she cried out for him to stop. "I wasn't making a request."

He released her with a shove. "Hand over the bag, or I squeeze your baby's head next."

Emma stumbled forward, twisting at the waist to put more distance between the lunatic and her son.

Henry screamed.

The man curled meaty fingers around the straps of Henry's diaper bag and jerked hard enough to leave material burns along her forearm as it slid. Before he separated it from her completely, Emma clenched a fist around one strap. "No!" she screamed.

"Stop!" Sawyer's voice blasted through the white noise of the street beyond the alley. A heartbeat later his livid face came into view across the crowded road. "Stop!" His eyes were fierce, and his voice boomed with authority. "Help her!" he yelled, motioning to Emma in the alley.

A few confused faces turned in her direction, gawking from the safety of the sidewalk just a few yards away.

Emma tried to hold on, tried to stall her attacker ten more seconds, just long enough for Sawyer to reach her, but the man's expression turned lethal. He reached a giant hand forward for her baby, eyes narrowed and darkening.

"No!" Emma screamed. She jerked left, spinning Henry farther away as a massive fist crashed into her cheekbone with a deafening thud. Her head snapped back and her vision blurred. Emma's knees buckled, and her back hit the brick wall of the credit union behind her. Air expelled from her lungs as she slid onto the filthy broken asphalt, Henry screaming in her arms.

The bag flew from her useless, flaccid fingers, and the man was in motion, beating a path down the alley, away from the crowd, away from Sawyer and away from Emma.

Henry wailed into her ear, arching his back in distress as Sawyer skidded to a stop at her side.

"Emma!"

She felt her strength giving way. Her arms knew to hold on, but her thoughts slipped into nothing. "Sawyer," she started, but the darkness rushed in to take her.

Chapter 4

Sawyer watched in horror as the man in black pulled back his fist and shot it forward at Emma and her baby. At *Sawyer's* baby. Fury burned in his veins, propelling him faster, erasing the final distance between them as Emma's body began to wobble and fall. She uttered Sawyer's name as his feet reached the curb only a yard from her side. The desperate, heartbreaking sound was nearly enough to land him on his knees.

Time seemed to stand still as her eyelids drooped shut, extinguishing the final glimmer of her awareness. Sawyer dove for them, catching Emma's body in a hug as it went limp and pressing both her and Henry to his chest. "Call 911!" he demanded, turning to fix a pointed look on the gathered bystanders.

Sawyer gritted his teeth as the assailant pushed

through a throng of pedestrians at the alley's opposite end and escaped his wrath, for now, with Emma's bag.

The soft whir of emergency sirens spun to life in the distance, barely audible over Henry's cries.

Sawyer focused on the lives he held in his arms. He repositioned them, allowing Emma's arms to fall to her sides, and getting a more comforting hold on Henry. "Shh," he whispered to his son. The seething anger he felt for Emma's attacker would have to wait. "I've got you, and you're going to be okay," he vowed, kissing the child's head on instinct, cuddling him tighter. And he would return the man's assaulting punch at the first opportunity.

Emma's lids fluttered open. "Henry."

"I've got him, and help is on the way for you." Sawyer took a moment to evaluate the rising bruise on her cheekbone. Her assailant's fist had been large enough to mark her from jaw to temple, and Sawyer felt his fingers curl once more with the need to return the hit. "The police and ambulance are almost here," he assured her.

The sirens were loud now. Emergency vehicles would arrive at any moment.

Then Sawyer could plot his revenge on the man who'd done this to his family.

A slow and gentle jostling roused Emma once more. The low murmur of a crowd and distant sounds of traffic pricked her ears. A cool and hearty breeze roused her with a snap. Suddenly, Emma's muddled thoughts pulled together in a sharp and deeply horrific memory. A man had attacked her and Henry outside the credit union. He'd taken all of Sara's things. Stolen the diaper bag from her hands. *And hit her.* "Henry!" Her eyes jerked wide.

"He's here," Sawyer answered. He appeared at her side, baby tucked safely in the crook of his arm. "He's okay."

Henry worked the small blue pacifier in his mouth. A broad grin stretched beneath the little soother when he caught her in his sight.

Emma sighed in relief. "Thank you," she whispered, fighting tears and taking inventory of the changes in her situation. The assailant was gone. Sawyer was here, and she was strapped to a gurney. An EMT pressed cool, probing fingers to her wrist. "Did he get away?" she asked Sawyer, craning her neck for signs of a policeman with the lunatic in handcuffs.

"Yeah," Sawyer answered. "I'm sorry."

She shook her head. "You saved Henry."

The muscle pulsed in Sawyer's jaw. His eyes were hard and cold. "The man who hurt you got away."

Sawyer's voice raised goose bumps over her skin. His calculating expression didn't help.

"Your cheek will be tender for a while," the EMT said. He explored the red-hot ache with a gentle touch. "Skin didn't break," he said. "There's no need for a bandage or stitches, but I recommend ice for swelling and aspirin as needed for pain." He flashed a blinding light into her eyes, and she winced. "Blurry vision?" he asked.

"No."

"Memory loss?"

"No." She frowned. That wasn't completely true. "I don't remember you arriving," she said, "but I remember being cornered, robbed and assaulted by a man in head-to-toe black. He wore a scarf across the bottom half of his face."

The EMT nodded, a small frown on his lips. "I'm sorry that happened to you and your baby." He pocketed the light. "If you develop any nausea or unusual neck pain, go to the ER. Tell them about this."

"Okay," she agreed, eager to get off the gurney and avoid an ambulance ride she absolutely couldn't afford. "I can go?"

He raised his attention to Sawyer, already moving into position so he could help her down. "You'll drive her?" he asked.

Sawyer reached for Emma's hand. "Yes."

"Not so fast," a vaguely familiar voice interrupted. The detective who'd come to her home to take the report of Sara's abduction moved into view, pen and paper in hand. "I have a few questions, if you don't mind. I've spoken to several witnesses, and I'd like to get your statement as well before the details become murky from time."

Sawyer stepped between the detective and the gurney. His pale blue eyes locked onto hers. "You don't have to do this now if you don't want to. He can come by later, or I can take you to the station when you're feeling better."

Emma took a deep, settling breath and lifted her chin. "I can do it now," she said, and then she slowly relived the second-worst experience of her life in vivid detail.

When it was over, she told Detective Rosen about Sara's hidden notebook, and he promised to pick it up personally, after he'd finished with the current crime scene.

At home, she showered until her skin pruned up, attempting and failing to wash the feel of the man's hands off her. Then, with Henry dozing in his crib, she cried herself to sleep in the middle of the afternoon.

She woke to an empty crib at her bedside and the tangy scent of barbecue in the air.

She was on her feet instantly in search of her son. The scents of her grill suggested all was well, that Sawyer was grilling, but she wasn't sure she liked him nabbing Henry without letting her know. She crept down the hallway toward the kitchen warring with herself. Henry was his son, but surely common courtesy dictated that he at least let her know before taking him like that. No one else in her world would have dared. Maybe Sara. The thought clogged her throat.

Emma found Sawyer on the back porch, manning the grill as suspected.

He turned before she spoke, as if he'd somehow sensed her arrival. "Hey," he said, his gaze lingering on her cheek. "Did we wake you?"

"No," Emma said flatly, "but I wish you would have. Instead, I woke to find an empty crib. I didn't like it." Across from the grill, aligned with the porch swing she loved, Henry swung cheerfully from a red-and-yellow baby swing fastened to the rafters of the porch roof. "You put up the swing," she said, unsure if she was doubly frustrated that Sawyer had helped himself to that too, or warmed by the gesture.

Sawyer opened the lid to her steaming grill and flipped a line of burgers with practiced skill. "I found it in the garage while I was double-checking the perimeter. I think I woke the little guy with your power drill, but he let me off the hook when I suggested he give the swing a try." Pride tugged Sawyer's lips, and Emma wondered if it was his handiwork or Henry that caused it. "If you don't want the swing there, I can move it," he said, brows dipping into a V. "Whatever you want."

"It's fine," Emma said, drifting toward her son. "He clearly loves it." She stroked Henry's soft brown hair and kissed his head, inhaling the soft scents of sunshine and baby shampoo. She'd come so close to seeing him hurt today. Her fingers found the aching skin of her cheek on instinct, recalling the moment of impact with perfect, bone-rattling clarity. Then she'd been rescued by the man of her dreams. A man she'd long ago assumed had walked out of her life permanently, only to turn up and move in with her on the night of their strange reunion.

Last night.

Her stomach churned with the weight of all that had happened these last twenty-four hours. Nearly forty-eight, if she started counting from the moment her sister had been torn from their home. Her heart raced, and her mouth dried. It was just too much.

Sawyer closed the grill lid and watched her for a long beat before speaking. "Do you want to sit down?" He poured her a glass of ice water from the pitcher sitting on the little table she normally shared with Sara. "I planned to check in on you when the burgers were done. It's been a long day. I thought you might want to eat."

Emma curled one arm around her middle, attempting feebly to hold herself together. "You didn't have to do this," she said.

Sawyer gave his spatula a little spin. "It's just burgers," he said smoothly, as if that was true.

But it wasn't *just burgers*. It was the attentiveness and compassion. The protection and security. It was all the things she'd missed so deeply when Sawyer had left, and it was like peeling the scab off a wound she'd worked very hard to heal.

Emma straightened her spine. "I meant you don't have to watch Henry so I can sleep or hang swings or cook for me." The gestures were clearly meant to be helpful and not intrusive, she decided, and she couldn't be mad that he'd taken Henry from the crib when he woke. It was a fatherly thing to do. The swing. The burgers. All acts of kindness. But Emma's gut still churned with anger. She didn't need Sawyer's help with those things. She'd been fine on her own all these months. Why should he get to walk back in and pretend he'd been here all along?

Sawyer narrowed his eyes. "It's the least I can do, don't you think?"

"No," she said honestly. "I called Fortress Security because I needed help keeping Henry safe and finding Sara. You saved us from that lunatic today. That's what I need from you. That and help finding my sister."

Sawyer's eyes went cold at the mention of the man in the alley. It was a new look on him. One she wasn't sure she'd ever get used to. "How are you feeling?" he asked.

"My face hurts," she said. "I'm mad in general. I'm also thankful Henry wasn't hurt."

Sawyer took a step in her direction, hand raised as if he might touch her swollen cheek. He stopped short, clearly thinking better of it, and lowered his arm. He raised his attention from the bruise to her eyes. "I'm going to find the man who did this."

"Good, because I think he was the same man who took Sara," she said through a tightening throat, "and that man is a monster."

"What?" Sawyer's already aggravated expression darkened. "Are you sure?"

She nodded. "I recognized his voice. So, I can tell you from experience that Henry and I were lucky. I stood by and listened as he strangled Sara with his bare hands, held her down, made her bleed, then dragged her away." The memory of mopping her sister's blood off the living room floor rushed back to mind, and she stood, ready to run. She didn't want to have an emotional breakdown in front of Henry. Or Sawyer. The day had been too difficult already. "Excuse me."

Sawyer was on his feet instantly. "Hey." He caught her in his arms and pulled her against his chest. The strong, familiar embrace felt so much like home, so much like everything she'd been missing for far too long. "I know I wasn't here for you before," he said, "but I'm here now, and I'm not going anywhere. You're not alone, Emma." He stroked her hair, and her heart gave a heavy thump.

She tried not to read into his promise. He wasn't going anywhere *for now*, but he'd be gone again when Sara came home. He would stay in Henry's life after that, but not in hers. Not really. Not the way her twisting heart wanted. Tears pricked her eyes, and her chest grew heavy with the need to cry.

"Excuse me," she blurted, bobbing free of him and running back inside.

Tears streamed over her cheeks with every footstep down the long hall to her room.

* * *

Sawyer knocked on Emma's door a few minutes later, then swung it open. The en suite bathroom door was ajar. "Emma?" he called. "Everything okay?"

She stepped out of the bathroom with red-rimmed eyes and blotchy skin. "Sorry. I needed a minute."

Sawyer set Henry in the crib beside her bed, a fresh cocktail of anger and regret mixing in his gut. "Feeling better?"

"No." She blew out a shaky breath, checking the corners of her mouth with her fingertips. "Not much. How's Henry?"

Sawyer gave his son a quick look. "He conked out in the swing. I wasn't sure it was good for him to sleep with his head tipped the way it was."

"Thanks." She moved toward the crib, toward Henry, and the urge to pull her against him was nearly too much.

He shoved his hands into his pockets. "You know that what happened to Sara isn't your fault," he said. "You couldn't have fought that guy and protected Henry at the same time. You did the only thing you could do. You were smart, quick thinking and brave."

"I don't feel like any of those things," she said, dragging her gaze from Henry to Sawyer.

He understood. Better than she could know. "Well, do you feel like a burger?"

Emma nodded, and Sawyer led her to the kitchen, where he'd set the table in her absence. She took a seat and downed the glass of ice water he'd poured for her. "How'd everything look when you checked the property?"

"Could be better," he said, hoping to sound less frustrated than he had been at the sight of the inadequate security measures protecting two single women and a baby. "Your locks are old. The windows are old. There are no security cameras. No alarm." He ran a heavy hand over his head and gripped the back of his neck. "I'll replace the locks and see what I can do to better secure the windows."

Emma set her empty glass aside and frowned. "I'd hoped to raise Henry on a farm, not inside a fortress."

"We all hope for a lot of things," Sawyer said stiffly. "But we have to adapt to the situations at hand, and right now, you need a fortress."

Emma placed a burger on her plate and covered it in mushrooms and onions, going through the motions, he assumed, but forgoing the bun.

Sawyer made his burger and bit into it, keeping one eye on her. He'd grilled burgers for her a dozen times during their monthlong whirlwind romance. In fact, some of his favorite memories with Emma had a grill in the background.

He'd been given a thirty-day leave last year after a particularly intense and dangerous mission, and he'd only expected to sleep in and veg out. Instead, he'd met Emma at a bonfire near a lake where he'd been fishing. He'd marched over to her, introduced himself. They'd hit it off, and he begged for her number when it was time for her to leave. He called her as she walked away. Invited her to fireworks in the park the next night. They'd spent nearly every day together from there. Until he had to go back.

Emma pushed the veggies around with her fork. "What if we don't find her?" she asked, pulling his thoughts back to the present.

Sawyer paused, the burger partway to his lips. "We'll find her."

"How do you know?"

"Because it's what I do. I search and rescue. I find people who don't want to be found, and I bring folks who are desperate to be found home." Images of his last mission flashed into mind. He'd taken his men on a rescue mission with bad intel. He'd assessed the risk, and he'd been dead wrong. He walked them into a trap, and that had cost five good men their lives. It darn near cost Sawyer his sanity.

"What if we find her and it's too late when we do?" The quaver in Emma's voice opened Sawyer's eyes. He hadn't realized he'd shut them.

Sawyer put the burger down. "We're going to find Sara, and she's going to be okay when we do," he promised. "Meanwhile, I'll be here to make sure no one gets near you or Henry again while we figure out what was going on. Okay?"

Emma shook her head, looking half-ill and pursing her lips.

"What?" he asked. They'd just covered her safety, Henry's safety and Sara's safe return. What else could make her look that way?

"I let go of the bag," she said. "I had everything from Sara's desk in that bag, and I let him have it."

"You didn't let him have anything," Sawyer argued. "I watched you fight him for it while holding a baby."

Emma shook her head. "Now he has what he wanted, and he doesn't have a reason to keep her alive anymore. Letting go of that bag might've killed my sister."

"Whoa." Sawyer raised his hands into a T for a time-out. "Look. You don't know any of that. Not his

motivation. Not his endgame. You don't even know if
what he wanted was in that bag. If he wanted the notebook with the numbers, the joke is on him because we
had that and Detective Rosen picked it up an hour ago
as promised."

Emma lifted hopeful eyes to his. "Yeah."

"Yeah," he said.

She nodded, steadying herself. "You're right." She
forked a stack of mushrooms, studying them, her
thoughts clearly somewhere else.

"Spill it," Sawyer said, wiping his mouth and then
pressing the napkin to the table. "I've been gone
awhile, but I know that face. You've got something
to say. So, say it. It's better to clear the air than try to
work through the smoke. Heaven knows we've got little fires burning everywhere."

She leaned forward, elbows on the table. "How did
you get through the things you went through overseas?
I know you're trained. You're smart. You're tough.
That's not what I mean."

Sawyer bit into his burger, locked in her gaze and
wishing she knew it was memories of her that had gotten him through the worst things imaginable. "Hope."

Emma pushed a forkful of mushrooms into her
mouth and watched him curiously. She nodded. "I can
do that." She chewed, swallowed, had some water, still
scrutinizing Sawyer until he itched to get up and move.
Her gaze shifted quickly away before returning to meet
his. "I spent a lot of time over the past year wondering
if you ever thought of me," she said, cheeks reddening.

He could see the honesty cost her. So, he would be
honest right back. "I did. Often. I used to think of the
things we'd done together. Now I'm just thinking about

all the things I've missed." He clamped his mouth shut and did his best to look less vulnerable than he suddenly felt. Things were complicated enough between him and Emma without him getting emotional. This wasn't the time for heart-to-hearts and personal confessions.

The mission was to find Sara and protect Emma and Henry at all costs. He took another angrier bite of burger.

Emma stood and left.

Sawyer groaned. He used to be a people person. He made people comfortable, at ease, even happy. Lately, he could clear a room with a look and a greeting. He hadn't particularly minded the change until now.

Emma returned several minutes later with a scrapbook. She set it on the table beside his plate. "Sara made this for me."

She returned to her seat and lifted her fork to finish dinner.

Sawyer examined the big blue book. Henry's name and newborn photo were glued to the cover and framed with red ribbon. A photo of Emma in a ponytail and "baby on board" T-shirt was positioned just below the first. Her beautifully round belly was tough to look away from, and it hit him again. She'd been pregnant. Delivered their child. Brought him home. Got to know him. Learned to care for him, and Sawyer had missed it all.

He opened the book and turned the pages with reverence, poring over every detail. Every photo. Every inscription. He admired the proud smile on Emma's face in each photo.

"What's wrong?" Emma asked, resting back in her chair. "You look furious."

"No." He closed the book. A swell of pride and gratitude expanded his chest. "Thank you," he said softly.

She quirked a brow. "You can't keep that. Sara made it for me."

"No." He laughed. "Not for the book. For Henry."

Emma's cheeks reddened again. "It's not like I made him on my own."

"No, but you did everything else on your own," he said. "I can't imagine how frightening it was to learn you were going to have a baby. Especially one whose father was literally MIA." He thought again of the monsters who'd taken those months and his men from him, but forced the images aside. He curled his fingers around the book's edge, grounding himself to the present. "You could've chosen so many other ways to deal with your pregnancy, and I swear I never would've judged you, whatever you'd decided, but—" he cleared his thickening throat "—but because you made these choices—" he lifted the scrapbook in a white-knuckle grip "—I'm a father, and whatever you think of me now, I am irrevocably indebted to you for this."

Emma's mouth fell open, then was slowly pulled shut. "You're welcome."

Sawyer's aching heart warmed at her acceptance of his apology. It was a step in the right direction. "What was it like?" he asked.

"Scary at first, then pretty amazing," she said, forking a bite of bunless burger into her mouth. "I got really fat."

Sawyer let his gaze trail over her, indulging himself in the admiration of her new curves. "Agree to disagree."

"I'm working on getting back in shape now," she assured him. "It feels good but getting chubby with a purpose was fun too." Her lips twitched, nearly accomplishing a smile.

By the time dinner was done, and Sawyer had cleared the table, some of the smoky air between them had cleared, as well. Emma joined him at the sink in companionable silence as they washed and dried dishes by hand before putting them away. It was dangerously easy to be with Emma when she wasn't looking at him as if *he* might be the one in need of protection *from her*. Easy to let himself think there could a future for them, that he could somehow make up for his absence when it had counted most.

But Sawyer couldn't afford to think that way. Couldn't afford to get distracted until he brought Sara home safely as promised. Only after he'd proved himself worthy of Emma's trust would he allow himself to dream of more. Until then, he had work to do.

Chapter 5

Sawyer's eyes snapped open, his senses on alert. According to the clock on Emma's living room wall, it was approaching 3:00 a.m., meaning he'd slept for four straight hours. It was the longest stretch he'd managed since returning stateside, and he felt unnervingly vulnerable for it.

Normally he woke to the screams of his fallen teammates or the pain of his own torture, but not this time. So, what had woken him?

He tuned in to the quiet home, suddenly acutely aware that it was his gut that had jerked him into the moment. *Instinct.* His pulse quickened as he listened. For what? He wasn't sure. Sawyer straightened, planted his feet silently on the floor.

The baby monitor on the coffee table caught his eye. He waited for an indication that Henry had stirred and woken Sawyer, but there was only the slow and steady breaths of a sleeping child.

"Sawyer?" Emma whispered, struggling upright on the couch, where she'd fallen asleep midsentence during the retelling of a pregnancy story. He'd been wholly engrossed in the details, but her words had turned to soft snores before she'd finished, and he hadn't had the heart to wake her or the guts to try to move her. He certainly had no right to touch her.

She frowned in the dark. "What's wrong?"

He considered telling her everything was fine, but he hadn't had time to confirm that yet, and the distinct creak of floorboards removed the possibility it was true.

Her eyes stretched wide. "Someone's in the house?" She flicked her gaze to the baby monitor, and panic drained the blood from her face.

Sawyer lifted a finger to his lips, then reached for his sidearm, tucked carefully between the cushion and overstuffed arm of Emma's chair where he'd rested. Then he reached for her. Much as he didn't want to bring her into harm's way, he couldn't afford to leave her alone either.

Emma followed closely on his heels, her small hands at his waist as they crept down the hall toward the sound.

Each bedroom door was open as they passed. Each light off. The laundry room. The guest bedroom, where Sawyer's things were stashed. Emma's room, where Henry slept soundly, unaware of the intruder or his parents' fears.

At her bedroom door, Emma released Sawyer and stepped over the threshold. She shot a pleading gaze at him, and he nodded before pulling the door shut with her inside.

He waited for the soft snick of the lock before moving on.

The bathroom door was open also. A night-light illuminated the narrow space, projecting the silhouette of a duck onto one wall.

When Sawyer reached Sara's room, the door was closed.

A beam of light flashed along the floor inside, leaking into the hallway at his feet. A sly grin slid over Sawyer's mouth. He hadn't imagined an opportunity to return the man's punch so soon, but he was glad for it, and unlike Emma, this guy wouldn't be waking up so soon after the hit.

Sawyer cast a look over his shoulder, confirming he was still alone, and he hoped Emma had taken Henry to hide wherever they'd gone the night Sara was taken. Someplace she could call the police and wait safely until help arrived.

He struck a defensive position behind the closed door and turned the doorknob carefully. The soldier in him rose instinctively and unbidden. His mind and muscles falling instantly on their training.

The door swung on noisy hinges, and the creaking of floorboards turned quickly into the loud groan and rattle of an aged wooden window frame forced upward faster than it was prepared to go.

"Not on my watch," Sawyer said, flipping the light on and aiming his gun toward the window. "Stop right there."

A man in all black looked at him from the bedroom window, one half of his body still inside the room as he straddled the casing, a black duffel bag over his shoulder.

"Release the bag and climb back inside slowly," Sawyer demanded, hyperaware that only one of the intruder's hands was visible from this angle.

The man shifted the duffel from his shoulder to his palm and stretched it into the room toward Sawyer.

"Drop it," Sawyer barked. "Now, show me your other hand."

The man dipped his chin slowly. His opposite hand came into view with a gun poised to shoot.

"Put your weapon down." Sawyer's voice slid into the deep authoritative timbre that forced most folks to obey his commands. This man didn't budge.

"I *will* shoot you," Sawyer warned. "I'm willing to bet my aim is better than yours." He let his mouth curve into a sinister smile, enjoying the weight and feel of his SIG Sauer against his palm and the flash of indecision on the man's face.

Henry's scream broke the silent standoff and Sawyer's concentration. A million terrifying scenarios thundered through his brain like a punch to his gut. Was there a second intruder? Had Sawyer overlooked him? Was Henry hurt? Was Emma?

The intruder's gun went off with a deafening bang!

Sawyer jumped back into the hall, pressing himself to the wall and cursing inwardly at the moment of distraction. "Emma!" he called.

Henry cried again, but Emma didn't answer.

Sawyer swore. He spun silently back into Sara's bedroom, already aiming for the window. He pulled his trigger as the muffled thud of the duffel bag hit the ground outside. The man took a second wild shot at

Sawyer, then toppled out the open window, smearing blood over the frame and Sara's wall beneath.

Sawyer's attention stuck to the hole in the drywall a few feet away from his head. The intruder's final shot had missed him by several feet, but the hole had punched through a wall shared with Sara's room. A wall shared by Henry and his crib.

Emma's pulse beat in her ears as she burrowed deeper into the walk-in closet that had been her refuge just two nights before. She could only pray it would be enough to protect her again. She shushed her fussing baby and tried desperately not to imagine Sawyer being injured while she hid. She couldn't live knowing another loved one had been taken from her while she sat idly by, but what could she do? She couldn't leave Henry, and she wouldn't risk making him an orphan, so she was stuck. Hiding and waiting. And praying. Again.

The dispatch officer insisted on staying on the line with her until the police arrived. "Can you see anything from your location?" she asked.

"No," Emma whispered. "Please hurry."

"What can you hear?" the dispatcher asked. "Can you tell me the number of intruders based on voices?"

Emma shook her head, unsure she could make another sound even if she wanted. Even if she wasn't terrified her voice would give away her hiding spot and put her baby in danger.

"Ma'am," the dispatcher began again, but a sudden gunshot reverberated through the silent home, stopping her midinterrogation.

Emma's heart seized and her chest constricted.

"Was that gunfire?" the dispatch officer asked abruptly, concern in her voice.

"I—" Emma nodded. "Yes." She stroked Henry's hair as he began to scream once more. "Help us," she breathed. "Please."

The blast that erupted next poured tears onto her cheeks.

Henry's eyes were wide in the glow from her phone. His lips pulled low into a full pout, startled to silence by the sound but ready to wail at any moment.

"Was anyone hurt? Do you need an ambulance?" the dispatcher demanded.

"I don't know." She covered her mouth with one palm to stifle a building sob.

The door to her room banged open, and she screamed. The door ricocheted against the wall, rattling the closet where she hid. "Henry!" Sawyer yelled. "Emma!"

A wave of relief pressed the air from her lungs. "Here," she croaked. "We're here." She inched forward as the closet door opened, balancing a crying Henry in her arms and the phone against her shoulder.

Sawyer dropped to his knees and pulled them into his arms. "Thank goodness." He took Henry from her, then offered a hand to pull her to her feet. "Call 911," he instructed. "I shot the intruder, but he got away with a duffel bag. I don't know what was in it."

Emma lifted the phone from her shoulder. "They're on the way."

He closed his eyes for a long beat, then reopened them to kiss Henry's hair and round cheeks a dozen times before kissing Emma's forehead and pulling her close. "May I?" he asked, sliding a hand up to take the phone. He spoke heatedly with Dispatch for several moments while Emma stepped away.

Her insides fluttered and her limbs quaked with excess adrenaline as she tried to follow Sawyer's explanation of what had happened inside Sara's room.

"I definitely hit him. There's blood. He'll need a hospital," Sawyer said.

A dark spot on the wall caught Emma's attention, and she moved across her room to inspect it through the bars of Henry's crib. A hole in the drywall. Inches from the place where Henry laid his head at night. She touched the hole with shaking fingers, and nausea rolled in her stomach. "He could be dead," she whispered.

Sawyer opened a pocketknife and dug the casing from the wall with his handkerchief. "I've got the brass," he said. "This might be all we need to track him. We can match the gun if it's registered. Match the print if he's in the system."

Flashers lit the world outside her bedroom window.

"Cavalry's here," he told Dispatch, pulling the curtain back for a look into the driveway.

Sawyer returned the phone to Emma, then headed for the front door with Henry to greet the emergency responders.

Emma tried not to look too long or hard at the crib or the bullet hole in the wall at its side. She doubted she'd ever be able to lay Henry there again, and she was sure she wouldn't sleep if she did.

She followed them to the living room, Henry lodged tightly against Sawyer's chest, silent and calm. Shocking because Henry wasn't good with strangers. Though

Sawyer wasn't really a stranger, she thought. Sawyer was his father.

She took Henry from him as he greeted the line of police officers, crime scene officials and the detective she'd spoken to earlier that day. She didn't have it in her to speak without crying, and tears would help nothing. Coffee, on the other hand, cured a multitude of things, and she could make a pot to be useful.

She moved to the kitchen as men and women in uniforms canvassed her home. There wouldn't be any more sleeping for her tonight, but honestly, she wasn't sure how she'd ever sleep again.

Sawyer paused outside the kitchen as a pair of uniforms passed by. "You okay?" he asked, concern and compassion plain in the words and his expression.

"Mmm-hmm." She nodded, pushing her attention back to the chore at hand.

Tonight's gunshots had punctured more than the drywall. The possibility she'd lost Sawyer again had wrenched her heart in agony and eradicated her carefully constructed walls of emotional protection. The realization that he was safe but would leave once Sara was home, made her chest pinch and ache in the extreme. She wasn't sure what that meant, but she was nearly positive it wouldn't end well for her raw and aching heart.

Chapter 6

Emma set Henry in his high chair once he'd calmed from the scare and offered him his favorite teether. At just over four months, his coordination wasn't great, but once he got the rubber cactus to his mouth, he normally chewed happily. Tonight was no different, and Emma marveled at the resilience of her son. If only she could suck it up so easily and move on to the moment at hand.

She turned to the counter and rubbed trembling palms down the legs of her jeans. Brewing the coffee and setting out the cups, cream and sugar would give her an outlet for the energy surplus buzzing around inside her.

Sawyer appeared a moment later, leaning against the jamb. "How are you holding up?"

"Not as well as Henry," she said, "but I suppose I

should expect as much from your son." She poured a mug of coffee and extended it in Sawyer's direction. "Coffee?"

Sawyer accepted the mug. He took a long pull on the steaming drink, eyes focused on her. "You did great tonight," he said. "With everything going on, I forgot to say that sooner, but it's true. Henry's a lucky kid."

Emma nodded woodenly. What had she done besides hide? *Again.* She was sick of being caught off guard and forced to react to all the villainous encounters. She wanted to *do* something that would stop them. Not hide until the situations passed. "We need to find out what he was looking for," she said. "It was a good sign. If whatever he wanted wasn't in the bag of things I took from her office, then Sara might still be alive."

Sawyer gave one stiff dip of his chin.

"If he found whatever he'd been after in her room tonight, then we don't have much time," she said. "We have to do something."

Detective Rosen arrived in the kitchen behind Sawyer. "Do I smell coffee?"

Sawyer nodded. "Help yourself."

The detective poured a cup, then offered Emma his hand. "I'm sorry to be back so soon, Miss Hart. I understand you were able to contact Dispatch while staying out of danger's path and protecting your son to boot. Nice work."

"Any word on Sara's whereabouts?" Emma asked, ignoring the comment about her spectacular abilities to hide and use a telephone.

"I'm sorry," Rosen said. "Not yet. We're running down every lead, but we don't have anything to share at the moment."

"Well, which is it?" she asked, working to control her tone and not upset Henry again. "Is there nothing to share or just nothing you're willing to share?"

The detective looked at Sawyer, who returned his level gaze. "Nothing worth sharing," he said.

"Try me," Emma dared. "You'd be surprised how little it would take to reassure me right now."

Detective Rosen rocked back on his heels and cleared his throat. "Well, we're working on the theory that this had something to do with her position at the credit union," he began. "We're unclear how her job and the abduction are related, but we believe they are."

Emma's hopes sank. She'd hoped the leads he'd mentioned were significant. Maybe even inside tips of some sort. Instead, it sounded like the police didn't have anything more than she'd come up with on her own.

Sawyer moved to her side, silently sharing his strength with her. "Any luck on deciphering the note-book's contents?"

"Not yet." Detective Rosen set his empty mug aside and fixed Emma with a patient look. "Mr. Lance said the intruder took a duffel bag with him. Do you think you might be able to walk through the room and tell me what's missing?"

Emma stepped away from Sawyer and pulled Henry from his high chair with a kiss. "I didn't spend much time in Sara's room," she said, moving into the hall behind the detective. "I'm not sure I'd notice if anything was missing besides the furniture, but I'll try."

A handful of men in various uniforms filled the space inside her sister's room, dusting the window frame for prints, taking photos and collecting blood from the floor.

Emma inched inside. Her pulse quickened and her breaths grew shallow. Seeing the policemen and crime scene people picking through Sara's things was like losing her all over again. The blood on the wall and windowsill reminded her of the broad smear she'd cleaned off the living room floor.

"Hey." Sawyer moved in front of her, the toes of his shoes bumping hers. "Take your time."

She snuggled Henry tighter and forced her gaze around the room. The items on Sara's vanity, bookcase and nightstand were scattered. The floor was covered with the contents of her closet. Her mattress was askew from the box spring. "Maybe if I clean up," she said. "It's too messy right now. I don't know where to look."

"All right," the detective said. "We're almost done. You can let us know once you've had time to reorganize." He handed Sawyer a business card, then drifted back down the hallway.

More than an hour later, the house was finally, eerily still.

Sawyer double-checked the door lock, then turned to face her. "What do you want to do?" he asked.

She shook her head, heartbroken and mystified. "I have no idea."

He pulled a set of keys from his pocket and raised them beside his handsome face. "Why don't we get out of here?"

He didn't have to ask Emma twice. When he'd offered to take her and Henry to his place for a while, she'd packed two bags without hesitation. Inside the cab of his truck, Emma watched her family ranch until it was swallowed by distance and darkness.

"What are you thinking?" he asked when the curiosity became too much.

"I don't know where you live," she said with a small laugh. "I was thinking that two days ago I would never have agreed to go home with someone without asking where they lived."

Sawyer locked his jaw against the complaint that he wasn't just someone. He was Henry's father, a man she'd called in to protect her and someone she'd once claimed to have loved.

She fiddled with the hem of her shirt. "I suppose you don't still live on base with four other rangers."

"No," he said. "They tend to cut off our housing once we're discharged." He glanced her way across the dimly lit cab. "I bought a place in the next county. We won't be more than an hour away if the police call with new information and you want to get back."

Emma turned curious eyes on him. "Where in the next county?"

"Lake Anna," he said, nearly crushed by a wave of nostalgia.

She swiveled in her seat, eyes wide with interest. They'd met at Lake Anna, and Emma had loved visiting the lake when they'd dated. She told him once that she wanted to live there someday, and he'd promised to buy her a home with a dock and lots of privacy so they could make love under the stars anytime they wanted. Sawyer assumed the rising color in her cheeks meant that she hadn't forgotten that conversation either.

He checked the rearview mirror as they moved along the desolate highway, one of only a few dozen cars traveling just before dawn. He passed his exit and got off on an unlit, extremely rural ramp instead, checking again for signs they'd been followed. By the time he backtracked several miles and made a few unnecessary turns to confirm they were still alone, the sun was rising.

Emma straightened and rubbed her eyes as they bounced down the pitted gravel lane to his simple A-frame cottage. The motion light snapped on as he settled the vehicle outside, welcoming him home. The lawn was still dark, shaded by the surrounding forest, but the lake before them was the color of fire, reflecting the sunrise over its glassy surface.

Sawyer bypassed the wide parking area near his back porch in favor of a smaller, narrower patch of gravel near the home's side entrance. He used this door as his front door, because the actual front of his home faced the lake.

Sawyer climbed out and grabbed Emma's things from the back, then met her on the passenger side. He took Henry's bulbous car seat carrier from her hands. "You'll be safe here," he promised, stepping onto the wide wraparound porch. "We weren't followed, and I've barely moved in, so even if the man I shot managed to get my name somehow, the only people who know where I live are my teammates in Lexington. The home is technically owned by the company, for privacy reasons, so it will take some time and know-how to track us here."

He unlocked the door and hit the light switch inside, then motioned for Emma to pass. Sawyer keyed in the code to the silent alarm system, then caught Emma's eye as she took the place in.

She folded her arms and made a circuit around the living room, stopping to look at the photos on his mantel, then out the stretch of windows facing the lake.

Sawyer set Henry's car seat near the couch and went to join her. "What do you think?"

"It's beautiful," she said.

"Thanks." He gave the space a critical exam. Packed boxes filled the corners. Stacks of paint cans and piles of new fixtures lined the walls and nearly every flat surface. He'd gotten the place at a steal, planning to use it as a safe house for Fortress until he fell in love with it. Unable to separate the cabin and its location from his memories with Emma, he'd decided to move in. That decision had led to a lot of unexpected work and added costs. Like updating *everything* and getting the place a mailbox and address. For the past fifty or so years, it had been little more than a cabin in the woods. Someplace someone had built to spend weekends, but never intended as a home. "It needs a lot of work, but they say it's all about location, right?"

"That's what they say," she said softly, still focused on the lake and rising sun. "I can't believe you've been this close and I had no idea."

Sawyer had thought the same thing the moment she'd told him he had a son. He was just one county line away, and he'd still missed the kid's entire life so far.

"How's Cade?" she asked his reflection in the glass. "I've been so wrapped up in my messes that I haven't even thought to ask you about your little brother."

Sawyer smiled at their reflections, side by side in his new home. "Cade's good. He's finishing up with the Marines soon, and he'll join Fortress when he gets out."

"Sounds like your security firm has become the

family business." She nodded appreciatively, a note of pride in her voice. "You had your doubts about going big right out of the army, but I knew," she said. "I've always known you could do anything."

Sawyer stepped closer and put his hands back into his pockets to stop them from reaching for her. "Wyatt put everything in motion." Sawyer had been scheduled for discharge with Wyatt, his closest friend and brother in arms, but his captivity had kept him from it and forced Wyatt to do everything on his own. Another case of Sawyer leaving loved ones to fend for themselves.

Wyatt, like Emma, had done a fine job without him.

Emma erased the final few inches between them, bringing her foot and leg flush with his. She linked her arm through his and tipped her head against his shoulder.

Sawyer raised the opposite arm across his chest and set his hand over hers on his arm.

Soon the sun gleamed orange and was well above the horizon, looking as if it might have risen from the fiery water's depths. Sawyer couldn't resist it any longer. He slid the patio door open and ushered Emma outside. She gave their sleeping son a glance before moving onto the deck, where Sawyer had spent every early morning since he'd moved in. If there was an upside to insomnia, it was that he never missed a sunrise.

"Where are all the other lake houses?" Emma asked, scanning the scene in both directions. "I remember there being so many."

"Those are closer to town. We're on a finger of the lake, tucked between a privately owned hundred-acre property and the national forest."

"Wow." She pushed a strand of windblown hair behind her ear and surveyed the scene again, this time with a look of remarkable appreciation. Pride swelled nonsensically in Sawyer's chest once more. Her approval of his home probably meant more to him than it should, but he didn't care, he liked it.

Emma turned to him; there seemed to be a question in her eyes, but she didn't ask it. "I should set up Henry's crib," she said. "I hate to see him sleeping in the car seat." She headed back inside and lifted the portable crib off the floor where Sawyer had left it. "Where do you want us?"

Sawyer bit his tongue against the truth, that he wanted her and Henry right there, with him permanently, but he knew that wasn't what she'd meant, and it was much too soon, not to mention unfair, to spring something like that on her. What he needed to do was find Sara. Complete the mission. Prove himself.

He showed Emma to the spare room across the hall from his, and watched as she expertly unpacked and set up the portable crib, then changed Henry and got him back to sleep with only the smallest cry of protest. She really was great at being a mother. His son was a lucky boy.

Sawyer's father had been a real son of a gun, and Sawyer had sworn long ago to never repeat any of his varied and extensive mistakes. *If* he ever had a family of his own. He'd already started off on the wrong foot by not returning Emma's calls. Even if he thought he was doing her a favor. He should've let her make that decision for herself. Now he could only hope that she'd forgive him. She might understand logically why he hadn't called, but the pain of feeling rejected and unwanted was a lot to overcome, and there was nothing logical about the process.

"Sawyer?" Emma asked, pulling him from his reverie. "Are you going to lie down awhile?"

"No." He bristled at the thought. He had far too much to protect under his roof now, and too much work to be done in the meanwhile. "I'm going to have another look at Sara's notebook."

Emma crossed her arms and frowned. "I thought you gave it to Detective Rosen."

He nodded. "I did. Right after I photographed the pages."

She smiled. "Okay. I'm not sure I'll be able to sleep, but I'm going to try. Once Henry wakes, he'll need me."

"Of course." Sawyer moved toward the door, longing to tell her she wasn't alone. She didn't have to carry the weight of single parenthood anymore. He could make bottles, change diapers, shake rattles. He was hardly a professional at those things, but he was a quick study and he wanted to learn. Instead, he settled for "I'll be here if you need me."

Emma curled her small hand over his on the doorknob. "Thank you," she said softly.

Sawyer's body stiffened at her touch, with the urge to pull her against him and kiss her the way he'd dreamed of doing for a year. "For what?"

"For coming to my rescue the other night. For protecting us now." She removed her hand from his and slid her palm up the length of his arm and over his shoulder. When her fingers reached the back of his neck, a firestorm of electricity coursed through him.

She rocked onto her toes and kissed his cheek. "Good night."

Sawyer nodded once, then pulled the bedroom door shut between them while he could still bring himself to walk away.

Emma woke hours later to the sound of Henry's laughter.

Her bedroom door was open and his portable crib was empty, but his laugh was brightening her day even before her feet had hit the floor. According to her phone, it was nearly lunchtime. She'd had more sleep than she'd expected, given the circumstances, and she felt almost hopeful as she padded down the hall of Sawyer's lake house toward the living area.

The sliding patio doors were open, and Sawyer was on the porch swing with Henry, a near repeat of a similar situation yesterday. Funny the difference a day made. Emma couldn't find it in her to be irritated now. A cool breeze blew off the lake, tousling her hair as she emerged onto the wide wooden planks and joined them. "Sounds like you guys are having a good time."

"We are," Sawyer answered. "We've already been down to the dock to feed the ducks and fish," he said. "Henry had a bottle and is on his third diaper. It's been a busy morning."

Emma stroked her son's cheek. "When did you learn to make bottles and change diapers?" she asked, enjoying the warm, easy smile on Sawyer's face. He looked at ease, even peaceful, holding Henry to his chest.

"YouTube," he said. "I considered asking you for instructions, but I didn't want to wake you."

"Well, that was one way to do it." Emma smiled at the sunlight winking across the water. She'd always wanted a place just like this one, and Sawyer had found one, complete with a boat dock and canoe. Now here they were, in the place they'd wanted to be, but time and circumstance had changed everything. Was there a way back for them, after all they'd been through? The electricity continually zinging in the air between them suggested there was, but was chemistry enough? She had Henry to think about now.

"I made coffee if you need a pick-me-up," Sawyer said. "Creamer's in the refrigerator if you want it."

"Thanks." She turned for the house, suddenly desperate for the caffeine.

Sawyer stood with Henry. "Why don't we make lunch and watch the twelve o'clock news? Maybe there will be coverage of Sara's disappearance. Cops can be tight-lipped, but reporters rarely are."

Emma nodded. "Good idea."

Sawyer beat her to the refrigerator and passed her the creamer. "How about BLTs?"

"Sounds good." She poured the coffee while Sawyer made the sandwiches and Henry bobbed in his portable high chair, attached to the side of Sawyer's table. She scanned the utilitarian space and smiled. Sawyer's decorating style was a clear reflection of himself. The only valuable items in sight were above the fireplace. In the event of a robbery, the television was the best a thief would do here. In case of a fire, Sawyer would go straight for the line of framed photos below the flat screen. She pulled her purse off the back of the chair and dug inside for another priceless photo and carried it to the mantel. "Do you mind?" she asked, setting the picture of her parents with her and Sara in line beside Sawyer's photos. "I took it from Sara's desk and put it in my purse for safekeeping. Luckily, that psychopath didn't get it when he took the diaper bag."

Sawyer moved into the space behind her and powered on the television. The heat from his torso warmed her chest as he reached around her. "You can put anything of yours anywhere you like around here."

She let herself lean back and rest against him a moment before returning to the kitchen. She had to stay focused. Had to remember what was at stake. Sara was missing, and that was why Sawyer was there, not to fulfill some long-suffering fantasy of Emma's. Her heart was already a mess of tattered shreds without giving in to a desire that would only leave her hollow and ruined.

Sawyer set the table, and they settled in to a quiet meal of chips and sandwiches when the local news began.

"Do you think they'll mention the break-in at my place last night?" she asked. "Or my mugging outside the credit union?" Did the whole town know what she was going through?

A woman in a gray pantsuit stood before the camera. "Here at the scene of an early-morning hit-and-run on Main Street," she began.

"A hit-and-run," Emma groaned. "What is going on in our town lately? Has everyone gone mad?"

Sawyer's eyes narrowed, but he didn't move his attention from the television. He lifted the remote and pumped the volume up to ten. "That looks like Sara's credit union in the background."

"What?" Emma set her sandwich aside and peered more closely at the flat screen over the fireplace.

"According to authorities," the reporter continued, "assistant branch manager Kate Brisbane was on her way to work this morning when a white sedan struck and threw her, leaving Kate with extensive injuries. She was taken by ambulance to Mercy General Hospital, where doctors have admitted her to the ICU for treatment and observation."

Emma covered her mouth with both hands. She'd just spoken to Kate yesterday before she was cornered outside the credit union, mugged and hit. Kate's accident couldn't have been a coincidence. Could it? She turned her gaze to Sawyer, who was still glaring at the television.

"Kate Brisbane is the one you spoke with yesterday before you were assaulted?" he asked.

"Yes."

He pushed to his feet, plate in hand. "You want to go to the hospital?" he asked. "Pretend to be family so we can talk to Kate and see if she remembers anything more than the color of the car that hit her?"

"Absolutely."

Chapter 7

Emma fought her surging emotions all the way to the hospital. The last few days were taking a toll on her both mentally and physically. Any one of the things she was experiencing would normally have been enough to keep her busy overthinking for weeks. Piling them up day after day without a moment to breath or process was making her half-ill, jittery and desperate for a break.

Sawyer watched his mirrors diligently, his gaze making a continual circuit from rearview, to sideview, to the road, then back again. She presumed the exercise was to be sure they weren't being followed, and for roughly the thousandth time since Sawyer's arrival, she was struck with overwhelming gratitude to have him there with her.

He followed the hospital signs to visitor parking

without a word, then helped her out of the truck before reaching for Henry's car seat. "Are you ready for this?" he asked.

"Not really," she admitted. She hadn't been ready for any of it, but here she was. She took Sawyer's arm as he beeped the doors locked on the truck and turned for the hospital entrance. She tried not to imagine they were a real family as passersby smiled at them. Though it was certainly a nice thought.

She let her mind slip past the reminder that this was only temporary as she stepped through the hospital's automatic doors, and she refocused on the reason they were there. Someone had tried to kill Kate this morning, and anything Kate could remember might be the key to finding Sara.

Sawyer hit the elevator button, and the doors parted. He scanned the partial list of floors and wards as Emma boarded ahead of him. She hit the number six when he stepped in behind her.

"How do you know which floor the ICU is on?" he asked.

"It's the same as Labor and Delivery," she said. "Opposite wings."

The doors parted a moment later, and Sawyer stepped out with their son. "I should have been here with you. I didn't even know."

Emma sucked down a shaky breath as they moved along the brightly lit corridor toward the ICU. "It's okay," she promised, "because now you do."

Memories of waddling down that same hallway a few short months ago rushed back to her. Water broken, doubled over in pain. It was the most beautiful and terrifying night of Emma's life. Sara had been a total mess, completely freaked-out, running ahead of Emma to clear the path and waving her arms like she was hailing a taxi. They'd both been sure that Emma might deliver Henry at any moment. They'd read all the books and still knew nothing. It had been another twelve hours before Henry made his big debut. Emma slept more than Sara that night, thanks to the blessed epidural. Sara sat vigil, reading the tabloids and retelling funny stories from their childhood when Emma had woken. She'd held Emma's hand through every contraction, been the perfect coach, a dedicated aunt and a devoted sister.

And Emma wanted her back.

She gritted her teeth against the urge to cry. She'd already cried enough these last two days to fulfill her quota for a lifetime. Instead, she hiked her chin up an inch and approached the desk with resolve. "Hello, I'm Emma Hart. I'm here to see Kate Brisbane."

The nurse gave her and Sawyer a long look. "Are you family?"

"Yes," she lied.

"Well, as I've explained to her other family members—" the nurse motioned to a waiting room full of people behind them "—Kate is still unconscious, and we're only allowing immediate family five-minute sessions. You can take a seat with your relatives, and when she's ready for another visitor, you can decide among yourselves who it will be."

Emma's cheeks warmed. She hadn't thought of all the real family members who might be there for Kate. "Thank you," she said, taking Sawyer's hand and moving into the waiting room. "Well, that didn't go the way I wanted."

Sawyer gave her fingers a squeeze.

A dozen heads turned their way. She recognized one as Detective Rosen.

The detective stood and shook the hands of the couple he'd been speaking with, then came to meet Emma and Sawyer near the doorway. "I guess you saw the morning news."

Emma raised her eyebrows. "I guess so. Were you going to contact me if I hadn't?"

"We didn't see a reason to reach out to you just yet," the detective hedged. "We're looking into Kate's accident to determine if there's a connection."

Emma barked a humorless laugh. "*If* there's a connection? There's no way this was a coincidence," she said, crossing her arms over her chest. "This happened because Sara worked with Kate, and someone probably saw me talking with her yesterday."

The detective opened his arms and stepped forward, corralling them into the hallway, away from Kate's family. "We don't know that," he whispered.

"You do know that," she countered. "First, some psychopath walks right into my home and tears Sara away, then I'm attacked outside the credit union where she works. Our home is broken into that night, and this morning Sara's assistant manager is hit by a car. You don't have to have a signed confession to know these things are all part of a bigger picture."

Sawyer angled himself in on the detective, voice low. "Have you at least matched the fingerprints or blood in Sara's room to someone yet?"

"No," Detective Rosen said flatly. "Those things take time, and as for the signed confession, it would be nice because I can't assume anything. The investigation must be based on facts for it to hold up in court, and we can't afford to play catch and release with murderers. They tend to not play nice upon release."

Emma pressed the heels of her hands to her eyes.

"What about you?" Detective Rosen asked. "Were you able to think of anything else that might help us catch whoever was in your home? Did you notice anything missing when you straightened up your sister's room?"

Emma shook her head and dropped her hands to her sides. "Not yet," she said, suddenly ashamed to admit she'd left the home right after he did. "Maybe they were looking for the notebook." She lifted her thumb to her mouth and bit into the skin along her thumbnail. "When will you hear back from your lab?"

"A few days to a couple weeks," he said, lifting a hand to stop her complaint before she had time to voice it. "Knox County doesn't have a lab. We have to send our work out, then it has to get in line behind the work of every other district in our situation." He pulled a phone from the inside pocket of his jacket. "Excuse me."

Emma frowned as the detective walked away. She turned to Sawyer, frustration stinging her nose and throat. "Can you believe this?"

He headed back for the elevator. "Let's take another look at Sara's notebook. It's the only real lead we have, and it'll keep us busy. I've sent photos of the pages to my team at Fortress. Wyatt is good with puzzles like this. Maybe we can at least figure out if the notebook is relevant."

"Okay," she agreed. She'd nearly forgotten about the notebook with everything else going on. Maybe it was nothing, but if it was something that would bring Sara home, she needed to get copies to anyone who could help.

Sawyer matched his pace to Emma's as they moved across the parking lot to his truck. She was clearly upset, and he understood why. Investigations didn't move as swiftly as they should, nothing like what was portrayed on television, and the truth was that finding Sara the old-fashioned way would be much quicker than waiting for feedback from a lab in the next county. Lucky for them, he had the men of Fortress Security at his disposal.

He beeped his truck doors unlocked, then secured a sleeping Henry inside. As much as Sawyer missed the kid's smiling face, he was glad someone could still rest. He certainly couldn't.

He slid behind the wheel, powered the windows down and waited while Emma buckled up. The warm autumn breeze fluttered her hair, sending her sweet scent over him. He gripped the wheel a little tighter in response.

"Why do you think someone tried to kill Kate?" Emma asked, gathering her hair over one shoulder.

"I don't know," he admitted. "Maybe she knew more than she let on when the two of you spoke."

Sawyer scanned the lot for signs of anyone who'd taken an interest in them. A man on a motorcycle in the next row caught his attention. His bike faced away from their truck, but he dropped his cigarette and ground it out with his boot when Sawyer started the engine.

Emma turned a guilty expression in Sawyer's direction. "Is it awful that this hit-and-run gives me hope for Sara?"

He settled back in his seat, watching to see what the motorcyclist did next. "How so?"

"Maybe the fact these horrible things keep happening is an indication that whoever took Sara is still trying to get all the evidence she has on him. I think he'll keep her alive until he's sure he's covered his tracks and collected everything against him. The night he took her, he kept asking who she'd told. 'Who did you tell? Who did you tell?'" Emma lowered her voice to something fairly menacing as she repeated the question. She rubbed her palms over the gooseflesh on her arms as she spoke. "And Kate's attack tells us something else. The man who took Sara has a partner or a team or something. You shot someone last night, and there was a lot of blood left behind for a flesh wound. I can't imagine anyone pulling off a hit-and-run only a few hours after taking a bullet like that." She looked over her shoulder at the hospital. "So there are at least two men. The one who took Sara and mugged me, and the guy who broke in last night. Do you think Detective Rosen thought to ask the hospital staff if anyone was admitted with a gunshot wound last night?"

"Yeah," Sawyer said, shifting into Drive as the motorcycle cruised out of the parking lot. "He would've reached out to them right away, and even if he didn't, hospitals have to report knife and gunshot wounds. It's the law."

Emma settled back in her seat. "Right. Good."

Sawyer took the next left and headed in the opposite direction as the motorcycle. Something about the man had put his instincts on edge, and there was little Sawyer could do about it with Emma and Henry in tow. For all he knew, the driver had intended to get his attention and draw him down a certain path where trouble awaited. On his own, Sawyer would have loved the opportunity for engagement, but for now, he needed to keep Emma and Henry safe.

"I can't stop wondering why someone would have hit Kate," Emma said. "You were right when you said she might've known more than she let on, but in what way? Was she part of the scheme all along, whatever it is? Did she become a loose end? Or did Sara confide in Kate when she hadn't confided in me? And why?"

"Maybe it wasn't like that," Sawyer suggested. "Maybe Sara stumbled across an issue at work and asked Kate about it. You said Kate told you Sara had questions. Maybe just knowing Sara's concerns was enough for the criminal to want to shut her up."

Emma pulled her lips to the side. "Maybe. I didn't ask her what Sara's questions were. I only asked how Sara had seemed the last few days, and Kate said Sara had been fine. Maybe a little tired, but she hadn't noticed anything significant or helpful."

Sawyer glanced her way. "Could she have been lying? If Sara had confided in her, then been abducted, it would make sense for her to hide what she knew. She could have reasoned that she would be taken too."

Emma bit into the skin along her thumbnail. "I should have asked her more questions."

Sawyer followed signs for the scenic byway. They could take the road through the national forest all the way back to his place without ever getting on the highway. The speed limits were much lower, but less traffic would make it easier to know if they were being followed.

His phone rang in his cup holder, and he recognized Wyatt's number immediately. He poked the speaker button to answer. "Hey," he said. "You've got me and Emma on speaker. We're in the truck headed back to the lake house now. What do you have?"

"Hey, Emma," Wyatt said, taking a minute to be cordial. "I'm real sorry you and your sister are going through all this."

Her eyes glossed with instant tears. "Thank you."

"We'll get her back," he said. "I'm working on these numbers now, and Sawyer's a force to be reckoned with on search and rescue."

Sawyer's gut wrenched at his friend's high praise. Sawyer's last search and rescue mission had gotten his team killed. "What have you learned about the numbers?" he asked.

"They're accounts, like you said, locals attached to overseas partners, I think. I want to call your cousin, Blake, at the FBI on this. He can dig deeper than I can—legally anyway—if he takes an interest, and I think he will."

"Blake's card is on my desk. If you can't find it, call his brother West. He's the sheriff over in Cade County, Kentucky."

"On it," Wyatt said. "And, Emma...congratulations on the baby. Sawyer sent me some pictures. He's handsome as a derby stallion."

Emma smiled. "Thanks." She slid her eyes Sawyer's way. "You'll have to meet him someday."

"Plan to," Wyatt said. "I'll be in touch about these numbers."

Sawyer disconnected and turned his attention back to the road. "I sent a few pictures of Henry to the team when I sent the notebook scans."

Emma's smile grew. "Good."

The road through the national forest was winding and peaceful, a stark contrast to their lives. Lush foliage on either side masked the brilliant blue sky overhead, but shafts of determined sunlight filtered between the leaves and branches to create a marvelous display on the blacktop stretching uphill before them. Sawyer had been to a lot of places around the world, but there was no place more beautiful than this. Tennessee had always had everything he needed. *At the moment*, he thought, glancing through his cab, he had everything he needed right there in his truck.

Henry fussed, and Emma twisted in her seat to reassure him.

"Sawyer?" she said softly, turning forward as the truck floated around another downhill curve. "Did you notice the motorcycle at the hospital?"

"Yes," he said. "Why?" His gaze flicked to his rearview mirror and found the answer. A black motorcycle with a rider in matching helmet and gear blinked into view, then vanished behind the curve of the mountain as the winding road carried them steeply down.

"It's him, isn't it?" she asked.

Sawyer didn't answer. He couldn't be sure at that distance, but his gut said it was the same man. "I'll let him pass on the next straight stretch," he said. "We'll get the number on the license plate and contact Detective Rosen." Even if the rider's reappearance was nothing, it was worth a phone call to be sure.

Sawyer pressed the brake gently, reducing his speed

around the next sweeping curve. The pedal was softer than before, working, but not quite right.

The motorcycle drew nearer, its pint-size Alabama plate clearly visible now.

The road straightened before them, and Sawyer powered his window down, reaching an arm out and waving the man around as he continued to slow.

The motorcycle fell back.

"What's he doing?" Emma asked, voice quaking.

"I don't know." Sawyer stepped on the gas as they headed up the next hill. "Give Detective Rosen a call. Maybe they can run the plate. Tell him we'll get turned around and head over to the station. I don't like this."

Emma dug her phone from her pocket.

Sawyer crested the next hill and began the sharp decline on the other side. There was a wide lookout and parking lot with multiple trailheads at the base of the hill. It would be a good place to turn and head back before their tail figured out they were staying in the next county and not just out to enjoy the scenic drive. It would also give Sawyer a chance to look at his spongy brakes.

"That's right," Emma said, describing the situation into her phone. She unfastened her seat belt and turned onto her knees to stare through the back window. "Sawyer, slow down a little more. I can't read the numbers on his plate."

Sawyer added pressure to the pedal, and it slid easily down. Alarm shot through his system and a curse slipped between his lips. The brakes were out. The motorcycle wasn't tailing them. He was monitoring them. He'd probably cut the brake lines at the hospital and was watching to see the efforts pay off.

"Emma," he said, eyes widening as a huge camper trailer headed up the mountain in their direction, barely between the narrow curving lines. "Turn around." He hugged the mountain on his right, looking for a way to slow them down, even as the grade of the road seemed to steepen.

Henry gave a small cry in complaint, and Sawyer's heart constricted further. "Emma," he growled this time. "Turn around," he ordered. "Buckle up."

"I can almost read the plate," she said.

Sawyer took the next bend at nearly fifty miles per hour. The sign had suggested thirty-five.

Emma fell against the door, thrown off balance by the speed of the turn. "Slow down," she snapped, fumbling for her seat belt.

"I can't." Sawyer ground the words out. He adjusted his white-knuckle grip on the steering wheel and pressed the limp brake pedal into the floorboards. "My brakes are out."

"What? How?"

He pulled the shifter down from Drive, dropping it into a lower gear. The engine growled in protest. "I think someone punctured the line at the hospital. The brakes were fine when we left, but every time I've depressed the pedal since then, I've been pumping brake fluid onto the ground. Now we're out."

She covered her mouth with one hand, and Sawyer knew she understood what they were facing. She relayed the situation to Detective Rosen in sharp gasps, voice cracking and breaking on each desperate word.

The road plateaued slightly before taking another downward turn. Sawyer pulled the shifter again, moving it into the lowest gear. The engine revved and groaned, shooting the rpm gauge into the red.

Before them, a line of cars plugged away behind a slow-moving school bus. *Beep! Beep! Beep!* He jammed his thumb against his emergency flashers and continued a battering assault on his horn. Silently swearing and begging the drivers to get the message. His truck was out of control, and if they didn't move, he was going to take them all out with him.

The cars veered sharply, one by one, skidding into the soft shoulder against the hillside on the right as Sawyer's truck barreled past. A thick plume of dust lifted into the air as the vehicles skidded to a stop.

The school bus continued on.

Henry cried in the seat behind Sawyer, probably startled half to death by the blaring horn. His protests grew steadily more fervent as the truck closed in on the school bus. Tiny horrified faces came into view, staring back at him through the dusty emergency exit.

The road curved again, and the bus's brake lights came on.

Sawyer yanked the emergency brake and the truck made a horrendous sound. Dark, acrid smoke clouded the air outside his window, filtering through his vents and causing Emma to cough, but the truck didn't stop.

With no other choice to make, Sawyer gritted his teeth and resolved to leave the road at any cost. Whatever he hit, short of a hiker, would be better than the bus full of children or careening over the mountainside. He held his position between the lines as he took the plunging curve around the mountain, seeking the first semilevel place to exit and slow his runaway vehicle.

At first sight of a trailhead around the bend, he

pulled hard on the wheel. The truck slipped beside the school bus and over the rough, rocky berm with a deep guttural roar. The school bus swerved over the yellow line, and the pickup tore off-road completely, cutting a wild path through the miniature parking lot at the trailhead and taking a wooden sign with the location's official name down with it. The windshield cracked as the wood splintered and deflected off it.

Beside him, Emma threw her hands out as if the windshield might burst, and she screamed loud enough to chill Sawyer's blood.

Outside, people screamed and ran. They yanked babies from strollers and lifted children from the grass, launching their families against the tree-covered hillside. A mass of children in matching T-shirts fled a pavilion beyond the lot, and Sawyer directed his truck toward the newly emptied structure, hoping the slight uphill grade and a series of small collisions could safely slow the vehicle.

One by one, the picnic tables exploded under the impact of his truck's grille. One by one, the damage lessened until the little table and the hill brought his truck to a whiplashing stop.

In the parking lot behind them, a black motorcycle cruised calmly past.

Chapter 8

Sawyer met the police and paramedics in the parking lot and directed them to where Emma and Henry sat on the grass. The path of destruction from the main road to the grassy bank opposite the pavilion was broad and littered with the fragments of state-donated picnic seating. Miraculously, no one had been killed, unless Sawyer counted the trailhead sign, row of picnic tables and his truck.

Detective Rosen joined them several minutes later, having stopped to speak with a number of witnesses and onlookers. "Are you all okay?" he asked, turning his eyes to the paramedic as he walked away.

"Yes, just shaken," Emma said, speaking for them all. "What did you learn?" She tipped her head to indicate the crowd behind them while Henry slept soundly in her arms.

"The Alabama plate was bogus," Detective Rosen said. "A bystander caught the motorcycle on video while taping your out-of-control truck. My guys ran the numbers, but that plate hasn't been in use in a decade. Probably thrown out and picked up by someone."

Sawyer lowered himself onto the grass beside Emma and looped a protective arm across her back.

She leaned against him, deflated, and said, "So even with a license plate number, a description of the vehicle and a hundred witnesses, we still don't know who did this?"

"Sadly, no."

Sawyer gave her a gentle squeeze. "What else do you know?"

"We know the truck's brakes were definitely tampered with," Detective Rosen said.

Emma huffed a disgusted sigh, then pushed onto her feet with Henry in her arms. "I need a minute," she said, walking away.

Sawyer raised a brow at the detective. He stood and dusted his palms against his pants. "You need to figure this out," he said. "Half those kids probably caught the whole thing on video with their cell phones."

"They did," Detective Rosen said, "and we'll review every frame, but the motorcyclist was in head-to-toe black. No one knows what he looks like under the gear, and we don't have a plate for the vehicle. We're doing what we can with what we have to work with, which isn't much."

"What about the hospital parking lot?" Sawyer asked. "My brakes were fine when I left. Then they got spongy and went out before I realized what was happening. The guy on the bike was there when we left. I think he might've punctured the lines while we were inside, so I wouldn't know what happened until it was too late. If you review the security feed from the cameras in that lot, you'll find him."

"We can try," he said, pulling a cell phone from his pocket. "But you should know the cameras outside the credit union, which would have been useful in identifying Emma's mugger or the hit-and-run driver, were out. I don't think it's a coincidence."

Sawyer tipped his head back and shut his eyes for a moment. "That's because it's not. These crimes were all planned. It's not good news for the police, or the victims."

"Mr. Lance?"

Sawyer opened his eyes. The tow truck operator lumbered in his direction. "Where do you want the truck taken?"

Sawyer eyeballed the extended cab of the logoed vehicle. "Wherever you recommend," he said. "Would you mind taking us to a local car rental company on the way?"

Two hours later Sawyer steered a rented SUV home from the police station, using the flattest and most low-trafficked route possible between counties. He'd rented the new vehicle under his company's name and given Fortress Security's address in case anyone tried to track him through the rental.

Sawyer's rustic A-frame house came into view through the trees, and he felt his shoulders relax.

He went straight to the kitchen for two glasses of ice water, and Emma curled onto the couch with Henry on her lap. She accepted the ice water with deep, thirsty gulps, but the fear and uncertainty in her eyes broke Sawyer's heart. He'd vowed to protect her and their son at all costs, but they'd nearly died at his hand today.

Sawyer brought up the photos of Sara's notebook on his phone as he made his way to the living room. He needed to put a name to their assailant before someone came at them again. He had a duty to protect Henry and Emma, *his son and his...* The thought twisted into a painful knot. Henry was his son, but Emma wasn't *his* anything anymore.

He hated that truth nearly as much as he hated the man who kept trying to hurt her.

Emma pulled her feet beneath her on the couch and turned wide blue eyes on Sawyer. "If the motorcyclist knew your truck, then he must know your name."

"Not necessarily," Sawyer said, determined to keep his cool.

"If he knows your name, he can find your address," she said. "He can find Henry."

Sawyer shook his head and offered her his hand. "It won't be easy," he said. "My truck, like my house, is registered to the company."

"But the company has a website," she said. "The website has a list of the Fortress team members' names. *Your name,*" she said.

"I will protect you," he said. "This looks dire now, but it will be okay. I'm sure of it." And he intended to do anything he could to keep that promise.

The fire in Emma's eyes dimmed, and she shook her head in a look of resignation. "He'll find us again, Sawyer. He won't stop, and it's only a matter of time."

Sawyer took a seat at her side. He wanted to encourage and reassure her, but he was having trouble believing she was wrong. Instead, he held his phone between them, a photo from Sara's notebook on the screen. "Then we'd better find him before he finds us."

Emma analyzed the notebook pages late into the night, but nothing had changed. The numbers were still too long to be account numbers from Sara's credit union. Emma had already compared her fourteen-digit account number to the massive thirty-digit ones in the notebook. There was definitely more to the number-cluttered pages than just account numbers. She only wished she had a guess about what that might be.

Emma padded softly into the kitchen for another glass of water. Henry was fast asleep in his portable crib, and she'd already showered and changed into her favorite cotton shorts and tank top after dinner. If things went well for a change, Emma might get comfortable enough to fall asleep soon. The stress was taking a toll, and she needed the break. As it was, there was no way to release the ever-mounting tension, but a little rest could go a long way to taking the edge off, and that was what she needed most. She'd considered a jog along the lake earlier, or even a swim, but knowing a psychopath could pop up anywhere at any time had kept her close to her baby. Sadly, there would be no burning off steam for Emma until the nightmare was over. Assuming she survived at all.

The soft snick of an opening door put Emma's senses on alert. She stepped away from the countertop and leaned around the kitchen doorway for a look down the short hall. Scents of shampoo and body wash wafted out of the open bathroom door on a cloud of steamy air.

Emma's body tensed for new reasons as Sawyer moved into view. He pulled a black Fortress Security T-shirt over damp, rosy skin, still hot and beaded with water from the shower. His wet hair dripped over his temples and onto his broad, muscled shoulders.

She forced her mouth closed with effort.

"Sorry it took so long," he said, a look of profound guilt on his handsome face. "I was trying to decide if I should shave." He ran a broad palm over the dark two-day stubble, and Emma's knees went soft with an onslaught of memories. She'd intimately enjoyed Sawyer's stubble in the past. She knew firsthand about the rash it left on the tender flesh of her breasts and inner thighs when rubbed just right.

"I like the stubble," she said a bit breathlessly.

Sawyer's brows rose, and a sly grin slid over his handsome face. "That so?"

"Mmm-hmm." She cleared her throat and pressed a palm over her racing heart to calm the climbing beat.

Sawyer kept smiling.

"What?" she asked, pressing the glass of ice water to her lips before she lost control and kissed him again, the way she had the night before. *No*, she thought. She wouldn't kiss him like that again. That had been a chaste kiss on the cheek. Not even close to the way she longed to kiss or touch him. Emma swallowed hard and set the drink aside before she dropped it.

"You know," Sawyer began, closing in on her with intense brooding eyes, "we never really talked about the fact you kissed me last night."

Heat rose in her chest and cheeks at the reminder. Her gaze lingered on his lips. "It was a friendly, appropriate, completely innocent gesture," she said, hating the quaver in her voice.

"Why'd you do it?" he asked.

Emma struggled to swallow. Her chin hitched upward. "What do you mean?" She crossed her arms over her chest to protect her heart.

Sawyer took another step in her direction and reached for her, unfolding her arms and resting his broad palms against the curves of her waist. "Why'd you do it?" he asked again, widening his stance to plant one foot on either side of hers, pinning her against the countertop with his stare and the weight of his body.

Emma gripped his arms for balance, enjoying the heat and strength of him. "I missed kissing you," she whispered, unable to catch her breath. "I miss *you* and it makes it hard not to touch you."

Sawyer raised his hands slowly up her sides, grazing her ribs with his fingers, the sides of her breasts with his thumbs, then cradling her face between his palms, careful to avoid the darkening bruise along her cheek. "I missed you too," he whispered. The clean scents of toothpaste and mouthwash teased her senses for a heartbeat before Sawyer took her mouth with practiced skill.

He kissed her as perfectly as he had a thousand times before, and she curled herself around him in response. The taste of him on her lips pulled a greedy, exhilarating moan from her core, and she drank him in, enjoying the release much more than any evening jog.

She ignored the little voice in her head reminding her that a jog wouldn't break her heart when it was over.

Chapter 9

Emma watched the sunrise over the lake, her legs draped over Sawyer's lap on his back-porch swing. They'd kissed until she was sure the burning need for more would turn her brain to ash, then she'd slipped away to gather her wits. The kiss had been enough for now, considering the excruciatingly complicated circumstances.

He'd found her on the porch swing, kissed her head and settled in at her side, pulling her legs over his and resting her feet on the cushion beside him.

"I think we should talk to the branch manager," she told Sawyer as the fiery sun finally lifted into the sky. "When I was at the credit union gathering the things from Sara's desk, Kate told me Sara had a bunch of questions for Mr. Harrison. Maybe her questions were related to whatever's going on here. Maybe he's part of this."

Sawyer stroked the backs of his fingers down her arm. "I'll give Detective Rosen a call."

"No." She pulled her legs away and planted her feet on the floor. "We can call Detective Rosen afterward, especially if Mr. Harrison says anything useful, but I want to talk to him without the detective there. Besides, the police have already questioned the credit union staff. Maybe he'll be less on guard speaking to someone without a badge. He knows me, and maybe he knows something that can help me find Sara."

Sawyer frowned. "I understand why you want to go. I just wish you wouldn't."

Emma pursed her lips, prepared to fight as long and hard as necessary to get her way on this. "It wasn't a request for permission."

His lips quirked, apparently tempted to smile but thinking better of it. "Two women at that credit union have already been hurt. If it was up to me, I'd keep you in my pocket until the danger passed. Or book us a room at one of those all-inclusive resorts under assumed identities so we could sleep with both eyes closed for a night or two."

Emma's heart sputtered. "I can't leave Sara," she said. "I won't."

Sawyer tucked flyaway hair behind her ear. "I know. I was just enjoying a daydream where I know you're safe."

She smiled. "Then you'll take me to the credit union when it opens?"

He tipped his head over one shoulder and released a heavy sigh. "The manager is a significant link between Kate and Sara, so it's worth a conversation. I just don't know if it's a good idea to cross his path. Like you said, he might know something, or he might be the one behind all this."

"That's exactly why we need to talk to him."

Traffic was light on the way to the credit union. At nine fifteen, the school buses had already delivered the students, most office workers were at their desks and lunch hour was another two hours away. Sawyer parked the rented SUV across the street at the end of the block, and went to join Emma on her side of the vehicle.

Henry was bright-eyed and smiling as she tucked him snugly into a thick circle of fabric hung over one shoulder and across her body. He looked like a purse with a pacifier, and it made Sawyer smile.

"Are you sure you don't need to hold on to him?" he asked.

Emma shot him a sharp look.

He raised his palms.

A few moments later he opened the credit union door for her, still eyeballing the strange circle of fabric. "Will that thing fit me?"

"I doubt it," she said. "A lady at church measured me for it, but Henry's also got a backpack he enjoys. That's one size fits all."

"You put him in a backpack?" Sawyer frowned. "Whatever happened to just carrying your kid?"

"Baby slings and backpacks keep your hands free," she answered softly. "Not everyone has someone to help carry the baby *and* haul their groceries or unlock the car door or pay the cashier."

The words tightened Sawyer's core. Emma had

needed help with those things, and help hadn't been there. *He* hadn't been there.

"Emma," a maternal voice cooed. A woman with a round face and salt-and-pepper hair motioned them to the transaction counter. "Come on over here and let me see that little man," she said.

Emma obliged with a smile. "How are you, Gladys?"

"Better than you, it seems." She frowned at the angry bruise on Emma's pretty face. "I heard about your mugging, the break-in. Sara, then poor Kate. It's a darn shame. Things are all but sideways around here lately. If there's anything I can do to help you, just ask. I can cook, clean, babysit. Whatever you need. I've already been praying night and day."

"Thank you," Emma said, wrapping her arms around Henry, something Sawyer had noticed her doing anytime she looked uneasy or afraid.

Henry kicked and stretched, discontent at standing still, Sawyer suspected.

"Here." Sawyer reached for his son. "I can take him. You can visit."

Gladys watched, wide-eyed, as Emma passed the baby to him. "Well, now I think you've forgotten to introduce me to someone important here. You never let anyone hold that baby."

Sawyer gathered his son high on his chest and kissed his cheeks.

"Gladys," Emma said, "this is Sawyer Lance."

Gladys sucked air. "The daddy."

Sawyer extended a hand in her direction. "Yes, ma'am."

Her smile grew as they shook. "I've been praying

for you too," she said. "These two have needed you something fierce."

"I've needed them too," he said, releasing Gladys's hand and pulling Emma against his side.

Gladys pressed her hands to her chest.

An elderly couple came to stand in line behind Sawyer.

"Well," Emma said, "we'd better get out of your way so you can work. Is Mr. Harrison in his office?"

Gladys dipped her head and lowered her voice. "No. He didn't come in today, and as far as I know he didn't call off. Instead, we've got that one." She pointed to the office where a vaguely familiar face sat behind the desk, staring at the computer. "His name is Christopher something or other from our corporate office."

Sawyer moved out of the way, and Emma followed.

"Thank you," Emma told Gladys before turning her back to the woman and trapping Sawyer in her sharp gaze. "Why do you think Mr. Harrison isn't here?" she asked. "And where do you think he is?"

Those were very good questions. "Let's see if Christopher from corporate knows," he suggested.

The tall blond man at the manager's desk stood when he noticed their approach. He met them outside the office and pulled the door shut behind him. "Good morning," he said. "What can I do for such a fine-looking family this morning?" His name tag proclaimed the words *Christopher Lawson*, and his clothes said he knew how to pick them. All quality, neat as a pin and fashionable down to his tassel-topped loafers.

Emma offered him a polite smile. "We were just looking for Mr. Harrison," she said. "We always say hello when we're in the neighborhood."

Christopher crossed long arms over a narrow chest and widened his lanky stance. "Well, I'm happy to pass the message on, but Mr. Harrison's not in today."

"Shame," Emma said, dropping the smile. "Is he ill?"

Christopher shrugged, curious blue eyes twinkling. "Hard to say. Is there anything I can help you with?"

"No." Emma slid her hand into Sawyer's. "I guess we'll have to stop back the next time we're in the area." She swung Sawyer toward the door and nearly dragged him outside.

They crossed the street at the corner before speaking. Sawyer repositioned Henry in his arms and unlocked the SUV doors. "What do you think?" he asked. "Is Mr. Harrison sick or halfway to Aruba?"

Emma frowned. "Maybe, but if he's the one who took Sara and he's leaving the country, then what happens to my sister?"

Sawyer didn't want to answer that. He buckled Henry into his car seat, then went around to climb behind the wheel. "What did you think of Christopher?"

"I don't know," she said. "He was strangely familiar, but I don't think we'd ever met, if that makes any sense."

Sawyer buckled up and checked his mirrors before pulling into traffic. "Any idea where Mr. Harrison lives? Maybe the best way to find out why he's not at work is to ask him ourselves."

Emma tapped the screen of her phone. "I might have his address," she said. "The office Christmas party was at his house a couple years ago, and the invitation was digital." She paused to look at Sawyer. "Maybe that's how I recognize Christopher. There were a few folks from corporate at the party."

"Which way?" Sawyer asked.

Emma called out the turns through town as Sawyer manned the wheel. Thirty minutes later they arrived at an upscale parklike neighborhood, befitting a middle-aged banker. "I think his house is the brick one-story at the end of the road," she said. "I remember parking in the back. There's a big concrete area outside a giant garage and a pool."

"Here?" Sawyer asked as they motored slowly toward the brick home. A cluster of people stood on the sidewalk across the street as Sawyer turned the corner toward the rear parking area Emma had described. Emergency vehicles came into view.

"What on earth?" Emma sat forward. "That's Detective Rosen's car. Do you think the manager has been keeping Sara here all along? Could they have found her? Why wouldn't the police have contacted me?"

Sawyer shifted into Park, and Emma leaped out. He unfastened a sleeping Henry from the seat behind his and took his time following Emma through the crowd.

A pair of older women smiled at Henry, and Sawyer slowed to let them admire the baby.

"Hello," he said cordially. "Do you have any idea what's going on here? We were just on our way over for a visit."

"Oh, dear," the woman on the right said softly. "I'm so sorry."

Sawyer raised his brows. "About?"

"I was walking Mr. Bootsy after breakfast, and I heard a terrible calamity coming from inside the house," she said. "I didn't want to seem as if I was being nosy, so we crossed the street, but then there was a loud blast, like a gunshot. I ran right home and called the police after that."

"Sawyer." Emma's voice turned his head in her direction. The horror in her eyes set his feet into a jog.

Beside her, a pair of EMTs guided a gurney toward the home, a folded body bag on top.

Chapter 10

Sawyer cut through the crowd to Emma's side. He wrapped his arm around her and pulled her against his chest, practically reading her mind. "The bag's not for Sara," he said, leaning his mouth to Emma's ear. "It's most likely for Mr. Harrison."

Emma swallowed hard as she looked up at him, her breaths coming far too shallowly. She looked to Henry, and Sawyer passed the baby into her arms. Emma snuggled him to her chest and nuzzled him tenderly. Her gaze trailed the gurney with the body bag on its path to the house. "How can you be sure?"

Sawyer took Emma's trembling hand. "Come on," he said, giving her fingers a tug. He pulled her away from the crowd and through the front yard instead. "Neighbors heard a commotion this morning." He caught Emma's eye as they approached Mr. Harrison's porch. Sawyer climbed the steps, silently towing Emma along with him. "My guess is that Mr. Harrison figured out what Sara was onto with all those questions before her abduction, and he asked the wrong person about it. That or the man who took her found out she'd taken her concerns to Mr. Harrison. Either way, I'm sure he was the fatality here."

"We don't know he's dead," Emma said.

Sawyer tipped his head briefly to each shoulder. "This is his house, and we saw the body bag."

Emma sighed. "We should talk to Detective Rosen."

Sawyer peered through one of the front windows before moving onto the next. "I'm looking for him." He tried the door and a second window, then went back down the steps and around the opposite side of the house with Emma in his wake.

A row of flowering trees and bushes cast long shadows over the side yard, making their movement across the lawn less noticeable to traffic and onlookers. "Here," he whispered, motioning her closer. "Listen."

The curtains were drawn on the next window, but a number of male voices warbled inside. Sawyer adjusted his position for a look through the slight part in heavy linen panels. From his new vantage, he could see the reason for the crowd and emergency responders as well as the body bag.

Mr. Harrison was splayed over a desk in what appeared to be a home office, a handgun near his limp hand and a bullet wound at his temple.

Sawyer stepped back to make room for Emma, who slid into the small space before him.

She rose to her toes to see above the sill, then fell

back with a gasp. "He killed himself," she whispered. "Why would he do that?"

Sawyer braced his palms on her waist, steadying her, then took her hand and finished the circle around Mr. Harrison's home. They crossed the small courtyard by the swimming pool and emergency vehicles, and let themselves into the kitchen.

Detective Rosen stood inside, rubbing his chin with one hand and speaking quietly to an EMT. He started at Sawyer and Emma's appearance. "What are you doing here?" he asked, skipping the pleasantries.

"Door was open," Sawyer said. "What about you?" He moved farther into the room, getting a better look at the crime scene. It took only a minute to know his gut was right. Mr. Harrison hadn't committed suicide.

The detective frowned. "I'm a cop. I belong here. It's your appearance I'm concerned about."

Emma moved between them, positioning her back to the open office door where Mr. Harrison lay. "We were at the credit union this morning, and the man taking Mr. Harrison's place said he hadn't shown up or called off today."

"So you rushed right over?" the detective asked dryly.

Emma swallowed long and loud. "I thought his absence might have something to do with Sara's disappearance."

"Murder would also explain his failure to call off or show up," Sawyer said.

Detective Rosen lifted his brow. "Murder?"

Sawyer stepped forward. "That's why you're here, isn't it?" He turned to face the office. "First responders probably noticed the angle of the wound is wrong for a suicide. Whoever held the gun before leaving it on the desk beside the victim's hand was standing over him. Mr. Harrison was shot at close range, but there are no muzzle burns around the wound. Most suicide victims press the barrel to their skin to ensure they get the job done." Sawyer had seen it firsthand, and more often than he cared to recall during his time in service. "Furthermore, the gun is beside his right hand, but his desk phone, mouse, pens and coffee mug are on his left, suggesting Mr. Harrison was left-handed."

Detective Rosen sucked his teeth but didn't argue. "There are no signs of forced entry," he said, casting a look at the kitchen door, where Emma stood with Henry, looking more than ready to leave.

Sawyer nodded. He'd noticed that too. "He knew the killer, or he had another reason to open the door to him. Someone posing as a utility worker, salesman, new neighbor…looking for a lost dog, could've been anything."

Detective Rosen rubbed his chin again. "The crime scene team is coming to check for prints." He opened his arms the way he had at the hospital and stepped toward the door, herding Sawyer back to Emma, then outside.

"Wait," Emma said, stepping out into the sun. "Could Sara have been here?"

"No." Detective Rosen shook his head. "There are no signs that anyone other than Mr. Harrison had been living here. Now, kindly remove yourselves from the property. Civilians aren't permitted at a crime scene."

Emma's skin crawled with tension and grief as they moved away from the home. Back through the shaded yard and past the window where she'd seen Mr. Harrison's body. The image of him slumped over his desk would never be completely erased from her mind.

"Hey." Sawyer's palm found the small of her back.

A thick bout of nausea and panic rose through her core to her throat. "Take Henry," she said, fighting the terrible sensation and passing the baby to his father.

Sawyer pulled Henry to his chest, and Emma bent forward at the waist, huffing for air and hoping not to be sick on Mr. Harrison's lawn. She counted slowly, forcing her lungs to take bigger and deeper gulps of air despite the burn in her constricted throat with each pull.

Sawyer leaned her against him and rubbed her back. "It's okay. Take your time."

A few moments later her knees were weak, but the black dots in her vision had cleared. She straightened her spine and squared her shoulders with feeble resolve. "Sorry."

"Don't be," Sawyer said.

Emma pursed her lips. A thousand horrific thoughts cluttered her frightened mind. "What if we find Sara like that soon?"

"No," he said. "Sara's smart. She's cautious, and she's a fighter. I'm sure that whoever has her is no competition for her will to get back to you. We just have to figure out where she is."

Emma hoped he was right. Sara was strong, but maybe her captor was stronger. Maybe her physical injuries had weakened her mental ability to stay focused and fight. "I've been praying that she'll escape," Emma said, stepping back into the sunlight of the front yard, "but she was in bad shape. You should've seen the blood on our living room floor. The way he choked her and climbed on her. The sound when he hit her." Emma's teeth began to chatter despite the morning's heat.

Sawyer helped her into the SUV and fastened her seat belt for her before shutting the door.

She watched as he did the same for Henry, then climbed behind the wheel.

"What?" he asked, reaching for the ignition and checking his mirrors.

Emma unbuckled and slid across the bench to him. She pulled herself against his side and buried her face in the warm curve of his neck. She gripped the strong muscles of his shoulder and breathed him in until her racing heartbeat slowed to the steady confident pace of his. "This lunatic hit Kate with a car and shot Mr. Harrison. What's he going to do to Sara?"

Sawyer pulled her onto his lap and cradled her in his arms, sliding the seat back gently to make room. "Sara's going to be okay," he whispered into her hair, "and so are you."

It had been a long time since Emma let someone else carry her burdens for her. Not since losing her parents had she truly let her guard down, and even then she shared the pain with Sara. Sitting there now, curled in Sawyer's arms made her dream of a life where she could trade off the work of being strong from time to time. Sawyer had been gone for a year, but he was back now. He was there with her and Henry, and maybe she couldn't make him stay, but she could make sure he knew that was what she wanted. That her heart had been torn open all over again at the sight of him, and only his enduring presence would heal her.

Sawyer's rough palm brushed the soft skin of her

cheek. He tucked strong fingers beneath her chin and searched her face with soulful blue eyes. "What are you thinking?"

"I don't know what I'd do without you," she whispered.

Sawyer lowered his mouth to hers and kissed her gently before resting his cheek against the top of her head. "I hope you'll never again find out."

Emma agreed, and tonight she'd make sure Sawyer understood just how much she wanted him to stay.

Chapter 11

Sawyer held Emma's hand as they drove back through town. He stroked her fingers with the pad of his thumb and imagined a life where the three of them—Emma, Henry and himself—could spend days together doing whatever they wanted and getting to know one another, not haunting crime scenes in search of stolen loved ones and debating murder versus suicide. He struggled to keep his eyes on the road and off the people inside the SUV. He needed to protect them at all costs and find Emma's sister, but he wasn't sure what to do next. His team members were on other assignments, and already working the numbers from Sara's notebook in their spare time. Sawyer was supposed to be the man on call. The extra hands. But he'd gotten this call, and everything had changed. His jaw tightened and his grip on the wheel intensified. Keeping

Emma and Henry safe made it impossible to go out on his own, and while there were some situations where a young family moved inconspicuously, the places he wanted to go would be dangerous for him alone, and he refused to be the reason Emma was ever frightened again.

If it was up to him, Sawyer would lock up Emma and Henry safely somewhere, maybe even back at Fortress Security with a few armed and trained bodyguards, then Sawyer would return to Emma's town. He'd start at the local pool halls and bars, asking anyone who'd had enough alcohol to loosen their lips if they'd heard about the missing woman or the hit-and-run. Surely in a community as small as Emma's all the thugs and lowlifes knew one another. Someone had surely bragged about the money they were going to come into. Someone would buy one too many rounds on him. There was jealousy among thieves, and Sawyer was sure he could find a lead the police couldn't if only he could divide himself in two to get to it. He gave Emma another long look, then glanced at Henry's sleeping face in the rearview mirror. They weren't officially his family yet, but he was willing to do anything in his power to make it that way, if Emma would have him.

She turned to face him at the stoplight, as if she'd somehow heard her name in his mind. "Can we stop at my place before we go back to yours?" she asked. "I'd like to pack some more of my things and what's left of Henry's. Maybe even bring his crib." The words were music to Sawyer's ears, but he hated the uncertainty he heard in them. Had he given her some reason to think he wouldn't be thrilled at the suggestion? Had their late-night make-out session not conveyed the fact that he wanted nothing more than to be with her, and with Henry, every day?

She watched him with an uplifted brow.

"All right," he said finally, simply. But he needed to do better. He needed to make his intentions crystal clear so there would be no room for misunderstanding. *Sooner rather than later*, he thought, *before anything else can go wrong.* There were already enough complications between them. "Why don't we stop by the outlets and buy a crib for my place?" Sawyer suggested. "There's no sense in hauling one back and forth when I need one now too."

"What?" Her narrow brows hunkered low between her eyes. "Why?"

"I want to spend as much time with Henry as possible now that I know he exists. It makes sense for him to have a room at my place too."

Emma's expression went flat, and she turned forward once more. "Okay."

"What?" Sawyer asked, taking the next right toward Emma's home. Clearly they weren't going shopping.

She bit into the skin along her thumbnail. "Nothing, it's fine."

Sawyer gave a dark chuckle. He hadn't been gone nearly long enough to have forgotten what *fine* meant. It meant she was mad, and for no good reason as far as he could tell.

She made a little fist and tucked her bitten thumb inside it, still forcing her attention outside as they took the final turn onto her long rural street.

He worked his jaw, determined to let her be mad about nothing. Except, she shouldn't be mad. She should be glad he wanted to be with his son as much as possible. Shouldn't she? Wasn't that the good, honorable and *right* thing to want? He squinted across the seat at her. "What's wrong?"

"Nothing."

Sawyer cut the engine in her driveway and turned toward her, throwing one arm over the seat back beside him. "Nope."

Emma's cheeks reddened. "Yep," she said, sliding out onto the gravel and shutting the door behind her. Hard.

Sawyer climbed out and met her at Henry's door, where she unlatched his car seat from the base. He considered taking the heavy carrier from her or at least offering to carry it, but Emma was upset, and he'd learned quickly that she kept Henry close at times like these. *Even if she was mad about nothing.*

He followed them to the front door and outstretched a hand, offering to hold the carrier while she dug for her key.

She hooked the seat in the crook of her arm and handled everything herself. A moment later she pointed her key at the lock and froze. She backed up a step and looked at Sawyer. "It's unlocked."

The frustration he'd felt toward her unexplained attitude bled away, and every instinct he had steeled him to defend her. He motioned Emma behind him as he turned the knob. She hurriedly obeyed.

The door swung easily inward, and Sawyer cursed. She was right. Someone had been there, and the house screamed with the evidence. He pulled his weapon and reached for Emma with his free hand, pulling her and Henry close behind him.

The house was in utter disarray. Every item in sight had been turned upside down. Someone was desperate to find something. *The thing that he had broken into Sara's room to find*, Sawyer thought. A good sign that whatever Sara had on this guy was still in play. A good sign because her life likely depended on that.

Sawyer ached to prowl through the upended room and shoot today's intruder the way he'd shot the last, but his legs locked and his muscles froze before he reached the center of the living room. He couldn't take his family one step farther into a potential ambush, and he couldn't send them out of his sight to wait. He stepped back, urging Emma onto the porch, then rushing her down the steps beside him to the SUV, where he locked them all inside and started the engine in case they needed to make a fast retreat.

His muscles ached to pounce on the man who'd done this, but that would have to wait. Right now, he had his family to think of.

The police arrived within minutes of Emma's call to Detective Rosen. He came later, having been caught up at Mr. Harrison's murder scene. Comparatively, she supposed Mr. Harrison's situation had probably seemed more pressing, but she disagreed. She and Henry were still alive, still in danger, and finding out who kept coming at them seemed paramount to finding out who'd killed a man after the fact. Maybe if the police got to the bottom of her situation now, she and Henry would never end up like… Emma's stomach coiled at the thought of Mr. Harrison's fate becoming Henry's.

Emma took Henry to the rocker in the living room as men and women in uniforms began showing up in pairs. It was both profoundly tragic and strangely reassuring that the faces were becoming familiar to her. She'd seen them all at least once these last few days, some after Sara's abduction, others after her own mugging, the first break-in or the runaway truck scenario. The small-town police force was only so big, and now she'd met them all, or at least it seemed that way. Thankfully, they all knew that this was part of a complex ongoing investigation, and Emma hadn't had to repeat any information for them. She wasn't sure she could without bringing on an emotional breakdown, and there was no time for that.

She kept Henry close, singing softly and stroking his hair and cheek until he grew tired of watching the crowd and he dozed in her arms. Henry was her life now, and keeping him close to her heart seemed to be the only thing keeping her from losing her mind. As long as Henry was safe, everything else would be too.

Even if her mother's dishes were shattered and the bookshelves her father had made her on her tenth birthday were ruined. Even if every sweet memory she'd made before her parents' deaths were slowly being chipped away and ruined by one murderous psychopath...

If Henry was okay, Emma would be okay too.

Emma tried not to think about the scene before her. She didn't let her gaze or mind settle on the woman dusting her door for prints or the photographer snapping shots of her destroyed things. They were just *things*. But her stomach clenched at the sight of her framed photos scattered on the ground, some torn from the frames. Photos of her parents. Photos of Henry. Images of her and Sara through the years. How could she go on in a life without Sara? Emma wasn't even sure who she was without her for context. They were best friends. Confidantes. *Sisters.*

Sawyer walked into the room, instantly pulling her jangled nerves together. Something about his presence had a way of doing that. Calming her. He'd stuck to Detective Rosen's side after his arrival, talking, listening and occasionally making calls. She admired Sawyer's unwavering confidence under fire. Ironically, of all the terrible things they'd encountered together these last few days, she'd seen him rattled only once, and that was in the SUV earlier when he'd offered to buy a second crib for Henry and she'd abandoned the conversation.

Her spine stiffened with the memory. He wanted to get his own crib for Henry instead of sharing the crib she already had. *What's wrong?* he'd asked. Was he kidding? Only the fact that it had been the worst way possible for him to say he had no intentions of making a life with her. What he'd suggested sounded like the behavior of divorced couples, not reunited lovers making a fresh start. She didn't want two of everything or to split her son down the middle, raising him separately but together. She didn't want to be a separated couple who'd never even had the chance to be together.

Her heart rate sped with fresh frustration. She supposed she should be happy Sawyer wanted to be with Henry as much as possible, but given the fact she'd just decided to tell him how badly she wanted to build a life with him, the notion of a second crib had been an unexpected punch to her gut. She shook it off. Sawyer didn't know about her plans. It wasn't fair to be upset when he had no idea why. And, she reminded herself, after she told him what she wanted, there was no guarantee that he'd want it too. She'd have no right to be mad about that either. She let her eyes close briefly. She needed to prepare herself for that possibility.

For now, she owed him an apology and an explanation for her earlier behavior. He'd been nothing but kind and comforting to her despite his own feelings about getting the surprise of a lifetime when she'd introduced him to Henry. Of course, she wasn't in the mood to give an apology or an explanation, and both would have to wait until the house was straightened and empty of police officials. Until then, she rocked and sang and hoped Sara would be home soon. She *needed* her to be home soon.

Eventually, Sawyer walked the last of the cops onto the porch, and Emma rolled Henry's crib into the living room, then laid him in it. She wasn't ready to let him out of her sight, and she couldn't leave him anywhere there was a bullet hole in the wall beside his head.

Emma started a fresh pot of coffee and collected her cleaning supplies from where they'd been thrown out of the hall closet. As if Sara had kept her biggest secrets at the bottom of a can of Comet. Emma started by putting her living room back in order and giving everything a good scrub so Henry wouldn't be surrounded by chaos when he woke. She folded afghans and arranged throw pillows, straightened the curtains and lined books, quietly, back onto the built-in shelves along the fireplace. She shimmied the furniture back into the correct positions and righted the overturned vase, which had blessedly not broken in the spill. Goose bumps rose on her arms as she sprayed the cleanser on every flat surface and pretended that with enough elbow grease, she could rub all traces of the intruder's grubby hands off her and Sara's lives.

Sawyer returned as she put the last cleansing touch on her living room. "Nice," he said, looking wholly impressed.

"Thanks. One room down, eight more to go." She puffed air into overgrown bangs, then tucked them behind her ear. "What did Detective Rosen say?"

"He thinks whoever did this was looking for the notebook we gave him."

Emma agreed. She moved into the kitchen and put her table and chairs back in place, thankful for the work to busy her hands and give her restless nerves an outlet. "Did you talk to your team? Have they made any more progress with the pages you sent them?" She'd seen him on the phone and hoped that was the case.

"Wyatt's working on it." Sawyer restocked the pantry with fallen cans and boxes, then lifted the broom into his hands and worked it over the linoleum floor. He stilled when his phone rang. "It's Wyatt," he said, looking at the small screen. He set the cell phone on the counter and pressed the speaker button. "You're on speaker. I'm with Emma. What do you have?"

"Hey," Wyatt began, skipping the niceties this time and getting right down to business. "We were able to make a definitive match on all the numbers in Sara's notebook. The first account number represents an account at the Knox Ridge Credit Union, more than one hundred of them, actually. The back half of each number is a second account, as suspected, coordinating with a bank in the Cayman Islands. That's why the numbers all end the same way. Sara began each line with a transaction date, which accounts for the initial set of numbers on each line."

Emma wiped large wet circles over her countertop, trying to channel the excess energy while she processed the information. "Was Sara tracking an embezzlement scheme?"

"Maybe," Wyatt said. "Blake's looking into it further than I can, but that's the direction we're leaning."

Sawyer crossed his arms. "Could be money laundering. Could be both."

The phone was silent for a long beat before Wyatt simply added, "Yep."

Emma shivered as the implication settled in. "This is a lot bigger than I thought," she said, her mouth going dry with anxiety. "I thought Sara caught one guy doing something big enough to get him arrested. Now I know she caught someone stealing from at least a hundred people? Funneling funds offshore? And the man behind it is so unstable he'd kill to cover his tracks." She swallowed the painful mound of emotions piled in her throat and wrapped her arms around her unsettled stomach. "He killed Mr. Harrison. He tried to kill Kate. And us too." She swept her gaze from the phone to Sawyer and saw the truth in his eyes.

Whoever was doing these things would do whatever it took to be sure his stolen funds were safe.

Even murder a pair of sisters and a little baby.

Chapter 12

Sawyer worked at Emma's side for hours, enjoying the steady pace and easy partnership they'd fallen into midway through the kitchen cleanup. He scrubbed. She tidied. They were an excellent team. Emma knew where everything went. She knew how things worked. He, on the other hand, was decent with a scrub brush and lifted fallen items with less trouble.

Emma adjusted the volume on her phone dock's speaker as a new song began. She watched as he emptied another dustpan of broken glass into the trash bin. "I know I've said it before, but thank you, Sawyer," she said. "For helping me with this mess. For being here when we need you most."

Sawyer let the smile budding on his lips break free. "Where else would I be?" he asked with a wink. He watched as her own smile bloomed in return, and some of the day's horrendous weight lifted.

Working beside her, even at a task as unfortunate as theirs, reminded him of how good they were together. Emma was his perfect teammate. The yin to his yang. He'd never experienced anything like it, not even with his brothers in arms after years of fighting side by side. With Emma, it was different. Seamless. Better.

She stretched to set a pile of freshly folded jeans on her closet shelf, and Sawyer had to force his gaze back on the floor and dustpan.

There were perks to their camaraderie besides companionship. He also enjoyed her taste in music, and the playlist she'd started to help pass the time was filled with his favorites. A few of the selections were deeply nostalgic, and most of those memories included her.

Another bonus was the conversation. She didn't push or prod for more when he answered her questions, and she always answered his with depth and sincerity. She took her time, and he appreciated that.

The other benefit to their evening was watching her dead-sexy body bend and stretch for hours, a little sweat beading in the most deliciously distracting places.

Sawyer met her at the closet doors and placed the next few stacks of clothing on the shelves just above her head. "I've got it. Move over, shorty."

She bumped him with her hip. "I could have done that," she said, grinning. "I've been short all my life, you know. I've learned to get creative."

"No need to get creative when you've got an extra set of hands," he said.

"And they are *very* nice hands." Emma flashed a

wicked grin but didn't say another word as she went to refill her drawers with freshly washed and folded clothing. Whatever she'd been upset about in the SUV seemed to have passed. He planned to circle back to that subject later, when the work was done, but for now, he was just glad to see her smiling.

He didn't hate seeing her in her "work clothes" either. A few hours ago when she'd announced that she would change to finish cleaning, he'd expected her to return in oversize sweatpants or a holey T-shirt. Instead, she'd emerged from her room in a pair of short black running shorts and a fitted V-neck T-shirt. He could understand why the outfit worked for her. It couldn't possibly be hot or cumbersome, two definite benefits with so much bending, stretching and sweating ahead. Her outfit worked for him too, but all his reasons were currently testing his integrity and willpower.

Emma finished refolding the rest of her clothing and reloading the dresser drawers, then wiped a line of sweat off her brow. "I think that's it," she said. The hem of her shirt rose above the waist of her little shorts as she reached to peel the elastic band out of her hair and free her ponytail. The strip of exposed skin drew his attention to her middle, and his fingers curled at the sight of her creamy skin. Determined not to touch the gentle sway of her stomach or curves of her waist, he braced his hands on his hips. Emma wasn't his to touch that way anymore. And this was hardly the right time to address the possibilities that she might reconsider him for the job anytime soon.

He dragged his gaze to hers. "I guess our work is done here."

She smiled, and he knew he'd been caught ogling,

but was that all? Could she see the shameless truth in his expression? That he wanted her in every possible way, even if this was a terrible time to want more than to keep her safe and bring her sister home?

"What now?" he asked, intentionally leaving the question open to interpretation.

"Now," she said, plucking the thin cotton fabric of her white T-shirt away from her sweat-dampened skin, "I need a shower." She shook out her hair and gave him the sexiest damn smile he'd ever seen before walking away. "I won't be long," she said, moving in the direction of her en suite bath. She hooked a finger at him as she crossed the threshold.

Sawyer swallowed a low groan and went after her.

A small, distant cry pulled him up short. He caught the doorjamb in both palms and dropped his head forward in disappointment, but only for a moment. He lifted a genuine smile to Emma's stunned, maybe even disappointed eyes. "Duty calls," he said, smile growing.

"Daddy duty," she said, smiling back.

He liked the sound of that. He turned on his heel and gave her one last look over his shoulder. "I'm going to have to insist on a rain check for that shower."

Emma laughed. "If you handle daddy duty so I can soak this day off right now, you've got more than a shower coming your way."

Sawyer gave a low wolf whistle on his way back to Henry's crib in the living room, where he would soon get to hold the other love of his life for a while.

Emma took her time in the shower, both soaping up and winding down. She let herself imagine Sawyer had joined her under the steamy spray, and a wave of similar memories pummeled through her. Emma's time with Sawyer, before Henry, had always been intense. He'd asked for her number the moment they'd met and called the same night, before she'd made it back to her car. He'd told her he didn't have much time. That he was a soldier on leave for thirty days, and he planned to make the most of his time. When he asked her out, the sound of her name on his tongue had felt like coming home. Maybe that was what people meant when they said "love at first sight." Whatever it was, being with him again had brought it all back in a powerful rush.

She spent a few more minutes enjoying the fantasy that she wasn't alone before stepping out of the shower and pulling herself back together. Thoroughly dried and relaxed, she paired a jean skirt and short-sleeved button-down with bare feet in sneakers, then blew out her hair until it was soft on her shoulders. A little lip gloss and mascara, and Emma was ready to face the rest of her night, whatever that might hold.

Sawyer's voice rumbled down the hall from the kitchen as she stepped into the hall. She followed the sounds of his singing until she reached the kitchen, where he two-stepped Henry through the room.

Henry looked tiny in Sawyer's muscled arms, his narrow body stretched against Sawyer's broad chest. Their matching blue eyes lit with each buoyant step. Just when she'd been certain Sawyer Lance couldn't get any more desirable, this happened. It wasn't fair. Seeing him like this with their son was more than she'd ever dared to dream for, and here he was, instantly devoted and obviously happy. It was exactly the way she'd felt the moment she'd realized she was pregnant.

She and Sawyer had created the most precious gift imaginable together, and the beauty of that truth tugged at her heart. Despite everything else going wrong in her life at the moment, her heart overflowed with gratitude.

Sawyer raised a smile in her direction as the song ended. His jaw went slack before his lips broke into a wide smile. "You must be going somewhere special looking like that."

"I am," she said. "I've got a whole night planned at the lake with two very important men."

"Two, huh?" Sawyer strode to meet her in the room's center, turning Henry so he could watch the approach. "Sounds like some lucky guys."

Emma pulled Henry into her arms and kissed his cheek. "I'm the lucky one," she said. And it was true. She hated knowing it would end soon. That Sawyer would go back to his new life in progress, and she'd only see him during the drop-offs and pickups when they traded Henry like a shared book or CD.

Sawyer planted a kiss on Henry's head. "What do you say we get out of here?" he asked. "The house is spotless. The work is done. Let's head back to the lake house. I think it's my turn for a shower."

Emma shut her eyes against the planted image. If the awful things she'd seen today didn't keep her up all night, the thought of Sawyer in the shower absolutely would.

They loaded more of Emma's and Henry's things into the SUV and hit the road at twilight. By nightfall, they were settled in at his place, and Henry was fast asleep. Emma carried the baby monitor back to the living area after putting Henry down for the night.

"That was fast," Sawyer said, looking impressed.

"He was exhausted," she said. "I hope he doesn't remember any of this when he gets older."

Sawyer's lips turned up in a small, sad smile. "He won't. Most people don't have memories until pre-school, and those are fuzzy."

Emma sighed. He was right. Her earliest memories were around age five. So, maybe Henry would have a chance at normal, and the things he'd experienced this week might not turn him into a neurotic, anxiety-riddled mess. "Do you think whoever trashed my house will be back?" she asked.

Sawyer seemed to consider the question for a long beat. "He overturned everything in sight. I'm not sure there's anywhere left to look at your place. Hopefully, he's satisfied that whatever he wants isn't there, and he'll leave the house alone."

She wrapped her arms around her middle and rubbed the goose bumps off her skin.

"Are you hungry?" Sawyer asked, moving toward the kitchen.

Her stomach growled audibly in response. The only person who'd eaten anything since breakfast was Henry, who'd never missed a bottle.

Sawyer washed up at the sink, and Emma found herself staring.

"Why don't you let me cook this time?" she asked. "I saw some trout in the refrigerator this morning. There's plenty of veggies for a salad. You can shower while I get dinner started. We can meet on the deck for dinner."

Sawyer lifted his brows and straightened his shoulders. "I accept."

* * *

Sawyer rushed through a lukewarm shower, hurrying to clean up and get back out there to guard and enjoy Emma before she fell asleep.

Fifteen minutes later he pulled a plain black T-shirt and his most comfortable blue jeans over still-damp skin, and ran his fingers through wet hair. He peeked in on Henry before heading down the hall in Emma's direction. He found her on the rear deck, lighting candles along the railing. The table was set with a tossed salad in the center and ice water at each place.

"Trout will be done soon," she said, looking him over from head to toe with an expression that bordered on hunger. When her eyes met his, she blushed.

Sawyer's blood heated. She was checking him out. "Everything looks great," he said, "and dinner smells delicious." The familiar pinch of conflict warred in him. He wanted desperately to tell her how he felt and work out every detail of what would happen to them next.

Unfortunately, Sara was still missing, and they weren't any closer to finding her, naming the killer or figuring out what she'd been up to. So far, Sawyer had failed his mission. If there was a worse time to attempt to woo a woman, he couldn't think of one.

Emma opened the grill and tested the trout with a fork, then squeezed a lemon over the tops of the fillets, and levered each off the grates and onto a serving dish.

They ate in silence. Fireflies hovering over the lake. Moonlight reflecting on the silver water. The tension between them seemed to grow exponentially, and Sawyer realized it might be bad news in the making. Emma pushed the food around her plate, rarely making eye contact. Was she getting up the nerve to let him down easy? Had she seen the way he looked at her and known it was best to nip this in the bud? Was she trying, in her own sweet way, not to hurt him when she gave him his walking papers?

Sawyer set his fork aside, no longer hungry. If he was right, it would explain her attitude earlier, when he'd suggested buying a second crib for Henry to use at his house. *Maybe she didn't plan to let Sawyer see him long enough at a time to necessitate a crib.*

That couldn't be right.

Could it?

Emma wiped her mouth and set the napkin aside. "Can we talk?"

"Yes." Sawyer frowned, prepared to vehemently plead his case. No, he hadn't returned her message when he'd gotten home, and he understood now that he should have, but he was trying to do the right thing by letting her go. He thought she'd moved on, and he had no right to barge back in, in search of something that was no longer there. Of course, he didn't know about Henry then, but now that he did, he'd never walk away from his son.

Sawyer didn't want to walk away from Emma either.

She flopped back in her chair, the hem of her shirt knotted around her fingers. "We need to talk about the crib situation and my behavior earlier."

Sawyer dragged his chair around the table and captured her fidgeting hands in his, overcome with the need to stop her from saying the words that would break him. "Me first," he said, swallowing his pride. He couldn't let her push him back out of her life until she knew how he felt. If she still wanted out after he'd spilled his guts, he couldn't stop her, but at least she would have all the facts before making a huge decision. "I should have called," he said.

Her mouth opened, then slowly shut without a protest.

"I was trying to do the right thing, but I can see now how wrong it was." He lifted her hands in his and pressed them to his lips. "Emma, you are the only reason I'm even here today. Thoughts of you were what got me through my darkest times. The memories we made together kept me fighting when I wanted to give up." He squeezed her hands. "I needed to get back here to you like I'd promised I would. Now here I am. I'm home. A civilian and a father."

Emma blinked. "And? What are you saying, Sawyer?"

"I'm saying that I don't know what kind of arrangement you have in mind for us with Henry in the future, but I'll accept whatever terms you give as long as I can be with him as often as possible. I've already missed too much. I don't want to miss another thing. Not his first word or first step. Not his first baseball game or fishing derby or car or college…"

Emma sniffled. "Sawyer."

"Wait." He steeled himself for the finish. He was only halfway there, and he needed to finish before some other calamity kept him from it. "Once I'd made it back on base, away from the insurgents who'd held me all those months, I thought things would get better, but they didn't. Being physically safe seemed to shift the stress. Once I was no longer in survival mode, I had time to think. And it's all I did, but then I had a hard time concentrating on anything other than what

I'd been through. I couldn't eat or sleep. I retreated into my head with the memories I didn't want. It was like falling into a black hole every day. By the time I made it back stateside and was discharged, I was spinning out of control. My team at Fortress helped. They kept my head on straight. Gave me renewed purpose. New missions to save lives. My guys checked on me, made sure I toed the line and wasn't slipping back into the darkness, and it made all the difference. I was only beginning to feel human again when I took your call the other night, but I hadn't felt like myself in a year before that. It was like I'd been lost at sea and you were the lighthouse. I saw your face, and everything changed."

Emma blinked fat tears over her cheeks. She lifted her hands to her mouth and released a small sigh.

Shame racked Sawyer. He never wanted to be the reason for her tears, and he certainly hadn't meant to burden her with his troubles, only to open up to her so that she could understand. "I want you to be happy, you and Henry, even if that's not with me. Just…be happy."

Her expression hardened, and she folded her arms. "Why wouldn't I be happy with you?"

He frowned. "Didn't you hear me? I'm a mess. A barely recovered nightmare who just promised to protect you a few days ago and has failed repeatedly."

"That's not true," she said, setting her jaw and shifting her weight.

His gaze slid to the angry purple-and-brown bruise across her cheekbone.

"I was mugged outside a credit union," she said, apparently knowing where his thoughts had gone. "No one could have predicted that. *No one*."

He opened his mouth to tell her that was his job. To

troubleshoot, to think ahead of the danger and keep her away from it, not stand across the street while she was assaulted and pretend it could have happened to anyone. He'd been lax, and it had cost her.

She raised a palm to stop the interruption. "You've done nothing but protect me every minute since you got here, so don't try to tell yourself or me otherwise, because I'm not buying it."

Sawyer's mouth snapped shut. He watched the hard line of her narrow jaw clench, and despite himself, a pinch of misplaced pride swept through him. He loved that fire in her. The spark for justice when she thought something wasn't fair or right. The internal defender. Emma was kindness and honor, love and determination. She was all the things he aspired to be, and seeing her so ready to defend him sent a wave of warmth and hope through his chest.

"You haven't failed me," she said. "Not once. Not even when you got home and decided not to return my message. I can be hurt that you didn't call, but it won't change the fact that I would've done the same thing in your position. I would've tried to protect you from me too, and I would've done exactly what you did."

Sawyer's heart clenched. "What?"

"I think you are a brave and honorable man, Sawyer Lance. I don't want you to ever think any differently. I'm proud to know you, and I'm proud that you are my son's father. I was only upset about the crib earlier because I didn't like the idea of dividing Henry between us. It sounded like you wanted to split custody, but I don't want that."

Sawyer raised his palms to cup her beautiful face. A reed of hope rearing in him. "What do you want?"

She fixed emotion-filled eyes on his. "You."

Sawyer closed his mouth over hers, unable to contain himself any longer.

He kissed her slowly, deliberately, until she was breathless and unsteady in his arms, then he carried her inside.

Chapter 13

The next two days went quietly. Too quietly. No news. No new leads. The few times Detective Rosen called with updates, the information had changed nothing. Security footage of the hit-and-run outside the credit union confirmed the vehicle was a rental registered to Mr. Harrison, but there was no clear shot of the driver. Kate had regained consciousness and was doing much better, but she hadn't gotten a look at the driver either. Sawyer suspected it hadn't been Harrison behind the wheel, but considering the bank manager had been murdered, there was no way to know for sure now.

Detective Rosen had also let them know a hospital in the next town had reported a male gunshot victim. The man's wound was consistent with one delivered by the gun Sawyer had used on the intruder sneaking through Sara's window. Unfortunately, the shot had been a through and through, and there was no way to definitively connect that man's injury to Sawyer's gun. Since Sawyer never saw his face, and couldn't identify him anyway, the man was released after providing a bogus story. The local detective was supposed to follow up with him. His blood was being sent to a lab where it would eventually be tested against the blood collected from Sara's windowsill.

None of this got them one step closer to finding Sara, and time was marching on. Six days had passed since she'd been dragged from her home, and Sawyer still had no idea who could have done it, or where she could be. Worse, Emma had been right that first night when she'd said the odds of finding her sister would diminish significantly after the first seventy-two hours.

He reached for Emma in the dark bedroom. He'd fallen asleep with her in his arms again, feeling happier and lighter than he had in a year. He could get used to what they had going, and he was determined to ask her to stay with him once he'd returned her sister safely. Sawyer knew that rescuing Sara wouldn't bring his fallen teammates back, but it would be a great step in regaining his peace.

Emma rolled against him, her long hair splayed over his pillow and her warm breasts pressed to his chest. He longed to take her again, but that was no surprise. He never stopped wanting her. He'd always thought the month he'd had with her when they met was perfect, but he'd been wrong. Hearing Emma tell him that she wanted him and that she was proud he was her son's father, *that* was perfect.

Sawyer stroked her hair and kissed her forehead

before settling back onto his pillow, smiling and thoroughly content.

Moonlight streamed across the ceiling, and he was immeasurably thankful for the rest he'd gotten these last two nights with Emma. Though he wasn't sure what had woken him this time. Another nightmare? He didn't think so. He couldn't recall dreaming. Henry? Sawyer set his senses on alert and listened hard in the darkness. His son's breaths came deep and steady through the monitor. Henry was fast asleep, but instinct tugged at Sawyer's chest the way it had when someone had been in Emma's house with them that night.

Sawyer rose onto his elbows and forearms, a sense of dread erasing the peace he'd had only moments before. A heartbeat later he heard it. The low growling of a small engine. Maybe even an ATV like the intruder at Emma's house had escaped on.

Sawyer slid out of bed and dressed quickly in the darkness, listening closely to every creak, breath and heartbeat within his walls. The growl drew closer, and he cursed as an unfortunate realization struck. He hadn't heard an ATV. He'd heard at least three.

"Emma," he whispered, nudging her shoulder. "Wake up."

She jolted upright, eyes glazed with fatigue. "Henry?"

"No," Sawyer said. This was much worse. "We've got company."

Emma scrambled out of bed and pulled one of his T-shirts over her head, making an instant dress that stopped midthigh. "What's happening?"

Sawyer slid steady fingers between the panels of his bedroom curtain and peered into the night. Emma slid in front of him. Four single headlights cut through the dense and distant forest. All were headed toward Sawyer's home. "Call the police." Sawyer gripped Emma's shoulders and turned her to face him. "Get Henry and hide," he said. He snagged his sidearm from the nightstand and tucked it into his waistband, then pulled another from a drawer and kept it in his right hand.

Emma dialed and pressed the phone to her ear. "I don't know where to hide," she said, moving toward Henry's crib. "I don't know what to do."

Sawyer dropped the curtain back into place. She had a good question. He'd never had to hide before, certainly not on his own property, and he had no idea what to tell her.

"Hello," she said into the receiver, "this is Emma Hart, and I need help." She rattled off an overview of the last few days with mention of the four ATVs headed their way.

Sawyer handed her the keys to the rented SUV. "Get to the truck and drive to the police station."

"What about you?" she asked, gathering her sleeping baby and his blankets into her arms, the cell phone clenched between her shoulder and cheek.

"I can handle four men, but not while keeping an eye on the two of you. You need to stay safe. Protect Henry. I'll focus on the intruders."

"I'm so sick of running," she said, frowning fiercely.

The debate was cut short when the ATVs went silent outside.

Sawyer parted the curtains again. The headlights were out, and the world was silent. They'd abandoned their vehicles. "They're moving forward on foot," he said, turning back to Emma once more.

She slid into her shoes and disconnected the phone call. "Local police are on the way," she said. "Dispatch is calling Detective Rosen for us. They'll fill him in on what's happening now."

"Good work." Sawyer ushered Emma down the hall toward his back door and pressed his back to the wall. Emma followed his example. Together, they watched a foursome of armed silhouettes drift across the lawn in the moonlight, heading for the front porch. Sawyer gave Emma a reassuring look. "I'll take care of them. You and Henry head for the SUV," Sawyer whispered. "Get in and drive. Don't stop until you reach the local police precinct."

Emma gripped his arm, unfathomable fear in her big blue eyes.

He set his hand over hers. "It's going to be okay. Get yourself and Henry to safety." Sawyer squeezed her fingers, then slid into the night, hating himself for leaving her behind, but it was for the best. Sawyer was well trained, but there was only one of him, and he had no idea who these men were. They could be former military or even mercenaries for all he knew. To be safe, Henry and Emma needed to get as far away as possible. The intruders had come via ATVs, which they'd left a significant distance away from the house. Even when they heard the SUV spark to life, there would be little they could do to stop it.

Sawyer jumped over the handrail at the side of the porch, steering clear of the motion sensing light, then crept around the side of his home, gun drawn.

Frogs and crickets sang in the grasses and near the lake. A sky full of stars arched overhead. The same stars he'd watched through the corner of a filthy window during the nights of his captivity. He pushed the memory aside and listened for the gentle stir of the SUV engine.

He stilled to listen as whispered voices rose to his ears. "You get the girl and the baby," one man said. "I'll take out the bodyguard."

Sawyer's jaw locked. *No one* was getting his girl or his baby. He lowered into a crouch and cut through the shadows like a lion after its prey, determined to stop them, incapacitate them, hold them until the police arrived, whatever the cost.

A brilliant, silvery moon came and went behind a mass of fast-moving clouds overhead. Memories of his last night-strike forced their way into his head. His pace slowed as the earth shifted beneath him. The scene morphed and changed before his eyes. Suddenly he was in uniform, outside an enemy stronghold in dangerous territory with his team behind him. He felt the drip of sweat slip from beneath his helmet and ride over his temple to his jaw. Saw the guards up ahead. Militants. Two at the door. One on the roof. One on patrol. He hadn't known about that one before. Sawyer stumbled to a stop. He blinked and rubbed his eyes, willing the images to clear, willing his heart rate to settle, his concentration to return. He sipped cool night air and cursed himself inwardly. He thought he'd put these episodes behind him. Thought his mind was on the mend.

One of the four trespassers came into view, keeping watch along the home's edge. The others had gone ahead. This was their lookout, and Sawyer had the element of surprise on his side. He could drop the man with a single shot. Not a kill shot, but one that would put him down and keep him there. The sound would pull the others from the home, and if it went well, Sawyer could lie in wait, hidden in the shadows, plucking them off one by one until he had a pile of bleeding criminals awaiting the arrival of local law enforcement. If it went poorly and they split up before coming outside, Sawyer could find himself surrounded.

He sighted his handgun, choosing the least lethal, most effective shot. But the memories returned, and his weapon grew unsteady in his outstretched hands. His finger grazed the trigger, then pulled back. Touched, then relented. During his last mission, it had been the sound of his fire that had given away their approach. He had gotten them captured. Gotten his team killed.

Sawyer's tongue seemed to swell, his throat tightened. He lowered the gun and shook his head hard, as if he might be able to clear his thoughts physically. He had to move. Had to do something. The others were surely inside by now, and Sawyer still hadn't heard the SUV's engine ignite. He had to act. He couldn't afford not to. His breaths were quick and shallow as he crept through the night, closing in on the nearest target.

The distinct sound of the back door caused his heart to sprint. The normally soft metallic click was like an explosion in the night.

The man before him turned. His curious eyes went wide at the sight of Sawyer a mere foot away.

Sawyer's gun was up on instinct, stopping the man from raising his, but Sawyer couldn't force his finger back to the trigger. He couldn't feel his fingers or toes. Fear had wrapped him like a wet, heavy blanket, and the knowledge he wasn't in complete control was enough to make him want to run.

But soldiers don't run.

He braced himself. Forced down the fear. Even as the dark world shimmied and brightened around him.

A sinister grin curled the man's lips, and he lunged.

"Dammit," Sawyer whispered, opening his stance and accepting the weight of the wild, untrained attack.

Three quick moves later, the thud of the man's falling body brought Sawyer back to the moment, and images of that long-ago night were shoved away. *One down and three to go.*

Emma held Henry close and listened to the night. She had the SUV keys in one palm and her shoulder pressed against the back door of Sawyer's home, preparing to run. All she had to do was find the courage.

The SUV was parked in the gravel drive twenty feet away. It would be simple, under normal conditions, to cross the small porch, hop down the short flight of stairs and be at the vehicle in seconds, even carrying Henry.

But these weren't normal conditions, and Emma's heart was seizing with panic at the thought of making a run for it now. She'd seen the silhouettes of the trespassers as they'd approached, and they were armed. She couldn't dodge or outrun a bullet, and she couldn't bring herself to risk Henry's life by trying. Her mind urged her to hide, not run. Hiding had saved Henry on the night of Sara's abduction and again on the night the intruder had broken into Sara's room. Hiding worked for them.

Running was a dangerous unknown.

Behind her, the front door opened with a heavy creak. Soft footfalls spread through the house, forcing her onto the back porch.

Help is on the way, she reminded herself. *The local police are coming.*

She released the screen door behind her, eyes focused on her goal. The SUV. She dared a small step forward, but something held her back. The tail of Sawyer's oversize shirt was caught in the door. Emma bit her lip and willed herself to remain calm. The moment she let panic take over, she'd make messy, potentially deadly decisions.

Henry squirmed in her arms, his small features bunching.

"Shh, shh, shh," she cooed.

The footfalls inside drew closer, headed her way.

Emma jerked forward, freeing herself from the door with a quiet thwap! She flew down the back porch stairs on silent feet. The motion light flashed on as she reached the base of the steps. The short distance to the SUV warped and stretched before her like a dream where the hallway never ended and no matter how hard or fast she ran for the door, she wouldn't arrive.

Move, she begged herself. *Run.*

The back door opened, and Emma scurried into the shadows against the house. It was too late to make a run for the SUV in the bath of security lighting. She'd missed her moment. Running now would only put a massive target on her back *and Henry's*.

She crouched alongside the porch, careful to keep her head low, and she scanned her dark surroundings.

"Where are they?" a man growled.

"I don't know," another man answered. "The car's here. They couldn't have gone far."

Emma listened to the footfalls as they paced the

porch. She ducked deeper out of sight as the men approached the railing at her side.

"Check the house again," the first man said. "Where are your brothers?"

There was a long pause. "I don't know," the second lower voice said.

"Well, find them!"

One set of footsteps headed back into the house and out of earshot. The other man lingered. Waiting. Maybe even sensing she was near.

Emma watched as he leaned over the railing's edge and scanned the darkness. He was dressed in head-to-toe black riding gear, like the man who'd cut the brake lines on Sawyer's truck and chased them through the national forest. This man didn't have a helmet, but she still didn't recognize his face.

A chilly autumn breeze whipped through the air, and Henry made a small discontented sound.

Emma jumped back, jamming her bare legs into the thorns and briars of bushes along Sawyer's home. She bit her tongue against the stings of instant bruises and cuts and pressed a steadying kiss to Henry's once again crumpled expression.

Her baby's eyes fluttered shut and pinched tight as he tried to hold on to sleep.

The porch boards creaked.

The man was coming.

Emma broke into a sprint through the night, clutching Henry to her chest to absorb the impact of her flight. He squirmed but didn't cry.

She paused at the front of the house. Where could she go? Not onto the deck, dock or lake. She peered at the dark forest across the field. The men had come from the forest on the opposite side of the home. Was this tree line safe? Or was it possible more bad men lurked there, as well? How many were there? *Where were they?* she wondered, nearly frozen with fear once more.

"Did you find them?" an angry voice asked. The sound echoed in the night, near the opposite end of the house now, but any one of the four men could be on her in a second.

"No," another low male voice answered. "No sign of the lady, the baby or the guy. I didn't find my brothers either."

"Come on," the other voice said. "We'll split up and circle the place. You go that way. I'll go this way. We'll meet in the middle."

Emma sucked in a hard breath. She had to move. If she ran for the trees, they'd spot her crossing the field. The SUV was far away now, on the opposite end of the house. Behind her, near the voices.

A new fear breached her thoughts. Where was Sawyer? Where were the man's brothers? Did Sawyer have them, or did they have Sawyer?

She pushed the thoughts aside. One problem at a time. Right now, she was on her own to save Henry, and that started by staying hidden and alive until the local police could arrive. She scanned her options once more, looked into Henry's precious face, and made her decision.

"I love you," she whispered against Henry's soft hair. "You stay still, and I'll do everything I can to protect you."

As if in acceptance of their deal, Henry gave a soft snore.

Emma counted down from three, then she hurried across the short lawn toward the water. She slowed at the sandy bank, choosing her footing carefully so there wouldn't be footprints to follow. She took easy steps into the cold water. Fall's shorter days and colder nights had taken hold of the lake, despite unseasonably warm days. She sucked air as she waded deeper, to her thighs, her bottom. Then she carried Henry toward the dock and pulled a large red-and-white cooler from the weathered boards. She took it with her beneath the dock.

Carefully, she placed Henry and his mass of blankets into the cooler, onto the sand-and dirt-lined bottom.

Satisfied the makeshift boat would hold up, she ducked beneath the dock, sinking to her shoulders in the frigid water, and floated Henry along with her.

Ripples moved across the previously serene surface, a hundred neon signs pointing out their escape route.

Emma held as still as possible and anchored the cooler in place before her. She closed her eyes, hoping the ripples would stop before the men came to examine the lake.

A frog jumped nearby, making a little splash. Henry squirmed in the cooler.

"Shh, shh, shh," she soothed, holding the little vessel as it rocked on the ripples ebbing around her.

His tiny lips formed an angry frown, though his eyes were determinedly closed.

"Did you hear that?" a man asked. The harsh whisper startled Emma with its nearness. "I think I heard something near the water."

Emma gripped the cooler, hating herself for choosing the worst hiding place in the world. If they spotted her, she couldn't even run. She hadn't saved Henry and herself. She'd made them easy targets.

Two sets of feet pounded onto the deck above them.

Emma cringed. Her heart raced, and her stomach lurched. She lifted a desperate prayer as her fingertips nudged the soft rubber tip of Henry's pacifier caught in the blanket folds. She plugged it into his twisted mouth and stiffened every muscle in her body, willing her baby to be silent and the ripples to stop announcing her presence.

"No boat," one of the men said, taking a few steps closer.

The second man paced overhead. "I'm sure I heard something."

"Fish," his partner muttered, "ducks, bats, frogs. Who cares? We've got to keep looking."

The weight of their combined retreat rattled the boards, shaking dirt onto Emma's head. She stretched a palm over Henry's slowly wrinkling expression.

"Achoo!" Henry sneezed in a tiny puff of air.

The men froze. "What the hell was that?"

"What?"

Emma could see their faces through the space between boards now. She could read their murderous expressions and see their hands on their guns. All they had to do was look down, and her life was over. *Henry's* was over. His little boat couldn't save him from a bullet.

Her limbs and lips began to tremble. Her teeth rattled hard in her head. Tears welled in her eyes.

Bang! Bang! Bang!

A trio of gunshots erupted in the distance.

And Emma's heart thunked hard and heavy.

She'd already lost her parents and possibly Sara. Had she just lost Sawyer, as well?

Chapter 14

The men on the dock lurched into desperate sprints, arms and knees pumping, guns drawn as they raced toward the sound of gunfire.

Henry flailed in his little boat, then broke into tears. The violent cries were masked by a shoot-out. Emma inched through the water, away from the dock, away from the muzzle flashes and gunshots on the west side of Sawyer's home, the same side where the intruders had left their ATVs. A rush of unexpected pleasure drove through her as she realized a gunfight meant Sawyer was still alive and conscious out there somewhere.

The jolt of happiness propelled her to action. She moved more quickly through the water, towing Henry carefully back to shore.

His temper quieted slightly as she pulled him into

her arms and left the cooler in the water to sink. His little breaths came hard and fast, and his bottom lip trembled, puffing in and out with each raspy gasp, but for the moment, the wails had stopped.

Emma ran in sopping, squeaking sneakers toward the woods on the opposite side of Sawyer's house, away from the national forest, the intruders and the gunshots. Hot tears stung her icy cheeks as she flew through the night, stumbling on frozen legs, her wet skin screaming from the chill of blowing wind. Could Sawyer hold off four armed men on his own? For how long? How much ammo did he have on him? How much had he already expelled?

Where were the local cops?

Her hand went to the phone tucked into her bra, intending to call 911 and check on the cavalry, but the icy feel of her shirt slid through her heart. Her phone was gone. Likely lost forever at the bottom of Lake Anna.

The night was suddenly still. Quiet. No more shots fired. No sounds of a struggle.

Nothing.

Emma sent up a prayer and kept moving.

Soon, the low and distant cries of emergency vehicles and first responders pricked her ears. A moment later a much nearer sound wound to life. The familiar growl of ATV engines fading quickly into the night.

She stopped. Turned back. What did the sounds mean? Had the shooting stopped because the intruders heard the sirens and fled?

Or had the shooting stopped because they'd killed Sawyer and would come for her again the moment the police left her unattended?

Her heart ached with the possibility he could be

gone. "Sawyer," she whispered. Surely it couldn't be true. She stepped back toward the house, drawn by the need to know he was okay.

She didn't want to know a world, or a life, without him in it. It wasn't fair. It wasn't right.

A hot tear fell from her eye to Henry's forehead. Startled, his arms jerked wide. His lips curved down in the perfect angry frown.

"Sorry, baby," she whispered through a growing lump in her throat.

"Emma!"

Her name boomed through the night.

She lifted her gaze to the house, senses heightened. "Sawyer?" she asked the darkness.

"Emma!" he hollered again, this time closer, his voice intent and demanding. "Emma! Come out. It's clear." The silhouette of a man appeared beneath the cone of the security light as he passed the back porch.

"Sawyer!" Emma gasped. "Here! We're here." She started back across the field at a jog. *He was okay*.

Sawyer ran at her, arms wide. "Emma," he croaked. "I thought I'd lost you." He stroked her hair and kissed her face.

She bawled ugly tears of joy.

Henry screamed. He'd had enough of this night. He was outside after bedtime. He'd been floated in the water. Put inside a cooler. Had his little eardrums tested by a gunfight.

"The gunfight," she said, teeth beginning to chatter. "What h-happened?"

Sawyer pulled back with a questioning frown. "You thought I'd lose a gunfight?"

"There were four of them," she said. "I h-heard dozens of sh-shots."

"I only shot four times," Sawyer said. "I missed twice. It's tougher than you'd think to hit a man dressed in black who's running through the night." He wrapped his arms around her and rubbed her frozen skin for friction. "I hit one in the leg before he got to his vehicle, and I hit the other's ATV before he drove away. The rest of the shots you heard were all theirs missing me. I took down the first two men hand to hand. They're out cold where I dropped them. The other pair fled."

Emergency lights cut through the night as a line of first responders rolled along the gravel drive to Sawyer's home.

Henry, Sawyer and Emma were safe again for now.

Sawyer pulled Henry into his arms and held him tight, then looked carefully at Emma for the first time. "Did you fall in the water?" He glanced back at Henry, who was completely dry.

"N-n-no." She considered where to start the story, then told it as quickly as possible while trying not to bite her tongue or break her teeth from all the shivers and chattering.

Sawyer felt his blood boil as he listened to Emma retell the events that had forced her into frigid waters with their infant son. He pulled her a little tighter, wishing that he'd been there for her instead of across the property, letting two trespassers get away.

The side yard teemed with activity when they rounded the corner. Two cruisers and two ambulances were parked behind an unmarked SUV, presumably the detective on duty. Sawyer led Emma toward the ambulance.

"Oh, sweetie." An older heavyset woman rushed to meet them outside the open ambulance bay doors. Her sweet spirit and nurturing nature were evident in her kind eyes and audible in her gentle tone. Sawyer relaxed by a fraction. The woman reached for Emma, ushering her to the ambulance. "You look like you're freezing. Come here. Let's get you warm." She caught a blanket by its corners and stretched it in Emma's direction, opened wide to wrap around her patient's trembling shoulders. "That's a start," she said, motioning Emma toward the vehicle. "Hop in so I can fix you up," she said.

Emma's teeth chattered. "H-H-Henry,"

The woman's expression faltered. Her warm brown eyes snapped in Sawyer's direction, hyperfocused on the blanket in his arms. "Was the baby hurt?"

"No," Sawyer said with confidence. If he had been, it would've been the first thing she said.

Emma shook her head. "He's just t-tired and sc-scared."

Sawyer rubbed the blanket covering her back. "Let her look you over. I've got Henry," he promised. "We're fine."

The older woman tipped her head and refreshed her smile. "I've got heated blankets and dry scrubs in the bus."

Emma nodded woodenly, pressing her lips into a thin white line.

Sawyer kissed her head, then helped her into the ambulance.

"We'll only be a moment," the woman said before pulling the bay doors shut.

Sawyer leaned in, listening through the panels.

"Here you are. Go ahead and change out of that wet shirt, then I'll get your vitals."

Sawyer breathed easier. Emma was in good hands. Now he'd find out who the four trespassers had been. He'd knocked two of them out cold. Maybe at least one of them would talk. He frowned at the spot on the lawn where he'd left the first man unconscious. Hopefully, he'd been collected by the local officers and put in cuffs somewhere for safekeeping.

"Mr. Lance?" A man in jeans, a T-shirt and ball cap called from his porch.

Sawyer changed directions.

The man was Sawyer's age give or take a few years. His boots were unlaced and there were creases on his cheeks, signs he hadn't been on duty when he'd gotten the call to come tonight. The sleep marks were also indicative of a deep sleep recently interrupted. Sawyer couldn't help envying a man who was able to sleep so deeply that the sheets had left marks that were still visible. Sawyer had only truly slept soundly a few times in the better part of a year, each of those times had been this week, always with Emma in his arms.

Sawyer shook the man's hand. "Sawyer Lance."

"Detective Steven Miller," the man said. "I spoke with Detective Rosen on my drive over, and he brought me up to speed. Were you or Miss Hart harmed tonight?"

"No."

His gaze slid to the blue bundle in Sawyer's arms. "Was your son?"

"No," Sawyer said, feeling his protective hold on Henry tighten. Was this the way Emma felt all those times he'd noticed her pulling Henry a little closer? "Emma's with the EMT right now."

The detective's mouth turned down. "How many trespassers were here tonight?"

"Four," Sawyer said, turning his attention toward the spot in the yard where the first man he'd knocked out had landed. "I left one right over there, and another in the hallway outside my bathroom. Two got away on the ATVs they rode in on." He raised a hand in the direction where the vehicles had been. "I hit one vehicle and one driver. A superficial leg wound. I'd aimed for the tires, but the trees are thick, and they were moving fast."

"And it's the middle of the night," Detective Miller said. "How far away were you?"

"About thirty yards."

The detective gave an appreciative whistle. "I'd say you did all right."

"What happened to the man I left outside?" Sawyer asked, avoiding the detective's next logical question. *Where did Sawyer train to shoot like that?* It wasn't a deviation in topic he wanted to take right now. Right now, he wanted facts and answers.

"Outside?" Miller shook his head. "We only found one man. Inside."

Sawyer opened his mouth to swear, then shut it. His gaze dropping to the infant in his arms. He'd never been one to take issue with cursing, but it just felt wrong to be the one introducing his baby to the words. "I guess he got away." Though he wasn't sure when. Sawyer hadn't seen a third headlight when the other two men fled, and he hadn't heard another engine rev to life after the other had run off. "I don't suppose you recognize the man you found in here?" he asked.

"I do," Miller said.

Sawyer felt his brow raise. "Is that right?"

Emma jogged in their direction and up the steps to Sawyer's side, dressed in pale blue scrubs that dragged the ground and sagged off her shoulders. She wound her arms around his middle and pressed a cold cheek to his chest. "I'm fine," she said, rolling her eyes up to his. "Shaken up and cold, but well. How's Henry?"

"Perfect," Sawyer answered. "This is Detective Steven Miller. Detective Rosen filled him in on the case."

The detective extended a hand in her direction and they shook.

Emma gave him a slow and careful look, stopping to examine the badge on Miller's belt. "I didn't mean to interrupt. You said you recognized one of the men?"

A uniformed officer appeared, tugging a man in cuffs along at his side.

"Yep." The detective raised a palm, halting the cop and criminal. "Miss Hart, Mr. Lance, this is David Finn, an occasional visitor at the local police department. Petty crimes mostly."

Sawyer ground his teeth, aching to knock David Finn back into unconsciousness for about a week.

"Your last name is Finn?" Emma asked, releasing Sawyer and squinting up at the scowling man and his big black eye.

"Yeah? So?" he snapped.

Emma chewed her bottom lip. "I just wanted to hear him talk," she said. "This isn't the man who mugged me or took my sister. His voice is all wrong, and it's not the man who broke into Sara's room. Sawyer shot that guy."

David Finn slid his gaze to Sawyer, and Sawyer smiled.

He reached for Emma, bringing her back against his side.

Detective Miller gave Finn an appraising look. "So, what's your big important role in this mess, Finn? How do you fit into the business of terrifying this nice family? You're certainly not the muscle," he said with a wicked grin, circling a finger in the direction of the man's swollen eye. "And I'm still trying to figure out when you graduated from graffitiing the corner store to the attempted murder of a new mother and her infant."

"Man," Finn drawled, "I didn't attempt murder on nobody. I didn't even touch that woman or her baby, and I ain't talking to you until I talk to a lawyer."

Miller motioned the uniform to take Finn away.

As they passed, Emma pressed closer to Sawyer, a small tremor playing in her hand on his back. "I heard his voice when I was hiding," she said. "He was looking for his brother or brothers. David had family here tonight. Why?"

David craned his neck for a look back as the officer hauled him down the steps. He didn't speak, but the fear was plain in his eyes. David knew Emma knew about his brothers, and they weren't getting away like he'd thought. That truth gave Sawyer a measure of satisfaction.

It also worried him to know that by failing the mission, the sloppy foursome had turned their target into a witness.

Emma rubbed her palms against her arms, still fighting the cold.

"Why don't we go inside?" Sawyer said. "You're probably chilled to the bone, and Henry will be more comfortable in his crib, away from the wind."

Emma nodded. She looked to Miller. "Can you stay for coffee or tea, Detective?"

He took a long look at the scene beyond the porch. The ambulances and cruisers were packing up and pulling out, leaving his unmarked SUV alone beside Sawyer's rental. "Why not?" he said. "I'll be hanging around until the crime scene crew gets here to collect empty casings from the shoot-out. I might as well warm up while I wait."

"Great," Emma said, her spirits seeming to lift a bit.

Sawyer held the door for Emma and Miller, then followed them inside. "Is there anything I can do to help tonight?" he asked. "Finding the casings, identifying the tread marks or tracking the escape route?"

"Nothing tonight," Miller said. "I'd like to have you both speak with a sketch artist tomorrow if you're willing. Anything you can remember about the fourth man's face. I have photos of the Finn boys you can use to identify which ones were here tonight."

Emma nodded. "Okay." She led the way into the kitchen and stared at the counter. "Tea or coffee?" she asked.

"Coffee," Miller said. "Black."

Sawyer stopped to admire the limited number of scratches on the front door's dead bolt. "One of those men knew how to use a lock pick."

"Yep," Miller responded. "Probably the one you saw

leaving in handcuffs. Petty theft is his idea of a good time."

Sawyer stared at the lock, hating what an easy mark he'd made Emma and Henry. He'd assumed the fact that his home was registered to the company, in another county and had only recently become a place with an address would be enough to keep them safe for a few days. He ran a freaking private protection company, and he'd failed to lock down his own home.

Sawyer excused himself to put Henry in his crib, then headed back to the kitchen. When the sun rose, his place was getting a security overhaul that would be worthy of his company name.

Emma lined mugs on the counter where his old coffee machine puffed and grunted against the back-splash. "Will Detective Rosen be out tonight?" she asked Miller.

"No." The detective scanned Sawyer's home casually as he spoke. "Rosen said he's got his hands full back in Knox County. Seems the sudden crime spree over there has taxed their force to the limits, and he's barely treading water."

"How much did he tell you about my situation?" she asked.

Miller tipped his head over each shoulder briefly. "He says your sister found and documented evidence of an embezzlement scheme at her credit union. Someone was pulling hundreds of thousands of dollars a year out of the accounts by manipulating the computer system."

Emma shot Sawyer a pointed look. "That's a lot of money."

"Did he say how they were doing it?" she asked, filling three mugs with coffee and ferrying them to the table in a tight triangle between her palms.

"Computers," he said. "Someone manipulated the program that determines the interest owed on folks' accounts. The system began directing a small portion of the interest earned into an offshore account. The interest owed on most accounts is only about one-and-a-half percent, and the portion diverted from each account was minuscule at best. Most people didn't notice a few extra dollars or cents gone. Most probably didn't bother to do the math on it, just trusted the bank to add their one-and-a-half percent every quarter. In the event someone noticed and called the credit union on it, a correction was made immediately, and those accounts were credited fifty dollars as restitution for the error. Then that account was removed from the list of accounts being attacked."

"Then Sara noticed what was happening," Emma guessed.

Miller took another long pull on the steamy black coffee. "According to Rosen, she started looking at every account. One by one."

Sawyer smiled, watching Emma's face light up at the mention of her sister. "That's Sara," she said, "and it explains the mass amount of numbers in her notebook."

Detective Miller sat back in his seat. "Your sister tracked every error and the date the error was made for the past twelve months, logged the details, built a case to show the credit union's interest program had a flaw. Then, somehow, she managed to get her hands on the matching offshore account numbers, and Rosen thinks that was when things changed. Probably, whoever she looked to for help was high enough up the food chain to have been part of the scheme she'd uncovered. She sounds like a smart, determined, resourceful woman."

"She is," Emma said. "I wish Detective Rosen would have told us all this. He knows I want to be kept in the loop, but he rarely calls. It's infuriating."

Miller finished his coffee and set the mug aside. "It's a lot of information, but none of it brings you any closer to your sister, and I think Rosen's hoping to call with news that matters. Men like Rosen and me got into this for the people. I'm guessing he doesn't give two flips about bank interest. He's working to get Sara home." He offered a small smile. "I wish I was officially on that case because it sounds a world more interesting than the junk I deal with over here in Tennessee's most rural county."

Sawyer rubbed a palm against the stubble covering his cheek. He lived in Tennessee's most rural county, on a finger of a lake sandwiched between two forests. "How do you think these guys found us out here tonight?" It had taken emergency responders at least ten minutes to arrive, and they knew exactly where to go. The remoteness, Sawyer realized, was great until he needed the authorities, then he'd have to be prepared to wait.

Miller cast a look at Emma, then back to Sawyer. "Rosen's men have been searching Miss Hart's land, looking for the bullet that went through the man you shot earlier this week. If they find it and match it to their suspect, they can arrest him. They haven't found the bullet yet, but they did find a listening device late this afternoon. You'll be hearing from him tomorrow about a sweep of the home's interior for additional devices."

Sawyer moaned. "The man with the duffel bag came to plant bugs while he snooped."

"Seems like."

Emma paled. "We talked about Sawyer's home while we cleaned. The lake. Our time here."

Detective Miller frowned and pushed to his feet. "I'd better get out there. See if I can find some of the casings from tonight's showdown. Match the bullets to the guns. Guns to their owners."

Sawyer followed Miller to the door. "Before you go, what can you tell us about David Finn and his brothers?"

"Not a lot. The Finns are a big family, and they keep to themselves. Dad's a mechanic. Mom stays home with all the kids. They're strapped for cash most of the time like a lot of folks around here. Some of the older boys have been in trouble from time to time, vandalism, shoplifting, petty theft. Nothing like this."

Sawyer mulled that over. "When you say the Finns are strapped for cash, how strapped are you talking? They don't have enough money to take the whole gang out for ice cream after T-ball, or they don't even have enough money for the kids to play T-ball?"

"More like the church delivers gifts every year so the kids have something to open on Christmas morning."

A whoosh of air left Emma's chest as she appeared at Sawyer's side. There was sudden and profound sadness in her eyes. "So, David and his brothers were likely the hired henchmen," she said. "Coerced into participation by their need to assist the family."

Detective Miller cocked his head. "It's nice of you

to jump to that conclusion. I'm not sure most would in your position."

Sawyer smiled. Emma's kind heart and compassion were two of his favorite things about her.

Emma looked at Sawyer. "What?" Her brows knit together. "Most people are good," she said with finality. "What wouldn't you do to feed your family?"

Sawyer considered ticking off a list. *Murder. Theft. Kidnapping.* But he wasn't sure. Wouldn't he steal to feed his son? Wouldn't he kill to protect his wife? Mother? Brother? The honest answer was that it would depend on the circumstances. That he honestly didn't know. He'd never, thankfully, been in the dire straits Miller described. He'd never been in the Finns' shoes, so he couldn't judge, but he'd like to think that he'd always side with the law.

Detective Miller's cheek kicked up in a lazy half smile as he watched the exchange between Emma and Sawyer.

Emma's shoulders drooped. "I'm not trying to make excuses for criminals," she said. "At the risk of sounding awful, David Finn didn't look, sound or carry himself like someone with a lot of education, motivation or discipline. So, I doubt he's the criminal mastermind behind all this. Couple that with his family's financial situation, and it's more likely that he's made a bad decision for what he sees as a good reason."

Miller slid his gaze to Sawyer and smiled. "She's observant."

Sawyer laughed. "Yes, she is. I also noticed that the leather riding gear they wore was high-end, and those ATVs were new."

"So, either this wasn't the Finn brothers' first job,"

Emma said, "or the one in charge bought new bikes for his crew."

Sawyer gave her hand a squeeze. "That's my guess."

"New bikes?" Miller asked. "Did you get a make and model?"

"Yeah." Sawyer grabbed a pen and paper, then jotted down a description of the vehicles. He stopped suddenly, a smile spreading over his face. "Emma and I saw four headlights in the trees when the men arrived. Four bikes. Four men."

Emma smiled. "David didn't leave on his ATV."

It was still out there.

Miller swung the door open. "Nice work." He tipped two fingers to the brim of his ball cap. "I think I'll go see about that vehicle. I should be able to find the owner through the registration or purchase order. Thank you for the coffee."

"Detective Miller," Emma said, rushing to catch him before he slipped back into the night. "Wait."

Miller stopped on the threshold and raised his brows.

"Did Detective Rosen say if there has been a new lead on my sister?"

The detective took his time answering, but Sawyer saw the slight sag in his shoulders, the downward curve of his mouth. No news. "No, ma'am, I'm sorry," he said finally.

Emma blew out a soft breath. "Okay, well…" She looked at the floor, at her hands, scrambling for something more. "Is there any chance that the Finns have her? Could they be keeping her somewhere?" she asked. "Maybe hiding Sara has been their role in this until now. If they were being paid to keep her hidden, the payoff might've been enough money to buy the ATVs and riding gear."

Sawyer slid an arm around her back, eyes locked on Miller. Was it possible? "Is there someplace on the Finns' land where that could be possible? There were three brothers here tonight. That's more than enough muscle to contain one injured woman."

Detective Miller paused. He scooped the ball cap off his head and ran his fingers through messy hair. "It's a big property," he said. "Family land. I haven't been there personally, but I hear it's landlocked. Good for hunting and not much else."

"No neighbors, then," Emma said. "Secluded."

Miller rubbed his chin. "I suppose much of it is. I'd need a warrant to go poking through the home or property."

Emma stiffened against Sawyer's side. "Does that mean you think I could be right? Do you have enough evidence to get a warrant?"

He tugged the cap back on, swiveled it just right. "Not yet, but I'll call the station, see if the officers were able to get David to talk, and I'll take a look at the ATV left in the forest. If I can get a confession or link the Finns to the embezzlement scheme or something else connected to your sister, I'll have enough to wake up a judge." He smiled and stood a little taller. "I'll see what I can do."

Emma grabbed onto his hand as he turned to leave. "Thank you," she breathed.

Sawyer folded Emma into his arms and kissed her head. What she'd asked of the detective was a long shot, but it was something.

Chapter 15

Sawyer curled Emma against his chest. She'd showered until her skin was hot and pink, then dressed in sweatpants and a sweatshirt and crawled into bed fighting a tremor. He'd kissed her head and shoulders and wrapped her in his arms until her rigid muscles relaxed. When he'd felt her soft, easy breaths on his arm, he knew she'd finally found sleep.

She jumped around 3:00 a.m. when the sound of crunching gravel announced that Miller and the crime scene crew had finished searching the forest for clues and were on their way out. One officer stayed behind, keeping watch indefinitely at Miller's request.

"It's okay," Sawyer whispered. He stroked her cheek with the back of his fingers, careful to avoid the yellowing bruise from her mugging, and he snuggled her a little tighter. "I've got you."

Emma shimmied in his arms, rolling to face him with sleepy blue eyes. "Do you think Detective Miller will be able to get the warrant?"

"I hope so," Sawyer said.

He kissed her forehead and gave her a warm smile, but he hated that the first idea they'd had about where Sara might be was just a guess. It was the first hope they'd had, and after all the bad things that had already happened, he worried about how Emma would handle it if this theory didn't pan out.

Emma didn't speak again for a long while. She drew patterns on his chest with her fingertips, leaving heated trails over the fabric of his shirt. "The judge might not think there's enough cause to issue a warrant."

Honestly, Sawyer didn't either. Not yet. "I know." Sara could be with the man who took her and not with the Finns, or she could be at a site not directly related to any of the people they knew were involved. She could be anywhere.

Emma rolled back an inch and looked up at him in the darkness. "What if you and I take Henry to see the Finns in the morning?"

Alarm struck through Sawyer at the thought of Emma going within a mile of that family. "I don't think that's a great idea."

"Why not?" she asked. "If Detective Miller can't get enough together to justify a warrant, maybe we can. We can stop by and introduce ourselves to the parents, let them know we're the family their sons broke in on last night, and that my sister's missing. We can tell them we're worried about her, and we're only there to see if they have any idea who their sons have been spending time with lately. Not to accuse them of anything. Maybe they'll talk to us. They might be defensive toward policemen, but mother to mother, Mrs. Finn should understand my fear and want to help me if she can."

Sawyer rose onto his elbow and rested his cheek in his hand. "I wouldn't want to do anything that could tip the other boys off," he said. "They know David was caught tonight, but they might not know that we know they were here with him, or that we're considering the possibility that Sara is being kept on their land. Knocking on their door and introducing ourselves could set off all the alarms, and if she is there, our appearance could be enough to make them move her. Personally, I don't like a plan with that much risk," he said. "Not with Sara's safety on the line. Not to mention, we don't want to muck up whatever Miller and Rosen are doing."

Emma dropped her head in frustration. She rolled back over and settled against him before falling asleep once more.

Despite her nearness and the steady sounds of Henry's breaths in the crib beside his bed, Sawyer didn't sleep. He wouldn't sleep until his home was secure and all the men involved in the break-in were behind bars. Instead, he spent the hours until dawn devising a way to keep Emma safe while getting a look at the Finns' land without upsetting the case authorities were building.

The next day was long and quiet. Sawyer arranged an early-morning delivery of enough security equipment to thoroughly lock down the cozy A-frame home. He upgraded the ruined security system and added a feature that would cause flashing lights and an earsplitting alarm in the event of tampering. The chaos would confuse an intruder long enough for Sawyer to drop him. He'd learned the hard way that a system that only alerted the police wouldn't be enough. His home was simply too far from the nearest police station.

After lunch he changed the locks and dead bolts on the doors, and reinforced the jambs to protect against an intruder intent on kicking his way in. Emma stopped him from putting bars on the windows, so he ordered bulletproof glass to be delivered in three to five business days. In the meantime, he set up cameras and a silent alarm system along the property's perimeter that reported to his main computer inside.

Emma spent the day playing, cuddling and napping with Henry. She'd eaten all her meals with Sawyer, but hadn't had much to say, except when Detective Miller had arrived with a sketch artist, eliminating their need to make a run to the station. Miller walked the property while Sawyer and Emma did their best to describe the men they'd seen last night. Afterward, Miller had brought her a surprise. Her cell phone was in the bushes along the house, dropped in her escape from the trespassers, instead of in the lake, where she thought it had gone.

Once Miller and the artist left, there was only endless silence. Whoever said no news was good news had clearly never had to wait on something.

When Emma slipped into the shower after dinner, Sawyer moved onto the back porch to call the detectives. He started with Detective Miller.

Sawyer gave the trees around his property another long exam. He doubted he'd ever forget the mess they'd been through last night, and he knew Emma wouldn't.

Maybe it was time to return the A-frame to the company and look for a place to put down roots with her and Henry. A place where they could make happy memories. Someplace near parks and good schools. Maybe Emma would help him find the perfect spot to raise their son together, if he didn't screw everything up.

"Miller," the detective answered.

Sawyer made a quick pass through the formalities before getting down to business. "Anything new since you left this afternoon? Were you able to get David Finn to talk, or have you traced the ATV to its owner?" Ice fingers dug into the hair at the base of his neck, then slid down his spine. Sawyer rolled his shoulders and stretched his neck, throwing a cautious eye toward the trees.

"Nah," Miller said. "Finn's not talking, but I located the store that sold the ATV."

"Great," Sawyer said, standing straighter.

"You'd think." Miller grunted. "The purchase order says the buyer paid cash for the bike left in the trees last night. The camera over the register is a dummy, and the teenage sales clerk doesn't remember what the customer looked like because that was the night her boyfriend broke up with her and she vowed to never notice another man again. She only answered the few questions she did because I had a badge."

Sawyer dragged a hand over the back of his neck and gritted his teeth.

"The sales receipt recorded the date and time of the pickup, so I've requested security footage from nearby businesses around that time. We might get lucky and catch a glimpse of the truck hauling the ATV away. If

I can get a plate on the truck, I can follow the registration back to the owner."

Sawyer crossed his arms and scanned the distance again. "Any chance you got that warrant?"

"Based on what I've got?" he asked. "No. I don't have anything to link Mr. and Mrs. Finn to Sara's abduction. David might be their son, but he doesn't live with them."

"Where does he live?"

"Ratty apartment downtown. No signs of Sara," Miller said. "I checked last night."

Sawyer said his goodbyes, then dialed Rosen.

Rosen was equally unhelpful, but he confirmed the listening device Miller said had been found on Emma's property. He thanked Sawyer for the message Emma had left earlier providing verbal permission to sweep the house for additional bugs, along with directions to find the hidden key kept in their greenhouse. He had a team out there now.

Sawyer wandered back down the hall to his room, a little defeated, and waited for Emma to finish in the shower.

"Goodness!" Emma gasped upon sight of him on the floor with Henry. "What are you doing?" She pressed a palm to her chest as she lowered herself beside them.

"We're playing airplane," Sawyer said, passing their son her way with some enthusiastic jet sounds. "You look beautiful," he said, dropping a kiss on her nose. "How are you feeling?"

She shrugged. "Hopeful, I think. I'm almost glad those guys came for us here because now we have the power of two county law enforcement groups helping us look for Sara."

Sawyer scooted closer. "I had an idea. Now that I've got this place locked down, except for the window bars." He narrowed his eyes at her.

She bumped her arm against his. "That was a ridiculous suggestion."

"It wasn't a suggestion. The bars are in the closet now."

Emma smiled, her head shaking. "Go on with your new idea, please."

"I think the men who were here last night are probably regrouping and planning their next move. One was definitely shot, and I don't know how big this crew is, but that makes two with a GSW inside three nights, so now might be a good time for us to make a move."

Emma settled Henry on her lap and fixed a curious look on Sawyer. "What do you have in mind?"

Sawyer filled her in on the calls he'd made while she showered, then he suggested what he'd been weighing all day. "I want to gear up and head over to the Finn property at dusk, alone."

Emma squinted. "What does that mean?"

"I don't want to knock on their door. I don't want to give them the chance to say no. I want to enter the Finn property at its most remote access point, walk the land, look for outbuildings, abandoned mine shafts, anywhere big enough to hold Sara. I want you to wait here with Henry. You'll be safe if you stay inside, and Miller's got a lawman stationed on the property in case you need him."

Emma cuddled Henry close. "You're going on a rescue mission."

"Yes." The idea of Sara being held against her will had weighed on him more heavily every day. He knew that pain and understood those complicated feelings too well. The heartbreaking belief that no one was coming. The guilt and remorse. Sawyer's decision to shoot the night guard had alerted other unseen enemies, ultimately leading to the capture, torture and murder of his teammates. Sara, no doubt, blamed herself for pursuing the issue at her credit union. "If I find her, I can bring her home. The police can't even look."

Emma set her hand against his cheek and pressed her forehead to his. She sucked in an audible breath.

"I won't go if you don't feel one hundred percent safe here without me. You and Henry are my top priority."

Emma sniffled softly, then pressed her lips to his, drawing a deep, involuntary groan from him before she pulled away. "Go," she said with a smile. "Find Sara. We'll be right here waiting when you get back."

Sawyer got to work immediately, dressing in black and gathering his weapons and ammo. A sidearm in his belt holster. A spare at his ankle. A duffel bag with night-vision goggles, smoke bombs, wire cutters and anything else he thought might help him on his mission. "I might be a while," he said. "Could be past dawn. I pulled the topography map off the county auditor's website, and there's a lot of ground to cover."

She gripped his wrists in her small hands, a fervent look on her beautiful face. "Just come back to me," she said. "I love you, Sawyer Lance, and I don't want to spend another day without you in my life or in Henry's. We're your teammates now."

Sawyer's heart swelled. "I will come home to you," he vowed, "and if Sara's anywhere on those hundred or so acres of Finn land, I'm going to find her, and I'm bringing her home." He slid his arms around her and delivered a deep and assuring kiss before stepping onto the porch. "I'll wait while you set the alarm."

Emma nodded. She punched in the code, and the little activation light flashed red. *Armed.*

Sawyer let the officer patrolling his property know he'd be gone awhile, then he jogged to the rented SUV and climbed behind the wheel. Twilight was upon him, but he had a map and a twofold plan: search and recover. Return home to his new team.

Night fell slowly over Emma's temporary home. She put Henry to bed around ten and knew he'd stay there dreaming contentedly until dawn. She, on the other hand, doubted she'd be able to sleep until she saw Sawyer's face again. There were so many things she should have told him. Her heart was full and warm with the knowledge that while she'd retreated into her head for the day, and he'd locked the house down like Fort Knox, he'd also been plotting a way to help her sister.

By two thirty in the morning, her nerves had gotten the best of her, and she set a kettle on the stove for tea. The pot whistled, and Emma went to pour herself a little chamomile tea. She tried hard to keep her mind off the possibility that Sara would come home tonight, but hope was stubborn, and she'd thought of little else since Sawyer had gone to look for her.

She filled a cup and inhaled the sweetly scented steam as she raised it to her lips.

Poised to sip, the lights flickered.

Emma braced herself against the counter and waited, listening to the wind whistle around the windows.

A moment later the lights flickered again.

Moving to the door, phone in hand, she dared a look outside for the officer on guard duty. When she didn't see him in his car, she dialed the number he'd given her when he'd arrived for his shift.

The officer didn't answer.

Her heart rate kicked into double time.

Sawyer had secured the home today. He'd barred the door. Installed a high-tech alarm system that would contact the police if the power lines were cut or anyone broke in while the alarm was set, which it was. He'd made every provision short of window bars or bullet-proof glass, she reminded herself She was safe as long as she didn't go outside.

She stared hard into the night, willing the patrolling officer to appear. Maybe he'd dropped his phone without realizing or had left it in his cruiser while making a sweep of the perimeter.

The tall grassy field beyond the glass waved to her in the moonlight. Trees arched and stretched. Fallen leaves spun in tiny tornadoes around the yard, but there were no signs of intruders. No growling ATVs. No telltale headlights or silhouettes of armed men. *Just the wind.*

She dialed the officer again. Maybe he'd just missed the call.

The lights blinked out before the call connected, leaving her in the dark as the call went to voice mail once more.

"We're safe," she whispered. "This is fine. Only a brewing storm." She turned from the window, determined to stay calm. Sawyer had worked on the home's wiring all day, replacing the security system, installing new lights and sirens. The wind had probably just knocked something loose.

But she couldn't explain away the missing cop.

She brought up 911 on her phone and debated.

A loud pop turned her toward the hallway. The sound was loud and strange. Like nothing she'd heard before and very close. The newly installed security lights began to flash in the hallway and living area. An alarm blared in short, sharp blasts. Gnarled fingers of fear curled around her heart and squeezed.

Henry!

Emma ran down the hallway to the bedroom, slightly disoriented by the intense, repetitive bursts of light and sound. Her phone's flashlight beam streaked the walls and floor ahead of her as she gripped the room's doorjamb and propelled herself inside.

Light from her phone fell over an empty crib.

"No." Air rushed from Emma's lungs in a painful whoosh. Her mouth dried. The muscles of her stomach gripped. *This couldn't be happening. It wasn't possible.*

"Henry!" She swung the beam around the room. There were no security lights in the bedrooms, and the continuous flash from the hallway only added to her fear and unease.

The picture window beside the bed was shattered, cracked into a thousand individual crystals, most of which were now on the floor, glittering under the beam of her light. *This was the sound she heard.* Someone had broken the glass, and taken Henry.

"Henry!" she screamed, flashing the phone's light wildly through the space. She ran to the window in search of someone taking off with her son outside.

Instead, she found the missing officer. Facedown and unmoving in the grass.

"Henry!" Her scream became a sob. Sawyer had taken the only vehicle. She was trapped. Alone. Helpless.

Emma turned the phone over in her palm and hit Send on the call she'd had at the ready.

"Nine-one-one, what's your emergency?" A tinny voice echoed across the line.

"Someone kidnapped my son," she said, working to calm her labored breaths. She couldn't report the crime if she had a panic attack, went into shock or passed out.

"What is your name?" the dispatcher asked. "And where are you now? I'll send someone immediately."

Henry's cries broke through the intermittent blares, and Emma spun back toward the hallway. "I don't think I'm alone," she whispered.

"Are you saying there's an intruder in your home?" the voice asked. "Ma'am? Where are you?"

A sudden scream sent Emma into the dark hallway, sprinting frantically toward the sound of her son.

"Ma'am?" the voice asked. "I need your name and location."

"My name is Emma Hart," she rasped. "I'm at a cabin on Lake Anna off of Pinehurst by the national forest." She slid to a wild stop on socked feet at the end of the brightly flashing hall.

Before her, a large man blocked the way. Tall and lean, he towered over her, making the baby in his arms seem impossibly more fragile.

"Henry," she whispered.

"Hang up," the man said. "Now."

Emma disconnected the call.

The man stepped closer. He wore the black leather riding gear she'd come to know and loathe. He also wore a ski mask. "Put the phone down." The eerie calm in his voice was familiar and impossibly scarier than any sound she'd ever heard. This was the man who'd taken Sara.

Henry kicked and arched his back in a fit of fear and anger.

Emma dropped the phone where she stood, outstretching her arms. "Please. Give him to me." Her voice quaked. Her eyes burned and blurred with tears. She couldn't allow this monster to have her son. "I'll do whatever you want. Just don't hurt him."

The man motioned her toward the door. "I'd hoped you'd say that." The sinister curl of his lips was visible through the ski mask. He liked her fear, she realized. This was an elaborate game to him.

And he would kill her when he finished playing. Her. Sara. And Henry.

"Now, turn off your alarm."

Emma pried her dry, pasty mouth open and willed her words to be level and calm. "The alarm is wired to all points of entry. Windows included. When you broke it, you caused an alarm. Someone is probably already on their way."

He pulled a handgun from behind him and pointed it at the number pad, easily balancing her baby in one hand and the firearm in the other. "Shut it off."

Emma's windpipe narrowed. She obeyed, praying the emergency call she'd made, coupled with the broken window, would bring help fast. She pressed the numbers on the keypad carefully until the red light flashed green. "It's off," she said, turning back to the man, arms outstretched once more. "Please," she begged.

"Outside." He pointed to the door.

Her stomach coiled, and her mind raced. She needed to get her hands on Henry. Needed to make a run for the woods or the road, get away and hide until help could arrive.

"Out," he repeated, this time with venom.

Henry screamed again, a loud, maddening demand nearly as loud as the siren she'd recently silenced. It was pure fear. Pure agony, and Emma felt each new cry in her soul.

"Okay." She choked. "Okay." She slid her feet into sneakers by the door and pulled back the security bar, flipped a line of new dead bolts, then moved into the windy night.

On the living room floor behind them, her cell phone began to ring.

"Go." Her abductor pressed the hard barrel of his gun against her spine and forced her ahead.

"To the trees," he growled. "And don't try anything stupid, or I could get confused and drop this squirming kid. I might even step on him while I'm trying to get my hands on you."

Emma lifted her palms. "I won't," she whimpered. "Just, please, don't hurt him."

"Move."

"Where are we going?" she asked. "Are you taking us into the forest to kill us?"

He sniffed a laugh. "I could've killed you in your house," he said.

"Why didn't you?" She moved as slowly as possible with the gun against her back. The pressure of it bruising her spine. If she wasted enough time, maybe help would arrive.

Emma watched the horizon for a sweep of blue and white lights against the darkness, desperate to hear the racing sirens.

The weeds grew taller with every step away from Sawyer's neatly manicured lawn. Sticks and weeds brushed against her legs and clung to her shoes. Bristles and briars tore at her skin.

Beyond the first rows of trees, a black ATV waited with a rifle attached to a gun rack on the back. "Get on," he said.

"I don't know how to drive," she cried, confused and desperate. "There's nowhere for Henry."

The man moved in close. "Get on the bike, and you'll get your baby."

Emma scrambled onto the seat, arms reaching, tears falling.

As promised, he placed her son into her arms. She pulled Henry against her. His small body was cold from the blasting wind. He was dressed in one-piece terry cloth pajamas, no coat, no hat. The psychopath who took him hadn't even taken his blanket from the crib to warm him. Emma hugged and shushed and kissed Henry before turning back to the man with the gun. "I can't hold him and drive. He can't ride on this. It's not safe."

The man fastened the strap of a helmet under his chin, then gripped Henry's thin arm in one black gloved hand. "Fine, we'll leave him here."

"No!" Emma screeched, panic racking her chest at the thought of leaving her infant on the forest floor.

What was wrong with this man? Who could be so cold and damaged?

"Move forward," he demanded, shoving her with his free hand.

"What?" Emma rearranged Henry in her arms, nuzzling his cold face against her warm neck and trying, uselessly, to shield him from the gusting wind. She looked at the narrowing seat and gas tank between her and the handlebars. "Where?"

The man swung one long leg over the padded area behind her, and she instinctively scooted up.

Her thighs gripped the icy metal of the tank.

The man leaned against her back, reaching around her for the handlebars and doubling her over in the process, his chest against her back, Henry clutched precariously to her torso. The engine revved to life, and the man kicked the beast into gear.

Henry gave a pained scream as the vehicle jolted into the night, his protests swallowed by the roaring engine beneath them.

The ATV slid around curves, throwing earth into the air as it bounded over hills and flew along paths nearly invisible to Emma. She clutched Henry to her, willing him to be safe, whatever happened next.

She couldn't imagine where they were being taken, or what the man's plan was for them once they got there, but Emma knew it wasn't good. Her tears fell hard and fast, blown from her eyes by the raging, frigid wind as they tore through the darkness, one slender beam of light to guide the way.

Chapter 16

Emma lost track of time, clinging to the bike for her life and to her son for his. Her face, arms and legs were numb from the biting wind, and Henry shook wildly in her arms. She kept her eyes and mouth closed as much as possible, fighting against the fear and nausea, trying to keep herself together for when they stopped. Whenever that might be. She peeked, occasionally, in search of something she could use to orient herself. A landmark for location or a ranger's office for help when she was able to get free.

The only thing she saw were trees.

Eventually, the ATV slowed. The engine quieted to a purr, and the force of raging wind became something more endurable. Henry's screams were audible once more.

The driver climbed off the machine, chilling her

back instantly where his body heat had warmed her. She struggled to straighten, thankful for the coldness that meant he was away from her, and she could arrange Henry more comfortably in her arms. The moon was bigger, brighter where they were now. On a mountain devoid of objects to block or filter the light.

Before them, the headlight illuminated a large ramshackle shed. There was nothing else in sight except trees and the collapsed remains of a home long ago given back to the forest. A thick metal chain and padlock hung strong and new around the shed's aged door handles, and another powerful round of fear pricked Emma's skin. Someone was storing something of great value.

Sara.

"Get up," the driver barked as he approached the barn. "This is the end of the road for you."

Emma swallowed hard. She climbed awkwardly off the bike and stood on numb, trembling legs.

Her captor turned to the building. His attention shifted to the lock.

This was Emma's chance to run. She twisted at the waist in search of an escape path. The forest was dense around her, and the slopes were steep in every direction, covered in rocks, leaves, twigs, a thousand things to trip on, fall over in the night. The path behind them was relatively clear, but her abductor had an ATV to give chase. Even without the bike, he was undoubtedly stronger, likely faster, and unlike her, he'd dressed for the weather. Even if she managed to stay out of his reach, she couldn't hide. Not while carrying a screaming baby.

"Let's go," the man snapped as the lock gave way. "Inside."

Emma swallowed hard. She couldn't move. The dilapidated shed suddenly looked more like a tomb. The fine hairs on her arms and neck rose to attention. She was certain that going inside meant never coming out, and she refused to sign her son's death warrant.

He wrenched the heavy lock off the loosened chain and thrust the door wide. "Inside," he repeated. "Now."

Emma shook her head, arms tight on Henry, lips trembling. She'd made things bad enough by getting on that bike. She couldn't keep obliging this criminal. The bully. The killer.

He turned on her. "I said…"

Emma ran.

Her feet pounded the earth, flying wildly over the path the ATV had taken, away from the shed and the man who'd forced her out of Sawyer's home at gunpoint. Heart pounding, mind reeling, she searched the darkness for a way off the path and into the trees without falling over the sharp cliff on one side or trying to climb the hill on the other.

Bang! A shot rang out, echoing through the hills and evacuating a thousand bats from nearby trees. Henry screamed.

Emma slowed, raising one palm like a criminal in surrender while holding Henry tightly with the other.

A heavy hand clamped over her shoulder and spun her around, shoving her back in the direction of the shed. The armed man stayed behind her. His thick angry fingers dug into the back of her neck and the flesh of her shoulder. He swore vehemently as he steered her to the open door.

She dug her heels into the earth as her baby cried and flailed in her arms. Terrified of what she'd find inside.

The man gave her another shove, and Emma stumbled forward.

She recognized the shadowy form on the filthy wooden floor immediately. "Sara."

Sara shifted, raising her face to squint at Emma. Her arms and legs were bound, her face bloodied. Clothes ruined. What had he done to her? "Emma! No!" Sara cried. "No." She slung a line of thoroughly emasculating swears at her captor, then spit at his feet.

He dealt Emma another powerful shove, and she lurched forward, across the threshold and onto her knees.

She released Henry with one hand to brace them against the fall, and her wrist gave a gut-wrenching crack upon impact. Shards of blinding light shot through her vision as the pain spread like a heat wave over her body.

Beside her, moonlight shone through a hole in the roof, lending an eerie glow to the horrific scene before her. Sara sobbed and begged their captor for Emma and Henry's safety. She was a thin and fractured mess. Bruised and battered, filthy and frail.

The man unzipped his jacket and reached inside.

Emma scrambled back, angling Henry away from the man and placing herself in front of Sara. "No!" she screamed, imagining the gun already pulled. "Don't!"

He produced a cell phone with one hand, then unfastened the chin strap on his helmet with the other. He removed the helmet and ski mask as he walked back through the door.

Emma held her breath, watching intently as he tucked the helmet under one arm and pressed the cell phone between his ear and shoulder. She shushed Henry and cradled her probably broken wrist, avoiding eye contact as the man turned back to close the door. His face flashed into view a heartbeat before the barrier slammed shut, and Emma's blood ran cold.

Christopher. The man who'd stood in for Mr. Harrison at the credit union on the morning the police had found Mr. Harrison's body. Christopher had probably murdered him, then rolled in for a day of work like nothing was out of the ordinary. He'd been cool, calm and collected when they'd spoken at nine thirty that morning. Her stomach lurched at the memory of his easy smile. It went beyond unhinged to something more like completely deranged.

Sara sobbed against the rough wooden floorboards, apparently half-out of her mind with fear and pain. Her face was battered and caked with dried blood. Her wrists and ankles were raw from the ropes used to bind them.

Emma crawled to her sister's side and gently laid Henry on the floor with her. "It's going to be okay," she whispered, low enough to keep the hope between sisters. "I'm here. We're together now, and we're going to be okay." Emma wasn't sure she believed the words, but they had always been true before. She was counting on them to be true now.

Sara shook her head, frantic. "He'll kill you. You aren't bound yet. You have to run."

Emma hooked her fingers into the ropes at Sara's wrists and tugged with her good hand. Her left hand. Her weak and uncoordinated hand. Nothing happened.

"Stop," Sara said, tears spilling over too-pale cheeks. "You've got to find a way out of here."

Emma relented. Sara was right. Christopher could return at any minute. "Okay."

Outside, the ATV engine kicked to life and slowly moved away.

Emma checked the door. Locked. She examined the hole in the roof. Too high. Nothing to climb on.

"I'm so sorry," Sara gasped. "It's my fault you're here. It's my fault you're hurt. That Henry's hurt. I tried to protect you from all this."

Emma gave Henry a long look. "I don't think Henry's hurt. He's just scared. Cold. Mad." She backed up to get a better look at her sister and their jail cell, then levered Henry into her arms to comfort him. Her wrist screamed from the motion.

"I should have told you what I'd been up to," Sara said. "Then you could have told the police everything right away."

Emma shook her head and gently shushed her baby. "I would have done the same thing."

"I found discrepancies at the credit union," Sara said. "I thought the system was miscalculating interest, but it wasn't an accident. Christopher was stealing."

"I know," Emma said, circling the small room. She needed to find a way out of the shed before Christopher returned. No windows. One chained door. One hole in the ceiling out of reach.

"The accounts weren't just being shorted a portion of their interest. The missing interest was actually being diverted to an offshore account."

"I know," Emma repeated. "I gave your notebook to the police. We figured out what was happening, but no one knew who was behind it or where to look for you." She cuddled Henry closer, and his cries begin to soften. "Now I know it was Christopher."

Sara nodded. "Christopher works in IT at corporate. He wrote the program that stole the money. Harrison helped me figure out what was happening when I brought my notebook to him. We downloaded all the evidence we needed to contact the police, and I saved it on a thumb drive hidden in the picture frame on my desk at work, behind the photo of us with Mom and Dad." She blinked back another round of tears. "I wanted to keep you out of this to protect you, but all I did was put you and Henry in danger."

Emma pressed an ear to the wall and listened. Silence. "I have that photo," she told Sara with a grin. "It's on the mantel at Sawyer's house. The evidence is safe." And best of all, the lunatic who mugged her for the diaper bag of Sara's things hadn't gotten it.

Sara stilled. Her eyes went wide. "Sawyer Lance?" She slid her gaze to Henry. "*The* Sawyer Lance?"

"Yeah." She pressed her good hand to the door and moved clockwise around the room in search of a weak link. In a cabin older than time, complete with chunks of missing roof, there had to be a board somewhere weaker than her. "I'll catch you up as soon as we get out of here." She pressed the toe of her shoe against the base of every wall board where it met the floor, testing the integrity of each dark spot for signs of rot. "Come on," she whispered.

Sara wriggled upright on the floor, calming like Henry and beginning to regain herself. Her tears were gone, and a fresh fire burned in her eyes. "You have the evidence," she said. "That means we can put Christopher in jail for a long time for embezzlement after we get out of here. Harrison will testify."

Emma sighed. "Harrison was murdered."

"Murdered?" Sara's lips parted in horror. "How?"

"Gunshot. Someone tried to make it look like a suicide, but they failed. I assume it was Christopher, but he has a crew of goons working with him now."

"The Finns," Sara whispered. "They bring me food and water."

"Yeah. I think there are others too. In the week that you've been gone, Christopher has added a lot to the embezzlement, including multiple counts of breaking and entering, a hit-and-run, tampering with brake lines, three counts of abduction, a mugging and assault." She thought it over. "The brake line thing might qualify as attempted murder, same with the hit-and-run."

Sara gasped, "What has been happening out there?"

"Nothing good," Emma said, reconsidering immediately. She'd been reunited with Sawyer. Henry with his father. She was in love. Those were all good things. And the thought of Sawyer sparked a new idea in her head. "Do you know if we're on Finn land?"

Sara nodded. "I think so."

Emma smiled. "Sawyer left at twilight to come here and search for you. He hasn't found you yet, which means he's still on his way." And that was very good news. "He must've covered a lot of ground by now. It's only a matter of time before he finds this shed."

She gave the next board a kick, and her foot broke through. "Here!" Emma kicked again. Then again. The wood crumbled and splintered under the force. Slowly the initial shoe-size hole expanded into something big enough to slide Henry through. Soon, they would be able to run.

"Keep going," Sara said, scooting in Emma's direction. "When it's big enough for you to get out, go. Get help."

Emma turned her attention on Sara as she continued to kick and press the decrepit board. "I don't want to leave you."

"I can't go," Sara said. "I can't run. My feet are bound."

"Maybe we can find a way to cut your ropes."

"No," Sara snapped. "I can't go, but you can. We always put Henry first. That's the rule, and we never break it. So, you'll take him and go. Come back with help."

Outside, the low rumble of an ATV returned, growing louder with each passing second.

Emma's gaze darted around the room in search of something sharp to work on Sara's binds, but she was right. There was only dirt and wood. Her next kick wrenched the board loose with a crack, and Emma lowered quickly to the floor. She planted both feet against the edges of crumbled wood and pushed. The planks snapped and groaned under pressure. Hunks of the wall fell into the grass outside, and Emma's feet were suddenly beyond the cabin. Her hips and shoulders would fit through, as well.

"You did it!" Sara said. "You did it! Go! Take Henry and run!"

Emma pulled her feet back and hurried to Sara's side. She threw her arm around her sister's back and hugged her tight, not knowing if it would be the last time she'd ever see her. The painful tightening of her chest, lungs and heart was nearly enough to make her stay. "I love you," she whispered. "You are my best friend. My sister. My hero. Always have been. Always will be."

The ATV arrived, and the engine was silenced.

Sara batted tears. "You be the hero tonight, okay?"

Emma nodded. "Okay." She kissed her sister, then turned for the newly made escape hatch.

Before she could cross the small space to safety, the chains rattled and the shed door swung open.

Chapter 17

Christopher ignited a flashlight, briefly illuminating his angry face. His helmet and ski mask were off, his hair messy from the aftereffects of both. He swung the beam of light over the floor in search of his captives. Shock tore through his scowl as the beam stopped on the generous hole Emma had recently kicked in the wall.

"What the hell?" he snarled, storming inside the dank and musty shed, fists balled. "Did you do that? How the hell did you do that?"

Emma stiffened, scooted back, but didn't speak. A tremor rocked over her limbs and coiled her nerves into a spring. She'd been hit by him once, outside the credit union, and she'd seen him strangle Sara. She knew what he was capable of, and she hated herself for not being faster on the escape. She'd been so close.

Another minute, and she and Henry would've been hidden in the shadows, on their way to find help.

Christopher squatted for a closer look at the hole, then turned to Emma with his signature sinister smile.

She swallowed hard, scrambling for an explanation, contemplating a run for the door. Though running from him hadn't gone her way the last time.

He jerked to his feet, and Emma angled away, blocking her battered sister from his view. "Let us go, and we won't tell anyone what you've done," she begged. The plea was little more than a whisper on her sticky, swollen tongue, her mouth dry and pasty with fear.

Christopher barked an ugly, humorless laugh. He pulled his phone from one pocket and stared at the illuminated screen. "In case you haven't noticed, I don't make deals," he said. "I give orders and I call the shots."

She imagined his inflated ego swelling until it lifted right through the hole in the ceiling. "Then what do you want from us?" she asked. "What's the point? Why did you bring us here?"

He stepped purposefully in Emma's direction, and she winced.

He smiled wider.

Emma widened her stance and prepared to dodge him if he reached for her, or duck if he swung. She breathed easier when he stopped moving and checked his phone. Still, she had no idea why he'd taken the three of them and delivered them to the godforsaken shed. If not to kill them, which he could have already done, then why?

Christopher returned the phone to his pocket, looking satisfied with whatever message he'd received. He leaned at the waist, cold blue eyes searching for Sara around Emma's side. "I worked on this for years, then you just jumped right in and ruined it. You couldn't let it go. You had to pursue it. Relentlessly. Even after you called corporate to report the problem, and I told you I'd handle it. You just couldn't let it go!" His tone grew louder and more hostile with every word.

Emma glanced at her sister's equally red face.

Sara glared past Emma to Christopher. "You're tech support. I called you for help with what I thought was a system glitch. I had no idea I'd contacted the person who'd created the problem," she said, "at least, not until the problem never cleared up."

"You weren't supposed to follow up! That's not your job!"

"You're just tech support?" Emma asked, recalling Christopher at the credit union in a suit and a smile.

"I'm not *just* anything. Except smart, rich and fed up," he snapped. "Harrison wouldn't confess to his part in the ongoing amateur investigation with your sister, even under threat of death, and you saw how that went for him. I used my corporate ID badge to pass as the stand-in manager because I needed access to Harrison's office computer to remove any evidence he kept there. I got that job done, but there's still the issue with Sara. She told me she has enough data to ruin me, but she won't tell me where it is or who she's told. Funny, because she had a real big mouth when it came to shouting the problem from the rooftops."

"I was trying to help people," Sara cried.

Henry gave a grunt and squeal of complaint against the angry voices.

Christopher blew out a breath of exasperation. "This

could have all ended with you. I asked you who you told, and you lied. Now all these deaths are on your head."

Who did you tell?

The vicious whisper from Emma's memories rocked her back on her heels. She swallowed another lump of hate and remorse. "I was there," she said. "When you came into our home and tore her away. I heard you hit her. Choke her. Saw you slam her onto our couch and climb on top of her, bullying, intimidating. You wanted to know who she'd told, but she'd never told anyone except Harrison. Then you screwed up. You took her from me, and you shouldn't have done that."

Henry stiffened his limbs and released a scream that seemed to come all the way from his toes.

Christopher's eyes flashed hot. The hard set of his lips and rigidity of his stance warned her to tread carefully, but Emma stormed ahead.

"You're going to jail," she said, bouncing Henry gently in her arms. "It's only a matter of time now."

He shot Sara a fevered look, then fisted his hands into his messy hair. "You," he seethed, glaring at the woman he'd clearly abused for a week.

"You," she yelled back, angry and suddenly looking utterly unafraid. "You stole hundreds of thousands of dollars from local families who were already struggling to pay their bills and buy groceries. You helped yourself to a portion of the interest they'd earned. You've killed to keep it. To cover your tracks. You're a criminal. A monster and a thief."

Christopher narrowed his eyes. "And you made me a killer."

"Greed made you a killer!"

He tipped his head back and laughed. "Now, we're going to play a game," he said, turning his attention back to Emma. "I'd originally hoped that with enough persuasion, Sara would tell me where she put the files and evidence she's collected against me, but she hasn't been very accommodating. I tried hurting her. That didn't work. I tried isolating her. That didn't work. Food deprivation didn't work. Now the police have one of my men in custody, and he's sure to squeal on me to save his idiot brothers, so I need to get out of town fast. I can't go without those files. I didn't work this hard to become a fugitive living on the run."

"What kind of game?" Emma asked, circling back to what mattered and not caring if Christopher had to live in a cave in Tombouctou.

He fixed her with a warning stare, then sidestepped until he had a clear view of Sara on the floor behind her. "The game goes like this—Sara either tells me where the evidence is, or Sara watches while her baby sister and tiny nephew die slow, ugly deaths."

Emma moved back another step, putting more space between Henry and Christopher. "What about the Finn boys?" she asked. "You said you're in a hurry because they're going to turn on you. Will you kill them too? All of them?" She wrinkled her nose in challenge. "Seems like you might get one or two, but whoever's left will either get the best of you or get away and turn you in."

"You're forgetting that accidents happen, and those guys go everywhere together," Christopher said.

"Another case of cut brake lines?" she asked. Emma struggled not to be sick. He spoke about killing three brothers as coolly as if he were talking about the weather.

The building sound of an ATV engine turned Christopher to the door. "Excellent. He's here." He clapped his palms together. "That game we talked about starts now. You have three minutes to give me what I want or choose who dies first."

"You'll kill us all anyway," Sara said. "Why would I give you anything?"

Christopher smiled and pressed the door wide. "Three minutes," he said, shooting his gun into the air for emphasis before letting the barrier slam shut behind him.

Sawyer had lost count of the number of acres he'd covered when he heard the gunshot. He'd been at it for hours and not found any trace of Sara or anyone else, and at just before dawn, the single gunshot seemed all kinds of wrong.

He'd left Emma and Henry inside a heavily secured home, protected by a state-of-the-art system, but instinct had his hand inside his pocket, seeking his cell phone anyway.

He frowned at the pitiful single bar of service, then dialed Emma, thankful to have any reception so deep in the forest. No answer.

He redialed and squinted at the slowly lightening sky while he waited. The sun would rise soon, and he'd be able to see farther, move faster, finish his mission and return to his family. That was how he thought of them now, he realized. *As his family.* His new team.

He dialed again, and the call went to voice mail.

Sawyer's intuition flared. He dialed the number of the officer posted outside his home instead.

That call went to voice mail, as well.

Sawyer broke into a sprint, running full speed in the direction of his vehicle. This time, he dialed Detective Miller.

"This is Sawyer Lance," he stated without waiting for the customary hello when the call connected. "Have you heard from your man outside my home?"

"No," Miller answered hesitantly. "Where are you?"

"Looking for Sara, but Emma's not answering, and neither is her security patrol. I've just heard a gunshot. I think someone's taken her and Henry like they took Sara, and I think they're somewhere on Finn land with her now."

"Whoa," Detective Miller cautioned. "Slow down and start over. Where are you?" he asked again.

"Detective," Sawyer said through gritted teeth, feeling his temper flare, "check on my family. Call me when it's done. I'll fill you in after." He disconnected. His mind spun with calculations as he ran. The amount of time it would take him to return home. The amount of time it would take him to reach the Finns' home. The amount of time it would take to find the location of the gunshot based on the echo and his best guess.

His phone vibrated in his palm as he slid behind the wheel of his rented SUV. "Lance," he answered.

There was a long beat of silence before the detective spoke. "Emma made a 911 call late last night, when responders arrived, the home was empty. Your bedroom window was broken. Our man was down."

Sawyer beat his empty palm against the steering wheel and floored the gas pedal. He reversed down the long dirt road at the edge of the Finn property with abandon. Dirt flew in a cloud around him. "They were home when I left," Sawyer said. "I have the car, so where the hell are they?" He thought for a moment about the situation. "Did you say she called 911?" He pulled the phone away to check the screen. He'd missed four calls. Two from a number he recognized as belonging to the new security system. Two from Detective Miller. His teeth gnashed as he swung the vehicle around at the end of the lane. "You called," he said. "It never rang." Cell service wasn't any good on the mountain. Nothing but trees and wildlife for miles. No signs of civilization.

Sawyer swallowed past a growing lump in his throat as numerous horrific images cluttered his mind. "Were there signs of a struggle?" he asked, unable to bring himself to ask the bigger question. Was there blood?

"Just the broken window," Miller said. "Someone shut off the alarm using the code, but no one answered when the contact number was called."

"It didn't ring," Sawyer said. He spun the SUV at the end of the lane and shifted hard into Drive. There wasn't anything to be done at his place. Emma and Henry were already gone. The cops would slow him down with questions for their reports, and time was already wasting. He needed a new plan. "I'm going to the Finn house."

"You are not," Detective Miller ordered, his voice thick with authority.

"I am," Sawyer corrected. "If you don't want me there, I suggest you try to stop me."

A siren coughed to life on the other end of the line.

Challenge accepted. "You've got no business—" Miller began.

Sawyer cut him off. Miller didn't get to decide what was or was not Sawyer's business, and Emma and Henry absolutely were. "I've been on the Finn property all night," Sawyer interjected. "Walking. Looking."

"Trespassing," Miller countered, the siren on his vehicle complaining in the background.

"Looking for places Sara might've been held. I didn't hurt anything. Didn't touch anything."

"Did you find anything?"

"No, but there's a lot more ground to cover, and I heard a gunshot. It was near, but not near enough that I could say where it came from specifically, and I don't have time to mess around trying not to infringe on other folks' rights when my rights and the rights of my family have been trodden over daily for a week. So, like I said, I'm going to talk to the Finns. If you don't want me there or you're just eager to charge me with trespassing, then you'd better come haul me in." He disconnected and dropped the phone onto his passenger seat, then depressed the gas pedal and tore up the quiet country road getting to the Finns' house.

He took his time pulling into the driveway, careful not to roll into an ambush. He parked several yards from the front porch and climbed out as the sun crested the horizon. Senses on alert, and one hand on the butt of his gun, Sawyer opened the driver's door.

The home's front door swung open a moment later. A man in bib-style Carhartt overalls walked out. His clothes were covered in old grease stains. His boots and ball cap looked equally well-worn. "Who's there?" he called, stepping onto the top porch step.

Sawyer remained partially behind the open door. "Sawyer Lance, Fortress Security," he announced. "I'm hoping you have a minute to talk."

"I have a minute," he said, "but the missus is making breakfast, and I try not to miss a meal. Can I ask what this is about?" Mr. Finn was pushing fifty, tall and lean with a mess of crow's-feet at the corner of each eye.

"Are you Mr. Finn?" Sawyer asked.

"That's right. I'm Mark Finn." He hooked his thumbs in the straps of his bibs, both hands visible.

Sawyer relaxed and shut the car door. "Mr. Finn, I'm here because my…" He paused, stuck for the word. His *what*? His girlfriend? The term felt far too juvenile for what Emma was to him. She was everything to him. She and Henry. He rolled his shoulders and began again, reminding himself that time was speeding ahead while he floundered in a stranger's driveway, worried about semantics and courtesies. "My baby and his mama were abducted last night, and there was a gunshot out this way not long ago. I'm worried she might be on your property somewhere and hurt." *Or worse*, he thought. But there had only been one gunshot. There were two of them. A mama and a son.

"I heard that shot," Mr. Finn said, trading his easy smile for a frown. "Could be anything. Everyone's got a rifle out here. Could be someone saw a snake. Maybe had target practice or whatnot."

"No," Sawyer interrupted. "It wasn't target practice. There was only one shot, Mr. Finn." He felt the tension in the air, saw the man's shoulders square, his chin rise. "I'm not here to accuse you of anything. I'm looking for your help."

Mr. Finn crossed his arms and whistled. "I think you should go."

A moment later a dog the size of Texas tore into view, shaggy, caked in mud and rocketing to a seat at Finn's side.

Sawyer divided his attention, wishing he'd left the door open between himself and the massive mutt. "One of your sons was arrested last night," Sawyer said flatly. "I know because he and his crew came into my home in search of my family. I held them off. Shot one. The others got away clean. David was arrested. I think the others came back while I was out today, and I'm afraid that shot was meant for either my baby or his mama."

Mr. Finn's face went pale. "My boys wouldn't do anything like that. You're mistaken and out of line for coming here like this, and you'd do best to go."

"No, sir," Sawyer said. "I can't do that. See, I need you to tell me where a woman could be held on your property without being noticed for a week. Maybe two women now and my baby. Then I want to look for them."

Mr. Finn's sheet-white skin paled further, leaning on a shade of green. "No."

The half bark of a police siren shut Sawyer's mouth, already open for a rebuttal.

Behind him, Detective Miller bounced his black truck over the pitted gravel drive, bubble light flashing on top of his vehicle.

The door to the home opened again. This time a woman in jeans and a button-down rushed out. She had silver in her dark ponytail and a kid on one hip. A boy half her height trailed after her. "What's this about, Mark?" she called. "I'm just about to serve breakfast."

Mark let his eyes shut slowly, then turned to repeat Sawyer's story with a gentler touch than Sawyer had delivered it.

Detective Miller slammed his truck door, then hastened up the drive to where they stood. He pressed his palms to his hips and glared at Sawyer. "Have you said your piece?"

Sawyer nodded. "I have."

"Good. Like I told you before, we can't legally access their land without a warrant. So, you need to leave or be arrested for trespassing."

"I'm not leaving," Sawyer said. He turned desperate, pleading eyes on Mrs. Finn. "Please, ma'am," he pressed. "My four-month-old son and his mama are missing. I believe they're both in grave danger, and I think someone is holding them on your property. All I want is the chance to look for them. If they're not here, I'll leave, apologize, refine my search. But I'm asking you—what would you do if you thought your spouse and one of your babies was being held on my property? What if I said you weren't allowed to look for them?"

Mrs. Finn shifted the kid on her hip and traded a look with her husband. She turned a serious gaze on Sawyer. "You got something of theirs with you?"

Sawyer scrambled to make sense of the question. "What?"

"A shirt, a blanket, a hair tie," she said. "It don't matter." She tucked her fingers in her mouth and whistled. A mess of kids came running. "These ain't all ours, but they'll help if they want breakfast, and you know they do. Blue will help too, if you've got something he can use to track." She nodded at the dog.

"Yes." Sawyer spun around, wrenching the SUV door open and digging behind the seats for something belonging to Emma or Henry. "Thank you," he said, fighting a punch of emotion. He came up with a blue blanket of Henry's and a hoodie of Emma's.

Blue gave the items a long sniff, then took off in search of more of those same scents.

The Finns, Detective Miller and a slew of kids from age five to fifteen fanned out across the backyard, headed into the woods.

"We've got a number of barns and outbuildings," Mr. Finn said as they crossed the wide, flat space behind the house. "The kids and I have built blinds, forts, tree houses, all that and more on this land over the years." He slowed as his family and neighbor kids slipped out of sight, no more than silhouettes against a brilliant morning sky.

Sawyer ached to run after Blue, who was long gone, but waited, anticipated what Mr. Finn had to say. The way he'd paled at the mention of his other sons had meant something. Sawyer hoped it meant he had a good idea where Emma and Henry might be.

Finn swung a worried gaze from Sawyer to Detective Miller and halted in his tracks.

Miller cocked a hip. "You got something on your mind, Mark?"

Mr. Finn scanned the trees. "When my oldest boy was in high school, he'd throw wild parties at a spot we call The Point. It's just a small plot of flat land where my great-granddad's house stood about a hundred and fifty years back, but the last time I was out that way, there was a shed still standing." He pointed in the direction opposite of where the others had gone. "There's an access road a couple miles from here that cuts back this way. Down near Pine Creek Road."

"I know it," Detective Miller said, pulling keys from his pocket. "I drove past it getting here." He smiled at Sawyer. "I can be there in about ten minutes. You coming, Lance?"

"No." Sawyer shook Finn's hand with gusto, then broke into a sprint. "I can be there in seven."

Chapter 18

"Go!" Sara whispered frantically to Emma. "Please." She struggled to hold back the silent sobs racking her battered body.

Emma fought the urge to lose control right along with her sister, but that was a luxury Emma didn't have. She was unharmed and unbound. It was up to her to get them all out of there. Alive.

Henry squirmed in her arms. He'd screamed himself to sleep during the argument with Christopher, but he was restless. Ready to wake. To scream again. Ready for a bottle. A new diaper. All the things Emma couldn't provide for him.

"Go," Sara continued.

"No." Emma tilted forward, locking determined eyes on her sister. "I'm not leaving you here to be murdered."

"Think of Henry," Sara sobbed. "If you're still here when that door opens again, someone's going to die."

"He's going to kill us all regardless," Emma said. "The minute you tell him what he wants to know, you'll no longer be useful and we'll no longer have leverage. We'll all be dead the next second. So pull it together and help me think."

"You have to try to get away," Sara begged. "You have no idea what he's capable of." Tears rolled over her bruised cheeks, through the squint of her swollen black eye. She pulled her knees to her chest, and the ideas of what Sara might have been through came at Emma like a tidal wave.

"If he comes back and we're gone, he'll kill you," Emma explained. "Henry will hear the shot and scream, giving away our position, then Christopher will kill us. That's if Henry doesn't start crying the minute I lay him down to slide through the hole. Once I get out—if I get out—I can't even hide in the shadows anymore. The sun is up."

Sara pulled in a sharp breath; her cries quieted. She blinked at the warm rays of orange and amber light cutting through the shed's ceiling. "Another day," she said, mesmerized. "Every night I think I won't see another day."

Emma paced the small room with Henry in her good arm, forcing her thoughts away from the pain of her broken wrist. Outside, the sound of an approaching engine grew louder, closer, before the silence. "We need a plan, or you're right—there won't be another day. Not for any of us."

"Maybe we can hold the door shut somehow," Sara suggested.

Emma shook her head. "If we try to stop him from coming in, he'll just shoot through the door and hit us both. Besides, I can hear a second voice. There are two men now, and we aren't stronger than two men. I think my wrist is broken, and you look like you haven't eaten in a week."

"I've tried," Sara whispered. "When they bring it, I try."

Emma leaned her forehead to the wall and angled for a look at the new arrival between cracks in the rickety wooden boards.

"Who is it?" Sara asked.

"I think it's one of the Finn boys," she said. Though she hadn't gotten a clear look at him in the dark, she thought he might have been one of the two men on the dock while she'd hidden in the water. If she was right, then he'd already come to abduct and kill her once. Considering that she was currently abducted, it was an easy jump to the reason he was there now.

The newcomer climbed off his ATV with a gun on his hip. His shaggy red hair was unkempt, and his eyes were wild. His gaze jumped from the shed to Christopher. "I was thinking," he said nervously. "I think we can get this done another way. There's no one at either house now. We can leave them here, and while everyone's out hunting for them, we can go through both places, take another look. Find what we missed."

"No time," Christopher said. "I need to go, which means they need to go. You got that? If I come back here on my way out of town and find any of them alive, I'm coming for your family. All of them. Maybe I'll build a nice middle-of-the-night fire to take care of all those young siblings. Maybe a brutal car accident for your woman and your baby. While you're griev-ing over their twisted carnage, you'll know it was your fault. All because you couldn't do this one simple task. You want that?"

"No, man," Finn said. "I didn't want anyone to die." He scraped a heavy hand over his cheek. "I never agreed to this. You never said anything about kidnap-ping and murder."

"I just did." Christopher climbed onto his vehi-cle and started the engine. "I've got to get this ride scrubbed down in case her or that kid drooled on it. They'll check it for DNA when they find it, and I don't need any other fingers pointed my way. I gave Sara three minutes to tell you where she hid the evidence. If she doesn't, then you've got to make her choose who to shoot first. Don't make me a liar."

"What if she tells me what you want to know?"

Christopher drew a finger across his neck. "Kill them anyway. No loose ends. Understand?"

"What about the baby?" Finn asked. "You said I could take it to a fire station. Give it a chance at a life."

"I'm going home to pack," Christopher said, ignor-ing Finn's question. "There's a hole in the back wall big enough for them to fit through. If you take too long going in, they'll force you to chase them. It's awful damn early for that, trust me." He stuffed the helmet onto his head and flipped the visor up. "I want to see three bodies when I come back, so do. Your. Job." He delivered the final three words with deliberate men-ace, then revved his engine to life.

Emma's heart leaped and twisted in her throat. "Sit up," she told Sara. "Scoot back, sit up. Hurry."

Sara obeyed. Bending her knees, she planted her bound feet on the floor and pressed her back to the wall, settling her bound wrists in front of her.

Emma set Henry on Sara's lap, fitting him into the sharp curve of her sister's body for balance, then she dragged them both against the wall beside the door.

Next, Emma ran for the hole. "Don't let him fall."

Sara gripped Henry's legs in her hands. "What are you doing?" Sara gasped. "You can't leave him with me. I can't protect him."

"I'm not leaving," Emma said, crouching to grab the edge of a broken board in her good hand. She braced her feet against the floor and leaned back, throwing her weight into the movement, arm straining, legs burning. "Come on," she whispered. Nothing happened.

She inched forward, rearranged her grip on the wood and tried again.

"What are you doing?" Sara repeated. "Get out and take Henry."

"I'm not leaving. I've only got one arm to hold Henry while I run through the forest in broad daylight with him screaming. We'll be dead inside five minutes." Her grip slid. She reset her efforts and tried again. "He'll give chase. He'll hunt us."

The board made a moaning creak.

"So what?" Sara asked. "You have to try. Why are you making the hole bigger if not to run?"

The board gave way with a sudden, shockingly loud crack, showering the floor in shards of rotted wood and sending Emma onto her backside with a thump. A smile broke over her lips. "I can't run, but I can fight."

Outside, a man swore, and the door rattled.

Emma grabbed her newly freed slat of weak, aged wood and ran to hide beside the door with Sara and Henry. And wait.

Sawyer's chest throbbed with the effort of an all-out run up an uneven, rocky grade toward the mountaintop where Mark Finn had suggested Emma and Henry might be held. Maybe Sara too. His leg muscles burned. His worried heart hammered from effort and fear. It had been too long since he'd heard that single gunshot. *A kill shot*, he thought. And even if she hadn't died immediately, she'd have bled out by now, with all the time he'd wasted asking Finn's permission to look. Then again, without Finn's input, he would have had no idea where to go. Now he knew there was a shed, and Emma might be there with Henry. The thought pushed him harder, faster.

Maybe Emma had gotten away. Maybe the shot had missed her, and she'd hidden.

Maybe she had made the shot.

Sawyer slowed at the low groan of an ATV and walked silently in the sound's direction. Through the dense growth of ancient trees, a black ATV rumbled downhill with only a driver on board.

Emma widened her stance, raised the board onto her shoulder like a baseball bat and waited as the door wiggled, then opened.

And she swung.

The wood connected with the man's face in a gush of blood and curses. Her weapon split down the center in response, one long ragged crack, splinters of rot flying over the both of them. He stumbled back, blood pouring from his nose and mouth, eyes blinking, ready to fall. The man's arms flailed, hands reached out for balance and caught the doorjamb with a thud.

The gun in his hand went off.

Sara screamed. Emma gasped.

Searing pain scorched through Emma's side and her hand lowered to the spot on instinct. Her palm slid against a strange, slick warmth, and the world tilted, but the man didn't fall.

Not good.

She needed to knock him out, steal his ATV and race her son and sister to safety.

"You shot her!" Sara screamed. "Emma!"

Emma looked at her side, then her palms, confused and swimming in adrenaline. Blood seeped through her shirt. The eye-crossing, relentless pain came next. She locked her teeth and swung the wood again, heart in her mouth, pulse beating like thunder through her head.

This time, the man's hand shot out and caught the busted board. He wrenched it from her grip and threw it out the door behind him. "You broke my nose!" he wailed. Blood trailed over his lips, teeth and chin. The skin along the ridge of his nose was red, broken and quickly swelling. His eyes flamed hot.

Emma stumbled back, pressing both palms to her side, where blood flowed freely around and between her fingers now. Her broken wrist no longer ached, but her knees wobbled. Her head spun, and the pain of the gunshot chewed its way straight through her. The unconscionable burn radiated across her gut and up her chest until it ate through her vision, and the filthy, aged floorboards rushed up to meet her.

* * *

A second gunshot. Sawyer pulled his phone and his gun, double-timing his pace up the mountain toward the peak, where he hoped to find a shed, and Emma, Henry and Sara alive.

"Miller," the detective answered.

"Another shot," Sawyer said flatly, forcing his mind and body to stay tuned to the task. "Hear it?"

"I heard it. Got an ambulance coming."

Sawyer's shoulders relaxed by a fraction. "Did you get the ATV?"

"Yes, I did. Stopped him at the crossroad. Says he didn't see the no-trespassing signs and was just out for a morning drive."

Sawyer cursed. Rage burst through him like shrapnel. "You let him go?"

"No," Miller said. "He was trespassing, carrying a concealed weapon without a license, and his vehicle fits the description of an ATV seen leaving the site of multiple recent crimes. My deputy is on his way to pick him up."

"Who is he?" Sawyer fumed. "A Finn boy?"

"No. ID says Christopher Lawson."

Lawson. "He was at the credit union, standing in for the dead manager on the day that guy was murdered." Sawyer pushed himself harder, faster, his breaths coming quick and a smile forming on his lips. "I think you've gone and captured the ringleader. Don't let that one go."

"No intent of the sort," Miller said in an easy, casual drawl.

Hope rose in his chest as the next plateau came into view, and the cries of his son rose on the wind. "I've got eyes on the shed. I can hear my son crying." And there was another shiny black ATV sitting out front. If the victim of that last gunshot wasn't the driver of this ATV, then he was likely to be the next one shot. "You'd better order up another ambulance."

The sounds of Henry's and Sara's cries warbled through Emma's fuzzy head, and she pushed to her hands and knees on autopilot. "You don't have to do this," she said, adding immediately to the pleas of her sister.

The gun shook in Finn's hand. His gaze darted around the dank, rotten, earth-scented shed. He muttered behind the other palm, which he'd clamped to his mouth.

Emma forced herself back on her haunches, deliberating, watching Finn and gauging what he might do next. Desperation drove people to do awful things, and Finn seemed as desperate as any man Emma had ever seen. "Please," she tried again. "I'm already shot, but you can save my baby and my sister. Get them away from here and tell Christopher you buried their bodies or threw them in the river. Anything. Not this for them." She lifted a bloodied palm. Fresh crimson drops painted a thick path down her forearm. "They're all the family I've got."

His face contorted with indecision. He looked at his gun, at Sara and Henry on the floor, at Emma, bleeding and weak.

"You would want to protect your family if you could, wouldn't you?" Emma asked softly, hoping that big family of his had taught him to respect and honor a genetic bond.

Finn swung in her direction, a belligerent look on his youthful face. "I have family too. He'll kill them if I don't kill you."

"He's going to kill you anyway," Emma said. "He's going to kill all of us so he can keep his stolen money and his secret, but you don't have to do this. I can see this isn't who you are, and it's not what you want." She hoped she was right.

"This was supposed to be easy money," he said. "My lady just had another baby, and we don't have money for food or diapers. My folks can't help. They're strapped raising my brothers and sisters. I can't find work without leaving town. I can't look outside town for work without a car. Can't buy a car without money." He raised his hands and pressed them to his head, pointing the gun at the ceiling. "I was going to be the muscle. A bodyguard for Christopher, a lookout when he needed me. I was going to earn enough to keep food, formula and diapers in the house until I got real work. Then he got his hands on my younger brothers, promising them everything. Buying them fancy ATVs and riding gear. He reeled them in and had them doing his dirty work before I even knew it was happening. Then he used them as leverage with me. If I walked out on him, he'd turn them in for the crimes he had them commit. The next thing I know, we're all doing terrible things and we're stuck."

"Now your brother David has been arrested," Emma said. "Christopher thinks he'll turn on him to keep you out of jail, so Christopher plans to kill you after you kill us."

Finn didn't blink. It was the second time she'd told

him Christopher's plans, and the second time he'd taken the information in stride.

"You already know," Emma said, letting the truth settle in. "You know, but you're still willing to become a murderer for him. Why?"

Finn paced. "It buys me and my family time."

"No, it doesn't," Emma said. "And you can't take your whole family on the run with you. Your girl and your kids, maybe, but what about your folks and all those siblings? Have you made enough money from Christopher to relocate all of them? To keep running if he looks for you?"

"He won't look for us," Finn said. "He'll be busy running from the law too."

"And if he gets caught? Turns you in to make a deal for himself?"

Finn's breaths came more quickly. A line of sweat raised on his forehead and lip. He pressed his palms to his temples. "Shut up so I can think."

Henry's cries grew desperate again, as if he was in pain. Hunger, Emma thought. When was the last time he'd eaten? Before bed last night. It was also the last time he'd been changed. Tears pricked her eyes. Her baby was hungry, and she couldn't feed him. Scared and she couldn't hold him.

Finn dropped his hands and looked from Emma to Sara. "Enough. Turn around. Both of you." He pressed his thumb to the hammer on his gun and pulled it back with a soft click that rolled Emma's stomach. "I just want this to be over," he said, exhausted. "Turn around. I'll make it quick. Three shots. Three seconds. You'll never know it happened, and it'll be over."

"Please," Sara cried. "Don't."

Finn scooped Henry into his arms and set him against the wall, near the hole Emma had made. He dragged Sara back against the far wall, opposite the door, and he motioned Emma into the space between her son and sister. Lining them up like bottles for target practice. "Close your eyes."

Emma gripped her side and reached for her baby.

Finn groaned. "Stop."

Emma couldn't stop. It wasn't in her. Henry was alone, crying, scared. He wouldn't die alone like that. She didn't care what Finn or anyone else said. "Mama's here," she called, working her voice into something less soaked in pain, less mired in grief. "Shh," she cooed.

"I said stop!" Finn raged, his boot connecting with her torso, spinning her into a hard roll that ended with a collision against the side wall, away from Henry and the escape hole. The impact stole her breath, knocked the wind from her lungs. She searched wildly through spotted vision for Henry when she stilled.

"Henry," she choked.

His cries were there, but he wasn't. Her gaze darted across the floor. Had he flailed and kicked himself through the hole? Had he fallen to the ground?

Emma's heart and stomach lurched.

Finn stormed forward, peering through the hole. "What the...?" He stood upright as Henry's cries grew distant and muffled. Panic colored his bloody face. "I should've just killed you all the minute I walked in here," he said, storming for the door. "I let you talk to me and get into my head, now..."

A blast of gunfire cut Finn's rant short. The sudden burst rang in Emma's ears and vibrated in her chest.

Finn flew backward, arms waving, feet twisting, until he landed in a lifeless heap beside Sara.

The door swung open and Sara screamed.

A pair of men marched inside.

Emma's mind reeled. What had happened? Who had arrived? Who had shot Finn? Christopher?

The first man kicked the gun away from Finn, then lowered to check his neck for a pulse.

"Emma." Sawyer's voice broke through her muddled thoughts. His face swam into view, marred with fear and concern. He crouched before her, Henry crying in his arms. He pressed his forehead to hers, then kissed her lips with firm reassurance. "Sorry I'm late."

Detective Miller stood, stepped away from Finn's body. "He's gone," he said sadly, then moved to Sara's side and cut easily through her ropes with a pocketknife. Once she was freed, he hoisted her into his arms and carried her straight outside and into the day.

Sawyer's expression fell. His eyes stretched wide as he lifted a bloodied palm between them. "Emma?" His gaze trailed over her torso, over the smears of her blood on Henry's pajamas between them. "You've been shot."

Emma opened her mouth to tell him she was okay, that she loved him, but the words didn't come. She felt the strength of his arms around her. Smelled the sweet scent of Henry's baby shampoo as her head rolled back. Her thoughts fell into darkness.

Chapter 19

Sawyer kissed Emma lightly under the canopy of lights outside her home. A lot had changed in the eight months since he'd ridden with her, breathless and terrified, to the hospital following her mountaintop rescue. His pulse still raced whenever he thought of that day. He still dreamed every manner of horrific scenarios where things went another way. Sometimes he arrived five minutes later. Too late to save her. He hated those dreams most. But when the nightmares of losing her woke him now, the way nightmares of losing his team had woken him before, he simply reached for her in the darkness and pulled her near. Then everything was right in the world.

"I love you," she whispered against his crisp white dress shirt, playfully flipping the end of his tie.

He kissed her again, at a complete loss for words.

Seeing her so healthy and beautiful under the endless rows of twinkle lights, surrounded by family and friends, it was hard to believe that he'd nearly lost her completely. She'd gone limp in his arms, and he'd felt the punch of it in his gut as clear and strong as if it would kill him too.

Eight months since he'd stood sentinel at her bedside following her surgery. Eight months since he'd prayed around the clock to see her beautiful blue eyes once more. Eight months since he'd fallen to his knees the moment she'd spoken his name and begged her to be his wife. He hadn't gotten halfway through the rambling proposal before she'd said yes. It was her first word after three long days of silence, and it had the power to change his life.

She cradled his cheek in her palm as she smiled.

Two hundred guests and she only had eyes for him. His chest puffed in pride and satisfaction.

"What?" she asked.

"Just thinking about how lucky I am. How thankful," he said. It was a reminder he gave her often. "The hospital staff wasn't sure you'd make it." They'd said she lost a lot of blood on that mountain, too much for good odds.

"But you knew I would," she said.

"Yes, I did," he agreed. "They didn't know you like I do." They didn't know what Emma would do, what she'd endure or survive for the chance to raise her son.

Sawyer knew, and he'd waited patiently at her bedside with Henry and Sara until one day, Emma simply opened her eyes.

"Well, that makes us two lucky, thankful people," she said, sliding her palms gently against his chest.

Sawyer lifted her left hand and kissed the knuckles beside her engagement ring. The ring had been her mother's, but Sara had insisted Emma wear it after the engagement. Sawyer had a custom wedding band in the works to go with her mother's ring. She'd wear that soon too. For now, they'd settled on an open house–style engagement party where friends, families and neighbors could get a look at the girls they'd read about in newspapers and gossip columns straight through Christmas. The community had followed Emma's and Sara's recoveries like their own lives depended on it.

"Enough of that," a familiar voice boomed nearby. Detective Miller approached with Sara on his arm. Their flirting had started at the hospital, both checking in on Emma, and it continued to the present. Sawyer thought it was nice. Emma was more cautious, expectedly protective of her big sister, despite the fact that, to Sawyer's opinion, Miller had been a perfect gentleman every step of the way. "Save it for the ceremony," Miller said with a broad grin.

Sawyer gave Miller's hand a hearty shake. He owed the detective more than he could ever repay. Thanks to his dogged follow-up work, Christopher Lawson was in jail and going to stay there for a very long time. The expected charges of murder, attempted murder, embezzlement, kidnapping and a half dozen of others were just the tip of the iceberg once Miller got started. He'd combed through Christopher's personal computer as if it held the secrets of the universe, and he'd uncovered a treasure trove of evidence against Christopher in the process. Miller linked him and his accomplices to a bevy of other criminal offenses within the month. As a bonus, and as no surprise to the detective, David Finn had confessed everything he knew in trade for leniency on his brothers. Christopher turned on everyone in the hopes of reducing his sentence, but the FBI had been particularly interested in the money laundering and fraud. And they weren't interested in giving breaks.

Sawyer released his hand. "Sorry, man, I just can't seem to keep my hands off of her."

"So I've heard" was Miller's quick response. It earned him an elbow from Sara and a grin from Emma.

She pulled Sara into a hug. "Thank you for doing all this," she said. "Everything is absolutely beautiful, completely over-the-top for an engagement party."

Sara stroked Emma's arm as she stepped back. "Consider this a test run for the big day."

Emma smiled into the apricot-hued horizon, lifting her chin to the warm setting sun. "I still can't believe I'm getting married on our land. Just like Mom and Dad."

"They'd be really happy," Sara said, tearing up. "I'm still just really glad you're alive."

Sawyer worked to swallow the brick of emotion that presented at the slightest reminder.

"Back at ya," Emma said.

Thankfully, Emma's broken wrist had healed as nicely as her gunshot wound. Both under constant watch and care from Sawyer and Sara, not to mention an endless string of casseroles and pies hand delivered by community members, a testimony and staple of courtesy in the South.

Sara leaned against her new beau's side, her gaze floating across the sea of people on her lawn. "I'd started thinking of Emma and I as alone in the world after Mom and Dad died, but there are nearly two hundred people here tonight, and we're expecting a hundred more for the wedding in September." She eyeballed Sawyer. "Though I think half these guests belong to you."

He smiled. "Probably so." The group near the stables, for example, now roaring with laughter as Henry toddled after a barn cat. He recognized every face from his team at Fortress Security, plus Wyatt's new wife and baby. The rest of that crowd was blood-related and soon to be Emma and Sara's family, as well. Most of them were Garretts. Cousins from Kentucky that seemed to have *protect and serve* in their blood.

For a pair of sisters so accustomed to being alone, Emma and Sara were in for a major adjustment. Henry would never know a day without someone to play with.

Sawyer's partner, Wyatt, caught him staring and led half the pack in Sawyer's direction. Wyatt's new wife laughed along behind them, leading Henry by one hand. His cousins' wives herded everyone else in his direction.

"Well, here comes a crowd," Sawyer muttered to his little circle, a smile already spreading on his lips. "What do you suppose they're up to?"

Wyatt pulled Sawyer in for a strong one-armed hug, then kissed Emma's and Sara's cheeks and shook Miller's hand. "We were just talking about the happy couple," he said, looking from Emma to Sawyer, then back.

Sawyer's senses went on alert. "What are you up to?"

Others from the lawn began a sweep in their direction, whispering and pointing as they moved.

Wyatt pressed a palm to his heart, feigning innocence. Poorly. "Henry was just telling us the story of how two quiet sisters single-handedly took down a psychopathic murderer, escaped abduction and ended a mass of fraud and embezzlement operations, armed only with wood from the dilapidated shed where they were held."

Emma laughed as Henry made a stumbling run for her calves. "Is that right?" she asked. "I know his vocabulary is up to fifteen words now, but I'm not sure he's mastered *dilapidated* or *psychopathic murderer* just yet."

"You'd be surprised," Wyatt said.

Sawyer hoisted Henry into his arms, awed as usual by the sensation of looking into a mirror or at a living photo from his youth. He kissed his son and felt the familiar tug of pride.

"What are you thinking?" Emma asked, smiling again, her skin aglow in the slowly setting sun.

"I'm just all kinds of happy," he said.

Emma beamed, all eyes on her as the crowd grew silent. "Well, I'm glad," she said, digging into the pocket of her pale pink sundress. "Because I have an early wedding present for you." She opened her palm to him, revealing a small scroll in the center. The little paper was tied with two thin white ribbons.

Sawyer dipped his head, unsure. "Is this a bride thing?" he asked, taking the scroll between his thumb and first finger for examination.

Emma smiled. "Open it."

He frowned, especially cautious with any surprise that his entire family and group of friends seemed to be in on. "You said it's a wedding gift?" he asked, removing and pocketing the white ribbons, then unfurling the white paper with his thumbs while Henry did his best to grab it from him.

"More like—" Emma paused and grinned impossibly wider "—Christmas gifts."

"Christmas gifts? It's the middle of summer." Sawyer made a sour face and kept unrolling. That clue didn't help him at all. Finally, he turned the paper over in his fingers. One heavy black square occupied the center of the slick white paper. A grayish semicircle centered in that. In the semicircle were two white peanut shapes. Some sparse text rode along the top. The date. *Yesterday.* His last name. *Lance.* The name of the hospital where Emma had been treated last fall. *Mercy General Hospital.* The word *female.* Written twice. "What is this?" He lifted his eyes to the group, who looked collectively disappointed in him.

He knew what he thought it was, but he didn't dare jump to conclusions that might bring him unnecessarily to tears in front of two hundred people.

"Here." Emma slid in close and pulled Henry onto her hip. She pointed to the first peanut. "This is your daughter." She slid her finger to the next peanut. "And this is also your daughter." She stepped back and watched him, one hand set protectively on her stomach.

"What?" He'd been right? Babies? He stared at the little paper through quickly blurring eyes. "You're really pregnant?"

She nodded, eyes glistening. "That's right, Sawyer Lance," she said. "In a few weeks, we'll marry and become an official family of three. But by the end of the year we'll be a family of five."

"Pregnant," Sawyer's gaze slid to her middle. He'd missed all this the first time. He'd longed for an opportunity to see her glow and bloom again one day. A day when he could be there for her. For anything she needed. That day was already here.

"Yes." She smiled.

"Twins?"

"Girls," she answered.

And like the day she'd opened her eyes in that hospital room, Sawyer knelt before her. This time, he kissed her belly through the soft fabric of her sundress, then rose to kiss her nose, her forehead, her cheeks and her mouth as the crowd burst into whoops and applause.

* * * * *

**IF YOU ENJOYED THIS BOOK
WE THINK YOU WILL ALSO LOVE**

INTRIGUE

Seek thrills. Solve crimes. Justice served.

Dive into action-packed stories that will keep you
on the edge of your seat. Solve the crime
and deliver justice at all costs.

6 NEW BOOKS AVAILABLE EVERY MONTH!

His hands cupped her face. She blinked up at him.

"They buried me," she said, fighting the emotion
trying to take over at the thought of never seeing him
again.

Anger flashed in his blue eyes, and his jaw muscles
clenched. "They better never touch you again. We can
make an excuse to get you out of here. Say one of your
family members is sick and you had to go."

"They'll see it as weakness," she reminded him. "It'll
hurt the case."

He thumbed a loose tendril of hair off her face.

"I don't care, Ree," he said with an overwhelming
intensity that became its own physical presence. "I can't
lose you."

Those words hit her with the force of a tsunami.

HIEXP0622

Neither of them could predict what would happen next. Neither could guarantee this case wouldn't go south. Neither could guarantee they would both walk away in one piece.

"Let's take ourselves off the case together," she said, knowing full well he wouldn't take her up on the offer but suggesting it anyway.

Quint didn't respond. When she pulled back and looked into his eyes, she understood why. A storm brewed behind those sapphire-blues, crystalizing them, sending fiery streaks to contrast against the whites. Those babies were the equivalent of a raging wildfire that would be impossible to put out or contain. People said eyes were the window to the soul. In Quint's case, they seemed the window to his heart.

He pressed his forehead against hers and took in an audible breath. When he exhaled, it was like he was releasing all his pent-up frustration and fear. In that moment, she understood the gravity of what he'd been going through while she'd been gone. Kidnapped. For all he knew, left for dead.

So she didn't speak, either. Instead, she leaned into their connection, a connection that tethered them as an electrical current ran through her to him and back. For a split second, it was impossible to determine where he ended and she began.

Don't miss
Mission Honeymoon *by Barb Han,*
available August 2022 wherever
Harlequin Intrigue books and ebooks are sold.

Harlequin.com

Love Harlequin romance?

DISCOVER.

Be the first to find out about promotions, news and exclusive content!

f Facebook.com/HarlequinBooks

Twitter.com/HarlequinBooks

Instagram.com/HarlequinBooks

Pinterest.com/HarlequinBooks

YouTube YouTube.com/HarlequinBooks

ReaderService.com

EXPLORE.

Sign up for the Harlequin e-newsletter and download a free book from any series at **TryHarlequin.com**

CONNECT.

Join our Harlequin community to share your thoughts and connect with other romance readers!
Facebook.com/groups/HarlequinConnection